TRIPLE WITCH

WICKED FIX

REPAIR
TO HER
GRAVE
Sarah Graves

BANTAM BOOKS
New York Toronto London
Sydney Auckland

REPAIR TO HER GRAVE
A Bantam Book / August 2001

ISBN 0-553-58225-9

Published simultaneously in the United States and Canada

Bantam Books are published by Bantam Books, a division of
Random House, Inc. Its trademark, consisting of the words "Bantam
Books" and the portrayal of a rooster, is Registered in U.S. Patent
and Trademark Office and in other countries. Marca Registrada.
Bantam Books, New York, New York.

PRINTED IN THE UNITED STATES OF AMERICA

OPM   10 9 8

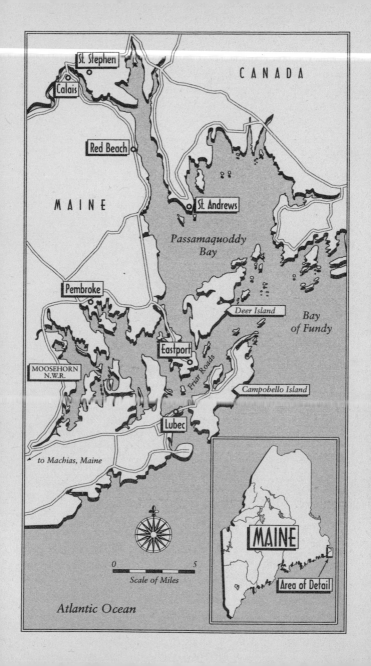

1 When I first moved to Maine, I missed my friends from the city so much that I would invite them to visit me. Shamelessly I lured them, promising steamed lobsters and blueberry pies, while they grumbled about the long drive and the probable absence of Starbucks mocha latte once they arrived.

Well, they were right about the Starbucks. Soon enough, though, they caught on: Eastport (population 2,000), located on Moose Island at the northeastern tip of the Maine coastline, is so remote it might as well be on Mars. And that, if you are a high-powered executive type—most of my friends had the kinds of jobs in which Maalox extra-strength is known only half jokingly as Vitamin M—can be a selling point.

Before I knew it, all my bedrooms were booked from the first of June right on through Labor Day weekend, and I began thinking of summer as a fine time to stock up the refrigerator, put fresh sheets on the beds, and leave town.

But this summer, I had decided, would be different. Anyone who angled for an invitation was told that the plumbing in my old house had exploded, and by the way, I was sure that it was only a coincidence, but also we all had hepatitis.

So on the morning when the whole awful business began, I was feeling pleased with myself. The guest rooms were empty and I had stripped down the faded old wallpaper. Armed with paint, brushes, rollers, and rags, I was about to begin giving the rooms a much-needed face-lift, the first they had received in decades.

Climbing the stepladder in the smallest room—I was also replastering a section of the dining room wall that summer and felt concerned about biting off more than I could chew—I began removing the screws that held up the cut-glass light fixture, a lovely old item that I did not want to get spattered with paint.

But when two of the screws had come out the fixture shifted, and with my arms extended it took both hands just to hold it up there. In this position I could not get the other pair of screws removed, or the first two back in. So it was a screw stalemate.

Just then my black Labrador retriever, Monday, wandered into the room looking bored until she spotted me up there on my perch. Instantly her tail began wagging and the back half of her body began slamming into the ladder. That was also when someone came up the back porch steps and knocked—shave-and-a-haircut!—on the back door.

Monday whirled to race downstairs and greet the visitor, in her haste delivering a final body blow to the ladder. I searched wildly with my feet, finding only thin air as the ladder toppled.

Falling, I recalled from the martial arts movies my teenage son, Sam, is so fond of that I should roll when I landed. So I did, and that, I imagine, is why I hit the wall so hard. But the stars I saw on impact were nothing compared to the sight of that lovely antique ceiling fixture beginning to fall.

Pushing off from the wall, I skidded on my back across the hardwood floor, arriving just in time for the heavy glass sphere to land hard in my solar plexus.

"Oof," I said.

"Nicely done," remarked somebody from the doorway.

"Who the hell are you?" I inquired irritably, sitting up.

He was tall, mid-thirties or so, wearing a white shirt open at the collar and faded denims. Shoving back a shock of straight blond hair that kept falling down over his forehead, he came in.

"Raines. Jonathan Raines? We spoke on the phone, you said I could come and stay here. . . ." He stuck out his hand, peering at me through a pair of thick wire-rimmed eyeglasses.

Good heavens. I remembered his call. But I certainly didn't remember telling him any such thing.

"Mr. Raines, if I did invite you, that was back in January. And since then I haven't heard another word from you."

He looked chagrined. "I know. I'm sorry, it was rude of me. But I've been out of the country and— Oh, dear, I hope you won't send me away. Because in addition to being very late on my Ph.D. dissertation—I've come all the way from Boston to research it here—I'm embarrassingly short of funds."

Jonathan Raines, I recalled very dimly, was related to three of those old friends of mine from the city, and he was a graduate student of music history.

Or something like that; he'd been fuzzy on the details and when he'd phoned I hadn't given them much thought, anyway. At the time, June had seemed very far away; winter in downeast Maine makes summer seem like something that only happens to other, more fortunate people, probably on some other planet.

I hadn't even made my no-summer-guests resolution until April. So I could have invited him, I supposed, then forgotten I had done it. Why else, after all, would he have called, if not to get me to do just that?

And now here he was.

"Please let me help you," he said, bending to take the glass ceiling fixture. And . . .

Dropping it. The crash was hideous.

"Oh, gosh, I apologize. I'll replace it, of course." Vexedly he began gathering up big glass shards.

"Mr. Raines. I'm terribly sorry, but no matter what I said months ago, you can see I'm in no condition for having company."

The house was an 1823 Federal clapboard with three full floors, an attic, a cellar, and a two-story ell, and much of it at the moment was almost as torn-apart as the guest room. In addition to my larger projects, I was repainting window sashes, tightening doorknobs that had taken to falling off and rolling all over the place, and planning to repair the tiny but wonderfully-convenient-when-it-worked downstairs hall bathroom, which we called (inaccurately, lately, which was why it needed repairing) the flush.

"And," I went on, waving at the glass bits, "I'm afraid that item is not replaceable. It was an antique, probably from—"

He was examining one of the shards. "Wal-Mart," he pronounced.

Squinting through the eyeglasses, he went on. "See? The sticker's still on it. Probably someone else broke the original one and replaced it with this."

Well, I'd never seen it up close before.

He looked up, smiling. "Not a bad copy. Funny, isn't

it? How an object can seem to be one thing and end up being another."

Hilarious. At the moment, I wasn't sure which was worse, believing the thing had been precious and irretrievably broken, or finding out that it wasn't.

He straightened, and right then I began thinking there was something not quite kosher about him, as I spotted the gold chain he wore around his neck. For a professional student it was a very strong-looking, muscular neck, and from it a small white pendant hung dead center at the hollow of his throat.

A shark's tooth. How unusual, I thought as he adjusted his glasses, scanned the room through them, spotted a final shard of glass, and dropped it onto the newspaper.

"Thank you," I said. "You can put that mess in the dustbin. Come along and I'll show you."

If I could get him downstairs, I could get him out onto the porch, and from there to a motel or a bed-and-breakfast. Waiting for him to go ahead of me, I put my hand on the doorknob. It was loose, like all the rest of them; patience, I counseled myself.

"Meanwhile," he asked casually, as if inquiring about the weather, "do you still think this place is haunted?"

Whereupon every door in the house but the one I was holding slammed shut with a window-rattling *bang!* TVs and radios began playing, the washer began filling and the dryer began spinning emptily, and Monday let out an eerie, piercing howl that reminded me unpleasantly of the Baskervilles.

Raines didn't turn a hair. "Well," he said cheerfully, on his way downstairs with the broken glass and newspapers, "I guess that answers my question."

We had reached the front hall, where the chandelier's crystal pendants were still shivering. From there I could see into the dining room, where one wall stood stripped of its gold-medallion wallpaper: my replastering project. At its center the remains of a fresh plaster patch gleamed whitely, cracked down the middle.

"Oh, for heaven's sake," I said, forgetting my fright in a burst of exasperation. "I'd take all the ghosts in the world if I could just get that plaster to set up right."

Which wasn't quite true, but I was very irritated. Raines returned from depositing the bits of broken glass in the dustbin.

"I'm not sure that's a bargain you want to make, here," he said thoughtfully. In one hand he gripped a brown duffel bag; in the other, a shaving kit. "May I take these upstairs?"

He looked hopeful, and utterly unfazed by the events he had just witnessed. The appliances all shut off abruptly.

"All right," I gave in crossly, thinking about having to mix plaster again. But considering the kind of visitor I'd been having around here lately . . . I narrowed my eyes at him.

"You *are* alive, aren't you?"

"Indubitably," he replied, grinning, "alive."

"Try," I advised him, "to keep it that way."

Which was the first remark I wished, later on, that I hadn't made. But not the last.

From the dining room where I began gathering up the ruined chunks of plaster, I heard Raines go upstairs, his step jaunty and the tune he was whistling somehow familiar. I should have put it all together right then, of course, but I was distracted by the wreckage. So it didn't hit me for several more minutes just what that tune was:

That it had been composed right here in my own house, I mean, by a man named Jared Hayes who had lived here before me over a century and a half earlier.

Lived here, that is, until he'd vanished from the house.

Without a trace.

My name is Jacobia Tiptree, and once upon a time I was the kind of person who thought home repair meant keeping the building superintendent's phone number on my speed-dialer. A sought-after, highly paid financial consultant and money expert, I lived in a townhouse on the Upper East Side of Manhattan with my husband, a noted brain surgeon, and my son, Sam, a noted baby.

Also at that time, I was the kind of person who survived on takeout. If it came in a cardboard carton and I didn't have to cook or clean up after it, I would eat it. And since my husband back then thought food meant whatever they happened to be serving in the hospital cafeteria, and Sam in those days was subsisting on the stuff that came in jars labeled Gerber, this worked out fine.

But after what seemed like fifteen minutes and was actually fifteen years, I learned that while I was still happily eating Thai noodles my son had discovered Thai stick, a very potent form of marijuana. Also, my husband had begun competing for the title of Philanderer of the Western World.

And my job was if possible even more miserable than my home life. Because look: you get up in the morning, drink your coffee, and yell at your son or he yells at you or both, assuming you even know where he is. The rest of the day you spend helping rich people make more money while paying, if you can imagine it, even fewer taxes.

Then I would go home, and Victor's messages would be there: on the answering machine, and in my e-mail, which he loaded with virus bombs. By then I'd divorced him, and he bitterly resented it, even though he was so promiscuous I felt lucky my e-mail was the only thing requiring disinfection. It got so I would stand at my apartment door with the key in my hand, staring at it, unsure whether I should even go in.

And then one day I didn't. Instead I found Eastport, and came here in the same sudden, oh-to-hell-with-it way that I might have eloped with a traveling salesman or joined a circus.

Which is the short version of why nowadays I am:

(a) adept at the sort of recipe that starts out by directing you to peel and seed five quarts of Concord grapes, then stew the pulp in a kettle big enough to float a battleship, and

(b) the kind of person who won't call for repair help unless orange flames are actually shooting from the electrical outlets.

It's also why I'm never going to make that kind of money again, that I made in the city. But Sam is happy and no longer a dope fiend, and when I get up in the morning it's not a toss-up: should I go to work, or just put a bullet through my forehead?

In other words, my personal bad old days are gone. But when Jonathan Raines arrived in Eastport that bright June morning, I was about to find out how easily the past—even someone else's past, if it is bad enough—can come back to haunt you.

The facts about Jared Hayes were simple. It was sorting them out that was so complicated, and if I didn't manage it soon . . .

But that idea was too unpleasant to finish, so I didn't. And Hayes wasn't my prime concern at the moment, anyway; Raines was.

He didn't add up. So as soon as he walked out of the house I tried calling those New York cousins of his.

Or at any rate I knew the three of *them* were cousins to each other. So I supposed—on very little evidence, I'll admit—that was also his relationship to them. But they couldn't be reached, so next I called every music department at every college and university in the Boston area, discovering that no registrar at any of those places had ever heard of him.

"How did he know you think it's haunted?" my friend Ellie White asked later that morning, shaking out a fresh sheet. The scent of lavender from the linen closet wafted sweetly into the guest room, triggering as always a burst of nostalgia for a time long gone:

Jared Hayes, born in 1803, had acquired my house in 1830 from its original owner, a wealthy shipbuilder and merchant. At that time, the wallpaper had been fresh and the floors level, the rooms bright and alive with housemaids hustling up and down the back stairs, which were located where the tiny bathroom just off the kitchen hallway was located now.

"I suppose his cousins must have told him," I said, digging another blanket from the cedar chest. "All three of them were up here last summer, and I confided to them my . . . feelings about it."

Feelings that no one else had any reason to share; the odd things that went on in the house were always explainable. Only my sense that they were also purposeful was out of the ordinary, as if the house were sending a message particularly to me.

"And the favor I owe one of those cousins is so massive, I might never be able to pay it back, guest privileges or no guest privileges," I went on. "So I can't just kick Raines out."

"But it didn't bother him?" Ellie asked. "When it all . . ." She waved her hands to indicate those slamming doors, which could be pretty startling even if you did think it was only the wind.

"Not hardly." We'd shoved a bed back into the room, and a reading lamp, and a desk I'd bought for a dime at a church tag sale earlier that spring. "He almost seemed to like it."

I tossed a quilt atop the blanket. Being from Boston, Raines wouldn't be accustomed to Maine summer nights; not unless the out-of-the-country trip he'd mentioned included plenty of Arctic exploring. And the fireplaces, one in every room, had been shut up years ago, after a chimney fire that by some miracle hadn't burned the place to the ground. Someday, I thought, I would have all the chimneys relined and open the fireplaces again.

Someday. But this thought brought back all the worry I was trying to repress; angrily, I slapped on the chenille bedspread.

"You're sure he really is from Boston?" Ellie asked.

"I think so. He'd written my address on the back of an old envelope sent to him in Cambridge. I found it in here," I added, "when I came in with his towels. So that much is true."

"Huh," Ellie said. "Interesting. You know, especially if he *believes* in ghosts, you'd think the woo-woo stuff would've got rid of him in no time flat."

The woo-woo stuff. It cheered me immensely, hearing her put it that way, making the unease I felt sound manageable, even trivial. Slender and pretty, with pale green eyes, red hair, and freckles like a sprinkling of gold dust, Ellie had been my friend since almost the moment I got to Eastport three years earlier.

"Drat, look at that," she said. "I've lost the tiny hinge screw out of my glasses." She took off the tortoiseshell pair she was wearing, frowned at the separation, and tucked the pieces into her sweater pocket. "Anyway, where is he now?"

"Walking around town. He had a glass of water while he was spinning me a few more moonbeams about himself, and then he went out."

I took a deep breath. "It's Jared Hayes he's researching, Ellie. For his dissertation. Or he *says* that's what it's for, anyway."

"Oh," Ellie said. "*Now* I get it."

When Jared Hayes, the Eastport musician and composer, looked out his bedroom window on an early nineteenth-century morning, he saw ships: great, many-sailed trading vessels gathered so thickly into port, the harbor seemed fairly bristling with their masts. The town swarmed with commerce: shipbuilders, chandlers, riggers and sailmakers, dealers in oakum, hemp, and galley provisions, not to mention the goods those ships brought in and out: rum and cotton, lumber and nails, peat from Canada, and of course the fish that swam so plentifully in the ocean.

There was work for everyone; recently released from the loathsome four-year occupation by the British army in the War of 1812—when the news came that the Treaty of Ghent was signed, local people dug out horns and fiddles and played "Yankee Doodle" up and down Water Street to pipe the hated redcoats on their way— Eastport boomed.

And when an economy booms, artists and musicians do well, too: parties and so on. People celebrating their comfortable circumstances. Only not usually quite as well as Jared Hayes had done.

Ellie gave the room a final look-over and dusted her hands together, indicating that we were finished. "But you think—"

"Of course I do," I said, pulling the door shut. "What else would it be? He's searching for that damned violin."

We went downstairs to the kitchen, where Ellie fixed

coffee and I put out a plate of cupcakes I'd made earlier, in a burst of suspecting that I might be needing them: chocolate with bits of chopped sweet cherries in the batter and dark chocolate frosting.

"There's no violin," she said as we applied ourselves to the cupcakes. They were pure wickedness, nearly as restorative as I'd hoped. I took another.

"No, there isn't," I replied, chewing. "*We* know that. Or," I temporized, because after all you can't prove a negative, "we're pretty sure."

A hefty dose of chocolate had smoothed down my hackles and settled my nerves. To balance the effect, I took another sip of the hot, strong coffee that Ellie produces like a magical elixir from ordinary Maxwell House; eat your heart out, Starbucks.

"How many people," I asked, "do you suppose have been through the house searching for it?"

During the decades when the house had stood empty, I meant. Before I came to Eastport on a whim and spotted the huge white structure looming at the top of Key Street like a ghost from a distant era and got the people from the real estate office to let me in. I'd spent hours wandering the vacant rooms, filled with a shimmering sense of having been in them before; by the next day, the house had belonged to me.

Now, through the bright, bare windows of the big old barnlike kitchen, yellow sunlight fell in pale rectangles on the hardwood floor. Outside, a breeze shifted the branches of the cherry tree I had planted the previous summer, sending white petals swirling to the green grass like a shower of snow.

"Half the town," Ellie replied dreamily. "Looking for Jared Hayes's famous lost Stradivarius. But they never found it. The only treasures ever found here were those dining room curtains, stuffed in a cubbyhole up in a corner of the attic, forgotten."

They were champagne brocade and we'd run them through the washer and the dryer. They'd survived, and hung beautifully.

"Because"—I held up an index finger—"how would an isolated small-town fiddler and minor-league musical composer like Hayes ever get enough money to buy a Stradivarius in the first place?"

That was the old story, told and retold over the years until it had begun sounding like the truth: that Jared Hayes had bought one of the famous instruments and hidden it, and then he had vanished.

And that it was still here.

There had been a few hopefuls who had wanted me to let them look again—just before Raines phoned, a charming fellow with an Australian accent had called three times and very nearly managed to persuade me— but I had been able to turn them all down with one excuse or another. The idea of the thing appearing someday, however, just wouldn't die.

And now out of the blue came a guy from Boston with a cock-and-bull story about a Ph.D. project.

Yeah, right. Ellie nibbled her cupcake delicately. "He had," she pointed out, meaning Hayes, "enough money to buy this house."

"If he bought it," I came back. We'd been over all this before. "Some say he won the house gambling in a saloon."

"And some say Hayes had enough money to buy the whole town," Ellie countered, "if he wanted to. Surely he had cash enough for some pretty fancy furnishings. You've seen the receipts."

Hayes's household account books still existed, and despite some irregularity in them—the way, for instance, the Grand Canyon forms an irregularity in Arizona—the *expense* sides of the ledger columns were clear enough for anyone to read. In the fine old copperplate hand of the classically educated man of his day, they listed furniture enough to outfit a castle, along with rugs from the far East, English china, and French crystal.

A harpsichord, originally crafted for the court of Frederick the Great, had been shipped here and reassembled in my dining room not far from where my attempt at a plaster job was crumbling right this minute. A Chinese lacquered cabinet so large and heavy no ship's captain would load it for the perilous journey around the Horn—at the time, of course, there was not yet any Panama Canal—had been hauled by a team of elephants over the Alps to Spain, where the shippers were more adventurous or perhaps only greedier; at any rate, it got here.

"Whether it was gambling money, though," Ellie added, "is another question."

"You can bet he wasn't earning it by playing the fiddle," I said. "Or not all of it, anyway. But . . ." I could already see which way her thoughts were headed. "But Ellie, we wanted a nice, quiet summer."

My son had at last made firm college plans for the fall. My ex-husband, Victor, had moved here to Eastport but had also stopped devoting himself—full-time, anyway—to driving me nuts. And my main squeeze, Wade Sorenson, had proven as fine and durable a romantic choice as I had known he must be back when I fell in love with him at first sight. In fact we had decided—in theory, anyway; in practice we were both still shying at the gate—to get married.

This for me was like thinking I might stick my hand in the fire again, and Wade was of the "if it ain't broke, let's not fix it" persuasion, constitutionally. Still, the idea kept recurring and gradually we were getting to feel easier with it, the way two people will when they are happy and comfortable with one another.

And Ellie knew all this, but now she brushed it impatiently aside.

"Nice, quiet summer," she scoffed. "If you don't get this place straightened out, you'll be in a nice, quiet asylum soon."

At which I nodded sadly because, as usual, she was correct. Lately I couldn't even go to sleep in the house without worrying whether something was going to sneak up in the dark and pull the covers off me and I would wake up with double pneumonia. And I couldn't help thinking that somehow it all had to do with Jared Hayes:

With whatever had happened to him. And with what, since to me it seemed clear there was something, he wanted done about it.

"If Raines isn't scared and he's already interested, that could be a good thing," Ellie said persuasively. "It might be, he will come up with something that we haven't."

If Ellie and I were both mad scientists, she would be the one whose laboratory is always exploding. On the other hand, her blithe, no-disaster-can-possibly-befall-me attitude does tend to get results.

"Maybe," I allowed. "And I do know those cousins. Probably they wouldn't send me an axe-murderer, or anything like that."

An understatement: all three of them were heavily involved in federal law enforcement. Any axe-murderers they came across would get sent somewhere, all right, but it wouldn't be Eastport.

She went on: "Because I've been thinking, and it seems to me there are two possibilities to explain the discomfort you've been experiencing. One is that your house is haunted. Or two, and this is my clear choice, that your *head* is haunted."

I just stared at her: trust Ellie to boil it all down for you that way. "Haunted," she said, "by the *idea* of what happened to Hayes, by your questions and wondering about it."

"But . . ."

"I know. You've experienced . . . phenomena." She pronounced the word judiciously, like a physician mentioning an unpleasant side effect. "Only they're never . . ."

Right; like I said. Never flat-out inexplicable.

"So in your view, it wouldn't be so much that the house is haunted," I said, "but that I am. By it."

"Uh-huh." She ate a cherry bit. "And if we're going to do something about it, we need more information about Hayes. So we can find out the answers to your questions and put a stop to it."

She got up, refilled our coffee cups. "*And* if this Raines person is here to look for Hayes's violin, maybe he can help. That is, if we help him."

"Maybe," I said, still not quite seeing how. "But Ellie, what if he only makes things in this house get *more* challenging?"

I didn't quite see how that was going to happen, either. But lately, anything seemed possible. Out in the street a car started suddenly with the roar of a bad muffler; I jumped about a foot.

Ellie sighed. "Jacobia, don't you see it doesn't matter that things might get worse? For one thing, they might anyway, and for another, you're already too unhappy. Whatever's going on around here is making you a nervous wreck."

She took a deep breath, the kind people take when

what they are about to say to you is painful but for your own good.

"I know you love it here," she said. "But we've got to get this place fixed so you can live here comfortably again, and by that I don't just mean your remodeling jobs. If we don't, worst case, you won't be able to . . ."

She stopped, allowing me to reach on my own a conclusion I'd been trying very hard to avoid. But at this point it was obvious.

"Worst case," I said slowly, "I'm not going to be able to stay in this old house."

"Meanwhile," said Ellie, breaking the heavy silence that followed my pronouncement, "there's another thing that ought to start concerning you, if it hasn't already. Isn't the Eastport Ladies' Reading Circle meeting in your dining room in"—she frowned in pretended thought—"just five days?"

"Oh, good heavens." Like my unexpected houseguest, it was another thing I'd completely forgotten.

"With," she went on, twinkling mischievously, "items like silver coffeepots and china teacups? Linen tablecloths, little sandwiches with the crusts cut off, and so on?"

All that and more: tiny lobster-paste-filled puff pastries. Petit-fours hand-dipped and decorated with candied violets. Ellie is by no means a fan of little sandwiches with the crusts cut off, but I always find it charming that someone has gone to all the trouble of making them.

Only this time the trouble-taking someone would be me. After three years I had been accepted into the rarified society of town women who Got Dressed and Went

Out every other Tuesday evening to Discuss Literature; now I was going to have to show I deserved my newly elevated status.

By, for instance, buying and wearing a pair of panty hose, an item of clothing I dimly remembered from my life in the city.

"I don't guess folded paper towels for napkins will do, will they?" I asked nervously. Like Raines's visit, the Reading Circle meeting had seemed so far off when I'd agreed to host it.

And now here it was.

"No," Ellie said. Her own great-aunt had been a founding member of the group, and Ellie while perfectly friendly to it in theory stayed away from it in practice.

But she knew the drill. "I think before I worried about the napkins, though, I'd do something about the wall," she went on. "Having one in that dining room, I mean. With wallpaper on it and so on. And there's the matter of the facilities."

Ye gods, the plaster and the flush. "Ellie, please, I'm on my knees, here."

Not literally, but metaphorically I was down there bowing and scraping. Ellie made the loveliest puff pastries and petit-fours this side of Paris, and with the number of snow-white napkins and tablecloths her aunt had left her, she had enough linen to supply a hotel.

"All right," she gave in immediately; she also has a solid gold heart. "I'll be in charge of the catering and linen supply. But I'm not," she warned, "going to be there."

Ellie's aunt had not precisely been a sainted character, and the activities she had pursued still gave Ellie the hives just by association. "No how, no way . . ."

And that went double for Discussing Literature; my

friend read voraciously, but as for displaying knowledge in public she would rather choke on her own spit.

"Fine," I said, knowing when I was well off. "Now, about Raines . . ."

Ellie rinsed our cups and put the Tupperware lid back on the cupcakes. In the corner, Monday looked up from her dog bed.

"Well, he's out there," I said reasonably. "Talking to people. So if someone's going to help him, I'd say now would be perfect timing, and I've got to . . ."

I waved at the hallway, where something that looked like a perfectly usable little guest bathroom lurked silently, waiting for the unwary. And considering the amount of coffee and tea that got consumed at your standard Ladies' Reading Circle meeting . . .

"It is a sort of a beverage-intense gathering, isn't it?" Ellie said thoughtfully.

Suffice it to say I believed that particular task had better go straight to the top of my to-do list. So I got out the tools: a big screwdriver, a pair of pliers, and the plumbing seal, like a doughnut made of wax, that I had bought at Wadsworth's Hardware Store months earlier when the job went on the list in the first place.

"You're doing it yourself?"

"Why not?" The truth is, almost anyone can repair or replace any reasonably modern plumbing fixture. But this fact—that people do plumbing, you are a people, therefore et cetera—is a secret, because when plumbers do it, it costs $75 per hour, while when you do it, it's $0 per hour. And dividing $75 by $0 yields an infinite number of dollars, which is how many the plumbers will lose if the secret ever leaks out.

"Well, okay." With a last doubtful look, Ellie went upstairs to wash her face and comb her hair before heading downtown. While she was gone, I got out the cleaning supplies and began my task by scrubbing the target area very thoroughly, this being another secret to successful plumbing:

Kill every germ within three miles before you start. That way you will possess a relaxed, confident attitude, and the body language to match.

Unfortunately my own body language was not as fully focused and confident as I might have wished, because the odd features in Jonathan Raines's personal presentation kept popping into my head like sour notes in an otherwise skillfully played piece of music.

He'd implied that he was an ivory-tower academic, and I was already fairly sure that story was hogwash. But none of the other occupations I could imagine for him would produce the muscles he had. Thinking this, I turned off the water in the little bathroom and pressed the flush handle, observing that the tank on the back of the bowl did not fill up again.

(Once I flushed first and *then* turned off the water, not noticing that the tank had refilled immediately, and when I took out the bolts that held the fixture to the floor . . . well, let's not proceed any further along with that little story.)

At any rate, I got rid of the water, thinking about the shirt Raines had been wearing when he arrived. An impoverished student, so short of money that he needed to stay with me: another obvious untruth. Back in my New York days when I was financial counselor to guys who kept London tailors' fax numbers in their Rolodexes, I'd seen enough custom-made, long-stranded Egyptian cotton dress shirts to know one when I spotted one, even if it did have the collar open and the sleeves rolled up.

Musing over this, I disconnected the filler tube at the back of the tank—that's what the pliers were for—and pried the two little white plastic caps off the tops of the floor bolts. Next, I unscrewed the floor bolts; that's what the screwdriver was for.

Just then Ellie came back, thinking along the same lines as I'd been. "What do you suppose Raines really is?" she said.

"Maybe an art dealer or a scout from an auction house. Or even a private investigator specializing in valuable antiquities, on assignment from a buyer."

Whatever he was, he'd picked up a rumor and decided to run it to its source, just in case. It was the only explanation that made sense.

"And since he *is* here, I guess it also makes sense to try to use him to find out what the heck this place *wants*," I conceded.

Which for me was like saying that maybe the earth is really flat. Three years earlier, the idea of a place wanting *anything* would've made me hoot with scornful laughter.

Nowadays, I was more likely to hoot at the sensation of an ice-cold finger placed suddenly on the back of my neck. And when I turned, of course no one was ever there.

So maybe Ellie was right and it was all in my mind. "By," I went on, "helping Raines try to find an old violin and paying attention to any old Hayes facts he digs up *while* he's looking."

I pulled out the first-floor bolt. "But what I don't get is, why would *he* need help? Raines, I mean."

Ellie rolled her eyes at me. "Because no one in Eastport is going to tell him anything at all otherwise. About the old days around here or Jared Hayes or anything else. You must understand that much by now, Jacobia."

Right again: in Eastport, people will know all about you ten minutes or so after your car tootles over the causeway onto Moose Island. Deciding what to think of you, though, and whether or not to give you the time of day . . . well, that could take years.

The final floor bolt snapped off as I was removing it. As it did so, I realized . . . "Ellie. How the heck did Raines *get* onto the island?"

If you didn't happen to be driving a car over the causeway, getting here was no easy matter. No bus, no subway, not even a pay phone at the stop on the mainland where the bus from Bangor would let you off. I said as much.

"But he didn't come in a car," Ellie said. "Or at any rate there's no extra car in your driveway. He walked downtown?"

"Yes. So how did he arrive in the first place?"

Ellie shook her head, clipping Monday's leash to her collar. "I guess we'll have to ask him."

"Just let me get this all straight, though," I said, "before you go."

I held up three fingers. "We don't know for sure that Jared Hayes hid anything of value. We don't know that it was a violin if he did. And we certainly don't know it was a Stradivarius."

I took a breath. "To the contrary, actually."

Back in the city I'd had a client who collected old musical instruments. And from him I'd learned that in the discovery department, it's all over: finding an unknown Strad—in Eastport or anywhere else—was as likely as going out to dig in your own garden and unearthing another Rosetta stone.

"All we *do* know is that Hayes's diaries mention a violin, a special one. *And* that they talk about a treasure."

It was how I imagined the story about a Stradivarius first got started: the diaries, along with letters, account books, and musical manuscripts, were at Eastport's Peavey Memorial Library.

"But nothing in his handwriting actually *says* a violin was what he meant. *And* we don't know his disappearance was linked to any of it."

"I'd say that sums it up pretty well," Ellie agreed.

"But," I went on, "we let Raines try to *find* a Stradivarius, anyway. And while he's looking . . ."

"We peek under every rock he turns over. See if information about Hayes's disappearance might be lurking there. And with it, a clue to curing your case of the heebie-jeebies."

Which didn't really give me a very good feeling at all. For one thing, when you turn over a rock what you find underneath is often slimy. For another, the term *heebie-jeebies* didn't please me when applied to myself, though I had to admit it was accurate. Finally, Ellie's plan still seemed nebulous to me: what rock?

But when you're up against a problem you quite literally cannot put your finger on, I supposed nebulosity might be as good a strategy as any other.

"All right," I said. "I'll go along with it."

"Good," she replied, as if there had been any chance of my saying otherwise. Ellie looks as delicate as a portrait of a lady painted on porcelain, but she has more horsepower than the Indy 500 once her mind is set on something.

"So, let's get to it," she said to the dog.

"Mmmf," Monday uttered, wriggling eagerly.

"Besides, if we don't pave the way for our new visitor," she said as they crossed the back porch, "he might ask nosy questions where he shouldn't and get dropped off the fish pier."

It was one of the things I had liked about Ellie right from the start: that she would speak to a cat or dog as naturally as to a human being. When they had gone, I went to the front of the house to watch them as they headed down Key Street under the maples shaking out new summer-green leaves in the June sunshine.

Ellie chatted animatedly while the black dog trotted beside her, listening. I thought how charming they looked going along so companionably together, and as I thought this a cup flew straight out of the dining room sideboard and smashed against the tiled fireplace surround.

I had a startled moment to wish that Ellie had been there to see it. Then the boom arrived: a blast so loud it shocked starlings out of the maple trees, a flapping cloud of them rising up in squawking confusion.

Simultaneously a distant fire siren began blaring; that was when I realized there had been some kind of explosion somewhere and the flying cup had been an effect of it, nothing more.

Peering out, I spotted a billow of black smoke coming from Campobello, the Canadian island lying directly across the bay; something, as the men around here would have put it, had gone up sudden.

But there was nothing I could do about it, so when I'd swept up the china cup pieces I returned to the task at hand: actually lifting that porcelain bathroom fixture off the floor.

And it took all my muscle power, but I moved the thing. Then I took out the old wax plumbing seal (like a collar around the cast-iron pipe in the floor), whose age and resulting leakiness were the source of the problem in the first place, and replaced it. And just about that time George Valentine happened to come in the back door, so he helped me lift the fixture again and get it settled back onto its original footprint.

Which was when it hit me, the first thing I'd noticed about Jonathan Raines: why was he wearing a shark's tooth pendant? Like his fit-looking physical condition, the daredevilish ornament didn't fit any mental picture of him that I could come up with.

But to this, as to so many other questions that had arisen that morning—such as where I would ever get enough chairs to accommodate the Ladies' Reading Circle—I had no ready answer.

"Hey, way to tackle it," George said approvingly, standing back to eye my plumbing handiwork.

George has dark hair, milky-pale skin, and a perpetual five o'clock shadow. Thin, permanent black lines were etched into his knuckles from the dirty work he was always having to do around town somewhere; in Eastport, George was the man you call for a dead car battery, a fallen tree limb, or an underground fuel line that has broken and needs to be dug up, pronto.

"Thanks," I said. "Big noise across the water a while ago."

"Ayuh. Don't know what, yet. Sent some of the fire crew over on the Coast Guard cutter, see if they can help. You're okay with the rest of the job?" He gestured at the little bathroom.

"I hope so." All that remained was to put in the floor bolts and turn on the water; the moment of truth was fast approaching. "I guess we'll see in a minute."

"Ayuh," he allowed evenly again. "Guess we will."

George was Ellie's husband and one of my main cheerleaders in the household fix-it department, partly because before I began attempting them I used to call him at all hours to come over and do things like unstick a balky window sash or flip the switch in the fuse box. Not that he ever complained about this or even mentioned it; what he did instead was, he began replacing his tools.

One at a time, he went out and bought himself new hammers, pliers, and screwdrivers. The old ones, somehow, always wound up living at my house, and eventually I got my own toolbox for them, too. Which was either the beginning of it all or the beginning of the end, depending on how you look at it.

At any rate, I put back the floor bolts. "Voy-lah," George said as I hooked the water up again and the tank began filling.

"Yeah, maybe, huh?" I said hopefully.

Noticing that no water was spreading out onto the floor, I allowed myself a small moment of triumph before hurrying to the basement to check that I had not inadvertently transformed the steps down there into a waterfall.

I had not. Well, this was looking auspicious. Cheered by the thought of the infinite number of dollars I had saved, I went up the basement steps, which was when I noticed that the water was still running in the little bathroom; it shouldn't have been. And whipping off the top of that porcelain tank, I saw why.

The filler mechanism was bent so the float had snagged on the tank's side, jamming the shutoff mechanism. As a result the water level had already risen nearly over the edge of the tank; flooding was imminent. Pressing the flush handle to empty some of it, I crouched to turn the small round knob on the filler pipe to stop the inflow.

Whereupon the knob popped off into my hand and water began jetting merrily. Reeling back in drenched surprise and forgetting what a tiny room I was in (this was, after all, originally only the entrance to the back stairway, and servants were not expected to take up much room any more than they were expected to make much noise) I cracked my head on the doorframe, my knee on the porcelain, and my elbow on the wall.

Well, I made a lot of noise, and luckily for me George was still around—after all those fix-it trips to my house, he'd gotten to feel at home there, and he was making a peanut butter and banana sandwich and pouring himself a cup of coffee when I yelled—and he remembered the

cellar location of the main shutoff. So I swore and sputtered while he ran down there and twisted the main
knob, which fortunately did not break off in *his* hand or
the house would have floated away.

"Huh," George said, coming back upstairs to survey
the pool of water spreading out into the hall. He
straightened his gimme cap, which was black, with GUP-
TILL'S EXCAVATING lettered on it in orange script.
"Guess that old filler pipe handle must just've been
ready to go."

"Right," I said through gritted teeth, thinking that
what plumbers really get paid for is aggravation. "Go
eat your lunch, George, okay? I'm not fit to be around
right this minute."

"Yep," he said prudently, and skedaddled.

Whereupon I cleaned up and went back to
Wadsworth's for a new filler pipe handle and a kit of
new insides for the toilet tank, the installation of which
turned out to be as complicated as rewiring the space
shuttle. And by then George was gone, but I managed it
by adding an extra part I devised out of a paper clip.

That, bottom line, is the thing about house repairs in
a very old house:

Any part of it that you touch is apt to be as fragile,
and as likely to topple over onto something else that is
even more fragile, as a row of dominoes. So on-the-spot
improvisation is often needed.

That floor bolt, for instance, that broke while I was removing it. If I'd tried getting the rest of it out of the floor
before proceeding, I would probably still be there trying.

Instead I'd tapped the stuck shaft of the bolt down
into the floor with a nail and screwed a new, slightly
larger bolt into the same hole right on top of it. The
new bolt had pushed the old one farther along into the
hole ahead of it and held just fine.

Voy-lah, as George would have remarked.

Meanwhile I kept thinking about improvisation, and about how I felt that somehow Jonathan Raines was doing it, too.

When he'd arrived, for instance, I'd assumed I must have invited him. He, anyway, seemed quite certain of it. But now upon reflection I thought something else was also possible: that he'd made the invitation up out of whole cloth. Heard of me from his cousins, phoned me merely to find out for himself what sort of person I was, and decided to wing it, not wanting to risk a refusal.

Trusting in his flim-flam talents to convince me that I had asked him here.

Which, if true, implied two more fairly interesting things:

First, he was an excellent con man; the flim-flam had worked beautifully.

And second, Eastport in general wasn't his target area.

A motel or one of the town bed-and-breakfasts wouldn't have suited him. No, he'd wanted to stay with me; had lied, perhaps, in order to engineer precisely this result.

He was after a priceless, probably mythical, old violin.

And I was his target area.

2

Hecky Wilmot was a short, wizened old fellow with dyed black hair, sharp, suspicious eyes that spied everything, and a lined, age-mottled face that looked as if it had been carved out of a walnut. A native Eastporter who'd lived here all his life, he was fond of saying he knew all about the town that a decent man could report, and plenty that a decent man couldn't.

"So," I said to Ellie, "we tell Hecky that Jonathan Raines is *your* cousin, right?"

I'd decided to get out of the house for a while, and had run into Ellie downtown. Between us, Monday mooched happily along the sidewalk.

"That's right," Ellie said. She'd been thinking. "My good old cousin Jon."

Like Hecky, Ellie was an Eastporter born and bred, and around here, being related to an Eastporter was almost as good as being one yourself.

"And then we ask Hecky please not to let it get public that Raines is my relative," she added. "Hecky will like the idea of a man who doesn't want to trade on his family connections, but you know he'll gab it all over the island that there are some."

"You bet," I agreed. If Raines was related to Ellie, then people would talk freely to him. And he would take, we hoped, new lines of investigation, ones we hadn't even thought of.

And later, I thought determinedly, I would pick his brain for whatever he'd found out: thoroughly, like a seagull cleaning the meat from a clamshell. Flim-flam me, would he?

We'd just see about that. Meanwhile we'd tracked Hecky, the nearest thing Eastport had to a public address system, to an art gallery and studio on Water Street, overlooking the bay.

Out on the waves, a couple of sailboats tacked against the breeze, making way for Deer Island which lay to the northeast in the whitecapped channel. Just off the dock's end, a flock of cormorants fished diligently, dipping and gulping with undulating movements of their long, curving black necks. The smoke from the earlier explosion on Campobello had dissipated, the Coast Guard cutter back at its mooring.

"That's how we can get it around town the fastest," Ellie finished. "By making Hecky think it shouldn't get around at all."

It was the beginning of tourist season and the shops and cafés on the street all sparkled with fresh paint, clean windows, and planters full of red geraniums under flags proclaiming the shops to be OPEN!

"But do we tell him what Raines is up to?" I asked. "About the violin?" In the fresh salt air, a hint of wood smoke mingled pungently with the smell of pine tar.

"I don't think so," Ellie replied. We turned to go in just as Eastport's police chief, Bob Arnold, went by fast in the town squad car, heading for the north end of the island.

Bob didn't wave; Ellie's eyebrows went up curiously.

"For one thing, Raines doesn't know *we* know, so we shouldn't mention it," she added as the squad disappeared up Water Street. "Besides, I don't think Hecky would like it."

This turned out to be an understatement. The little gallery had been a candy store in its previous incarnation; local boys had gathered there in the old days and many of them had not lost the habit. As we entered the shop, Hecky and half a dozen of his cronies were gathered around the little black woodstove in the corner, hashing over the latest news.

Like him, they were smart, spry old men who would relish town gossip for as long as they had blood pressures, and they all looked glad to see us in case we'd brought interesting fodder.

At first. But when he caught sight of us, Hecky scowled and the rest followed suit; in Eastport, Hecky was an opinion-maker.

"Young feller's staying with you was in here a little while ago," he said, fixing me in a severe gaze.

"Yes, he's—"

"Asking a lot of questions about Jared Hayes and his hidden Stradivarius," Hecky went on accusingly.

Straddy-varryus. Oh, damn Raines's eyes; couldn't he see out of them, that when you went at a guy like Hecky you had to go by the circular route?

But then I made a mistake that was just as bad. "Yes, because he is writing a dissertation on—"

Ellie glanced sharply at me, but it was too late; I'd put my foot in it by mentioning writing, especially any that anyone but Hecky might be doing.

"Just finished m' book, y'know," Hecky said darkly.

"Yes, I know," I began. It was about Eastport and he'd even managed to find a regional publisher for it; *Downeast Deeds: An Eastport Story* was due out any minute.

"I'm looking forward to—"

Reading it, I'd been about to say. But he stopped me. "Don't see as there'll be any need for another," he said flatly.

Of course not; the notion that someone else might trespass on his literary territory wouldn't be welcome, especially now. Another local author's warmhearted Maine memoir, for instance, entitled *Clyde Found Fruitflies in the Berries,* had gotten the sharp side of Hecky's tongue on more than one occasion lately.

"He's doing it for college," I hastened to explain. "Raines, I mean. Like a term paper, not *real* writing like yours, Hecky."

"Hmph," he retorted, not much mollified.

The shop was a combination art gallery and working studio that ordinarily smelled sweetly of oil paints and turpentine. But now the atmosphere in it soured further as Hecky glowered at me.

"And he's got no business muckin' about with Hayes nonsense. Damned fool violin and all that other old clattertrap."

He glanced around at the brightly colored water scenes and landscape portraits decorating the walls. Behind the counter the shop's proprietor, Jerome Wallace, worked on another one.

"This"—Hecky jerked a gnarled fist at the paintings—"is what we show the folks from away, want to come and see the real downeast Maine as it oughta be. All bright an' cheerful."

He frowned thunderously at me. "Not them old stories about murder and mayhem. Bad women"—*wimmen*—"an' dark deeds such as ought to've stayed buried with the men who done 'em."

I tried not to look as curious as I felt; this was the first I'd heard of Hayes doing dark deeds or being associated with bad wimmen.

From behind Hecky, one of the other men in the shop winked elaborately at me. Truman Daly was tall, wiry and white-bearded with a gleam in his eye that could turn to lightning if you got him riled. As courtly a gentleman now as forty years ago, lively and involved in everything that was interesting, he was Eastport's best-known citizen—welcome in the fanciest parlors and lowest saloons, though he visited the latter very infrequently and only for soft drinks—and he treated Hecky Wilmot as if Hecky were a younger, less diplomatic brother.

Now Truman smoothed his long, white beard with one expressive hand and made a discreet yap-yap motion with the thumb and finger of the other, as he and the other men began edging toward the door of the shop.

When Hecky got on a rant, the best thing was to leave him alone to it. As the little bell over the shop door jingled, I caught a sniff of wood smoke again, decided it was only the stove downdrafting.

Hecky leaned toward me, his bushy white eyebrows beetling in sharp contrast to his dyed black hair.

" 'Twas a curse old Jared Hayes lived under," he intoned, "and another as took 'im. I ain't such a fool as to dabble in it, nor should you be, or anyone from away. *Especially* from away."

He glared around. "It oughta be let alone," he declared, his old voice quavering with emotion, and with that he stomped out, leaving Ellie and me blinking at each other.

"So much for helping Jonathan Raines get accepted in town," Ellie said after a moment, laughing weakly.

"Right," I agreed, still a little shocked by the old man's fervor, "and we never even got the chance to tell our lies. Maybe we should've told Hecky that Raines was a literary agent."

"It sounds to me as if he's just jealous of his turf," Ellie said, echoing my own thought. "With his book coming out and all."

"Do you think he's getting nervous? I mean, that somebody like Raines, with his supposed academic credentials, might decide to say that Hecky the hometown amateur has gotten it all wrong?"

Jerome dragged his gaze away from his painting. "Hecky's pretty touchy lately about that book of his, all right," he said. "Way he talks, it's going to set the whole town on its ear, what he's written. Truman Daly says he thinks maybe Hecky put in a few things he wishes now that he hadn't."

"Huh." Now, there was a thought worth pondering. It would be poetic justice if for once Hecky was worried about what other people were saying, instead of him doing all the saying himself. "Whose old skeletons has Hecky been rattling, do you suppose?"

Ellie shrugged, spreading her hands. The smoke smell was stronger; not the woodstove, I realized. And now I heard sirens.

"Something's put a bee in his bonnet," Ellie agreed, peering out the storefront window.

Across the street in the parking area by the fish pier, a small antiques-and-crafts fair was being set up: quilts, jellies and jams, and a variety of other homemade items covered the red-and-white-checked cloths.

"Oh, dear," Ellie murmured, "the quilt for the crafts fair."

In what she laughingly called her spare time, she and the other ladies of the Quilt Guild were completing a sampler quilt; the squares were finished, but the quilting—all hand stitching, in red and blue for the Fourth of July—was Ellie's job, as she has the finest quilting hand in all of Washington County.

"I've got to buckle down," she instructed herself firmly, at which I managed not to laugh out loud; Ellie is one of the most buckled-down persons on the planet. But I promised to remind her about it, meanwhile continuing to observe the activity across the street.

Among the workers I spotted Lillian Frey, a tall, rangily constructed woman in her late forties, with wiry, pale blond hair and a deeply tanned face. She had a nail gun in her hand, a big stapler sort of device with the nails in a strip hanging down like ammo in an old-fashioned machine gun, and she was fastening lengths of two-by-four, *bam-bam-bam* one after the other, bracing the legs of the table in her booth.

As I watched, a photographer from the local newspaper, the *Quoddy Times,* showed up; reflexively, Lillian backed away. From this distance the scar on her cheek didn't show much, but it was common knowledge she didn't like having her picture taken. When the photographer moved to another booth, she went back to work.

Beside me, Ellie frowned. "Hey, who's that?" she wanted to know as a car swung into the lot and skidded to a halt.

In her outfit of pencil-slim jeans and black sweater Lillian looked smashing as usual, like the country antique items she sold as a sideline to her main business: handmade musical instruments. The scar only added a rakish touch, though I was sure she didn't feel that way about it.

But her smile of satisfaction at finishing the nail job vanished as a girl slammed from the car Ellie was squinting at. "That's Jill. Lillian's daughter," I said.

She was built more like her mother, athletic but long-boned and with finer, more delicately-modeled features. The scowl on her face spoiled her attractiveness, though.

"Wow," Ellie said, "she looks tough."

"Right," I sighed. "As usual."

Piled in the back of Lillian's station wagon were handsome old things—a banjo clock, a Thomas Moser chair, a wicker plant stand, and some very nice hooked floral rugs—along with several small musical-instrument cases that I supposed held violins: the hand-built instruments that were Lillian's specialty.

Jill slammed her fist on the wagon's fender as she went by; the women began arguing about something.

Which didn't surprise me; the chip on the girl's shoulder was already legendary. "She's been hanging around Sam," I said.

I was not best pleased to see her. "She's been in town about a month. I keep hoping she'll leave again any minute."

"She looks old enough to be out on her own," Ellie appraised the girl, "that's for sure. And plenty older than Sam."

"Right," I agreed sourly. I thought so, too: old enough to be on her own with a job and an apartment, preferably on the other side of the country.

Or the world, even. The argument reached its peak, Lillian and Jill standing flat-footed, face-to-face. Then the girl turned, stalked to the car, and sped off. Lillian stood looking after her a moment, the nail gun still in her hand, then got into the station wagon and followed, her face grim.

I had a moment to feel sorry for Lillian and to wonder why she didn't let things cool off instead of going after Jill while they were both still so angry. But it was none of my business, and we'd started out to clear the way for Jonathan Raines, not snoop into Lillian Frey's obviously unhappy family matters.

"He's probably gone over to the diner," Ellie said, meaning Hecky, so we set off to try to locate him there. But he wasn't in the diner, or the hardware store, or the five-and-dime. He wasn't at a table in the Happy Landings Café or on a barstool at La Sardina, Eastport's Mexican restaurant.

"We really need him," Ellie said. "Right now he's out there somewhere doing the opposite of what we wanted. In Eastport Hecky and his big mouth can fix it so that not only will people refuse to help Raines, they won't even look at him."

"I know," I said, frustrated. Ellie's plan had actually started seeming possible to me. But an hour after we'd begun we were back where we'd started, at the art gallery.

Suddenly a heavy *thwap-thwapping* sound filled the air and an aircraft swooped low over Passamaquoddy Bay. It was the Coast Guard helicopter, its red markings clearly visible on its chunky white body as it beat its way north.

"What in the world is going on out there?" Ellie said. The smell of smoke had never really gone away and grew stronger again now, hanging over the town in a pale haze; not a woodstove or anything like it. Something around here was burning like hell.

Jerome Wallace came outside. He was a big, rawboned man with faraway blue eyes, a thatch of greying hair, and a quiet manner, his clothes habitually paint-smeared.

"Just talked to the dispatcher," he said. "Some guy went off those high bluffs up at North End, into the water. No one seems to know who he is and they're all out there trying to find the body."

Ellie and I looked at each other.

"Some guy," Jerome finished, "from away."

That night, Jonathan Raines sat cheerfully un-drowned at one end of the dinner table, and George Valentine sat at the other. George was chief of Eastport's volunteer fire department as well as its unofficial man of all work, so he knew the whole story of what had happened at North End.

"From away," he repeated, forking up some of the bay-scallop casserole that Ellie and I had prepared. With it we were having steamed endive vinaigrette, cheese biscuits, and some of the new baby potatoes that Ellie had dug that morning, with fresh parsley and butter.

"It doesn't matter that he was somebody from away," I said, and George looked up kindly at me.

"Course it doesn't, Jacobia. But it's all we know about him so far, 'cause the car he drove has come up on a stolen list in Massachusetts. Must've had his wallet, ID and all, on him when he went over. Keys, too, if he had 'em."

Also with us at the table were Sam and his friend Maggie Altvater. The two of them were taking advanced scuba lessons this summer and had gotten in just in time for dinner.

"How do you know for sure he went over at all?" Maggie asked reasonably. "I mean, just because the car is there and he's not. If it's stolen, maybe he just abandoned it."

In the candlelight her creamy complexion glowed with health, her hazel eyes bright with good humor and quick intelligence. And her honey-colored hair was a wonder, falling in masses to the middle of her back.

Unfortunately, it was her habit to spoil the effect with plaid flannel shirts, baggy jeans, and thick-soled hiking boots, none of which did anything to flatter her ample figure.

An unhappy picture of Jill Frey flashed before my eyes: slim as a switchblade and dressed fit to kill. Maggie was a wonderful girl, accomplished and mature; on top of everything else, she was a volunteer emergency medical technician complete with a scanner and a cherry beacon on the dash of her pickup. But Sam treated her like a comfortable old shoe, partly on account of her always presenting herself as if she were one.

"Wonderful library you've got here in town," Raines said, apropos of nothing. "I saw it this afternoon," he added with an odd, intent look at me.

Meanwhile, Sam took another forkful of scallop casserole and chewed happily; at eighteen, he was as strong and good-looking as a healthy young horse, and as stubborn.

"To the library," Jonathan Raines repeated significantly, still looking at me, "after I went everywhere else that I went."

Later I understood that I'd been meant to hear it, that it was important. But I was still thinking about Sam.

It would never occur to him that a girl like Jill Frey could do him any harm; he'd spoken to her twice on the phone already this evening, and I was sure it would ring again anytime now.

"Fellow's camera equipment, tripod and so on, piled by the edge," George answered Maggie's question. "Lady walking her dog found the stuff. No camera."

He swallowed some Budweiser. "Probably had it with him on a strap around his neck. And you can see by the branches all broken off fresh where he scrambled down for a better view, that's the way he went."

The phone rang; Sam jumped up to get it.

"And mainly," George finished, "if he didn't go over, where is he?"

Ellie looked skeptical. "He might not've scrambled, though. Maybe he fell down right from the top. We don't know what he was doing out there, not for sure."

She sipped some wine. "There ought to be a sign there, you know. That edge has been crumbling for two hundred years. It's a safety hazard."

At the north end of the island, she meant, where the view takes in the whole bay: Deer Island, the Canadian waters beyond, and mounded in the distance the hills of New Brunswick and Nova Scotia. Sam came back, his eyes bright and his cheeks flushed, a secret smile he couldn't quite manage to hide on his lips.

"It's enough to tempt anyone who doesn't know how shaky it is, the soil at the very edge of those cliffs," Ellie said. "To get too close, and . . ." Her hands made a *whoops!* gesture, indicating what could happen next.

Having given up on the topic of the library, apparently, Raines glanced up from his plate of potatoes, salad, and cabbage rolls. He was, it had turned out, a rabid vegetarian; he'd made the cabbage rolls himself, steaming the purple cabbage and saving the water for, he said, a health drink.

The notion of which made me shudder. But he'd been a perfect pleasure to have in the kitchen, cleaning up after himself as he went along, and he was so matter-of-fact about his diet that even George—who thought meat and potatoes were two of the five major food groups—wasn't holding it against him.

"So this isn't the first time?" Raines asked. "I mean, that someone has fallen?"

Sam shook his head. "Nope. Every couple of years somebody goes over, usually a visitor. Mostly they get rescued, but . . . see, it looks real safe. But you get out there, step just a little too close—not everywhere, but in some spots—and bingo." He took a swallow of milk. "Next thing, you're in the water, and the current there is vicious. That body's halfway to Lubec by now, maybe farther."

The next town to our south, he meant, along the wild, rocky coast where the land tumbled into the water. And you would tumble, too, if you didn't watch yourself carefully.

"If," Sam said, "it didn't wash up into one of the caves." He ate some more casserole. "Man, they say that some of the caves at the north end run clear to the other side of the island, like a honeycomb. Course," he added with a cautious look at me, "I've never been in any of them myself."

"Right," I said, not believing him for a minute. The idea of him spelunking in underwater caves still gave me the willies, and he knew it. So he—and Maggie, too, I strongly suspected—tended to shelter me from reports of their more outrageous adventures.

On the other hand, I was pretty sure Jill Frey wouldn't be joining Sam on any of these strenuous capers. Despite her athletic build, from what I'd heard of her she didn't seem to be the outdoor type. As a result, I bit my tongue when the topic of sporting activities came up; however dangerous, they were still better than the indoor ones that Jill might suggest.

"Anyway," Sam went on, "it's a cinch he's not alive anymore. The water in Passamaquoddy Bay's about fifty degrees," he told Raines. "Which makes survival time maybe fifteen minutes, even with your head above water. Your muscles lock up and you go into hypothermic coma even before you drown."

Sam related these sobering facts with some gusto, but Raines absorbed them gravely and the rest of the company went quiet, too; I thought it was time to edge the table talk away from dead bodies. Besides, I had some questions that I wanted answers to, from Jonathan Raines.

"So," I invited him brightly, "tell us about your life in Boston. It must be an exciting place to be, lots of intellectual activity and all. I suppose if any new musical manuscripts turn up, I mean of the old historical pieces, you'd be among the first to see them. As a graduate student of music history, I mean," I added, letting him hear the edge in my tone.

"And the music clubs," Maggie said wistfully. "Bluegrass and jazz." Maggie had a lovely, note-perfect contralto singing voice and was a dedicated country-fiddle enthusiast.

"Do any sculling?" Sam asked. "I hear that's a big sport in Cambridge, on the river, there." He ate another cheese biscuit.

Even George joined the interrogation; usually taciturn, he seemed to have taken to Raines. "Got a girl?" he asked joshingly.

Raines laughed but seemed uncomfortable at being the focus of so much interest, which under the circumstances I thought was not surprising. Considering, I mean, that he was lying through his straight white teeth.

"Not, alas, anymore," he replied to George's question a bit sadly. Removing his thick glasses, he polished them with the hem of his white napkin; true to her word, Ellie had raided her linen closet, so we were well supplied with them.

Now, if I could only deal with the rest of the Reading Circle arrangements so handily; at the moment, redecorating requirements were looming rather large. The hole in the plaster, for instance, gaped yawningly at me from across the table.

"The girl—well, she dumped me," Raines said ruefully.

Sam looked surprised. No girl had ever dumped him, and his confidence in this department was so extreme, he didn't realize that not everyone in the world shared it. I watched him turn the notion over in his mind, then discard it.

Raines turned to Maggie. "There are lots of clubs in Boston, but I don't get to go much. Studying," he explained, with a quick look at me. He hadn't forgotten my question or missed its reason. Jonathan Raines, it was turning out, didn't miss much.

Across from him, the broken plaster patch gleamed whitely amid the mottled grey of the older material: horsehair plaster. In the nineteenth century builders added horsehair to make it stronger, and looking at it always reminded me of sunny pastures.

But if you didn't happen to be as fond of horsehair plaster as I was, it was hideous, especially since my patch was centered like an irregular bull's-eye in another, earlier one. A hundred and fifty years ago, someone else had faced the same problem as I did now—a hole in the wall—and had solved it.

I wished I could consult that old fix-it expert; the patch's edges were straight, smooth, and clean, as if someone had simply cut a square opening in the wall, then filled it in. In the morning, I resolved, I would take care of it: yet another patch, then the wallpaper. I had a spare roll of the old gold-medallion pattern, fortunately.

"You and Sam should go down there, though," Raines went on to Maggie, "make a weekend of it. You can hear any kind of music in Boston, and play it, too. There are jam sessions in the clubs. You do play?" he added, sounding sure of himself.

Her face lit up at the thought of going somewhere with Sam, as well as at the idea of a jam session. And, of course, at the attention Raines was paying to her. "How did you know?"

"Your fingers," he smiled. "Calluses on the left hand, and your nails on that hand are clipped short. Marks of a musician."

Maggie beamed and I began liking Raines a lot in spite of myself. All day long I'd kept trying to phone his cousins again, but one had gone upstate with a federal prisoner, one was getting ready for a RICOH trial, and one was undercover. So it would be a while before I talked to any of them.

And meanwhile here was Raines, behaving like a perfect, gentle knight of the Round Table. What he said next didn't hurt my opinion of him, either.

"Oh, I almost forgot." He brought a package up from under his chair. "Your light fixture," he said, offering it to me. "I went up to Calais, to the Wal-Mart, and they had another one."

"Why, thank you. But—how?" It was twenty miles to Calais, our nearest big market town. "For that matter, how did you get *here*?" I asked, taking the package.

Raines stuck his thumb up in pantomime. "Caught a ride with the same man who brought me over to the island," he said. "White panel truck, dog in the cab, maybe you know him?"

Ellie and I looked at each other: we knew him, all right. Wilbur Mapes worked as an urchin diver in season, when he worked at all. The rest of the time, when he wasn't out hunting, he went to farmhouses, barns, anything that was being torn down, scavenging odd items.

Besides a shotgun and a dog so mean, people said, that it would bite you as soon as look at you, the other thing Wilbur had in the cab of that truck was a canning jar full of homemade white lightning.

"Interesting man," Raines remarked dryly, at which point I liked him even more. The jar, the white lightning, and Mapes himself were infamous in and around Washington County. A ride with him could scare the hair right out of your head, unless you possessed a considerable amount of intestinal fortitude.

Still, I wasn't about to let Raines completely off the hook. "I suppose if a rumor got started about a lost violin, a very *valuable* lost violin, way up here in Eastport, Maine, you'd be in a position to hear about it in Boston?"

George got up, taking his cleaned plate out to the kitchen. The blast on Campobello, he'd told us, had been the full fuel tank of a big pleasure boat, the property of an inexperienced, sozzled mariner from Montreal: flashy but noncatastrophic, except to the hapless mariner who'd lost his vessel and barely escaped going up in the explosion.

The smoke Ellie and I smelled downtown, however, had been a grass fire raging in the dry fields above Pirate's Cove, not far from Eastport's freight docks: much less dramatic but potentially a lot more dangerous. Now George was going out with the rest of the fire company to check for hot spots.

Raines looked transparently at me. "Yes, I suppose I would hear about such a violin. And being as the last one—I assume you're talking about a Strad—sold for one-point-three million, it might be an interesting rumor."

The candles flickered warningly, but of course it could have been a breeze from the open window. Raines swallowed some wine, folded his napkin, and placed it beside his plate.

"If," he added, "I were the unscrupulous type."

"Which you're not." I was trying to hide my shock; the last time I'd looked, the going price had been $750,000. It was what my client had paid for the one he bought, back in the city.

Raines held my gaze. "Which I am not. Unscrupulous, I mean. But enough about me," he segued smoothly, turning back to Maggie. "Do you know what makes the tone of a real Stradivarius so fine?"

Maggie smiled shyly, surprised at being made again a part of the conversation. "Well, the whole aging process, I guess. Being old. And something about the wood they used?"

Raines looked wise. "Pickling," he pronounced. "They're just finding out that the Strads—there was a whole family of them in Cremona, building great instruments—well, it's coming out that those guys soaked the wood in brine and it altered the molecular structure."

"Salt water," Sam said thoughtfully. "That makes some sense. Some of the stuff we find while we're diving, well, you wouldn't think it'd have lasted so long. Leather, and even some wood."

He turned to Raines. "You should see it down there. One spot sand, washed clean as a whistle, and right next to it'll be some little fragile clay pipe or something, so perfect it's like it'd just got put there. And things we find that should've rotted."

"Well, but a lot of that is the peat," Maggie pointed out. "The effect of it, I mean. They shipped it in the old days from the port, and I guess they must have spilled lots," she explained to Raines.

"The acid in it preserves things," she went on, "and if it collects in the sort of backwater places that the tide doesn't wash out, whatever got buried in it seems to last forever."

She frowned. "But not always. Remember that leather sack we found, Sam?"

"What was in it?" George asked interestedly, returning for the cups and glasses.

Maggie shrugged. "We don't know. We touched it and it just fell apart, like it was dissolving." She turned back to Raines. "When the silt cleared, whatever was in it had just"—she made a *presto!* gesture with her hands—"washed away."

Sam nodded, letting her talk, wearing a patient expression that reminded me of my ex-husband. I didn't enjoy it and Sam looked a lot like his father anyway, with his green eyes, lantern jaw, and dark, curly hair. And it didn't help any that Sam had been acting like such a knucklehead about Maggie: as if when he wanted her around, well, naturally she would always be there for him, and if he didn't, she wouldn't.

"It's the tone that would have made Jared Hayes want one," Raines said. "A Stradivarius. I don't play, myself. But musicians say it's not a matter of degree, the difference between them and any other violins. They say that it's like playing a whole other instrument; the music flies out. Like," he finished, "the music was just *in* there, waiting to be released."

Behind him on the gold-medallion wallpaper the tiniest spot of red appeared suddenly, like a droplet on a pricked fingertip.

Or didn't. When I blinked and looked again, it was gone.

Maggie nodded dreamily, thinking I suppose of the music just flying out, and she and Sam got up together. They'd made a small business of selling things they'd discovered underwater, listing the items on the Internet via Sam's computer: old china, coins, those clay pipes. Just now they were selling a clay Schweppes jug, and the proceeds from it would buy Sam's books for the fall semester.

"We'll do the dishes, Mrs. Tiptree," Maggie said graciously, "and thanks for dinner." Sam, looking put-upon but with no good way to escape, followed her out.

"So it's not just hype, then," Ellie said when the two had gone. "People thinking that because the violins are so rare, there *must* be some special something about them. Some mystery."

Raines shook his head as the happy blare of a Cajun dance tune came from the kitchen; Sam was a fan of distant sports-radio programs we could sometimes pull in on clear nights, but Maggie liked the Montreal stations.

"No," Raines said. "The specialness is real."

As he spoke, an odd look crossed his face: one part heartfelt longing, another part rationally assessing. But in the next instant it was gone, as George returned to rest his hand briefly on Ellie's shoulder, waiting to say something.

"There were only eleven hundred or so Strads ever made," Raines went on musingly. "I say only, but it's a big number, really; the old man worked practically until the final moment of his life. Into his nineties."

The music from the kitchen cut off and a man began talking about a batting streak that somebody was having.

"And this was when?" George asked, still waiting. He looked straight at me, so I would know it was me he wanted to talk to.

"In the 1700s," Raines replied. "No electric light to work by, no power tools. Just an artist, making musical instruments."

"By hand," George said approvingly.

"And by ear," Raines added. "Now only about six hundred and fifty instruments are left. Not all violins; the family also made harps, guitars, cellos, and violas.

And the reason no more will probably ever be found is, almost every instrument they made has already been accounted for."

Almost. He knew a lot about them, I realized. "Lost in shipwrecks, burnt up or exploded—the fire-bombs in Dresden during World War II got a lot of them," he continued. "The ones that do still exist have individual names of their own, like Greatorex or Messiah."

"So if somebody finds one in their attic . . ." Ellie began. "I mean with a label inside, that says it's a Stradivarius . . ."

"Right. Chances of its being real are a zillion to one against."

Which seemed like stiff odds, considering what I thought he was really here for. Still, when he turned back to Ellie and me, his eyes held a spark of teasing merriment: *I've got a secret.*

"All right, now," I began, annoyed. "I think I've had just about enough of—"

"But I hear from some of your neighbors that you two have been involved in some mysteries yourselves," he remarked, deftly changing the subject.

I just stared at him; I knew how to interrupt people that way, too, and make it seem to everyone else as if I hadn't. It was a technique I'd learned while steering wealthy people into financial plans that did more for their portfolios than for their egos. It took nerve and practice. And he was good at it.

Too good. "Solving crimes in a small Maine town? It's too wonderful to be true," he added. "So, like the rest of the place, I guess it must be." Smooth, very smooth.

"Wade back tonight?" George asked casually. It was what he'd been waiting to say, and I understood; he liked Raines, so far. So far, though, was as far as it went. Back in the city I could have had a street gang in my apartment and they could have murdered me, and if they didn't let my body decompose too badly, no one else in the building would even have noticed. Here it was different.

"After midnight," I said.

Most of the time, Wade Sorenson was Eastport's harbor pilot, which meant he guided big vessels in through the deep, tricky channels, shifting currents, and treacherous tides that led to the port. But starting two days earlier he had become part of a two-vessel team delivering a tugboat to its new berth on Grand Manan Island, and right now he was still out on the water, the lights of Eastport not yet even in sight.

"They promised to radio Federal Marine if they're delayed," I told George. "I'll let you know if they do."

Satisfied—George would fight dragons for me and Ellie, and probably would manage to slay quite a few of them, too, if push came to shove—he went out, as we gathered the remaining serving plates. In the kitchen, Sam and Maggie had formed an efficient assembly line for the dishes; not for the first time, I saw how well and happily they worked together.

Sam, I thought, you dunderhead; I'd tried to raise him right, but he was nevertheless an eighteen-year-old American male, so naturally his idea of female beauty was like Jill: tall, blond, and just enough older than he was to seem sophisticated. Twenty or so, I calculated. Sam was just eighteen.

"It's true," I admitted to Raines, averting my eyes from the spectacle at the kitchen sink: unrequited love on Maggie's side, obliviousness on Sam's. Really, it made me want to swat the kid. "There was a string of deaths," I went on, "and we got to the bottom of them. Untimely," I added reluctantly, "deaths. And unnatural."

And somehow Ellie and I had developed a knack for revealing the skulduggery behind such events; for a while, people in town had begun joking that Ellie's nose actually twitched at the smell of blood. Recently, however, things had quieted down.

Or they'd quieted down until now. I wasn't happy at the thought of an unidentified man, driving a stolen car, coming to Eastport and then immediately falling off a cliff.

Still, no one was calling it murder. "Mostly we were just in the right place at the right time," I said to Raines.

He found a roll of plastic wrap and covered the casserole. "I've heard of that," he said. "But I've got a feeling it's not going to happen to me. Not here."

Also, he put the butter, salt and pepper, and salad dressing away without anyone having to tell him where they went. Then, knocking my socks off, he found the dog biscuits in the cookie tin on top of the refrigerator, opened it, and fed one to Monday.

"Jared Hayes's story would make a wonderful Ph.D. dissertation," he said. "It would make up for my being late with it, I'm sure. Something fascinating, not dry like so much academic writing is. A real man, a talented composer, with real secrets and real . . ."

He paused, as if thinking perhaps he'd said too much, and I agreed; while he was talking the lights had dimmed briefly, but he hadn't seemed to notice. And of course it could simply have been a power dip; out here on the island, you could get a hefty brownout if the PTA scheduled a food sale and everyone decided to bake cookies on the same night.

Still, a prickle went over the little hairs on my arms.

"Even after one day I can tell I'm not going to get any-where with Hayes," Jonathan Raines went on. "Eastport people seem warm and friendly," he allowed. "Really charming, not fake at all. But I'm a stranger here, and of course they think I've come because I want something. That I'm using them, or that I'm trying to."

He finished wrapping the leftover cabbage rolls and put them in the refrigerator, right next to the jug of cabbage juice, which resembled purple ink.

"Not," he added with a chagrined little laugh that didn't sound happy, "that I'm having any success at that, either."

It was what I thought, too, that he was using us. And reports of his activities around town had only hardened my heart on the matter: that Raines, dressed in a many-pocketed fishing vest like some mad angler trolling for information, had been spotted trying to interrogate Eastport's dourest citizen, Elmore Luddy, actually chasing the old man across his own lawn before Luddy slammed the porch door in Raines's face.

That he'd visited the Waco Diner, where the vest would have been about as popular as a red flag in a bull ring. The fishermen who ate in the Waco wore plain rubber boots and sweatshirts from the discount store and disdained hats until the gale warning had been up for twenty-four hours. A fancy fishing outfit bought from the Orvis catalog was the kiss of death to the guys in the Waco.

But according to Ellie, who heard everything that went on in town, Raines had stood out at the end of the fish pier in that vest, too, where everybody downtown could see him in it, and in a pair of silly yellow Wellington boots.

And of course he'd met Hecky Wilmot, antagonizing him with talk of writing and of old, unsavory Eastport secrets, both of these being Hecky's private property in Hecky's opinion.

So, as Raines himself suspected, in the snooping department he'd screwed up royally. And too late he seemed to have realized this, so crestfallen that I couldn't help but feel sorry for him. I could confront him later, I decided, turning from his harmless, suddenly boyish-looking face.

Sam was putting the wineglasses away on the top shelf of the cupboard, while Maggie rinsed the sink. "Want to get our gear ready for tomorrow before we check the bidding on the Schweppes jug?" she asked, wringing out the sponge.

The suits, gloves, and other insulating garments they wore in the cold water lay in the hall awaiting maintenance. With them stood the pair of outrageously bright yellow Wellingtons.

As Maggie turned, Sam stood on tiptoe to put the last glass up, his arm outstretched and his face unselfconsciously young and attractive. "Yeah, good idea," he said. At which Maggie's own face suddenly was suffused with such melting affection that it embarrassed me to look at it.

Maggie gave the sink a final, unnecessary wipe. When she finished, there was nothing but her usual good humor in her expression.

But I'd seen, and so had Jonathan Raines, whose sympathetic sorrow he concealed by frowning down at his hands. *She dumped me,* he'd said lightly, but I sensed he didn't feel light about it.

Maggie must have picked something up from the cooling of the atmosphere, as well. "You could get her back, you know," she said quietly to Raines. "You could call her and apologize."

He looked up gratefully. "It's too late now, I'm afraid. But thanks for the thought, Maggie."

"Come on, Mags, work to do," Sam broke in, and a moment later I heard them chattering happily, dragging their gear out onto the porch to ready it for tomorrow.

"You two could get to the bottom of it," Raines said

when they had gone, meaning Ellie and me. "What happened to Hayes, for example, why he vanished. All I need to know, and more. You could find out because everybody knows you, and they'll talk to you."

Ellie sat down across from him. "We've tried," she said. "We got out Hayes's papers in the library, old issues of newspapers, everything we could find."

It struck me, then, the other thing I'd been wondering about Raines. A zing of suspicion went through me as I thought just how unusual it was.

"How'd you know where to find the plastic wrap? Where I keep the butter and condiments and so on? And how in the world did you know the dog biscuits are on top of the refrigerator?"

But his answer was ordinary enough. "Oh, well." He shrugged modestly. "That's not hard. Things are usually where you expect them to be, aren't they? If you think about it."

He let out a heavy sigh. "Only not this time. And the trouble is, I can almost smell it. You have no idea the difference it would make to me, and it's here, but I don't have the tools to get at it," he finished, his voice hardening in frustration.

Then he caught himself. "The information, I mean," he added. "About Jared Hayes, to write my dissertation. Get the degree."

"Jonathan," I began. *Stop lying to me,* I was about to say to him. *Play straight with us and we might even be able to help you.*

But at his mention of Hayes, the lights dimmed suddenly once more and flared again. Up in the attic, something thumped loudly and threateningly three times.

Monday whined. "It must be unnerving," Raines said, angling his head sympathetically. "Having things so unsettled."

I could have told him how unnerving it was. But Raines

hadn't confided anything, so I didn't, either, and that worked out in the end about as well as it always does.

"Squirrels," I said shortly. "They get into the attic and bump the wires and knock things over." I was annoyed, so I didn't feel like telling him anything but a few ground rules.

"Listen," I began sternly. "You're welcome to stay here—"

Back in the city, one of Raines's cousins had once saved my bacon. I won't bore you with the details; suffice it to say that when Raines's relative finished chatting with the district attorney, my wealthy client no longer had a room reserved for him at a federal prison and I wasn't being sued anymore.

"—as long as you want," I finished.

Noting my tone, Raines eyed me contritely. And mad as I was at him, I still liked this strange creature with his gold shark's tooth necklace, his thick spectacles, and custom-tailored shirts.

"However," I went on briskly, noting with satisfaction that my sit-up-and-listen voice still worked, "there are some things you're going to do, and not do, from here on out."

I pointed an index finger. "First, you will confine yourself to library research. Manuscripts, diaries, letters, and account books and so on, things Jared Hayes left behind in the house when he vanished."

Raines opened his mouth to object, but I got in ahead of him; two could play that game. "But when the rubber meets the road, my friend Ellie White and I will be in the driver's seat, not you."

I took a deep breath. "No more blundering around in Eastport demanding that people talk to you," I went on. "If you need that sort of question answered, and I suspect that you will, ask it of us, and we will try to find the answer for you."

Ellie's eyebrows went up in the *wow, good plan* expression she saves for when I have really outdone myself, and I felt the small burst of pride I always experience on these rare occasions.

Thank you, I telegraphed at her. "Also, I want you to watch out in general about who you talk to, where you go. Not just when you want to know something, but all the time. And don't argue," I added as he made as if to object again.

". . . tanks and regulators," Sam said to Maggie on the porch. "And a few more dive flags."

I closed my ears to this; the idea of Sam being underwater at all was just one of the many notions I was having to learn to ignore—some more successfully than others—in the process of cutting the apron strings.

"Guys like Wilbur Mapes, for example," I went on to Raines. "He's no joke, Jonathan. You should stay away from him. People around town like his dog better, because the dog at least growls before it bites you. Wilbur just turns mean in a heartbeat."

Raines looked impressed. But I wasn't finished. "Finally, I don't believe for a minute your story about your Ph.D. dissertation. I think you're really here to try to find a certain rare violin."

Once more he tried to interrupt; I waved a hand at him and he fell gratifyingly silent.

"And you won't. But if you insist on sticking with it," I went on, "kindly at least refrain from flat-out rubbing our noses in your denials. We're not stupid even if we don't live in Boston and attend graduate school, which by the way I've already learned that part of your story isn't true."

He examined his fingernails, looking like a kid who knows he deserves the scolding he is getting.

"I don't think you're stupid," he said. "I never

thought that, honestly. And your plan sounds fine, except that there's one thing you haven't thought of."

"Which is?" Ellie asked.

"That I've made such a hash of it already," Raines replied. "I thought this was just going to be another small town. You know, with people dying to talk. Flattered, thrilled to be asked."

He shook his head. "But Eastport . . . well, I was too eager and people didn't like it. And now"—he sighed heavily—"if you ask questions on my behalf, they'll *know* it's for me, and they won't answer *you*, either. If only there were a way to . . ."

He hesitated, then seemed to gather his courage. "And there is another thing. I hadn't wanted to tell you. It sounds so . . . so melodramatic. But there's someone who wants to stop me."

Great: now we had a villain, opposing the lovesick hero in his brave, solitary search for . . . Oh, for heaven's sake.

"Jonathan, it doesn't only sound melodramatic. It sounds absurd." For one thing, why would a villain want to stop someone from writing a Ph.D. dissertation? "You can't even keep your . . ."

Stories straight, I was about to say. But, "Look, let's just cut to the chase, shall we? First of all, I want to know where you heard that tune you were whistling. Earlier"—I looked hard at him—"when you first got here."

Maggie and Sam had finished with the drysuits and were now in the back parlor powering up the computer. "While we're on-line we can upload pictures of the jug," Maggie said. "I borrowed my Dad's digital camera while he was up here."

Maggie's dad was a salesman in Bangor; he and her mom were on decent terms and he visited often. "See," she said, "they're on this disk. Sure wish he'd left the camera, too," she sighed.

I heard the computer's disk drive whirr as it accepted the pictures, which was a process I no more understood than I caught the drift of quantum physics, but it worked.

"Great," Sam said. "Um, you'll write the captions?"

"Uh-huh." Maggie finished whatever arcane maneuvers it took to get snapshots of a two-hundred-year-old seltzer jug onto the World Wide Web, and snapped the floppy from the drive. "That's the bargain, right? I do the words, you do the numbers."

"You got it." Sam was dyslexic, a handicap that made reading and writing laborious, but he drove a hard bargain; Maggie, smoothly literate, tended to low-ball. So they made a good team for the Internet auctions where they sold their finds.

And in other ways, I thought. But I reminded myself that it was none of my business, as Raines looked puzzled.

"Tune? I don't know. Guess I heard it somewhere." He tipped his head, thinking.

Or acting as if he were trying to think, while knowing where he'd heard it.

"Not in Boston," he mused aloud. "I think I'd recall. Hmm, that is a riddle—maybe from you? Did you happen to be whistling it yourself when I came in? Because I'm sure I heard it when I—"

"No, Jonathan." My patience was wearing thin. "We all know the tune."

It was a dervish of a virtuoso fiddle number; local players had tried it, and although they could reproduce the melody, the tempo was demonic and in the end they all confessed that it had beaten them.

"But I can't whistle," I went on, "and Sam wasn't

here, and when Monday tries to whistle all she does is spit out little dry bits of dog biscuit. So tell me the truth, for once."

What I wanted was the rest of the story: not just how he'd known the music or why he was here, but why he was so sure a country fiddler named Jared Hayes had really had a Stradivarius.

And why he thought it was still in Eastport. That was what I wanted that night, safe and sound at the kitchen table.

Instead, as he whistled the tune again, the old music books in the library seemed to rise in my mind's eye: thickly quill-penned with eighth- and sixteenth-notes, the heavy old vellum foxed and faded but still thrillingly legible, even to me.

The pieces, mostly dance tunes with titles like "Jo's Jig" and "Mandalay Reel," painted a portrait of Hayes as a man with energy and style. When they were played at musical evenings put on by the Eastport Historical Society, you could almost hear him laughing merrily in the background.

But there were darker pieces, also, as *presto* yet filled with minor-key flourishes and throbbingly sad melodies, hinting at an awful yearning. Like . . .

" 'Pirate's Revenge.' " Raines snapped his fingers, smiling with the happy surprise of a man who has answered a difficult game-show question. "But for the life of me I couldn't tell you *how* I know," he said.

Whereupon all the lights went out.

And stayed out. We lit candles, which didn't do much for our activity level; really, there are few things anybody wants to do nowadays by candlelight, with the notable exception of one thing. But Wade had not gotten back, yet.

We called the power company to no avail as the blackout time lengthened to an hour and then another.

And we played a few games, trying to tell Go To Jail from Park Place in the gloom. But we were a dull company, and finally when George stopped back to get Ellie and Maggie had gone home, we went to bed. George had promised to fix whatever had gone wrong—it wasn't the fuse box, and no one else in town had lost power—in the morning.

Lonesomely, I got under the covers. Of course, the house was well stocked with emergency storm supplies; after all, this was downeast Maine, where a three-day blow is referred to by the natives as "a little weather." But candles in the bedrooms were forbidden as fire hazards and reading by oil lamp has never been a habit of mine, since the lamp wicks must be trimmed with near-microscopic precison or they stink.

And since Raines was tired, he said, from traveling, and Sam was planning to go out early the next morning, by ten o'clock I thought everybody in the house was asleep.

Except for me. I just lay there with my eyes open, half of me cursing Jonathan Raines for disrupting my summer and the other half still wondering curiously what the heck he was up to. Even with Monday taking up most of it, the big bed felt empty, as it always did with Wade still out on the water. I wished he would get home early, but I knew he was still several hours from shore, on a boat in the dark.

Somewhere out there a man's body was floating, too: a man whose whole story I felt certain we hadn't heard yet. The Coast Guard search for the fallen stranger would start again in the morning, but as Sam said, strong tides and currents could have taken the body anywhere, as they took everything that floated, sooner or later.

Around midnight the phone rang shrilly and I jumped, but it was only Ellie. "You all right?"

"Fine," I said. "You?"

"Okay. Working on the quilt. The stitching is in two colors, red and blue, so you can't see the pattern until all the quilting is finished. But it's going to be great when it's done."

I waited, imagining her with the quilting frame in her lap, her hands moving patiently.

"George went out again," she said.

"That fire at Pirate's Cove?"

"Uh-huh. It was arson. He just didn't want to say so at the table."

"Oh," I said, understanding immediately. Not too many topics could make George Valentine lose his temper. Arson, though . . .

"So the guys are taking turns on night patrol in Eastport, and over on the mainland, too," she said resignedly. "They are carrying," she added, "guns."

Which anywhere else might have seemed like an overreaction, but on the rural mainland, especially, night patrol could be scary duty. The midnights there were unbroken by streetlights, so dark and deep that even familiar places felt like another country. And many of the inhabited structures were miles off-road, so it was essential not to let an arsonist's habit get established.

"George says the gun rack in his truck's not a decoration," Ellie said, and I could see it: George's face wearing the closed, purposeful look Eastport men's faces get when they mean business.

"He'll be all right," I said, thinking of Wade. When he was home he had a small business appraising and repairing firearms out of a workshop in the ell of my house.

"I know," she replied quickly. George was nearly as handy with a shotgun or rifle as Wade was. "It's silly, isn't it? How we worry about them."

I agreed that was true, and after a while we hung up, knowing it wasn't. Because out there in the dark, on the back roads or on the water, anything could happen.

Anything at all: a few months earlier, three men had gone out fishing like they always did. Solid, experienced men, and the boat was fine, too. But without any warning an aft compartment filled with water: gone fishing. That time, one of the men came back and two didn't.

So one way and another I didn't feel the least bit sleepy. Still, I must have dozed, because several hours later when I came downstairs, flashlight in hand, to go down to the breakwater and meet Wade when he arrived home on the tugboat, I found that the hole in the dining room wall had been vastly enlarged.

A hammer lay on the hardwood floor beneath it. Another flashlight lay there, too, still switched on, its battery dying and its bulb emitting a weak yellow glow. Pried chunks of plaster littered the floor around it, and on the table, as if he had only taken them off for a moment, lay Jonathan Raines's pair of thick-lensed, wire-rimmed eyeglasses.

Raines himself, though, was nowhere to be found; luckily for him, since if he had been there I'd have throttled him.

But I looked everywhere, Monday padding along behind me in the silent rooms.

And he was gone.

3

Furiously I pulled a sweater on and strode downtown, past the old mansard-roofed Bainbridge mansion at the corner of Key Street. Of late a sad relic with boarded-up windows and rotting trim, in its heyday a ballroom had occupied the mansion's third floor; now whenever I glimpsed it I thought of the music played there all those years ago, and of the people gorgeously dressed in ball gowns and tuxedos. Lately I found myself wondering, too, if they were all still up there somehow, dancing in the dark.

I shook off a chill, though the night was not very cold. *Funny,* Raines had said when he arrived, *how an item can seem to be one thing and turn out to be another.*

Yeah, I thought at him; the way you seemed at first to be a minor annoyance, and instead you're a major pain in the tail.

I headed downhill on Key Street toward the bay; next came a row of clapboard cottages from the 1800s, gleaming by moonlight, their window boxes brimming with flowers. At Water Street I passed the red-brick Peavey Library, its front-lawn cannon aimed at the waterfront as if to ward off any redcoats who might be returning. Across the street, the Happy Landings Café stood dark and silent, its deck umbrellas folded like the wings of sleeping birds.

At the breakwater, Wade's boat had already arrived. Under the dock lamps, the men on the *Ahoski* worked to make her fast to the massive dock pilings, with lines as thick as their arms tied around the cleats on the tugboat's rail. Beyond, the moonlight sketched the wave tops with thin lines of silver; below, the dark water heaved sluggishly with the tide, reminding me again of the fellow floating somewhere out there, drowned and alone.

The dampness made me shiver again. But then Wade appeared, ascending the old ladder up the dock's side as easily as climbing a flight of stairs. His wiry hair gleaming in the lights and his grin visible even at a distance, he hurried across the breakwater and caught me in a bear hug.

"Hey." Smelling of lime shaving soap and cold salt water, he pressed his cheek to my hair.

"Hey, yourself." I put my face into his down vest. "Trip go okay?"

"Piece of cake." He glanced back at the tubby old vessel, waved to the guy still at the helm behind the big wheel, shutting down the electricals. The bridge lights went out, the radium glow of the navigation and communications equipment on the consoles like sparks of green fire in the sudden darkness.

"Everything good at home?" Wade slung an arm and we started back uphill. "Sam okay? And did I get a package?"

"You got a package. I brought it in." A new Lyman shotgun-shell reloading press, I happened to know, and it weighed a ton.

"And Sam's fine. Well, not perfectly fine; he's got a huge crush on an unsuitable girl. I'm hoping it will fade. But . . ."

I told him about the day. "So when I see him again I'm going to kill him," I said, meaning Raines, "and that will be that."

I didn't really mean it. Probably cutting his thumbs off and feeding them to the seagulls would be punishment enough.

"But the way things are going around here, I'm going to have to host the Ladies' Reading Circle meeting in a tent out in the backyard."

Wade laughed, a deep, rumbling sound that made me feel much better. "Do them good," he said. "Fresh air."

By which he meant he thought Reading Circle meetings were excessively refined. "Tell you the truth, I'm a little surprised at you," he said.

I'd wondered about it, myself; china teacups tend to make my little finger rise in parody, and just thinking about the elastic waistband on a pair of panty hose can give me a cramp. But when winter returned and it started getting dark at two-thirty in the afternoon, and I had been wearing ice cleats on my boots for what seemed forever, the ladylike refinement portion of the program would start looking pretty good to me.

"Don't worry," I said. "You're not going to have to attend. In fact—"

Men sometimes hovered around the edges of Reading Circle meetings, or were present as invited guests. As a rule, though, it was a girl thing.

"I'll make myself scarce," he assured me. "Don't worry about that."

Wade had his own little house on Liberty Street, to which he repaired when he wanted to throw an all-male bash, bourbon and cigars. Or if he just wanted a stretch of solitude. Early on, I'd felt rejected when he did it, but then I noticed two facts: (a) his mail and his packages kept coming to my place, and (b) sooner or later, so did he. If—when—we got married, I would want him to keep the place on Liberty Street.

And so would he. "Meanwhile," I went on, "the power in the house is . . ."

But then I stopped. We were cresting the hill on Key Street, under the big old maples looming massively along the sidewalk.

". . . out," I finished. "Or it was."

Beaming through the branches, turning the new, transparent maple leaves a luminous gold-green, every window in the house blazed. All but the ones in Sam's room; he must have woken up and switched his off, not realizing that the rest were on, too.

Monday woofed suspiciously once and fell silent as she caught our scent; when we got inside she did a doggy buck-and-wing in the hall to greet us, then settled back into her bed.

Raines hadn't returned. "Lucky for him," I said grimly as Wade got a beer from the refrigerator and took it to the dining room to survey the damage. "When I get hold of him . . ."

"Um, Jacobia?" Wade's voice sounded curious. "How big a hole did you say he made in here?"

I'd been turning out lights, but at his tone I stopped and went into the room. And wished I hadn't: half an hour earlier, the gap in the plaster had been about two feet square. But in my absence, the old-house domino effect had gone to work with a vengeance: with such a sizable section of old plaster missing—and therefore not available to hold the rest up against the forces of gravity—a whole section of wall between the door to the butler's pantry and the window pantry had collapsed.

In other words, a two-foot square hole—not minor, but it had been manageable—had expanded to six-by-twelve: disastrous.

"Oh," I said inadequately.

"Now, don't panic," Wade said, seeing my face.

"I'm not panicking," I said.

Also, I wasn't screaming. But I felt like it. Ragged ends of plaster chunks hung from the ceiling trim and dangled along the window, clinging only there by virtue of the strands of horsehair still embedded in them.

"Inside the fortunately very solid containment vessel that is my body, I am exploding," I said carefully.

"Let's just go make ourselves a few scrambled eggs and an English muffin," Wade said, putting his big hand on my shoulder. "And a couple of double whiskies. I can open the Lyman press in the morning."

And that, in a nutshell, is Wade. To him, disaster is green water over the helm and a fire in the engine room; little else signifies.

"Right," I said. There was nothing to be done about it now, anyway. So I went around turning off the rest of the lamps, glancing into Raines's room to make sure he hadn't sneaked back in.

He hadn't, but his duffel still lay by his neatly made bed; that and his eyeglasses, still out on the dining room table, told me he would return to the scene of the crime sooner or later.

And when he did, boy, was he ever going to be sorry.

Wade and I had whiskey and eggs at the kitchen table, Monday delicately accepting the little bits of muffin and egg I fed her.

"People giving you a hard time, huh?" Wade asked.

Now that he was here, I felt the muscles in my shoulders and neck relaxing. The house had an entirely different feel about it when he was in it.

I shrugged. "Not so bad." Wade had warmed the whiskey very carefully in a saucepan, and I could sense it putting a fuzzy, artificial blur on my miseries. Fortunately, there wasn't much of it left in the bottle.

"This visitor guy. All the house repairs. And Jared Hayes." Wade knew how caught up I'd gotten in that old story.

"Still feeling spleeny about it, are you?"

Spleeny: a downeast term for being jittery without cause. Most of the time Wade let me alone about it, for which I was grateful; if he had been solicitous on the topic I'd only have felt more foolish.

"And Sam. Really it's him I'm most worried about," I said.

Wade eyed the second half of my muffin. I handed it to him. "I probably shouldn't be so paranoid that Sam's going to turn out like his dad," I said. "I mean, after they made Victor, I think they broke the petri dish they fished him out of."

Wade chuckled. "Sooner or later any young guy gets wild over girls, Jake. Sam'll get through it, just like he's gotten through everything else."

Everything else: like being dyslexic, getting addicted to a variety of drugs and kicking them, growing up in a household that had been perpetually at war. I could argue that Sam deserved a little irresponsibility, a little selfishness. As a child he'd had to be as sensitive as a cat's whisker just to survive.

But it made me nervous. "Did you? Get wild about girls when you were his age?"

Wade looked down at his plate. "Well, I was a little busy. Not too much time to raise hell. Of any kind."

Wade's own dad had been a hell-raiser there at the end of his life, only the hell he'd raised had been with his fists. He'd been beaten to death in a brawl in Derry; after that, with a mother and younger sister to support, Wade dropped out of school and went to work on a fishing boat.

"I used to feel cheated, tell you the truth. Never dated any girls, figured I was missing out on something. But now I know." He smiled quietly, poured the last half inch of spirits from the saucepan into his shot glass.

"Know what?" Wade never talked about this stuff much.

He looked up, still smiling. "That I was waiting for you."

And there it was; he would go along so silently, sometimes, that I would start wondering. Or he would go to Liberty Street for a week. Then he would blindside me with something so simple and matter-of-fact, I wondered only how I'd gotten so lucky.

Wade got up and stacked our plates and silverware in the sink. "Don't let Victor give you too much guff," he advised. "A lot of shipping coming into the harbor this week. I don't have time to take off, find Victor, punch him in the nose."

That was another thing, the psychological place Wade located my ex-husband: in the margin where he belonged.

"I'll remember," I promised, and he ruffled my hair easily.

"Good." He pointed at my glass. "Now finish that up."

Once the whiskey was gone, we went to bed, Wade wrapping his arms around me before falling almost instantly into the sleep of a man who has spent all day working hard outdoors.

And so, much to my surprise, did I. And whether it was the whiskies or my relief at having Wade home off the ocean that made me sleep so hard, I'm not sure; all I know is that the next time I opened my eyes it was—egad!—eight in the morning.

Wade had gone out already—the new shotgun-shell reloading press had been opened and hauled upstairs to the ell workshop, the carton it came in broken down and stowed with the rest of the recyclable stuff—and so had Sam. Raines's room remained empty, but his duffel was still here and so were his glasses.

And the house felt very silent, as if the spirit world had gone on hiatus. All of which might have made for a day in which I could just possibly get the dining room repairs going, but in the kitchen, Eastport's police chief Bob Arnold sat waiting for me at the table: drinking coffee, eating a doughnut, looking unhappy.

Very unhappy. Also, sooty and exhausted. "Another fire?" I asked, and he nodded glumly.

"Looks like we've got ourselves a firebug in town. But what else is new?"

Because it was summer, he meant; in Eastport it was the dark side of an old tradition. Burning fields of tinder-dry grass from the year before, heaping last autumn's leaves in bonfires, and on the mainland searing off acres and acres of old blueberry shrub to make way for fresh growth: all of it remained common practice.

Every year, too, a few houses went up in flames; un-occupied, mostly, but sometimes not, and tattling on a firebug was as good as putting up a placard: BURN MINE. Tradition wasn't all church suppers and the Fourth of July in downeast Maine.

It was why a grass fire had made George Valentine so angry. But that wasn't what Bob Arnold wanted to talk to me about. "You had a guest? Jonathan Raines?"

The past tense alerted me. "What's happened to him?"

Drinking with Mapes, maybe, or poking his nose where someone decided it shouldn't go. I thought about the possibilities for Raines's current whereabouts: the hospital or jail. Arnold eyed me, his round, pink face full of imminent bad news.

"Seem all right to you when he left, this Raines fellow? In his right mind, and so on?"

Uh-oh. "Bob, what *is* it?"

He put his cup down. "Looks like last night, at midnight or so, he went off the end of the dock. Drowned."

A thump of disbelief hit me. "But . . . how do you know? I mean, are you sure it was him? You've found a body?"

If they had, it could've been the other one, I was already thinking. The one who'd gone off the bluff at North End. Hoping, because Raines was so troublesome that by then I'd have done anything to get rid of him; his boyish charm was a point in his favor, but even I drew the line at torn-down walls.

The thought of his face, though, blue and motionless . . . and his Ph.D. work. Now, I thought irrationally, it would never be finished.

"Oh, Bob." Suddenly I was heartbroken. "*Are* you sure?"

" 'Fraid so. Wore a vest, did he? Fancy one, a lot of small pockets in it, like for fly-fishing?"

"You mean he isn't even recognizable?"

I don't know why that felt as if it made things worse. Maybe because I could see Jonathan's face so clearly in my mind's eye: handsome, and with a quiet kind of competence half hidden behind the youthful features. A face with a future . . . but not anymore. Monday came up and pushed her cold nose anxiously into my hand, sensing my distress.

"I mean," Bob said gently, "so far the vest is all we've got. Couple of fellows working on a dragger in the boat basin saw him; they were up late, hoping to get out fishing today."

So by the time I went down to meet Wade, it had all been over. What search there would have been in the darkness would've halted, to start again in daylight: recovery, not rescue, because as Sam said, the cold water would finish a person off fast.

"Put in an emergency call as soon as they saw him fall," Bob went on. "They said he had just pitched off the end like maybe he lost his balance."

Which made sense timing-wise, if he'd gone out while I was asleep. "Anyone else see him?"

"Ayuh. Teddy at La Sardina"—the Mexican place on Water Street across from the dock—"he said Raines came in eleven-thirty or so, had a drink at the bar."

"Just one?" I asked, but Bob didn't know. "Teddy won't talk about his customers, you know, 'less you ask a direct question. Even to me. He's too good a barkeep for that." Discretion being the key to success in the bar business in Eastport, just as it was anywhere else. "He did say Raines wasn't loaded enough to mistake the dock for a stretch of sidewalk."

Which happened now and again, in town. But if Raines was not drunk, there went that explanation.

"Fell off the end of the dock," I repeated musingly, trying to picture it. "Well, I *guess* it could happen."

In the dark, the end of that pier was a wild place, with wind gusts that could knock you off your feet and the half-glimpsed, half-felt movement of the rolling waves to upset your equilibrium, especially if you weren't used to it. Wade handled it fine, but I kept well back from the edge myself.

"Time we got there, there was already no sign of him. Early this morning, found the fishing vest hung up on a snag in one of the pilings. And that's all she wrote," Bob finished in tones of regret. "Who was he, anyway? Friend of yours?"

I shook my head. "Hardly knew him. Friend of a friend, you know how that goes."

He nodded wisely. "Summer complaint."

It was the term Maine natives used when describing summer visitors, especially ones who lingered, offering no certain date of departure.

"Talk in town already," he said, swallowing some coffee. "He have any problems that you know of?"

"Talk? You mean about problems that might have made him jump off the dock?" I had to laugh at the idea; Jonathan Raines had been about as darkly brooding as your average ball-chasing pup.

"I doubt it," I told Bob. "He wasn't the type." Which I was sure had been said of many unexpected suicides, but this time I thought it was true. "I'm sure it must've been an accident."

Another possibility was beginning to niggle at me, though. It was true that there was no guardrail on that dock. And it was a dicey spot if you lost your balance easily.

Still, plenty of people did stand there, even at night.

"Least his wallet was in the vest," Bob said, "not like

the other guy. Startin' to look as if we might never find out who *he* was."

A lot people seemed to be falling into the water around here suddenly, I thought, my suspicion index rising.

"I notified," Bob added, "the woman on his emergency card. She's the girlfriend."

Oh, boy; I'd forgotten about her. *She dumped me,* Raines had said. "You talked to her?" I asked. "Was she . . ." I waved my hands to indicate emotional upset.

Bob shook his head. "Cool as a cucumber. I doubt you'll even hear from her," he replied.

"Excuse me," said a woman from the back hall, peering into the kitchen at us.

I hadn't heard her at the door and neither had Monday, who blinked in affronted surprise: *Where'd you come from?*

Which was my question, also. She was the prettiest girl I'd ever seen, with hair dark and glossy as a raven's wing. She wore no makeup—on her, it would have been gilding the lily—but her red lips, pink cheeks, and violet eyes framed in dark fringelike eyelashes made her face as richly colorful as an oil painting.

"I'm Charmian Cartwright," she said, holding out her hand.

I took it; it was cool and trembling perceptibly, her voice shaky with the effort it was costing her to keep it controlled.

"The lady I mentioned to you," Bob Arnold said, getting up.

Lady was right; it wasn't so much her costume— beige silk slacks, a tunic top in yellow with silk frog closures, sandals that looked like—and probably had cost—a million bucks.

It was the way she wore them: perfectly. Carelessly, and yet with a great deal of quiet care. Nary a chip in her pink-beige nail polish, and if that black hair didn't get a hundred strokes every night, I was willing to eat my hat.

"You're Jonathan's . . ." I paused, looking for the right word.

"That's right," she agreed, not supplying it. "I flew up as soon as I heard." Her eyes, the same dark purple-blue as the tiny flower their color was named for, glistened with emotion.

"Miss Cartwright, I wonder if I could have a few words with you later," Bob Arnold said.

She glanced sharply at him. "I'd like a few words with you, too," she retorted, at which point any thoughts I might have been having about purely decorative value went out the window. Getting a charter to Eastport on sudden notice was no mean feat, either.

"Please sit down," I offered a little tardily, as Bob went out, no doubt to recover from the effects of having just met this elegant young creature.

She did so, accepting a cup of coffee and, after a moment of hesitation, a piece of toast. "Thank you," she murmured as I set it in front of her.

I liked the way she ate: manners aplenty but businesslike, putting fuel in the machine. On her left ring finger she wore a gold ring with an opal in it, the stone glowing with blue fire; it was her only jewelery.

Just then Sam came in with a clunk and clatter of dive gear, talking animatedly; I expected to see Maggie behind him, but it was Jill Frey. I hadn't heard her car pull up, but it must have; oh, this was just terrific.

"Anyone here?" Sam began, then saw Charmian and dropped a diving weight onto his foot. "Ow."

Behind him, Jill's ice-blue eyes narrowed for a competitive instant.

"Where's Maggie?" I asked, feeling mean and not bothering to squelch the emotion, especially since Sam had apparently stiffed Maggie on the plans he'd made with her for this morning.

"I don't know where she is," Jill said carelessly, flipping back a wisp of white-blond hair while still eyeing the stranger. "Off lifting barbells or something. God forbid she shouldn't be able to keep up with the men, since she obviously can't compete with the girls." Her laugh was a brittle, dismissive sound.

Sam had already raced upstairs; Jill wouldn't have said that about Maggie if he'd been listening, I thought.

Hoped. "Hurry up, Sam," she added with irritation.

"Coming," he called, and when he came down his hair had been slicked back and his T-shirt exchanged for a clean polo shirt.

"See you later, Mom," he said, peering curiously at the woman at the table as Jill put her hand possessively on his arm.

I could tell he was torn between wanting to know who the visitor was and anxiety to get Jill Frey out of here; he was well aware of my opinion of her.

"Got to stop at Dad's, he owes me ten bucks," Sam said. Then: "Jill's joined the dive class," he added, wanting to push something positive about her. "Isn't that great? We're going out on Dad's boat with him to practice with the gear."

He smiled at Jill, who simpered at him in return, and of course I did not poke my finger down my throat right there at the kitchen table.

"Great," I said flatly. "Don't let her stay underwater too long."

Sam ignored the clear meaning in my remark, but he heard it, and so did Jill, whose icy eyes flashed at me in sweet triumph as she tugged my son's arm. "Come *on*, Sam."

Then they were gone, and I was left with a collapsed

wall, a dead houseguest, and a grief-stricken fair maiden.

"I'm so sorry for your loss," I said.

I was, too; that cool-as-a-cucumber stuff Bob Arnold had mentioned was really just well-bred manners. Maybe the girl was as steel-spined and capable as her actions seemed to indicate; getting from Boston to Eastport as she had, for instance, showed some fairly machinelike efficiency.

But she was obviously heartbroken. Despite her high color and good grooming, her violet eyes were tragic and her squared shoulders suggested a soldier marching to doom; if she let her guard down even the slightest bit, I sensed, she might lose all her desperate control.

She bit her lip hard. "I'm sorry," she began, but couldn't go on; a sob escaped her. Producing a handkerchief, she dabbed her eyes with it, then gathered an inner strength I'd already begun suspecting might be considerable and straightened bravely.

"I'm sorry to trouble you," she began again, her voice shaking faintly. "But he hasn't any family to make arrangements, you see. So I came as soon as soon as . . ."

"Oh, you poor thing," Ellie said, coming in and assessing the situation immediately. "George went down," she went on to me, "last night when the call came. I didn't know then who it was, or I'd have called you. They're out again now, looking."

Charmian gazed brokenly at us. "You mean he hasn't . . . Jon's body hasn't been . . ."

"No. The tides are strong, and there's a current around that pier. And it seems he was wearing a pair of boots?"

Ellie looked questioningly at me. She had on her spare eyeglasses, the ones with the pink frames that made her look like an absent-minded librarian, especially with her red hair twisted into a French knot from which a few curly strands escaped.

"Those Wellingtons," I agreed sadly, understanding what she meant. They'd have filled with water and carried him down where the currents ran like cold submarine rivers, to sweep him away.

"So I can't take him—" Charmian's voice broke on the word *home*.

"No. I'm so sorry to have to tell you," Ellie pronounced kindly, but firmly, too. I remembered suddenly that as George's wife—the wife of Eastport's fire chief, that is—Ellie spoke to many people who had suffered misfortunes.

And it would be no kindness to raise false hopes. "They may find him, and certainly they're going to make every effort to do so. But you need to prepare yourself for the possibility that you may never be able to take his body home."

At this, I fully expected a sudden torrent of tears. But Charmian Cartwright received the bad news with grave dignity. Only a tiny stiffening of her shoulders betrayed how hard it hit her.

"I see. Thank you for telling me. Would it be too much trouble to . . . that is, exactly what's supposed to have happened to him? Was he doing something foolish and dangerous, as usual?"

"Oh, no. Nothing like that." I decided not to mention the violin we believed he'd been looking for; it wasn't pertinent anymore, I thought.

"He didn't seem careless to us," I went on. "He was just a very nice, mild fellow, said he was researching his Ph.D. A bit absentminded-professorish, maybe," I added as another pang of affectionate regret struck me.

"Drat," Ellie said. "Can you believe it?" She frowned down at the stem of her glasses in one hand, a tiny screw in the other. "Twice in two days."

"Give them to me, please," Charmian said softly but in tones of command, like a schoolteacher so accustomed to obedience that it is given unquestioningly.

Ellie looked surprised but handed them over.

"And of course you know he was a little . . . well. Clumsy," I went on. But even as I said this, I felt my memories of Raines clashing confusedly:

Muscles, a lithe appearance, but those thick glasses, and he'd dropped that cut-glass ceiling fixture as if his fingers had been buttered. Short of money, too, yet dressed by a London shirtmaker and out of the Orvis catalog.

"He said himself," I went on puzzledly, "that he wasn't the deftest person in the world. . . ."

But Charmian apparently was. From a soft leather bag that looked too tiny to hold much more than a lipstick, she produced a small ornate penknife. Opened, the implement revealed a multitude of attachments, including a miniature screwdriver.

With it, she reattached the stem of Ellie's glasses, then handed them back to her. The whole operation took approximately thirty seconds.

"Why, thank you," Ellie managed.

"Go on, please," Charmian said, closing the penknife.

"Well. That's what they think happened. That he missed his footing in the dark or lost his balance at the edge of the pier."

It sounded reasonable as I said it, but Charmian stared as if I'd suddenly begun speaking gibberish. "They think he *fell*?"

She turned to Ellie. "You can't be serious. There must be some other explanation."

Ellie looked regretful. "Well, yes, actually. He could have jumped. I must say I don't think that's very likely, but . . ."

"But," I put in gently, "he did mention being short of money, as well as extremely late on his dissertation. And"—I hesitated—"he'd touched briefly on his breakup with you, too."

"Oh, that." She waved a manicured hand dismissively. "That wouldn't have lasted. It was . . . I mean, surely he *knew* . . ."

Her voice wavered; she pressed a knuckle to her perfectly even, porcelain-white front teeth.

"We'd have reconciled in time no matter how we quarreled," she managed. "But now . . . oh, Jon," she finished brokenly, "what in the world have you *done*?"

Something she'd said struck home suddenly. "You mentioned his not having any family? What about his cousins in New York?"

The ones whose assurances, even secondhand, I'd accepted so blithely. Whose implied vouching for Raines, without my having ever even spoken to them directly about him, I'd swallowed whole, taking them as a guarantee that he would at least be harmless, if not the most forthcoming person in the world.

"You mean he wasn't related to them at *all*?" So that if I had called them . . .

Charmian looked confused; all at once I understood just how thoroughly I'd been flim-flammed. Talk about *chutzpah* . . .

"I'll be damned," I said, and Ellie nodded comprehendingly.

"Probably he had some more moonbeams ready to spin for you," she said, "if he got caught."

"But that's not important now," Charmian insisted. "What's important is that . . ." She fought tears, mustered control.

"Jon was cheerful and clever," she declared, "and not a bit clumsy. I can't imagine where you got that idea. He couldn't have jumped—*or* fallen. Do you know what he took up last summer for a joke, just to show that he could do it?"

Her violet eyes challenged me. "Tightrope-walking. He had already mastered rock-climbing, bungee-jumping, and parachuting."

She dug in the little handbag again, pulled out a snapshot. "Look," she demanded.

It was a shot of Raines at the edge of a snowy canyon, with what looked like half the earth and all the sky spread gloriously out behind him. He was wearing canvas shorts, thick socks, hiking boots, and a white T-shirt; the backpack he bore towered over his head, a pair of cross-country skis strapped to the pack.

"That's Jonathan," Charmian stated flatly.

It made me feel a little better, that I'd gotten that much right about him: athletic. But probably nothing else. The yuppie garb he'd been wearing had been a good disguise.

I'm an idiot, I thought at Ellie, and she shrugged minutely.

Hey, you can't win 'em all, she telegraphed back.

"As for money, that's the silliest . . . I have enough for both of us even if we lived forever, and Jon knew that perfectly well. And as for a *dissertation* . . ."

The girl gave the word an odd, scathing twist, then stopped troubledly, as if she'd been about to speak ill of the dead.

Or tell a secret: that, for instance, he wasn't writing any dissertation.

"Well," she went on, "let's just say there was no urgency about it. Furthermore," she added with quiet emphasis, "his death was no accident. *Or* suicide."

A stab of unease pierced me. He *had* said someone was trying to stop him. But I'd brushed it off. "So what you're telling us is . . ."

Ellie looked significantly at me, her eyebrows raised.

The thought had occurred to me, too, when I tried picturing the scene on that pier in the dark; that there had to be something more.

But even now I didn't really believe it. I still thought Jonathan Raines had fallen off the dock in a mishap, or maybe—this was a long shot, but possible—on purpose.

And despite my own questions about either of those scenarios I thought Charmian's memory of him was obscured by grief and by her own guilt on account of their broken affair.

Still, I wanted to know if she would come right out and say it, the word we were all thinking.

She did.

"Murder," Ellie repeated as if testing the idea. "But Jake, you don't really think . . ."

"She does." I angled my head at the ceiling.

Charmian was upstairs in Jonathan's room; we'd decided she should stay here instead of going to a motel, so I had another guest, which I wanted about as much as typhoid fever. But I just couldn't bear the thought of sending her to stay alone.

Now Ellie and I were in the dining room, cleaning up chunks of plaster. Rag ends of wallpaper clung to the plaster pieces and broken sticks of lath. "What a mess," I mourned.

Raines's eyeglasses still lay out on the table. "He meant to come back," Ellie said, picking them up.

"If he was going to jump, he wouldn't be needing them," I countered. Experimentally, Ellie took off her own and put his on.

"Criminy," she said, peering through them.

I thought she was talking about the glasses being so strong, about how if he'd been wearing them, as perhaps he ought to have been, he wouldn't have fallen.

"Take a look," Ellie said, handing them to me.

But when I put them to my eyes, I saw . . . nothing. Or nothing different, anyway. "Plain glass." I got more distortion looking out through the old panes of the dining room window.

"These are fakes," Ellie said. "No prescription at all. But for what? So he would look more intellectual?" She peered through them again. "Or to make it look as if he needed them. Like a disguise?"

"I don't know, Ellie. And what difference does it make now, anyway?"

I dropped the last chunk of plaster into a trash bag and swept up the dust, already making a mental list for the hardware store: more plaster, and new filters for the respirator I'd be wearing when the plaster dried, so I could sand it all down again without having to get in line for a lung transplant.

And that sanding needed to be complete inside of four days, since last time I looked, the untimely death of a mysterious visitor that no one knew anything about was not grounds to cancel a Ladies' Reading Circle meeting.

I tied the trash bag with a wire twist—wondering if maybe I could just crawl inside the bag and stay there—and set it in the butler's pantry, which was turning into ground zero for the repair project.

Tools, tarps, a bucket, and a jumbo packet of sandpaper like a harbinger of the dark days to come stood where the good china and crystal had resided, in the golden days before I moved here. Once upon a time, this house had been home to people of quality: vigorous businessmen and ladies whose housekeeping outranked mine by several orders of magnitude.

Sadly I regarded the pantry shelves, where now the only eating or drinking implements were a set of plastic cutlery, paper plates, and a thermos for when we went on picnics.

And then I spotted it, glittering in the corner beneath the low shelf: some kind of high-tech gadget. Battery-pack handle; it was obvious that it twisted, to turn the device on. . . .

At the other end, the glassy, rounded tip of a long, stalky appendage glowed suddenly. Ellie peered over my shoulder to get a closer look at the thing. "Is that an eyepiece?"

She pointed at a roundish, eye-sized aperture in the body of the thing. "May I see it?"

She grasped the black stalklike part in one hand to keep it from waving around, held the cylindrical body of the object with the other hand, and peered into it.

"Oh! Jacobia, it's a . . ."

I'd figured it out: a fiber-optic viewing device. Victor, my ex-husband the philandering brain surgeon, had brought this sort of thing home sometimes to show to Sam, in case Sam might like to follow in his father's footsteps.

The thought made me shudder, especially since right now Sam was with his father and, probably, one of his father's young lady friends. Victor found them even here in downeast Maine, and when he couldn't find them, he imported them. And of course Jill Frey was with them, too.

I frowned at the high-tech gadget. "What the heck's it doing here?"

"Raines must have had it," Ellie concluded. "No one else in the house would have one, would they? Sam wouldn't, for diving?"

"I don't think so. He'd have been showing it to us at dinner last night if he had." Perhaps due to his father's influence, Sam adored fancy gadgetry, could fix just about any of it, and vastly enjoyed demonstrating it for other people.

Ellie frowned. "But what would Raines want with . . . Oh."

Her face intent, she approached what was left of the wall: a two-foot-high section of intact plaster extending upward from the floor trim. Carefully she placed the stalk's long end behind the plaster, twisted the device to make the light go on, and . . .

"There's something down there."

"You're kidding."

"Nope. It's a . . ."

My mind was racing. "I'll bet Raines meant to take that wall down all along."

Or take some wall down, anyway, to peek behind it, in case a Stradivarius happened to be hidden there. I'd inadvertently focused his attention on *this* wall by removing the wallpaper, so he saw the old plaster patch centered behind my new one.

Then he'd done just what we'd been hoping he would do: he'd *seen* with fresh eyes. The old patch was square, with clean, straight edges; it hadn't been put in to fix something broken. It had been done to fill a hole that was deliberately cut.

And he had realized this. "Oof," Ellie said, craning her arm down. "I think there's something . . . What have you got in the house with a hook on the end? Maybe we can fish it out."

"Nuts." I'd had enough. "Take that gadget out and stand back." With the claw hammer I gave the remaining plaster a smack.

Naturally, however, when you are trying to break plaster it becomes durable. So it was ten minutes and a lot of claw hammering before we got at it: a thick packet of papers bound in leather.

An old manuscript: eagerly, we opened the cover.

The pages were blank.

"Well, darn," Ellie said indignantly as Monday nosed in to find out what we were excited about: hidden dog biscuits?

"No, Monday, there's nothing here." I flipped through the empty pages in disgust. "Well, that's par for the course lately. Raines tore down the wall for nothing."

But Ellie looked dubious. "Why would anyone hide a book of blank pages?"

I snapped the book shut, dust clouds from it billowing into the air. The soft antique-leather binding seemed to mock me with its aged look of importance, its sense of having been hidden away for some secret reason.

"I don't know," I said. "And I don't care. What I do know is that the Reading Circle meeting is getting closer by the minute, and if I don't want those little sandwiches with the crusts cut off to be full of plaster dust, I need to get busy."

Because it was obvious now that there was no percentage in further effort. Raines was a stranger, he'd showed up here, and now he was gone: end of story.

Blank pages, indeed; I yanked sharply at the last scraps of wallpaper. "And Charmian?" Ellie asked.

"Waiting for the body to be found, that's all. And talking to Bob Arnold this afternoon. I hope he convinces her that she shouldn't wait around forever."

I picked up the hammer and pulled out the rest of the broken plaster. Plaster mix, I said stubbornly to myself. Lath pieces, nails, wallpaper paste. Tools and materials for reconstructing what was broken. Doggedly, I swept up the plaster bits.

But Ellie wasn't ready to quit. "Fake glasses. A high-tech snooping device. And a book without words," she said. "There's something connected about those ideas. But what's the link?"

"They're all part of an annoying and ultimately meaningless puzzle," I said. "One that at the moment resembles my life."

I emptied the dustpan into the trash bag with an impatient shake. "Why couldn't Jonathan Raines have picked some other house to demolish? Darn it, I wish I'd never heard of Hayes. I've got half a mind to burn the place down and see how he likes *that*."

Then I waited: for all the alarm clocks to go off, or the smoke detectors to begin shrieking, or the windows to slam open and closed by themselves.

But nothing happened at all, and it struck me suddenly that my haunted old house (or my haunted old head, if you subscribed to Ellie's theory) had been eerily inactive since the power came back on.

Or since Jonathan Raines had disappeared.

"Why would he leave it there?" Charmian asked.

I didn't know how long she'd been standing in the hallway at the foot of the stairs. She came into the room.

"If he had the eyepiece and had torn down the plaster, why would he leave before he looked? He'd done all that work, so why stop at the critical moment? And if he did look, why go out just as he might have discovered something important?"

Good questions, but I didn't have answers to them, either. "Did you know what he was searching for?" I demanded.

She flushed slightly, biting her lip. "Yes. An extremely valuable violin. A Stradivarius. Everyone else says there'll be no more ever found. But Jonathan . . . well."

So there it was, out in the open. "What convinced him that everyone else was wrong?"

Those remarkable violet eyes were pink-rimmed; she'd been weeping. "Jon . . . well, he marched to a different drummer, that's all. He got hunches and went along with them. I'm not sure where he got this one from, but it would make his career if he found an unknown Strad. He said he would find it if it killed him."

She laughed brokenly. "And now . . . the instrument didn't kill him, but someone did. I'm absolutely sure, because I know Jon, and he would never have just walked away from a clue that might have put a Stradivarius in his hands in the next moment. Someone *lured* him. That's why he left just when he was about to discover something. And then . . ."

The conclusion was obvious. She still believed that someone had killed him.

But the objection was obvious, also: "Men on fishing boats saw him out there on that pier," I said. "Saw him alone, saw him go over, no one to push him."

Unless a ghost pushed him off that pier, I simply didn't see how it could have been done.

And that far, even I was not yet ready to go.

Ellie put her hand on Charmian's arm. "Would you like to come with me and talk to the men?" she asked. "It might calm your mind to know from them how it happened, to hear it from a person who was there at the time. Then you could . . ."

Rest easier, she had been going to say, or something like it. But Charmian refused this comfort, as I'd expected she might. She didn't look like the rest-easy type.

"No, thank you. I appreciate your offer. But I don't want to talk to people who think he fell or jumped, because he didn't."

Now that she'd seen what Raines had been doing just before he died, in fact, she looked like a young woman who was bound and determined to find out exactly what was rotten in Denmark.

I waved at the table. "What about the eyeglasses?" I asked. "They're fake."

She nodded. "He did that sometimes. When he wanted people to think he was . . ."

"Geeky?" Ellie supplied.

Charmian smiled. The effect, on that portrait-pretty face, was of sunlight shining through rain. "He wouldn't have meant any harm," she added. "I mean, he wouldn't have stolen it. The violin, if he'd found it."

I wasn't so sure. She sounded convinced, though.

"But as I told you, he was the least geeky person you could imagine," she finished.

Her own use of the past tense made her lip begin trembling again. Troubledly, she fingered the leather of the old book on the table, opening it without seeming to look at it.

Over the years, the glue in the old binding had loosened and become brittle. With a faint *crack!* the spine separated and the book lay open flat. "I still can't believe he's gone."

Gravely she picked up Raines's glasses and set them atop the blank pages. Through the dining room windows the morning sun shone onto the paper, two brighter small circles illuminating the yellowed paper where the lenses focused light on them. The moment lengthened as she seemed to debate whether to say more, finally deciding against it.

"Thank you," she said finally when Ellie repeated her offer. "You're very kind, both of you. But I think I'd better stay here and wait to hear from Mr. Arnold."

She fingered the corner of the book. "I wish it could talk," I said, not meaning anything by it, just filling empty air.

Meanwhile, in the back of my mind I was thinking about the hardware store. Maybe it was cold of me, but leaving the wall in a mess wasn't going to bring Raines back. Like the bright day outside, life would go on, and I didn't even know these people.

Or so I argued with myself. Just the night before, I

had worried over someone who was out on an adventure. Only in my case that someone had returned safely home, hadn't he?

"I wish it could tell you what happened," I said.

Charmian frowned speculatively at the book. "Maybe it can."

But I didn't take that remark to mean very much, either. Books can't talk unless someone reads them aloud; like me, she was just making noise to fill the unhappy silence.

Before I went out, I did my best to make her as comfortable as possible. This, for a girl of her manners and breeding, turned out to be easy.

"Please don't trouble." She managed a smile, took my hand. Hers was smooth and cool, and she was wearing a good perfume, its faint scent reminding me of tinkling music.

"If I'm thirsty," she assured me, "I'll find something to drink, and if I get hungry, something to eat."

I did want to go, and she saw my hesitation. "I've already found the bath."

The one upstairs, she meant. The hall bathroom still wasn't working; that paper clip improvisation hadn't served as well as I'd hoped. I might fix it again sometime when I didn't feel I was being nibbled to death by ducks.

"And I see there's an ironing board out in the kitchen," she went on. "So I'll touch up a few things from my bag."

A cloth overnight bag, it stood in the hall like a harbinger of houseguest doom. I stifled once more the impulse to suggest that she take it somewhere, anywhere else; she was bereaved, I reminded myself, and I couldn't just send her to a motel.

But I was tempted to go there myself: one where all the plumbing worked and the walls were not falling

down. Too bad I had something else on my calendar entirely; a lunch date with my ex-husband, Victor.

"And then I might lie down for a little while,"
Charmian finished. "So do what you need to do, please.
I'm fine here. And I appreciate your letting me stay."

Which, according to the highbrow code she had obviously been raised in, translated to: *Please leave me alone.*

So I did, with a final glance at the old book lying
open on the dining room table, Raines's fake eyeglasses
sitting atop its blank pages, looking nowhere.

4 Wadsworth's Hardware Store in Eastport
was started in 1812 by Henry Wadsworth
Longfellow's cousin, Samuel. As the black let-
tering on the glass over the door proclaimed,
it was the first ship's chandlery ever established in
the United States, and until the Groundhog Day Storm of
1977, it had stood on a wharf directly across from its
present location overlooking Passamaquoddy Bay.

But on that fateful day in '77, a low formed over the
Outer Banks and raced up the eastern seaboard, gathering strength as it came. By the time it reached the Gulf
of Maine, it had hurricane-force winds fed by freakishly
warm coastal waters for that time of year; like a
whistling teakettle on a hot stove, the storm was sucking energy from below and spewing it out.

There was little warning. Some say a ring formed
around the full moon the night before, others that the
sun rose red. What is known is that the storm came on
so fast there was not much time to prepare, and that in
any case no preparation could have been adequate for
what happened next.

It hit like a freight train. People who were there watched the Wadsworth's building lift up and float off the wharf, tilting slightly as it careened on the massively high tide, rocking on waves that rose impossibly against the streaming sky. The two-story structure and everything in it sailed across the heaving water, broke apart, and sank into the boat basin, while the wharf buckled and collapsed. Even today, if the tide is very low, you can still find odd items from the old Wadsworth's store shelves in the mud at the foot of the boat launch ramp.

Thinking about this, I glanced at the stubs of the old wharf pilings sticking up from the low water, then went into the new store, its walls covered in tiny wooden drawers filled with nuts and bolts in all sizes. You could buy a hatchet, a tide clock, a sink trap, or roofing nails weighed out in a counter scale and dumped into a paper bag. Buckets of deck paint and paint remover stood side by side, testimony to the constant scraping and painting that is a major feature of work-boat life.

I still had a couple of hours before the lunch date from hell with Victor, so I got a ten-inch spreading blade for plaster smoothing, a putty knife, and a twenty-pound sack of plaster mix. I paid the nephew of the original storekeeper, Charlie Wadsworth, and asked him to deliver my purchases to the house.

But Charlie was out of the quart tins of stain-killing white shellac, and I wanted to apply some before I started the wallpaper patch. You never can tell how old wallpaper and new materials will act together, and I figured a coat of stain-kill right now might save a lot of problems later.

The working men in Eastport however, are not accustomed to buying quart tins of anything, and Charlie had just sold his last small can of shellac to a woman from away, who wanted it because she was painting a gazebo.

"What's a gazebo, anyway?" Charlie wanted to know. "Sounds like some kind of exotic zoo animal."

Which in Eastport it very nearly was; our lawn ornaments run more to wooden whirligigs shaped like lighthouses. I explained to Charlie what a gazebo was—realizing only as I finished that he was putting me on; he knew perfectly well—then strolled up the street to the Quoddy Marine Store by the Quonset warehouses on the freight dock. There I asked Zeke Watkins if he could help out a person who did not need a whole tanker-truckload of shellac, which is what a gallon of it seems like when you only want a quart.

Zeke eyed me silently from under his thick, salt-and-pepper eyebrows, then went to the back of the store and returned with a fast-food Big Gulp cup.

"Better pour this into a jar, something, you get it home," Charlie advised, saying it the Maine way: *Jah*.

I took the cup, a little dazzled as always by the glimpse of another world that the marine store afforded me. There were five-ton towing blocks, nine-inch lobster bags, and four-man life rings, as well as whole aisles full of propellers, cotter pins, lines, lubricants, and fuel additives. There were spinning rods and packing compounds—both synthetic and genuine oakum—for pounding in between the seams of deck planking.

"Fellah visitin' you was in heah," Zeke said. "Too bad what happened to him."

"Right," I said distractedly, gazing around at many-hooked mackerel jigs, fly tying supplies, and an old Johnson seven-and-a-half-horse trolling motor, perfect for the wooden rowboat George Valentine was reconditioning.

"Zeke, put that away for me, will you, please?" I wrote out a check unhesitatingly; George has been so good to me since I came to Eastport that I couldn't make it up to him sufficiently if I went out on the water and rowed him around myself.

"Fellah needs to be careful, foolin' around that dock," Zeke commented, and I agreed that a fellah did.

Then I went back downtown, carrying the Big Gulp cup that was already getting soggy and wondering what to do with it. By the time I reached the massive old four-square granite post office building, the stink of shellac had begun competing heavily with the sweet perfume of the wild roses massed along the waterfront, just now unfurling their big wine-pink blooms.

Even in the open air the fumes were making me dizzy; passing the police station storefront, I spied Bob Arnold inside and decided to beg him for a better container.

"Here, here," Bob scolded, seeing me with the seeping mess of waxed drink cup and dripping shellac. He grabbed an empty coffee can from the shelf underneath the coffeemaker, dumped the smelly white stuff into it, and put a cover on it.

"I swear, Jake, the monkeyshines you get up to," he groused. "What're you doing slopping that messy stuff all over town? Why, I oughta charge you on a count of littering."

"I'm trying to keep an Eastport architectural treasure from falling down," I retorted. "Although this morning I'm not having much success."

I updated him on what Charmian Cartwright had told Ellie and me about Jonathan Raines, and what we had found.

"Fake eyeglasses, a blank manuscript book, and someone who supposedly wanted to stop him from whatever he was up to," I said. "This someone, of course, has not yet put in a personal appearance. And," I added sorrowfully, "meanwhile, once I get all this paint stripper home, I have to go see Victor."

Bob nodded in sympathy, saying nothing. He'd been a witness to my struggles with Victor since I'd moved here. "Sam getting along with him all right?"

"Oh, yes," I said, hearing the acid in my voice. "And I used to think that was a good thing."

He nodded again. In the role-model department Victor was one half of a wonderful fatherly example: gainfully employed, not a substance abuser, and so hell-bent on maintaining some kind of a relationship with Sam that he had actually relocated here.

Unfortunately, the other half resembled a case study from a sociopathology textbook. And in summer, the other half reared its ugly head with thrilling abandon, because in summer Victor drove his sports car around town—a new one, to replace the one he'd sold when he moved here—and ran his sleek, bullet-shaped power boat at high speeds up and down Passamaquoddy Bay.

"Playing his old tricks?" Bob asked.

" 'Fraid so." The toys, chosen in part by Victor for their bright colors and shiny surfaces, attracted females in the same way—and, I was convinced, by pretty much the same biological mechanism—as flowers attracted butterflies.

Or in Sam's case, I was afraid, the way blood drew sharks.

"Women," I sighed. "Or girls, when we're talking about Sam. Not that there's a difference between the two in Victor's mind, of course, if they are over eighteen."

Victor's main question about any good-looking female that he met was the same as his question about any car he admired and had a hankering for: street-legal or not? After that, it was merely a matter of strategy.

"Ayuh," Bob commented tactfully. He'd seen it as often as I had: Victor tooling around with the latest in a

series of young ladies decorating the passenger seat in
shorts and halter tops. Or if they were in the boat she
would always be wearing a teeny bikini, never mind
that this was downeast Maine and when you got out on
that water even in August, what you wanted was a
heavy parka.

"Anyway," I said, "I'm going to try to talk to him
about it at lunch." Which I knew would be about as pro-
ductive as shouting down a well; when he first came here,
I'd harbored high hopes of his having reformed. But the
calm we experienced in the few months following
Victor's arrival was, I realized later, caused by culture
shock, not by any real change in his character.

Still, there was no point recapping all this to Bob,
who had enough troubles already with the firebug, the
guy who'd fallen off the cliffs, and now Jonathan
Raines.

Glancing around, I spotted a garment on the rack by
the soda machine: a tan, many-pocketed sleeveless item.
"Is that it?"

He nodded: Raines's fishing vest. I reached out
and touched it, almost superstitiously, but the wicked-
looking thing stuck into the front of it made me pull my
hand away again.

It was a mackerel jig like the ones I'd just seen in
Quoddy Marine: about four inches long, roughly cylindrical, with black and silver paint approximating the
scale markings on a fish.

"Nasty item," I remarked. From the cylinder dangled
a dozen barbed fishhooks; a broken length of high-test
fishing line was knotted to the eye at the end of the lure.

"Guess somebody lost it," Bob said. "You know
how the hooks snag on the pilings sometimes when
people are fishing off the end of the pier."

He poured himself some coffee from the inky-
looking pot on the warmer. "The only way to get it freed

up again, you do that, is to cut the line, say goodbye to your mackerel jig," he said, waving the pot at me.

I shook my head. On a good day, Bob Arnold's coffee makes a fine substitute for crankcase oil. And the sight of the mackerel jig stuck to the vest had popped a picture into my head:

Someone under the pier, casting upward to hook that fishing vest. And *pulling* . . .

"That's it," I said. "That's how you could make it look like someone was falling, with no one nearby who could've pushed him. From a distance, it would seem as if he'd lost his balance, but he'd be getting pulled from underneath."

Bob was quick on the uptake, but his voice when he replied was full of skepticism. "How'd you know he was going to be there? Your victim, if you are deciding to pull such shenanigans."

He waved his cup at the window. "You just wait forever by the dock, hoping he's going to wander by? Too damn cold in the water, I can tell you. And where else, he wouldn't see you?"

I gazed at him. It was all so clear to me. "Maybe you agreed to meet him there. When you saw him coming, you could duck out of sight yourself."

That could be why Raines had gone out just as he was about to investigate the hole in the plaster; because he'd made a date to meet someone.

"As for where, that dock has wooden crosspieces under it, like scaffolding. You wouldn't have to be *in* the water. You could scramble out from shore, one crossbeam to the next, to the end. Or at high tide you could float out there in a little boat, tie up underneath where it wouldn't be seen. Then . . ."

"Cast up, hook the guy, pull him in. Cut the line, he drowns and you get away clean." Bob wasn't looking so skeptical now.

But then he changed his mind again. "Wouldn't be easy. It's slippery under there. And you'd have to know the way. Have it in your mind ahead of time, how you'd get out there."

He held a finger up. "Also, you might get there in a boat, but you couldn't stay there. Need solid footing, pull hard enough to be sure you'd yank a guy off. And that gets you back to . . ."

He had a point. Sooner or later you would have to be on some solid spot. And the stuff that coats a wooden dock piling, green and slimy, makes Vaseline seem like tar paper. Also, although in theory your route might look very simple and straightforward, in practice—and in the dark—it would be something else again.

But all that was minor compared to the one thing Bob Arnold needed most, to get interested in any serious way in what I was suggesting: a decent motive.

"Raines just got here," he said. "Cops in Cambridge called his landlady there for me, let her know what had happened, ask a few questions. He had rooms in her house, it turns out, and she knew him pretty well."

"And she said?"

Bob shrugged. "Same as the girl. Far as she knows, he's got no relations here. None anywhere, says the landlady. And she says he never talked about knowing anyone here, either."

So Charmian had been telling the truth about there not being a family to claim his body, or not any that would easily be found.

"So I guess if the body does turn up, it's all hers," Bob went on. "The girl's, I mean. Point is, though, what reason would anyone here have, go to the trouble of killing him? And it would have to be someone from here, know how to get out to the end o' that dock quick."

And be crazy enough to try it, he didn't say, but I got the drift. It was the kind of thing only a guy from around here would do: wild-ass daring and potentially fatal.

In other words, the kind of thing half the guys around here did for a living day in and day out: diving, fishing, dragging for urchins, cutting down eighty-foot trees, loading them on trucks. Their daily bread.

"So who . . ." Bob didn't finish the question.

". . . would want to kill him, and could do it. I don't know, Bob. I'm just saying. The whole thing's so crazy and unlikely."

Briefly I explained what I thought Raines was really up to: finding an old instrument whose very existence would make his career.

And whose sale, despite Charmian's protestations of his honesty, would surely make his fortune, if he managed to find it and to sneak it out of Eastport unnoticed.

"I'm not sure about that last part," I admitted.

I left out the business about worrying whether my house was being haunted, also; Bob ranked ghosts right up there with alien abductions, fat-free snack food, and guys who are only holding the murder weapon for a friend, in the believability department.

"But what if someone else were after the Stradivarius, too?" I went on. "The person he said wanted to stop him. Someone from here who knew he was coming. Or someone from away who followed him here, who *knows* someone here?"

It was time for me to go. "Either way," I finished, "one-point-three million reasons for murder are waiting for whoever does come up with a previously undiscovered Strad."

Bob drank the last of his crankcase oil, made a face

at the empty cup. "Which, if what you're telling me is right," he said, "all the real experts say there isn't one. And everyone in town has looked for the thing, not found it. And now all of a sudden not one but two crackpots get so het up about it, one of 'em ends up dead and the other one—*who,* may I remind you, no one has seen—is the one who killed him?"

His expression said pretty clearly what he thought of that. He'd have been likelier to believe in ghosts.

"You're right," I admitted. "It does sound far-fetched. Some mysterious unknown person opposing him: when he said it, even I thought it was a ploy just to get my sympathy."

Now, though . . . "He's stopped, isn't he? Stopped cold."

Just then a siren sounded from a vehicle coming our way, and the radio on Bob's desk crackled to life. I couldn't decipher the sputter-and-crackle of it, but he could.

"Damn," he uttered, and headed for the door. "Another fire. First one was just trash, but . . ."

But you never knew. I followed him out as another siren in the distance howled nearer.

"Let it go, Jacobia," he advised as he slid into the squad car and fired up the engine. "We've got our own problems around here, real ones. For all I know, Raines stuck that mackerel jig in his vest himself, for a souvenir or to make it look authentic."

I blinked. Trust Bob for the commonsense angle. With a businesslike wave, he pulled out and sped away, while Charlie from Wadsworth's and Zeke from the marine store and the other men, fishermen and carpenters and truckers, hopped into their own trucks and raced off to try to stop the latest in the string of mischief done by this year's firebug.

Probably another brush fire, I thought as I headed

home with the shellac in the tin can. But that, like so much else that day, was too much to hope for.

"Two hundred years," Ellie mourned, striding up the sidewalk beside me. "A little old wooden schoolhouse, not hurting anybody. *How* could someone be so mean?"

I'd met her on my way home; she had been visiting the Happy Landings, arranging to borrow a coffee urn for my Reading Circle meeting, when the call came in for any fire company members who were in there: to get on the stick.

But the damage was done, according to Millie Wilkins, who had taken the call when the tiny, picturesque building on the Shore Road, over on the mainland, was already a heap of embers. The task now was to keep the fire from spreading to the dry fields and brush lots beyond, Ellie said sorrowfully as we passed the library.

But then she changed the subject. "I saw Sam a little while ago with Jill Frey," she said.

Uh-oh. "And?"

"They were kissing on the breakwater," she said. "They were sitting in her car necking. Sort of, um, enthusiastically, if you catch my drift."

Oh, great: my son the exhibitionist.

"It was quite the show," she went on, not liking to have to tell me this. It's another of her pleasant traits, that she thinks bad news doesn't need her help to spread around.

"So I thought I'd better give you a heads-up," she said, "before Hecky Wilmot or somebody walks up and asks you about it right out in front of God and everybody."

"Right. I'm seeing Victor later, to talk to him about this very topic. Not that it'll do much good, but I've got to try."

She nodded, and we finished climbing the Key Street hill to my house. The big old white Federal loomed ahead of us, its crisp green shutters and massive granite foundation making it look like a three-story beacon of solidness and safety.

That is, it did from the outside. Inside, it still resembled a remodeling project being attempted by monkeys who had recently escaped from the zoo.

Patience, I counseled myself for the millionth time as once again I had to slam the back door hard merely in order to get it to latch. Also the radiators needed painting again, as there was not enough stain-kill in the world to keep red enamel—what *had* somebody been thinking?—from coming through white semigloss, so they were all turning a hideous sort of mottled shrimp-pink.

I left the can of shellac in the hall as Ellie stopped ahead of me in the kitchen doorway, tipping her head curiously.

"Quiet in here," she remarked. Then: "Why, hello," she said to someone as I peered past her.

"Hello," Charmian returned the greeting matter-of-factly, just as if she were not standing at the ironing board, wielding my steam iron over the pages of the old book we'd found earlier in the dining room wall.

"Remember when I said maybe these pages really could talk?" she asked. "This is what I meant."

"Invisible ink," I said as understanding washed over me. I could already see the lines of handwriting, a translucent, pale greeny-brown color, spidering across the pages.

"Charmian, I'm impressed."

Her fragile laugh tugged at my heart. "Jon's glasses

and his fiber-optic eyepiece gave me the idea. Plus a book without words: you had to *look* for something."

The connection Ellie mentioned; Charmian had sensed it, too, and taken the next step.

"After you were gone, I examined it again, and where the sun shone through the glasses, something showed. Like a photograph being developed. It was the heat, I thought, through those glass lenses. So I applied some more heat, and—voilà."

Or voy-lah, as George would have put it. "This girl," I said to Ellie, "has possibilities."

"Clearly," Ellie agreed, and Charmian looked pleased. She wouldn't have, if she'd known what else I was thinking. A pretty girl, a story of heartbreak, but she'd been Johnny-on-the-spot as soon as Raines met misadventure, hadn't she? As if, once he was out of the way, she could move right in.

"I suppose the clipper ships carried lemons," she said, "to prevent scurvy, in the old days. And lemon juice makes a fine invisible ink. Any acid will, really, especially if you spray it with cabbage water to reveal it. But I didn't want to stain the book purple unless I had to."

"She's right," Ellie said. "Until the sailors realized that Moose Island's wild rose hips are full of vitamin C—well, they didn't know it was vitamin C, of course, but they did know about scurvy—the ships carried lemons."

All at once the significance of Raines's cabbage rolls, and the perfectly disgusting-sounding health drink he'd said he would make from the purple water, was coming clear: another tall tale. But how could he have known in advance that he might find a book with invisible writing in it?

Charmian warmed another page. "The Elizabethans," she went on conversationally, "used spoiled wine. Vinegar, you know. They were big on secret writing, although mostly they used codes. All the fights over the English throne they had, so they had lots of secrets."

She peered at the book, touched the iron carefully to one spot. "And in the Revolutionary War ferrous sulfate was a common one. Nowadays there are new chemicals like ferric chloride, potassium thiocyanate, and invisible inks that reveal themselves under ultraviolet light, for secretly marking things."

I was familiar with these latter methods. Paper money has UV-sensitive ink in it, so it can be distinguished from realistic but non-UV-sensitive counterfeit. Stock certificates, too.

But none of this was the kind of thing a person just fell out of bed already knowing. So how did she?

"That kind of secret printing," Charmian recited, "began in the 1940s, in Moravia, I think, although at the time it was just fluorescent, of course."

Of course. She was chattering nervously, building herself up to something but not yet quite able to say it.

"The newest is the kind that shows when a sort of magnet is applied. Electrophoretic invisible ink, it's called. But I still think the cleverest invisible writing was done by a Roman soldier in 50 B.C. who shaved a slave's head, wrote on his scalp, and let the hair grow back. When the slave was sent past enemy lines to the allies, his head was again shaved, and the message appeared."

She looked up. Ellie and I were staring at her.

"Oh, dear," she managed weakly.

As she spoke, I'd been moving nearer to the book on the ironing board. Now I could see its pages clearly and the tantalizing lines of writing moving across them.

Tantalizing but illegible. The elaborately penned letters had come back only partially, creating a sort of connect-the-dots puzzle. A manuscript-reconstruction expert might have been able to decipher what the pages said, given hours of work and plenty of other samples of the author's handwriting.

Or if the pages had only been a copy or draft of something, and that something were available, then the text could have been figured out.

But not otherwise. One page was particularly infuriating: comprised of lines that formed the shape of Moose Island, dotted with circles, crosses, and tiny legends that didn't even look like English, it might almost have been a readable map.

Almost. Charmian looked over my shoulder. "That's Latin, I think. If only there were a little more of it, I could . . ."

Right; Hayes had been classically educated in the European style, which at the time meant languages ancient and modern. The natural sciences were big in those days, too: gentlemen bent on ruling the world not only financially but intellectually.

"Charmian," I said, "I think you'd better tell us the rest of your story. Bob's busy for a while, so you'll have plenty of time. Which," I added, eyeing her sternly, "I suspect you're going to need."

She sighed, her violet eyes regarding each of us in turn.

"Yes," she agreed, switching the iron off. "I suppose I'd better. Let's walk outside a little and let some light onto more of the story than this old book tells. Which is nothing."

She made a tiny frown at it. "Lemon juice, what a letdown. You can see why modern methods are so much more satisfactory."

Right, and it was especially disappointing if it was your wall that had been torn down to get to the book.

"Besides," she said, "the one thing it doesn't tell even

if we could read it is the thing I'm going to learn before I leave."

She regarded its yellowing pages sadly. "Who killed Jon, and why?"

"Enough," I snapped at her, and she looked up, startled.

"Don't play dumb," I said, "it doesn't suit you. You knew he was coming here. You knew how to get a charter to Eastport; if you hadn't, it would have taken you much longer. Probably the way you knew is that Jonathan had done it first. I doubt he ever rode anything so slow as a bus from Bangor in his life. And he probably discussed his plans with you."

I turned to Ellie. "Wilbur Mapes didn't pick Raines up on the mainland at the bus stop. He picked him up at the airfield."

Back to Charmian: "Which I'm sure Mapes will confirm if we ask him. And when I finally get to talk to Jonathan's so-called cousins, I'll learn they've never heard of any Jonathan Raines, won't I? That was a story just to get me to let him stay here."

Raines had done his homework, all right: on me. Somehow, he found out that I owed one of those fellows a big favor. And if I'd discovered his lies—if, for instance, I'd managed to get a phone call through and find out about the whoppers he was telling—he'd have talked his way around them somehow.

He'd been good at that: talking around things. Charmian reddened silently, confirming at least part of my opinion. There was no longer any point in leaving more messages in New York.

"Jonathan had to testify in an art-fraud case," she said. "That was last autumn, he was a prosecution witness, and when it was over he had drinks with the three government lawyers. I think they even played squash together or something. Are they the ones you mean?"

"Yes." They were the Three Musketeers of the squash courts *and* of the federal courts. I could just hear them telling Raines about their vacation in a house up in Maine—one that the owner thought might be haunted by a ghostly musician—and about the rumored Strad, which they'd have known would be of interest to him.

And I could see him listening carefully, filing it all away for future reference and research.

"There's something else, isn't there?" I was taking a stab, but from the way she flinched I knew I was still on target.

And I'd had it with silly stories. "Pretty brave statement, saying you'll find out how and why Jonathan Raines died. Unless of course you already think you know who did it. I'd say that ups your chances of succeeding, wouldn't you?"

"Let's take a walk," she said quietly again, "and I'll tell you all about it."

"Nuts," I responded. "We're staying here. I've got more to think about than your problems, you know."

I waved toward the front of the house. "I've got twenty ladies due in that dining room in four days. So I'm going to work on the plaster right now, and you're going to talk *and* help."

"First of all, Jonathan was no dorky academic guy the way he wanted you to believe," Charmian began slowly.

In the dining room, I prepared the section of the wall for replastering: knocking away the rest of the loose bits around the edges, brushing out the crumbs, and identifying the lath pieces that would need fixing.

"So you've told me."

There were a couple of old wooden pallets in the

cellar and I'd decided that I could use those to repair the broken lath. It didn't need to be pretty, only strong enough to hold the weight of what would cover it. So I'd set Ellie to work with the small hand axe, splitting crosspieces from the pallets into strips.

"He was a professional finder of fine things," Charmian went on. "For museums, mostly, or private collectors. He specialized in musical items: instruments, manuscripts, letters of famous musicians, and even rare old recordings."

"I see." Ellie delivered a small bundle of what looked like stove kindling and was really the future skeleton of my plaster repair. The lath was the bones and the plaster would be the flesh securely suspended from them. I hoped.

"Sometimes he had to figure things out, or travel, to find what he wanted," Charmian said. "Sometimes both, working on only a few clues he picked up in a library or from conversation. But once he was on the track, Jon would go anywhere, do anything. He was like a cross between Lord Peter Wimsey and Indiana Jones."

I thought this a somewhat romanticized and idealized version of Raines, but I let it pass. Also, she hadn't yet confided how a pretty girl who'd obviously had a lovely upbringing knew so much about invisible ink. But I figured I would find that all out in good time, too; in fact, I was determined to.

"That's why he didn't call you for so long," she said. "He was diving off the coast of Australia."

So that's where the shark's tooth had come from. At the time I'd been just a promising little gleam on his horizon, no doubt, but he was shaping up to be the kind of fellow who got all his ducks in a row well in advance.

"He wanted to come here right away," Charmian

went on, "but he'd promised to . . . Well. Anyway, first he had to finish up that other assignment."

Finish it from inside a shark cage; pillaging some sunken ship's hold or some such thing, no doubt. I selected a piece of wood, measured it against a gap in the lath inside the wall, and found it satisfactory.

"Go on," I said. Holding the repair piece against the gap, I used a power drill to make pilot holes for each of the screws I would be using; nailing the lath, smacking the fragile structure with a hammer, might damage more lath or the existing plaster.

"Last year when you two found one of Jared Hayes's old diaries," she went on, "in the library, the story . . ."

The final volume of the old musician's daybook, it had said nothing useful and ended, ominously, in the middle of a sentence.

". . . the story got to Boston. That it existed, I mean, and that it talked about the Stradivarius."

"It doesn't," I mumbled around a mouthful of tiny screws, "*say* Stradivarius."

And how, precisely, had the story traveled? I centered a screw in a pilot hole and used a screwdriver drill bit to drive it in with a quick buzz of the power drill.

"But Jonathan thought it *might* be one," Charmian said. "And for him that was enough."

I drove the screw at the other end of the lath splice and tested the result: solid. So I went ahead and patched the rest of them, Ellie handing me lath pieces as I needed them, working more quickly now that I thought the method had a chance of being successful.

"And Jonathan knew that no one from around here would talk to him about it if he told them what he was up to or behaved like what he really was," Charmian said.

"A freelance," I managed around the fasteners,

"historical daredevil." And they hadn't talked, anyway. But I let her go on.

Charmian nodded, sighing. "That's a fair description. So he got up a sort of a disguise. Because otherwise he looked like . . ."

"A storybook adventure hero." In the snapshot, without the glasses and the goofy outfit, he'd looked very different, just as he'd said: *A thing can resemble one thing, and be another.*

"Yes," Charmian said. "Just like that."

By now I'd got the rest of the lath breaks patched. It is another standard feature of old-house fix-up: you try things, and if they work you keep on doing them. This time, matters were going swimmingly.

"So basically," Ellie put in, "what he was up to was just what Jacobia and I suspected from the start: finding the violin, and then stealing it. Getting it out of town to sell, or maybe keep for himself, without anyone ever knowing he had it."

"Probably," I said, "for a client. A customer all lined up to take it off his hands, privately."

Charmian frowned. "No, that's not it at all," she defended Raines stoutly. "He wanted to protect it."

Yeah, right. Protect it right out of here. I cleared away the unused wood strips, preparing for the next stage.

"There's someone else who wants the violin. Someone who will destroy it if he finds it"—Charmian's voice rose urgently—"to protect his own reputation."

She lifted her chin in a gesture of, I thought, misplaced loyalty. By now it was clear that Raines could have bamboozled her, too, with the same hoary old tale he'd tried using on me: the race against the villain.

Unless she was as bad as he was. "Jonathan wanted to get to it first, to stop him," Charmian declared.

"That's very touching. And who, may I ask, is the

ogre we're talking about here? Whose reputation one violin could destroy?"

"He's . . . my uncle Winston."

For the first time she sounded a little embarrassed. I thought she ought to, considering the number of lies she'd told me since she'd arrived.

But I didn't think she was lying now. For one thing, this part of the story could be checked. "He's an authority on the subject and he's been saying for years that no more Strads will be found," Charmian went on. "And he's getting old, with younger men taking over the field. So for one to be discovered at this late date in his career would spoil his reputation, not only for the future but retroactively, too. If you see what I mean."

She took a breath. "It would call into question other things he has said. His whole eminence. And he's not a man to be crossed easily, Uncle Winston. He knew what Jonathan was here for. That's why I'm so afraid . . . afraid he's . . ."

"Killed him?" Ellie said, and Charmian nodded.

As a motive it actually had some substance. Unfortunately, it was unrealistic in its practical aspects. "Hand me the pitcher of water, please," I said.

Charmian did so, distracted momentarily by the process I was getting under weigh. Or way, as non-nautical types misspell it; since moving to a place where boats were almost as numerous as people, I'd become sensitive to such things.

"How do you know how much to put in?" she asked as I began pouring water into a large plastic basin.

I'd bought the basin to use for washing lacy underthings, but since the habit of wearing these items had faded about twenty minutes after I'd arrived in Eastport, I was sacrificing it to the old-house cause.

"Recipe on the bag. Give me the mixing spoon."

Stirring the mixture caused clouds of white powder to rise from the basin.

"Don't breathe the dust," I warned, cautiously adding more water. The texture is crucial: too thick, and it dries too fast. Too loose, and it falls back out of the wall.

"There. Out of my way, now. This won't wait." Turning my head from the basin, I took a deep, fortifying breath and plunged into the crucial part of the job.

With a trowel I slopped a big dollop of mixed plaster onto a metal palette and scooped some up with the spreading blade. Then, quickly, I began spreading it over and between the slats of lath; imagine spreading peanut butter thickly onto an English muffin, working it in, and you will have the idea.

"I don't suppose this Uncle Winston fellow would show up driving a stolen car," I mused aloud.

Charmian looked surprised. "Uncle Winston doesn't drive. He has himself driven."

So much for that theory. And it would have been too much to hope for anyway that the guy who'd taken the dive off the bluffs could be explained so neatly.

"Stepladder," I said. Ellie shoved it over, and I went up. "Describe him, please," I told Charmian. "Your uncle."

She proceeded obediently. "Old," she repeated. "Well, not *so* old; mid-sixties. But old for his age, because he's very large, and he has gout, and smokes a pipe though his doctor forbids it, and drinks red wine."

She paused, thinking. "He uses a cane, and wheezes climbing stairs, and sometimes won't take his pills, so his blood pressure gets to be terrible."

Fascinating. "Hold the basin up here." I scooped out more plaster; it was already stiffening. I would have to work faster or mix a whole new batch. I chose the first option: slap-slap.

"He's also very stubborn, ill-tempered, and opinionated," she ended with a flash of anger. "And he has an enormous ego. And he *despised* Jonathan for being what he couldn't be anymore."

"So in his youth, your uncle was just as devil-may-care as Jonathan in the finding-the-goodies department?"

She nodded. "More so, even. What else do you want to know about him?"

"Plenty, actually. But that's enough for now." I climbed down from the ladder. "To sum up, you believe that a very large man, of more than middle age and with serious health troubles, has sneaked into Eastport without anyone noticing him and murdered Jonathan Raines."

I finished pressing plaster into the lower part of the hole and began scoring the surface of the material with the spreader. This gives the next layer, which I could apply by this evening, I hoped, a good surface to cling to.

"By," I continued, climbing the ladder again to score the top part, "scrambling out under the end of the pier, or taking a boat out there, which for him just getting onto one would be a good trick, if he's as large as you describe him. *And,* once he'd got purchase on the slippery dock, casting a barbed line up to snag the front of Jonathan's vest and pulling"—I demonstrated, giving the spreader a sharp yank downward—"so as to make Jonathan topple off the pier, and cutting the line as he fell past."

The plaster surface was fully scored. "It would all take," I finished, "a considerable amount of agility, and familiarity with that dock. And you'd need some way to get him to meet you there; Jonathan, I mean. I gather that under ordinary circumstances, he would not have been eager to meet your uncle Winston for a chat."

Charmian and Ellie followed me as I carried the

plaster basin past them into the kitchen and ran hot water into it, and all I have to say about this process is that if you don't do it immediately after you finish plastering, you are going to wish heartily that you had, next time you want to use that basin.

"Jake, that's quite a theory," Ellie said.

"Thank you." I ran hot water until it began steaming. "It certainly has all my favorite qualities in a theory: far-fetched, poorly strung together, with many loopholes for other perfectly good explanations . . ."

That Raines had put the mackerel jig onto the vest himself, for instance. He'd been in the marine store, and he might have just wanted it for a souvenir as Bob said.

". . . and physically impossible, to boot."

I left the powder mix standing on the newspapers spread on the dining room floor for good luck, but took the palette, the spreader blade, the spoon, and the drill to the sink, also.

"But if you like it, you're welcome to it," I finished.

The drill I disassembled and set up on the hall shelf where it lives because I always need it for something; the rest of the things I began scrubbing.

Ellie took the tools from me and dried them with paper towel after I rinsed them. Last came the basin, which cleaned up nicely, so there was still hope for frilly underthings.

Like maybe in some other life.

"So you don't really think that's what happened," Charmian said, crestfallen.

I turned from the sink. "No, I don't. It's ridiculous. No gouty, old, overweight uncle climbed out underneath those dock pilings and hung there, waiting and wheezing. The water is cold, the surface is precarious, and the exertion would be tremendous."

"He could have paid someone," Charmian countered.

You had to hand it to her; she didn't give up easily. And it was the other thing I'd been thinking: that if it had happened, it was probably someone local, as Bob Arnold had also said.

Not a welcome notion, or very real-world likely, either, which was why Bob had barely touched on it; Eastport is not well supplied with killers for hire.

But: "He has money enough? And people to ask?"

"More money than God," she affirmed. "And over the years, he's had to deal with some pretty slimy characters. He's the man you go to, or he used to be, if you have had valuable art stolen and you want to get it back."

Then all at once I made the connection I should have made a lot earlier: valuable art. "Good heavens. This is *the* Winston Cartwright we're discussing?"

Oh, for Pete's sake, of course it was. She nodded. "Why, do you know him?"

I nodded back. "By reputation."

Suddenly the idea of someone paying for a murder didn't seem quite so outlandish. "The same Winston Cartwright who got back the *Terra Forma*? That big silver . . ."

Well, I didn't know what it was, actually. It was a silver *something*, meant to be hung on a wall, and it had been worth a fortune when it was stolen off the airliner transporting it from an exhibition in St. Louis back to its home in the Big Apple a half dozen years earlier.

"The same," she replied gravely, meeting my eye.

Offices in Cambridge, with branch offices in penitentiary visiting rooms all over the country: if a con had a secret and it involved stolen art, Winston Cartwright could coax it—or threaten; one time he was said to have sent a thief's family to Disney World for two weeks, keeping them incommunicado while telling the thief that they were chained in a rat-infested basement, and faking torture tapes to convince him—out of the miscreant. Among owners of valuable art he was legend, which made it all the more curious how few people could actually say they'd ever seen him.

I hadn't, for instance. "He keeps a low profile," Charmian said, apparently catching my thought. "But when you do meet him, he's . . . impressive."

"Another reason I doubt he's here," I said.

On the other hand, it didn't *have* to be someone local. In summer when the town is full of visitors an ordinary-looking guy could blend in. A minion: do the dirty deed, stick around to find the violin if he could. Then he could spirit it away.

Or *she* could. But I didn't say that part out loud.

"One more thing. I don't quite see what this all has to do with you." I took the dish towel from Ellie and dried my hands on it.

"I don't mean finding his body and taking it home," I added as Charmian opened her mouth to protest. "Or," I went on, "wanting to know who killed him. *If* someone did. Because we don't know that, either, do we?"

She'd have protested that, too, but I didn't let her. "What I mean is, you seem pretty urgent about this whole situation. *And* I get the sense Uncle Winston isn't just some distant relative you see at Thanksgiving."

She was shaking her head in denial but her face said *You've caught me*. I pressed on.

"So what's the deal, Charmian? The minute you got the call about Jonathan, you chartered a plane like your hat was on fire and your pants were catching."

I hung up the towel. "Also, you know a lot about a lot of things they don't teach in finishing school. Invisible inks, old languages. You learned from your uncle, I imagine. Probably you share his interests. So, are you sure an old violin isn't really all *you* care about, here?"

By now she was very near tears, and furious at me. Which was exactly the way I wanted her: ready to hit back with anything and everything she had in her.

And in her anger, she might tell me the rest of the truth.

She took a shuddering breath. "All right. My parents died when my sister and I were very young. Uncle Winston took us in and raised us. He's still my sister's legal guardian; she's only sixteen. When I got out of college, I went to work for him, in his . . . Well."

She straightened. "Everyone calls it a research firm."

Right; that was a nice, socially acceptable term for what good old Uncle Winston did. Other people might call it *fighting fire with fire*.

Or hand-to-hand-combat. She turned the opal ring on her finger. "That's where I met Jonathan. He's like Uncle Winston, smart and adventurous. But not so . . ."

"Ruthless," I supplied, and she nodded gratefully. "You've met Jon. He couldn't hurt anyone, not for anything, no matter how valuable. To get back the *Terra Forma*, Uncle Winston actually . . ."

Her face creased in remembered horror. "I can't say it."

But I already knew. He'd kidnapped the baggage guy who'd had the keys to the airline storage warehouse. And then, using a pair of ordinary hardware-store pliers, he'd pulled out one of his own teeth.

If the guy wanted similar dental work done, Cartwright had said, well, Uncle Winston would be happy to oblige. Otherwise, he should spit out the identities of the men who'd stolen the *Terra Forma*, and its current whereabouts, or he'd soon be spitting out one of his own incisors.

As in, *right this very goddamned minute.*

"It wasn't a real tooth," I said, and Charmian gazed at me in astonishment.

"But . . ." Obviously even she had thought that it was.

"Sorry, but I can't tell you how I know," I said.

It was my old buddy Jemmy Wechsler, onetime banker to the mob, now a man with a price on his head—especially if the head was "severed off," as the man who'd put the price on in the first place had expressed it—who'd told me the story. Jemmy and I had crossed paths fairly often back in the city and a few times since then; now he was evading the Mafia, whose money he'd stolen, with humor and élan.

But to everybody else's knowledge, he was dead. And far be it from me to contradict this—for Jemmy—convenient notion.

"Trust me," I said, "it was a fake tooth." With a realistic-looking fake root. Jemmy was hilarious about it.

"Anyway, the rest of your involvement. This is all personal, you mean? Between you and your uncle?"

She nodded. "As I said, Uncle Winston didn't like Jonathan. He didn't want us to see one another. We fought over it all the time, my uncle and me, until in an angry moment I made him a bet: if he got to the violin before Jonathan did, or if it was never found, I would go on working for him for as long as he wanted me to."

"And otherwise?" Ellie put in, though by now we both knew what the answer to that must be. Charmian didn't disappoint us.

"If Jonathan won, I would marry him, and he and I would be a team. Traveling all over the world, finding exotic items that no one ever thought could be found. Having adventures," she finished wistfully, "together."

"And that's what you and Jonathan fought about," Ellie said acutely. "The bet you made with your uncle."

Charmian nodded brokenly. "He said, what if he failed? But I was so sure he wouldn't, and now . . . now I can't welsh on the deal because of my sister. I can't stay with Uncle Winston after what I think he's done. But if I leave, he'll make her life hell just to punish me. I've *got* to find that violin."

She pressed her clenched fists to her lips. "Jon was awfully angry when we met last. So was I. But how could he have believed me when I said I never wanted to see him again?"

She twisted the ring. "How *could* he?"

Interesting question, I thought as I went upstairs to clean up for my meeting with Victor. But it was not among the questions that I now most wanted answers to.

Those were: (a) could I believe Charmian? And (b) why did I care so much? Because . . .

(c) darn it all, I definitely did.

The Cannery Restaurant was built on the remains of the old sardine-processing factory at Rice's dock overlooking the ferry landing. From a window table you could look past the decorative buoys, heaped lobster traps, and the tiny gift shop operated out of the hut where the sardine tins used to get their labels pasted on, to the blue water spread out like somebody's daydream of a Maine island summer.

Victor was already there, drinking what he liked to call a "martooni." He would pronounce the word with an impish smile as if no one had ever thought of calling it that before; then with his eyes still on you he would eat the olive, crushing it between his strong white teeth as if daring you to try to stop him.

He glanced pointedly at his watch as I sat down. It was the classic black Movado museum piece, black face and no numerals on it, just the gold dot. Victor loved that watch.

"Nice of you to make time," he remarked, chewing the olive.

I let the comment pass, recognizing it for what it was: a reflex. He'd heard someone say it sometime or another, and he'd admired the sound of it. Now he was repeating it like a parrot.

"I'll have a Pepsi," I said when the waitress returned, and he rolled his eyes at the hopeless gaucherie of my choice. Real grown-ups, he believed, drank martoonies with their lunches.

"Are you gaining weight?" he asked, by way of opening the conversation.

"No, Victor," I said patiently. "I'm not."

He made a careless, have-it-your-way gesture. "Oh. I thought you had."

It was not, as anyone else would have known, a promising start. But then, Victor had always been an idiot savant of human-beingness. If a patient needed something, he would know it and take care of it immediately, even if he'd already been up twenty hours or if the patient couldn't pay. He was kind to them, too, hearing their fears and complaints and inquiring about their lives with genuine interest.

Which made it the more strange that, outside the clinical sphere, Victor had all the keen interpersonal perceptiveness of a colony of toenail fungus.

Eons later, or it felt that way, anyway, the waitress had arrived and gone away again, and our orders came. "You should chat with your son," I said. "About girls."

He glanced up from his chef's salad in wry surprise; he was capable, actually, of flashes of insight. It's one of the things that made him so dangerous. "Who, me?"

I ate some haddock. Lunch with Victor was a routine

we'd developed after he moved here; I thought of it as vaccination, exposure to a small, controlled dose of toxic substance to keep my system ready to deal with a no-holds-barred onslaught.

Which Victor still managed to deliver, on occasion. "Yes, you," I said. "He's picking up your attitudes, and it's not good for him. You know that it isn't."

He bridled uncomfortably, a tall, still-attractive man with green eyes, a lantern jaw, and a just-between-you-and-me smile he used to his advantage at every possible opportunity.

"Just because we couldn't make a go of it . . ."

Him and me, he meant. I drank some Pepsi. "That's not what happened."

He will do this: work it around in his mind—and in mine, if he can—so that I bear most of the responsibility for ending our marriage.

"There's a girl who's in love with Sam, and he's behaving like she's some sort of fashion accessory, something he can put on and take off whenever he happens to feel like it."

Victor frowned as this description hit a little close to the bone in the personal behavior department. "And?"

"And you zipping him around in the power boat every weekend, or in the car, bringing a different woman along each time, that's what. That debonair act you put on when he's with you. He admires it. He wants to be like you, don't you see that?"

His face softened. "Huh. Sam admires me. Thanks for telling me that, Jacobia. It means a lot to me, really. Thank you."

He smiled sincerely; seeing this, I gathered my wits about me. Just sitting at a table with Victor, inside his personal force field, makes you believe against all your better judgment that he is a nice, normal man with normal feelings. A conscience.

That you can trust him.

"Come on, Jake, what's the big deal? He's a kid, he's going to behave like one."

I suppressed my impatience. "He's not just any kid. He's had too many chances to go off the rails already, and barely escaped them. Now he's just about to get into college."

At the University of Maine in Machias forty miles away; he could come home weekends. Also, Sam had a part-time job at the local boatyard set up to start again in fall, with mentoring from the boatyard owner, Dan Harpwell. It was perfect.

"He wants to be a boat designer, he's lined up a future for himself, and I can't stand to see him tiptoeing around the edges of another pitfall," I finished forcefully. "And your lover-boy act makes Sam think that it's okay behavior," I said.

Victor looked innocently at me. "Well, but it is. For me."

Sudden fury struck me speechless for a moment, because this is the other thing Victor will do every time. It's all about him.

"It's not as if I'm married," he went on reasonably. "There is no reason I shouldn't have an active social life. And I don't promise these women anything, Jacobia. Not ever."

Calmly he drank some of his second martini while I struggled with the small, shrill voice in my head, the one that in spite of everything I'd been through with him kept crying out:

But you did. You promised me.

"Fine," I said finally. "Seeing as once again you have managed to make a conversation refer to yourself and *your* wishes, maybe *you* could just point out to *your* son that if he wants *your* life, then behaving like *you* is the way to get it."

Alone, I meant. Emotionally impoverished, dimly aware that other people had something he didn't. I still wasn't sure if Victor was unable or just unwilling to do what it took.

Victor once broke up with a woman he'd been seeing a long time, after our divorce; she'd suffered a serious back injury and was in traction for a number of weeks. And when I asked him what had happened to the relationship—he split with her right after the injury—he told me with a straight face that she was no fun anymore, so he had stopped seeing her. Not ironically, but as if this were the most reasonable thing in the world.

"Maybe," he allowed now, "I might mention it to Sam." Like I say, he has these flashes of insight. "I'm moving a bunch of my medical books out to the clinic soon, maybe he'll help me."

After he got here, I'd helped Victor establish a new medical facility whose purposes were:

(a) giving emergency care to badly injured people who would otherwise have to be Life-Starred to Bangor or Portland, and

(b) keeping Victor occupied and out of my hair.

"Anyway, I'll talk to him," he added, as I must have looked impatient again. He sipped at his drink. "So, who's the girl you have staying at your house? I saw her," he added, "go in with an overnight bag earlier on my way to work."

This was his way of letting me know he still kept tabs on me, and I found it about as charming a remark as you may imagine. But it was also my cue to let him change the subject, unless I wanted a battle that made Normandy look like a church picnic.

"Girlfriend of the guy who fell off the dock last night," I said. "She's here to claim his body if it can be found."

Eyebrows up. "Really. Sounds cheerful. Sam said she

was lah-di-dah. His term, not mine," Victor added with a grin.

Then: "I'll talk to him, Jake. Honest. I will."

A beat, while I decided how much to say. "Okay."

Then, to let him know I didn't lie around all day eating chocolates and watching soap operas—if I didn't impress him otherwise, he would accuse me of this—I related the events of the busy morning and described Charmian further.

"She knows languages," I finished. "Latin. Probably others." I went on to detail her deftness with small tools and knowledge of spy and/or crime techniques like invisible ink.

I drank some soda. "So, considering who raised her," I went on, "she can probably pick locks, fake early masterpieces, and forge passports."

"Not to mention forging the signatures onto the early masterpieces," Victor joked. He wasn't taking this seriously.

He finished the good parts out of his chef's salad and began picking at the greens. "Are you going to eat your roll?"

"What? No, have it." It was another annoying thing he did, eating off my plate as if we were still married.

"And there's one more thing that still bothers me, too," I said.

Just thinking aloud. My conversation with Victor was already over, for practical purposes. He tipped his head, chewing.

"That guy who went off the bluffs at North End," I said.

He swallowed. "But that was—"

"I know. Before the dock accident Raines had. If that's what it was. But *his* body hasn't been found, either; the guy from the bluffs."

I finished my Pepsi. "And I'm just thinking: if people

saw you come into town—which you could hardly avoid because there's only one way over the causeway, isn't there?—and then you wanted people to think you were gone . . ."

He'd stopped listening again; it made him the perfect person to bounce random ideas against. Maybe after they caromed off that invisible shield that surrounded him, they would fall into order.

I thought a minute more, working it out. "But you couldn't be seen *leaving* because you weren't *really* gone, then. . . ."

What I meant was, you can't come *or* go unnoticed here. And maybe the guy who'd gone off the bluffs wanted people to *think* he had drowned, but instead . . .

"You should leave this to the police," Victor said, ignoring my line of thought entirely in favor of his own. He was wearing his patented wise-and-superior expression now; to go with it, he was using his poor-foolish-Jacobia voice.

"I see," I said evenly. "And this would be because . . ."

"There's absolutely no reason for you to be involved in it," he said. "You don't know any of these people. You've got the girl in your house right now, for all you know she's tearing down more walls and so on even as we speak. She could be a co-conspirator in crimes which might possibly include murder."

"She's sitting at the kitchen table with Bob Arnold," I demurred, "or she's with him looking at the dock where it happened."

Bob had arrived as I was leaving. The schoolhouse fire on the mainland had been put out, but no suspect was in custody.

"Be that as it may," Victor said, dismissing easily my

attempt at parrying his comments. In a debate, Victor was like nuclear weapons against a rock pile, some primitive clubbing instruments, and a couple of sharpened sticks.

"It's none of your business," he pronounced primly, glancing at his watch again. "You should get rid of her."

Which of course was when I decided for sure that I would do no such thing.

"You'll talk to Sam," I said as we went out into the June sunshine: seagulls crying, a salt tang in the air, the snapping *whuff!* of sails as a couple of boats came around in the practice race course marked off by yellow buoys out in the channel.

"I said I would," Victor replied impatiently.

And maybe it was only that it was such a beautiful spring day, with the summer stretching goldenly ahead of us. Or maybe it was that my house had gone so serenely silent, after months of having my hair stand on end every time I walked into a darkened room. Maybe I thought that after one such unlooked-for miracle, another could follow.

"If you're so worried about it, I won't wait. I'll speak with him today," Victor said, getting into his little sports car.

Anyway, I believed him.

5 The day of the Eastport Ladies' Reading Circle meeting dawned damp and chilly, with fog filling up the shallow basin of the bay like cold soup in a bowl. It had been this way for two days, now, and the plaster patch in the dining room wasn't drying at all, a dark, ominous wet spot remaining at the center of it like the middle of a half-baked cake.

As a last resort I'd cut a wallboard square, glued it in there with Krazy Glue, and slapped wallpaper over it. The result wasn't anything the TV home-repair shows would have approved, and it was going to be the devil to take down and redo properly. But it worked for now, and I was admiring it when the phone rang.

"Jacobia? This is Clinty Havelock, over to the garage? I rented a car to a lady a little while ago, she says she's staying with you? And now Homer says . . ."

Homer was Clinty's husband, the town mechanic.

"What?" Ellie said from across the room, seeing my face.

"She's rented a car," I said exasperatedly.

Charmian had been spending her time at the library reading Hayes papers; Raines's body still had not been found, and I'd thought it was as good a way as any to keep her safely situated.

She hadn't said anything more about doing any investigating herself, and I'd hoped she'd given up the idea. But now I guessed she had gotten impatient.

Or something. "Go on, Clinty, what did Homer say?"

"Says that car ain't fit to be rented, he wasn't done on it and I should call you 'fore it . . ."

Oh, fabulous. ". . . breaks down," Clinty finished.

I told Clinty not to worry, that I would take care of it, and then I hung up to try to start figuring out how. But before I could, the phone rang again.

"Bettah come get the guhl," a surly voice advised, a voice so full of downeast twang it took a moment to understand: *girl*.

Damn. "Wilbur Mapes?" I asked, although I already knew.

In the background, his famously grouchy dog was barking as if a team of burglars were in the act of breaking into the place, which meant that a single,

solitary stranger might be somewhere within five miles
of Wilbur's property.

"Ayuh," he said. And unfortunately, I knew who
that stranger probably was: Charmian.

"I'm coming, Wilbur. Just wait for me, all right?"

In the background, something that sounded like a
pile of empty tin cans fell with a clatter. Then Charmian
came on.

"Jacobia?" Her voice was breathy and frightened, whether of Wilbur or his dog, I wasn't certain.
"Oh, Jacobia, I'm so sorry to put you to this trouble,
but my car died out here and this house was the
only—"

"Don't worry about it, Charmian. Just sit tight.
Their bark is worse than their bite."

I hoped. "Oh, blast and damnation," I said, hanging
up, but there was no help for it; she had to be fetched.

A little wildly, I looked around the kitchen, now so
full of fragile crockery I was almost afraid to move in it.
Ellie had arrived bearing china teacups, sterling silver,
more napkins, and a collection of cake plates for serving the cookies, petit-fours, and sandwiches to the
Circle. Also we'd lugged the coffee urn in and set it up
on top of the washing machine, which was the only
place where we could fit it.

Fortunately, I was not in charge of providing the
meeting's speaker; there was a committee for that, and
it had chosen, of all things, a mystery writer who'd recently moved to Eastport. Personally I thought this
choice was a bit lowbrow, but as I say, it was not my
decision.

"I'll come with you," Ellie said as I grabbed my car
keys.

"No. We still need sugar cubes for the tea table."

The house was as clean as a house with a teenage
boy in it ever gets. The sandwiches were made and cov-

ered with plastic and the puff pastries and petit-fours were stowed safely away in the refrigerator; we would cut the crusts from the sandwiches, set the table, and frost the petit-fours later.

In short, we were coming down to the wire on eleventh-hour preparations, which for a shining instant I'd actually believed I could complete successfully.

"Wade?" Ellie said. When the ladies arrived, we wanted our decks clear of unnecessary personnel.

I searched for my bag. "Ship coming in. Peat and particleboard. Won't be back till late."

"Sam?" She found the satchel, shoved it into my hands.

"Out with Maggie. The dive class members are still in the team that's looking for Raines's body down the coast."

The search would've been called off by now, only Charmian was being a thorn in everyone's side about it. Still, at least it kept Sam out of Jill Frey's clutches for a while; she had begged off the search party efforts. Too much like work, I guessed.

"I don't know about after that," I finished on my way out the door. "If they show up, give Sam a heads-up to steer clear. Pay him if you have to."

Drat Charmian. She'd been talking about retracing Raines's footsteps, but I hadn't thought she would do anything about it. Slamming into the car, I headed past the Moose Island Shellfish Co-op, the farmers' market on Route 190, and the clam beds in the inlet below Redoubt Hill. Crossing the causeway, I spotted the vessel Wade was coming in on, white and massive in the fog as it awaited an earlier vessel's departure. Finally I slowed for the 35 mph zone through the Passamaquoddy reservation at Pleasant Point.

Then it was onto the mainland, across Route 1, and out the winding two-lane road past the old grange hall.

When the pavement ended I juddered along on wash-board dirt, crossed the old rail line whose rusting trestle spans a salt marsh thick with sawgrass and cattails.

The fog thinned mischievously, then slammed down again like a grey wall. Half the time I crept along, knowing I was on the road only by the feel of the tires on the rough surface. A mile felt like ten; then suddenly the fog lifted and I was there:

A rock-strewn clearing, barren as the surface of the moon, reached uphill from the dirt road. A rutted, dusty track served as a driveway, at the head of which stood a house trailer, added onto with ramshackle ac-cretions of wood, tar paper, and tin.

Mapes's beat-up pickup truck was parked there, with a sheet of streaked, age-greyed particleboard propped against it. In big red letters with dried drips of red paint running down from them, the signboard read: NOTHING HERE IS WORTH YOUR LIFE.

With which sentiment I absolutely agreed; stretched over the clearing, peeking out of the last wisps of the thinning fog, was the tag sale from hell. A row of used toilet seats, three stacks of galvanized buckets, two an-chors, and a thick coil of rotting hemp rope lay under a broken ping-pong table beside a rusted-out tractor. Cardboard boxes of paperback books in a stack four boxes high and half dozen long were turning to papier-mâché. Juicers, coffeemakers, toasters, waffle irons, and crock pots stood on a board-and-sawhorse table.

And there was more, including whatever was in the falling-down shed at the rear of the property; picking my way toward the back of the trailer where a rickety-looking set of steps led to a back door, I shuddered to think how much of the moldy, scabrous, rusting, and all-around depressing detritus of daily life Mapes had managed to collect back there.

The door opened. "Ain't none o' that your business. S'posed to use the front door," he growled.

If there was one, I hadn't noticed it. What I did notice was how quiet it was out here, nobody around.

No cars had passed since I'd come up the dirt driveway. I'd seen none since leaving the paved part of the road several miles earlier, not even Charmian's.

"Why don't you just . . ."

Send her out, I'd been about to say to Mapes. But then I saw three things simultaneously:

The first was how swiftly nature was attempting to reclaim the barren clearing. A grassy trail leading to the shed from the trailer was bordered with red clover, lushly green in the damp, brightening sunshine, though the trail itself was well trampled, as if it had seen a fair amount of foot traffic recently.

The second was something that appeared to be a Tasmanian devil, equipped with a muscular body, blazing eyes, and a full set of large, sharp, impossibly pointed canine teeth, every one of which looked to be in absolutely perfect working order.

One moment, this ridiculously fierce, snarling creature was exiting the shed. In the next, it was nearly upon me.

The third thing I saw was . . . well, at the time, the third was only a flash of yellow, as I covered the distance to the trailer door in what felt like a single bound.

"Good move," Mapes uttered as a heavy *thump!* accompanied by a snarl made the trailer tremble. He was a tall, big-boned man with high cheekbones, very pale blue eyes, and light, curly hair.

Behind him, Charmian looked up in relief. "Jacobia."

The trailer inside was like the outside: a jumble of things, the largest of them peering glassy-eyed from the walls. A moose head, a deer head, a whole mounted fox . . . there was even a bear's head, for God's sake, and a ratty black bearskin spread out on the plywood floor.

But the items tucked in among the trophies weren't junk. Just about every exotic wood I could think of was there among the tables, hutches, desks, chairs, headboards, and sideboards in the collection: ebony, mahogany, even Brazilian rosewood. And the air smelled like furniture polish.

Also, there were guns everywhere: rifles, shotguns, and at least a dozen different handguns, just lying around or standing in racks. But I wasn't here for a tour of Wilbur's antiques or of his firearm collection.

"Well, this is a fine fix you've gotten us into," I began, angrier than ever with Charmian. "Where's the car?"

"Down the road," she replied miserably. "I passed this place and was trying to find a spot to turn around—"

"Ain't no turnaround for miles," Mapes said dourly.

"Come on," I said. "I'm running late already, so let's go. How the hell did you ever find your way through the fog, anyway?"

I turned to Mapes, whose primitive country-boy act I'd just about had up to the gills; there was a sharp intelligence glinting in those pale blue eyes. "Wilbur, will that yard dog of yours really tear us limb from limb?"

Because most of them won't. Some may rush in so close, you can feel their hot breath blowing right up your nostrils. But . . .

Mapes scowled, acknowledging it; dogs don't really like to bite people. They've been tight with the human race too long.

"Not 'nless I tell 'im to."

"All right, then." I had a last curious glance around at Wilbur's indoor stuff: good Staffordshire pottery, a very nice collection of cranberry glass, a lovely old amberina decanter from the New England Glassworks—I don't know much, but even I know to keep my eye peeled for these—and a table that unless I missed my guess was real Chippendale.

And more, but I didn't have time to examine it. "Come on, Charmian," I said, and went out the way I had come in, ignoring Mapes's protest: "Dammit, I *told* you, you just can't march around my property like—"

But I was already outside, with Charmian right behind me. I picked my way around Mapes's urchin diving equipment—drysuit, a regulator, gloves, and a tank harness—and made a beeline for the car, making sure the girl's footsteps were keeping up with me and darting a cautious glance toward the shed in case Mapes's opinion of the hell-dog turned out to be less than accurate.

The dog was nowhere in sight. But what I did see—clearly, this time—turned my heart to an icy lump, especially as Wilbur Mapes was now chasing us, his features dark with fury.

That yellow thing I'd glimpsed as I was rocketing toward the trailer turned out, actually, to be two things, stuffed between an old deep-fat fryer and a stack of moldy *National Geographics*.

It was a pair of yellow Wellington boots.

Charmian stared straight forward, silently, not protesting even though I was driving like somebody was going to step forward and start waving a checkered flag.

I didn't talk, either. For one thing, my teeth were clamped together too tight until we got back to the paved road. A dust cloud had been swirling up behind us, so I couldn't tell whether Mapes was still chasing us or not. But once we reached the pavement I saw that he wasn't; I slowed on the macadam, catching my breath and getting control of my urge to wring this girl's neck.

"What the hell did you think you were doing?"

She didn't look at me. "You saw them," she uttered. "You saw Jon's boots just as well as I did. Out with all the junk."

"That's not an answer to my question. You shouldn't have gone out there alone. What made you—"

Think of it, I would have said, but she was already answering. "He's a junk man. Mapes is, or that's what he wants people to think. I asked around, people in town. Who buys fine old things? Who's on the lookout for them? And they told me."

With Raines gone, people sympathized with Charmian. Heck, I did, too, when I wasn't trying hard not to swat her.

Like now. "And everyone mentioned the same names," she said. "Wilbur Mapes and Lillian Frey."

She said nothing more but I knew we were both following the same line of thought: that the fishing vest was one thing. Raines could've struggled out of that.

The boots, though. In my experience, it took both hands to pull a Wellington boot off your foot. Or someone else's.

The fog had lifted. Antique homesteads on either side of the road crumbled quietly, surrounded by gnarled remnants of apple orchards and staggering fence posts. Soft clouds of moisture rose from the damp earth.

But I was late, so I didn't slow to appreciate the view. And with home now almost within striking distance I began to realize:

I would still have time to shower. Ellie had promised

to be at my house again by early afternoon; she could put the finishing touch on the refreshments, we would throw a fast supper together, and she could leave before any early arrivals appeared.

And—wonder of wonders—even the little bathroom worked, with the recent addition of a bigger paper clip. It could all still turn out okay, but only if I got back quickly.

Thinking this, I stepped on the gas pedal, glanced in the rearview mirror, and got an unwelcome eyeful of the green Passamaquoddy police van right behind me, its lights flashing. I pulled over.

"License and registration."

I handed them to him. The land under Route 190 had been taken by eminent domain from the Passamaquoddy tribe when the road was built; ordinarily, I wouldn't dream of speeding here. It was rude and disrespectful; also dangerous.

But I'd forgotten. "Sorry, Officer." He gave me a flat look and the warning card that promised dreadful consequences should I be caught speeding here again.

"Have a good day," he advised unexpressionlessly in parting.

But I wasn't going to. Pulling up in front of my house ten minutes later, I saw to my horror that cars were parked three-deep in the driveway and lined up on both sides of the street.

An awful thought struck me. Surely I would have remembered if the Eastport Ladies' Reading Circle had scheduled an *afternoon* meeting, instead of an evening one?

They had. In the kitchen, the coffee urn burbled and the teakettle whistled. Wearing my apron and a look that said doom was being held off by inches, Ellie was frosting petit-fours with one hand and cutting the crusts from little sandwiches with the other.

"They're here," she said. "I couldn't do anything about the wall, so I improvised."

"The wall," I managed, hearing the murmur of women's voices from the dining room. What had happened to the wall?

"Better get in there," Ellie added, filling the sugar bowl. The faster she works, the less she talks, and right now I needed her speed-demon qualities very badly. So I did what she told me to do, which was how I discovered that Krazy Glue is not a good wallboard adhesive. The patch I'd set in had fallen out, bringing along with it the new wallpaper, the plaster patching, the lath, and an important-looking chunk of the tin ceiling.

Now it all lay on the dining room floor by the door to the butler's pantry. But that wasn't the worst part.

Tacked over the hole was a large, rectangular piece of black velvet. Painted on it—daubed—was a life-sized portrait of the young Elvis Presley, clad in one of the spangled pink jumpsuits he wore during his Las Vegas period and holding a guitar.

DON'T BE CRUEL, read the words in gold glitter across the bottom edge of the velvet. Ellie looked in from the kitchen. "It was the best I could do on such short notice."

"It's . . . striking," said Charmian.

"The highlights in his pompadour are especially effective," I agreed. "That Day-Glo blue."

Ellie returned to the kitchen while I studied Elvis, wishing I could get into the painting with him and drive away in the gold Cadillac artfully depicted in the portrait's background.

"I'm so sorry I've ruined your plans," Charmian said.

"That's all right," I said, reminding myself with an effort that this wasn't (a) green water over the helm or (b) a fire in the engine room. "But if you could just"—I gestured inarticulately—"get rid of some of the wilder lies. The evil uncle, for instance. I know Winston Cartwright does exists, and probably you are related to him."

"But—"

I'd been thinking about this. "But to expect me to believe he killed Jonathan or had him killed, that he takes any interest at all in what happens in Eastport, Maine, is—"

Ridiculous, I was about to say. Then I heard a man's voice from the parlor. Sam, I thought, but the voice was deeper.

Not Wade; not George Valentine or Victor. It was . . .

"Uncle Winston," Charmian said, aghast, and hurried into the parlor; I followed, dreading further disasters but fairly certain that they were imminent.

"Charmian, my dear," the bass voice boomed, "I am delighted to see you looking so well. I was concerned about you."

"Oh, I'm sure," Charmian replied, twisting her opal ring in surprised distress. "What are you doing here? Come to gloat over Jonathan's murder? Well, you're not going to get away with it. I should call the police right now and have you arrested."

While this charming family reunion played out, I surveyed the room. In it were twenty-five or so well-dressed women, each with her hair done, her makeup on, and her good jewelry donned for the occasion.

I was wearing a pair of old jeans and there were still bits of wallboard material stuck in my hair, and my hands were gritty with dried wallpaper adhesive. But it was too late to worry about that; besides, they weren't looking at me. Instead they gazed at the person in the parlor chair: a large man in a disreputable-looking slouch felt hat, wearing a voluminous trench coat.

In one huge hand he gripped an ornate carved walking stick; in the other he held a glass of something red and syrupy-looking. On the table beside him sat a small electronic device: a camera, I realized. But an odd one.

"How do you do?" he intoned gravely, noticing me. "Pardon my not getting up, won't you? At my age, I must save my energy."

He didn't look energy-deprived; sharp eyes, pink cheeks, an alert expression under wildly bushy salt-and-pepper eyebrows. Charmian's sigh at his words only reinforced my opinion: here was a fellow, past middle age but by no means elderly, who let people think he was fragile, the better to surprise them later.

"Charmed," he murmured, taking my hand and fixing me in a glance so penetrating that I felt as if my bone marrow were being biopsied.

He was so naturally attention-getting, it wasn't until I'd stepped right up to him that I saw Sam seated on the floor beside him, an object cradled reverently in his lap.

"Hey, Mom. Look what we found."

It was a human skull, minus lower jawbone, with what looked irresistibly like a broken arrowhead lodged in its cranium.

"Isn't that interesting?" I managed faintly.

The ladies looked fascinated, except for the one I thought must be the meeting's speaker, the mystery writer.

She fainted, two ladies crouching swiftly next to her. I thought of helping; after all, I was the hostess here.

Instead I reached wordlessly for the glass Winston Cartwright was holding, and he gave it to me. Draining it, I noticed that its contents were at least a hundred proof.

"Thank you," I gasped, handing the glass back to him, and he nodded, refilling it promptly from a silver flask he produced from among the folds of the trench coat.

"Blackberry cordial," he said. "Anyone?" he offered.

When my eyes stopped watering I saw that Maggie Altvater was here, too, hanging back behind the ladies. While they lined up to accept Cartwright's offer, she moved toward me.

"We found it diving," she said, meaning the skull. "At Pirate's Cove. We'd given up on looking for Raines for the day and gone out to hunt for another batch of old bottles to sell. It was packed in sort of vegetabley stuff with a funny smell to it when we got it up to the surface, like wet peat moss."

At my inquiring glance, she explained. "Not like packed by hand, or anything. Just in the stuff. Like it rolled there and got covered up and just . . . stayed there. Until we dug it out."

Stained brown, obviously ancient. "Peat moss. Isn't it what they find prehistoric skeletons in? Peat bogs, over in Europe?"

It had been on a public television program one night. And if old submerged bottles remained in backwaters the currents and tides didn't reach, then I guessed a skull might, too.

Maggie shrugged unhappily. "I just wonder who it was. And I wish we hadn't kept it. It half scared the pants off me, seeing those two eye sockets staring at me underwater."

Just then Ellie came to the door and announced that since the writer wasn't feeling well enough to give her presentation, the meeting would proceed to the refreshments.

Great: no speaker, an uninvited guest—two, if you counted the skull—and now we would have little cakes and sandwiches in a room that looked as if the wrecking ball hadn't quite finished with it. Trying to distract myself from the social debacle about to ensue, I sidled closer to Cartwright and the gadget lying on the table by him.

"It's a digital camera. I sometimes take photos of objects I find and send them to other people," Cartwright explained. "It's simpler and quicker to send them via the Internet from wherever I may be. And since I never know when I might run across such an object, I keep a camera handy."

"I understand." I'd never seen one close up before, though; unlike Sam and Maggie, since moving to Maine I'd left the high-tech revolution behind.

"You know, I've never really quite understood how it works," I said. I didn't see any film advance mechanism, or in fact any place to put film at all.

"I mean, does the picture stay inside the camera, too? For you to keep after you've sent it? Or . . ."

Cartwright looked at me. From his expression, I supposed he was about to embark on a difficult-to-understand explanation that would leave me gasping. He picked the device up, turned it over in his hands, readying to expound on it.

"The music goes 'round and 'round," he began gravely. "And it comes out"—he pressed a button and a small square plastic wafer popped from a slot with a little *click!*—"here."

"Ah." I nodded slowly. You put the wafer into the camera like film.

"I wonder how long it would've taken me, figuring that out."

It certainly wasn't obvious from looking at the thing, although I supposed if you bought one and read the instructions it would be clear.

"Oh, you'd have gotten there eventually," Cartwright said, eyeing me acutely, and seemed about to say more.

But just then one of the ladies approached: Nan Fairbrother, a bright-eyed little person with the whitest hair, the cleanest house, and the sharpest tongue in town. I had no doubt that Mrs. Fairbrother would be telling the story of my disastrous meeting to anyone who would listen, for weeks to come. But, as Eastport people so often do, she surprised me completely.

"Never mind, dear," she said. *Dee-yah*. "The first time I had a meeting at my house, I got so nervous I forgot what day it was entirely. I was in a housecoat and pin curls when they arrived."

They were in the dining room now: fallen plaster and Elvis. "What did you do?"

"I ordered pizza," she replied, "and jugs of Gallo wine, and had them delivered chop-chop. It was," she confided with her bird-claw hand wrapped around my arm, "a smashing success. Now go on like a good girl, and have a good time at your party."

The kindness of downeast people is like a rose, blooming with sudden, unexpected sweetness in a rocky place. I swallowed hard to get rid of the lump in my throat, which was lucky, since moments later I had a teacup in one hand, a lobster-paste sandwich with the crusts cut off in the other, and the party was going wonderfully.

Also, informatively: "Do you know," Winston Cartwright asked portentously of Maggie, "whose that skull almost certainly is?"

Charmian's threat to call the police, I gathered, had not intimidated him. Nor had she acted upon it. Meanwhile, the ladies were all agog.

"No, whose?" asked Rita Farnham, the tips of her manicured fingers pressed together. She ran the Clip & Curl on High Street.

"Yes, do tell," said Wanda Perrone, who looked as if she'd stepped straight out of *Vogue* magazine; this, I thought, was half the value of the Reading Circle, all

these women way out here at the back of beyond
bravely keeping the side up, armed with plenty of
Camay soap.

"This skull," Cartwright intoned, "belonged to Jared
Hayes."

Well, even I gasped at that. "How do you know?"

He glowered wisely at me. "Isn't it often the way
that a man may be little-known at home, yet famous in
the greater world?"

"Indeed it is," said Hester Sawtelle, who had
been a great beauty in her day and was still knock-
out gorgeous at ninety. "You all remember Dr.
Honigsberger."

Murmurs of agreement: Honigsberger had retired in
Eastport to raise, we thought, garden-variety dahlias.
Not until after he died did we learn he'd been one of the
greatest plant geneticists of all time, much published
and world-respected.

Cartwright went on: "The same is true for Hayes.
Although," he added wryly, "perhaps not for the reason
he might have wished. You see, Jared Hayes . . ."—
here he paused for effect—"was a pirate. Oh, he didn't
go out on raiding parties himself," Cartwright added.
"But . . ."

Another pause, more dramatic, then a growled decla-
ration: "But he *shared in the booty*!"

It wasn't as far-fetched a story as it might at first
have seemed. Eastport is perfectly situated for all varieties of waterborne criminality, surrounded by so many
coves, inlets, and other hiding spots for small boats that
it would take an army of customs officials to monitor
them all.

And to the ladies, many of whose male relatives were
engaged in, shall we say, *interesting* activities as we
spoke, it sounded entirely reasonable.

"Hayes traveled often to Boston and New York," Cartwright said, "as a touring musician. Which gave him a good excuse; he was, in today's parlance, a 'fence' for the pirate treasures of a man by the name of Josephus Whitelaw."

At this point the ladies began to look knowingly around at one another; the Whitelaw name was familiar to them, apparently.

"Whitelaw's angle was pirating the pirates," Cartwright said. "And pestering the British, in his younger days. So locally he became a hero. But later he began preying on American vessels, and that was his downfall."

"Don't forget about Jane Whitelaw," Priscilla Ware put in. An unmarried lady of a certain age whose white collar was trimmed with lace she designed and made herself, she was an incurable romantic.

"Indeed," Cartwright replied. "Jane, daughter of Josephus. What shall we say of her other than that she undoubtedly presided over many an elaborate dinner in this very room?"

Cartwright looked at me. "A gentleman musician, a pirate's beautiful daughter. It's a pairing worthy of literature, wouldn't you say? Tragic," he added, "literature."

"Why tragic? And how do you know so much?" I demanded again.

"Hayes and Jane Whitelaw were lovers," he replied. "The sort of lovers people write operas about, passionate and doomed. It was Hayes's plan to win her heart by becoming wealthy beyond even Jane's greedy dreams."

Maggie looked up. "Doomed? But why?"

"Because, unfortunately for Jane's father Josephus, he was in the act of looting a local vessel when several ships belonging to the U.S. Navy hove into view in

Passamaquoddy Bay. The sailors seized Josephus, clapped him in irons. Hayes was in Boston; when he returned, the authorities were waiting for him, as well."

"And then?" I glanced at Ellie; she was listening intently.

"Even then, Josephus might have talked his way out of it. As I say, he had been a great favorite. But when Hayes got back, he found a reward had been offered for information against Josephus and a warrant had been issued for his own arrest, the Navy having got wind of his part in the piracy. So to save his own skin—and for the reward—Hayes ratted."

I thought of those old account books, full of expenditures yet devoid of comparable income. That was where it all had come from: piracy. No wonder he hadn't kept records of it.

"Wow." Sam scowled down at the skull. "You jerk."

Maggie nodded in assent. "Turned in his girlfriend's father. That's pretty harsh." There was a moment of silence.

Then: "Eeeuw, what's that thing?" came a petulant voice from the dining room doorway. "Sam, I thought you were going to meet me downtown. I had to drive up here."

It was Jill Frey, her pixie-cut blond hair making her resemble an evil sprite and her narrow face tightening in further annoyance as she caught sight of Maggie.

At Jill's appearance, Sam jumped up as if flicked with a whip. "Oh, hey, I'm sorry. I forgot."

He thrust the skull at Maggie's not-entirely-willing hands. "Let me just go clean up a little in the kitchen. Everybody, this is my friend Jill Frey."

Jill bestowed a smirk on the assembly and said nothing, but took a petit-four. Not until she had eaten it did she spot the camera Cartwright had put down again on the table in the parlor, whereupon a look of frightened guilt suddenly came over her face.

She snatched it up, then seemed to relax as she examined it more closely; I had a moment to wonder what nerve in her rudimentary conscience the little gadget had plucked so strongly.

In the end, though, I didn't care; it was my own son whose conscience I thought needed attention, and plenty of it. Maggie bit her lip, looking away as I followed him into the kitchen.

He was washing his hands at the sink. "Sam. You should be ashamed of yourself."

He slapped water on his face, wiped it. "Huh?"

"Maggie's your friend, too," I said. "Don't you realize what you just did to her in there?"

"Oh, hey, Mom, you think Maggie and I are—"

"I'm talking about what *she* thinks. What you let her think, until somebody *you* think is more glamorous walks in."

His face hardened. "I know what this is all about, you know. It's about you and Dad."

Nobody's ever accused me of raising a stupid kid. And the parallel was pretty obvious. But—

"Let it alone, Mom. I hate to say this to you, but it's none of your business."

"Sam," Jill whined from the hall, "are we going, or what?"

"Mom."

"Yeah." I didn't look up.

"See you later."

"Yeah." Neither one of us giving an inch. I guessed Victor hadn't been in any rush to get to that father-and-son talk he'd promised to have with Sam.

If he'd meant to have it at all. Jill's car fired up, roared away; when I got back to the dining room Maggie was gone, too, out the front door to avoid running into Sam and Jill, and the skull sat on the sideboard staring at me with its empty eye sockets.

"So Josephus was hanged, and his ship burnt to the waterline in what is now called Pirate's Cove," Winston Cartwright finished.

Which didn't explain why Hayes's skull should be found there almost two hundred years later. "Who put the curse on Hayes?" I asked, remembering what Hecky Wilmot had said.

But my heart wasn't really in that question, either. I kept wanting to follow Maggie Altvater, say something useful to her. Or consoling. Not that there was anything.

"My great-grandfather said *his* great-grandfather saw Jane," Winifred Cooley said. She was a big, white-haired woman who ran a vegetable farm on the mainland and made molasses doughnuts so light you had to snatch them out of the air to eat them.

"No one knows what she was searching for," Winifred added, "but she was seen running on the bluffs at North End at midnight, a flaming torch in her hands, with the baby in her arms."

"Oh, yes," Hester Sawtelle agreed. "My great-aunt Hepzibah told the story, how they searched all that night on the water in the dark, towing rafts with bonfires on them to light the way. But they never found her."

"A child? Hayes and Jane Whitelaw had a child?" I looked at Cartwright, who nodded solemnly back at me.

"Heard her shrieking," Winifred recited, "damning Hayes and all who would deal with him to her own fate. And then—"

"Yes, the curse. And then she fell," Cartwright pronounced, "just one day before Hayes vanished. And *someone* saw her, because she was never found but the infant, Micah Whitelaw, was saved. A fortunate turn of events, indeed."

As he spoke, it occurred to me that in all the excitement of the past few hours, I had yet to tell Ellie about Charmian's trip out to Mapes's place, or Raines's Wellington boots.

"The arrowhead, by the way, is what clinches identification on this old fellow," Cartwright said, picking up the skull. "It's not what killed him, however."

He turned the thing in his hands. "Earlier in his life, Mr. Hayes had been shot by a Passamaquoddy gentleman whom he'd tried to cheat in a trade. By some miracle the wound was not fatal, but the point of the weapon broke off and stayed in Hayes's head. A birdtip"—he fingered the foreign object stuck in the cranium—"just like this one."

"Oh, now," I objected, "how could you possibly know that? In fact, how could you know any of this?" I was beginning to wonder if Winston Cartwright was just putting us on.

"No Hayes papers have ever been away from this town, to my knowledge. And even if they had, we've been through them and they don't mention any of what you have been telling us. So how—"

Cartwright beamed darkly, as if he had been waiting for just this objection. "Ah, but Hayes wasn't the only diary-keeper. And in my spare time, I happen to be a keen collector of volumes such as diaries, daybooks, and so on. Like the ones . . ."

He produced from his coat a tattered, leather-bound article. "Like the ones kept all his life by Micah Whitelaw, son of Jane Whitelaw and the mysterious Mr. Jared Hayes. Wonderful Micah," he enthused, "excellent fellow. The tale was still fresh when he was a young man, and he *wrote it all down*."

He brandished the volume, tucked it in his coat again. "The point of all this," he finished, struggling up from his chair at the table, leaning on the walking stick, "is that Jared Hayes was a scoundrel. If he said there was a violin in his possession, then saying so was a part of some scheme that he was planning."

He looked at Charmian, who stiffened under his gaze. "For Jared Hayes, musician and blackguard, *everything* was a scheme. You've been taken in by him, my girl. As was that young fool you thought you loved."

"No," she retorted, her voice quavering fresh anger. "It's you who made the mistake. You let that horrible Mapes person keep Jon's boots."

Cartwright grew still. The ladies, too, listened with keen attention. "What do you mean?" he asked finally.

"I *saw* them, today at his trailer. A trailer full"—she looked around wildly at the ladies—"of mean dogs, and guns, and moth-eaten animal heads, all mixed in among them all these amazing, valuable antiques."

She swung around to face Cartwright. "He's got masses of fine old things; you must know him, you know *everybody* like that. Horrible people with wonderful things—like you. And you *hired* him to kill Jonathan!"

In that moment Cartwright's much-rumored professional history came back to me, and I could believe every bit of it. He reminded me of an enormous, possibly venomous old spider, motionless but ready in the next moment to move with deadly speed.

"Mapes has his boots? You're sure?"

"Don't lie, Uncle Winston," she said. "I know you too well."

Oddly, it was this remark that seemed to wound him. "Do you, now?" he answered quietly. "Do you, at that?"

The ladies of the club had tactfully begun carrying

plates and cups to the kitchen, stepping around the heap of the wall wreckage to reach stray teaspoons and crumpled napkins.

"Jacobia, dear," said Mrs. Bentley Little-Barnes, who had been known even to her sister by her full legal name since the day she married Mr. Bentley Little-Barnes fifty years earlier.

She was also the membership secretary of the Eastport Ladies' Reading Circle. "You have fulfilled your hostess duties in fine style," she pronounced. "I am delighted, on behalf of the entire membership, to finalize your welcome to the Circle."

For a minute I thought there ought to be trumpets fanfaring. Through blizzards and nor' easters, pea-soup fogs and cold snaps to forty below, the ladies of the Circle faced an uncaring world with teacups lifted, makeup on, and stocking seams straight; when not drinking tea or discussing books, they did charitable deeds all over the county, and I was proud to be one of them.

"Thank you," I said humbly. Several of them actually did wear stockings with seams, I noticed as they went away down the sidewalk, looking like an army in good dresses in search of a cause to fight for.

"Good-bye," they called, waving back at me.

"Good-bye," I called in return. "Thank you for coming."

I closed the door, feeling drained and exhilarated. "Well, that went smoothly enough," I said to Ellie, who had begun soaping spoons. "Thank you so much for staying."

"You're welcome. I didn't mind it nearly as much as I'd feared. It's sort of . . . uplifting, somehow. The company of women." The sweet smell of hot, soapy water rose from the sink.

"And of course it went fine, Jacobia. What did you expect, to be judged by a point system? Though if you were," she added, "I believe the entertainment portion of the program would have put you over the top."

Which reminded me. "Where's Cartwright?" If he was a killer, or even an employer of them, he was an awfully charming one.

Not that charm meant anything; Jemmy Wechsler was charming, too, but I wouldn't like meeting him in a dark alley. And so, for that matter, was Victor. When he wanted to be.

"He went out the front like something shot out of a cannon, right after Charmian told him about the boots," Ellie said. "I never saw anyone that big move that fast before. And what about those boots, anyway?"

I brought her up to speed while I took the spoons out of the tray and began drying them; Ellie filled the tray with sudsy cups and began rinsing. "And Charmian?" I asked.

"Upstairs. Meeting her uncle again took the wind out of her. She took some aspirin, said she thought she'd lie down."

"Good," I said. "You know, there are a lot of things about all this, not even counting the boots, that—"

"Bother you," Ellie finished. "Me, too. Such as, I can see why Hayes might tell people he was getting a Stradivarius when he really wasn't. Or," she added, "some other very valuable item."

The violin that was also the treasure. Or was not. I wiped another teaspoon.

"It could have been part of a scam," she said, "especially now we know what a rascal he was. Can you imagine getting your own child's grandfather hanged?"

"Yeah," I said, remembering what Sam had said about it and wondering where Sam was right now. "I mean, no. What a jerk."

"But why lie to his own diary? In a diary, if it was a

scam you'd say you were *telling* people you had something, not that you really did." She surveyed the kitchen, took off her apron, and hung it on its hook, having done enough dishes for an army mess tent in about fifteen minutes.

"I don't know." I flung my towel down. Not wanting to jinx matters, I hadn't said anything to her about how peaceful the house was lately. Now I thought about it, decided again not to.

Besides, I had another subject entirely on my mind. "Ellie, if you were new in Eastport, how long d'you think it would take you to locate Wilbur Mapes?"

She blew out a breath. "Oh, I guess about twenty years."

"But Raines *and* Charmian both found him right away. Raines even got a ride from him, which probably means Mapes knew he was coming."

She nodded. "And Charmian found that trailer of his," I went on, "way out on the dirt road, drove there with no hesitation."

"You don't suppose it *wasn't* those boots that upset her so much? I mean, what if she already knew they were there? What if she just didn't like *you* seeing them, so she put on an act?"

"Then I'm not sure why she called me in the first place," I answered, feeling more confused. "Unless she and Mapes are in something together and they wanted to make it look to me as if they aren't."

I thought some more. "He was angry that I went around back. Maybe he didn't want either of us to see them? Me or Charmian? I mean, maybe he'd kept them for himself, and . . ."

Ellie shuddered. "A dead man's boots. Still, it *is* Wilbur."

People in Eastport liked to say Wilbur would sell his

own kidneys if he could get at them, a thought that made me feel a bit shivery about the absence of Raines's body. Whatever he was up to, though, the boots hadn't walked out there by themselves.

"You know what I wonder about most of all?" Ellie said. "I wonder why Hayes wrote in English, in all the other manuscripts and so on that we've got of his. But in that one . . ." She waved at the antique volume we'd found in the wall. "In that one, he wrote in Latin *and* used invisible ink."

"Pretty secretive," I agreed. And how had his head ended up in the bay? And then there was the fact that, nearly two hundred years later, Jonathan Raines had come to Eastport and immediately shared Jared Hayes's watery fate.

. . . damn Jared Hayes and all who would deal with him . . .

Did trying to find his violin count as dealing with him?

I don't believe in curses, but right about then, with purple twilight gathering stealthily in around the old house, I couldn't help wondering.

Maybe Jane Whitelaw's curse was finally coming true.

6 Early the next morning, Wilbur Mapes glowered from the rickety back porch built of scrap wood at the rear of his awful dwelling. The dog barked inside, its body thumping against the door of the trailer.

"Now, Wilbur," Bob Arnold said calmly, "you know I have got to follow up on things, might have to do with that young fellow."

Mapes uttered a profanity.

"I'll take that as permission," Bob said. Mapes slammed back inside. I hoped he wasn't in there loading one of the shotguns.

"All right, Jacobia," Bob said. "Let's have a look."

"They were right over here somewhere. . . ."

We picked our way between rusty bedsprings, wringer-style washing machines, rot-bottomed coal scuttles. The sheer volume of junk was overwhelming; where had I been when I saw the boots?

"You're sure, now? The boots you saw were the same ones. . . ."

"I'm sure," I said. But I was getting a sinking feeling.

I'd snagged Bob Arnold just as he was getting to his office and persuaded him to come out here with me, luring him with a bag of pastries from the IGA and a thermos of coffee.

On the ride we'd been silent, me because what could I tell him? That (a) the poltergeist or whatever it was in my old house was gone—or anyway, it had quit bothering me—but now (b) an old curse had got linked up somehow with Eastport's busiest junk collector, and the result killed Jonathan Raines?

I didn't say anything about keeping Charmian in residence with me, either. It probably wasn't the most sensible course of action on my part. But I knew how it felt to be a young woman in love and in difficulties, with no one to turn to; if I forgot, I had my memories of my years with Victor to fall back on. Maybe she was a pain in the neck, but I felt sorry for her, and with each passing day I was also feeling more stiff-necked stubborn about it, like the ladies of the Reading Circle who just hung in there come hell or (more often, in downeast Maine) high water.

Bottom line, I wasn't going to dump her, but I didn't think I needed to invite any arguments from Bob Arnold by saying so; at this point, he was so exasperated by her insistence that the search for Raines's body be continued, he was about ready to send her off the end of the dock, too.

Meanwhile, he was bone-tired after another night of trying—and failing—to catch the firebug. Happy just not to be driving, he'd ridden along contentedly enough, eating pastries and sipping coffee in a blur of fatigue. But now in the pale grey morning behind Wilbur Mapes's trailer, he wasn't happy anymore.

Me either. No yellow boots. Mapes slammed out again, thumped down the steps. "You want to say what you's are lookin' for, I might be able to set you on the track," he allowed sullenly.

"Pair of boots," Bob said. "Yellow, expensive ones. You got anything like that around here, Wilbur?"

The grassy path I'd noticed the day before led from the shed back into the fields, old pasture land bounded in the distance by windbreak cedars. Wilbur's face didn't change.

"Nuh-uh. Pair o' galoshes, you want them." He eased between a car engine and a row of bald truck tires, pulled the galoshes down.

Bob looked at me. "No," I said, wondering if the confusion of worthless things gathered here was really random, as it seemed to me, or if it mimicked some bizarre pattern in Mapes's head.

"We go in?" Bob asked, and Mapes nodded grudgingly. "Suit yourself. Watch the dog."

Inside, the dog was doing enough watching for all of us as we made our way through the clutter. I saw again the many valuable items, several that hadn't been here the day before, among the hunting trophies: a Queen Anne wing chair, a pewter tankard, two long-stemmed clay tobacco pipes.

"You know the fellow?" Bob asked Mapes. "One supposed to've fallen off the fish pier the other night?"

He didn't mention the guns lying around; in Maine, if Mapes wasn't carrying a weapon concealed, he didn't need a permit.

"Ayuh," Mapes replied, startling me. "I sold him some stuff now an' again. Old stuff, like he 'us always lookin' for."

Bob ignored my urgent glance; so there was a *connection.* "Sold him anything lately?"

"Nuh-uh. I'd call him, I got anything I thought he wanted. Old music stuff a while back. Ain't had nothin' like that lately. Damn fool."

My impatience got the better of me. "If you haven't sold him anything lately, how is it that you're the one who gave him the ride into town *and* took him up to Calais to get that replacement light fixture he'd broken? And how did you get his boots?"

Mapes turned, his eyes without expression. "Saw him on the road. Gave him a ride. Ain't no law against it." *And you can't prove otherwise,* his empty look added mockingly.

"Don't know about boots," he finished. "I'm a junk man."

But his treasures said he was more. The plain wooden table in the corner, for instance, had never been refinished; on closer inspection, it showed the rare mottling of old bird's-eye maple.

He saw me looking at it. "Folks want to get rid of stuff, they're gettin' new. Take it off their hands, couple of bucks."

Right, and because Mapes was just a junk man, no one thought about the stuff maybe being worth larger sums, the way they might if a city boy like Raines came around trying to buy it from them.

"You're a front man, aren't you?" I asked sharply. "A rep for the antique buyers. To the local people around here, you're the guy."

It was a good arrangement, profitable for Mapes and for his buyer in the city. And it could be how Mapes and Raines had come into contact in the first place. But I couldn't help thinking about the people whose houses that good stuff in Mapes's trailer had come out of: houses that needed reroofing, new furnaces, and insulation. People, mostly elderly, could badly use the cash the old stuff would bring at the Sotheby's auction.

Mapes just shrugged. "Wouldn't know about that. Anyway, if I was, it wouldn't do me no good to get rid of Raines. Ain't that what you're sniffin' around about? Think you saw them boot's o' his'n an' I had somethin' to do with what happened to 'im?

"Anyway," he went on, turning away, "you done? Morning's wastin', I got things to work at, man's got to make a living."

"Yeah, we're done, Wilbur," Bob said. "You hear anything in your travels, might shed some light on a certain subject, I want to know that I am going to hear from you."

"Ayuh," Mapes replied dully and unconvincingly. "Get on with you, now, I got to let the dog out."

We went, backing down the rutted drive past the big sign in red letters, whose message despite all Wilbur's guns I now found somewhat less convincing: NOTHING HERE IS WORTH YOUR LIFE.

Maybe so, but back in the city many of my wealthier clients had been collectors of old things, and while none would exactly have given their lives for that pewter tankard, I knew some who would have used the idea as a starting point in the bargaining process.

I gripped the wheel while the washboard road beat hell out of the car's suspension. "Bob, those boots were there. And Mapes is not precisely the most upright local citizen. For Pete's sake, he goes around tricking people into selling him valuable things, probably not giving them anywhere near what they must be—"

"Wrong." He said it mildly but definitely.

"What?" I glanced at him, then jerked my eyes back to the road as something white flashed across it: the flaglike tail of a twelve-point buck, bounding over the roadway and into the brush on the other side. "Did you see that deer?"

"Uh-huh. Big old fella, wasn't he? Blackflies start drivin' 'em out toward the roads this time o' year."

He watched it until it blended into the undergrowth. "Wilbur pays value. Him and his sister, only ones do, in my opinion."

We reached the paved road. "Used to be a dope grower," Bob went on. "Out on all that good land, the back of beyond."

Those fields behind his house, I realized as Bob added:

"I broke him of that. Stove in his boat bottom three or four times before he got the idea maybe someone was trying to save him a whole lot worse trouble. Him and his pals.

"Pals?"

"Ayuh. Hecky Wilmot and a guy named Howard Washburn, lives even farther out in the sticks than Wilbur."

My eyebrows went up. "Hecky a dope smuggler? But he's . . ."

Way too old, I was going to say, forgetting that the youth culture had not yet arrived in downeast Maine; in Eastport no man is too old for much of anything until he is permanently horizontal.

"Oh, ayuh," Bob said. "Hecky was a hell-raiser till he got the literary bug. Still got a streak of it, you ask me. Eye for the main chance, what's good for Hecky, and hell with the rest."

We passed the grange hall, got to Route 1. "But Wilbur's been pretty straight with me since that one little interlude we had," Bob went on. "Maybe I'm too soft, but I don't like to think he's involved with any really bad business."

In front of the police station he turned to me. "I believe you about those boots, you know. But he could've found 'em on the beach."

"Then why is he lying about them? Because he is, Bob, and that means he's involved somehow."

A carful of kids went by, the driver snapping a lighter. Bob didn't let his eyes follow them, but he noticed.

"I said that I didn't like to think it, not that he couldn't be. But I'll tell you one thing, those boots aren't on his place now. Mapes has some bad qualities, but bein' a damn fool was never among 'em, that I've noticed."

In other words, even if Bob got officially involved—beyond, I mean, looking for the body of an accidental drowning victim or possibly a suicide—at this point it wouldn't do any good.

"Those boots," he said, "are long gone."

"Yeah. Okay. Thanks for riding with me."

"Thanks for the doughnuts." He got out, straightened his shoulders against the effects of a sleepless night, and strode toward the little storefront building that was Eastport's police department headquarters. Then I remembered.

"Hey, Bob. The other one you said pays right for people's things, Mapes's sister?" The idea of his having sprung from a human family at all seemed unlikely, but I guessed he must have.

Bob turned, a pen and a notebook already in his hand: noting the plate number of the car with the lighter-flicking kid in it.

"Oh, yeah. Lives up on Hart Road? Big old California-lookin' house, used to be a lot of old back-to-the-land hippies there?"

The other shoe dropped. "Clamshell Cove." I knew the place.

"Mapes's sister," Bob said, tucking away his notebook, "she only dabbles in antiques, though. Mainly, she builds musical instruments. From around Boston, originally. Name's . . . Tarnation. What the heck is it, again?"

I knew that, too, drat the luck. Charmian had mentioned it.

That wasn't why I recalled it so clearly, though. It'd been on my mind in another context entirely.

But I let Bob have the satisfaction of snapping his fingers, anyway. "Got it," he said. "Lillian Frey."

"Funny how his clothes keep showing up, but not him," said Wade Sorenson. He was disassembling a Remington shotgun in his workshop in the upstairs ell. It was the only modern place in the house and I came here sometimes when I needed to see what a shipshape building looked like: square corners, level floors.

"Yeah." I sat on a milk crate by the steps leading up to the storage area. Wade had installed overhead lighting, benches for the big tools that did the metal-grinding and stock-cutting procedures, and the new Lyman shotgun-shell reloading press.

"But the thing is this," I said. "Bob Arnold hasn't got a clue how cutthroat the antiques business can be. And he's got a soft spot, for some reason, for that pack rat Wilbur Mapes."

"Who you think is involved?" Wade wound bubble-wrap around the shotgun parts, in preparation for shipping the weapon back to its owner.

"Well, how could he not be?" I asked impatiently. "Bob would think so, too, if he knew how much money might be at stake. That is, he does know. But that kind of money just isn't real to him. He feels fat and happy on thirty-four grand a year, plus the money Clarissa earns."

Bob's wife is a defense attorney. But around here, that job's no ticket to the higher tax brackets, either, since for big-time white-collar criminal cases that produce big attorney's fees, first of all you need some white collars.

Wade sealed the box up, slapped the label on it. "He's no slouch in the character assessment department, you know. Tends to pick out bad apples."

"I know. Another reason I'm so confused."

"Well. You could just let it all go by." His tone, and the amused crinkles around his eyes, expressed just how likely he thought that was.

He put the box in the bin with the others he'd readied for FedEx. "What strikes me, though, is what people from away know that you don't."

He pulled up another milk crate, sat beside me. Being up in the workshop with Wade always made me feel I'd been invited into his tree house.

"Because, look: Mapes and Raines already had something going. And obviously Charmian Cartwright knew about it, too. Enough, I mean, to know where he lives, and that she should talk to him."

"Uh-huh." Outside the high windows the clouds faded abruptly from rose-red to lavender as the sun dropped below the horizon, and fog moved in.

"But she didn't tell you," he went on. "Which means she was in on what was going on all along, or—"

"Or whatever it was, maybe she wants in on it now."

Wade nodded. "Or maybe she just doesn't know who to trust. The problem is, you don't know how much of any of their stories is true. You don't *know* she's on the outs with the old uncle. For all you know, they could be in on it together, and Mapes could just be a fall guy. Maybe she stuck those boots out there herself."

Brr. That was a bad thought. And she was an awfully capable young woman. "Mapes saw them afterwards, got scared, got rid of them," I tried it out aloud.

Wade stood up. "It could happen. The other thing, though, is still the whole idea that Raines was murdered at all."

I'd told Wade my theory of how it could be done: someone under the dock, waiting. Cast up a big hook, pull Raines off, cut the line.

"Well, maybe that's not so far-fetched, either." He was pulling his jacket on. "And I can see that it's eating at you. So why don't we just get it settled? What say we go down there and have ourselves a look?"

I smacked a hand to the side of my head. "Why didn't I—"

"Think of that?" he finished for me, giving me a hand up. "Because climbing out under that dock is slippery and scary, not to mention legitimately dangerous. Your mind didn't want to raise the possibility because then you would have to do it. Right?"

"Um, right." I followed him down the stairs. That's the thing about Wade: when *his* mind raises the possibility of doing something legitimately dangerous, his body is generally already full speed ahead.

Twenty minutes later, we both were. "It's not going to prove anything on the positive side, mind you," he said, pulling the rope on the little outboard. "But it could rule out something."

It was dead calm and about an hour away from high tide, just about as it had been when Jonathan Raines went off the dock; the rowboat putted smoothly out of the boat basin, around the stern of the tugboat tied at the fish pier.

Wade tossed a line, snugged it, and cut the engine. We were floating alongside the treelike pilings of the dock, dark and dripping with watery vegetation.

"Seaweed's been there a long time," he said, pointing to the long, leathery-looking fronds of it. "Anyone climbing in there, they'll have knocked down chunks of it with their boots, maybe marred the soft wood with a rope. And they'd have to be up high, 'cause the tide's the same as it was then."

He grinned at me in the darkness. He was wearing leather boots and work gloves, carrying a coil of line. "Sit tight."

"Wade . . ."

Maybe we should rethink this, I added mentally. But he was gone, swinging over the side into the dark looming structure of pilings and timbers. And then silence except for the creaking of the dock under the pressure of millions of gallons of cold salt water.

The neon lights of La Sardina on Water Street gleamed through the thick grey fog a hundred yards away; it could have been miles. A bat whuffed by, brushing my cheek, and a fish jumped with a watery smack.

"Wade?" No answer. A foghorn sounded distantly, and the ocean smell was briny, so sharp it was almost acidic.

The dock lamps didn't reach out here, and at first it was so dark, it was like sitting in a puddle of ink. But as my eyes adjusted I began to see into the forest of dock pilings. No Wade.

A splash, and a muffled oath. *"Wade?"* Damn, I was going to be made a widow before I'd even managed to get remarried.

I grabbed a float cushion, untied the boat, and was

just about to give that motor cord a pull when a white face appeared out of the dripping gloom.

Wade. "Hey. Where you going?"

"Oh, criminy." I tossed him the line. "I was getting ready to come in under there and rescue you."

He chuckled. "Why, thank you, ma'am. That's right neighborly of you." He stepped from a dock timber to the boat's rail, from there into the boat, so deftly that the boat barely bobbled.

"The annoying thing is, you make that look so easy," I said, starting the outboard. I aimed us back out around the end of the dock.

"You wouldn't have thought so, you'd seen me a minute ago."

"Why, what happened?"

He motioned me amidships, sat in the stern, angled the boat back in toward the pilings and then between them, idling down.

"Look up there." He aimed his flashlight up so the beam lit the green-shrouded works of the old dock structure. "See it?"

Suddenly we were surrounded on all sides by the massive old pilings, hemmed in by the support works of the timbers and rising steadily upward with the movement of the tide.

"Wade? I think . . ."

We should get out of there, was what I thought. Another few minutes of rising tide and there wouldn't be enough clearance to sit upright.

"Just look," Wade said calmly. So I did, and there it was: a plywood platform.

"Like a hunting blind," he said quietly. "Nobody scrambled out here. I was wrong about that, it's too slippery."

It was raining steadily under here, the water from last high tide not all drained before it rose again. A dollop of wet seaweed touched my neck. Wade, busy doing something I couldn't see, ignored the little shriek I made.

Another splash. At that moment, I wanted dry land more than anything in the world. "What was that?"

He turned to me, his face ghostly in the reflected light of the flash. Its glow, bouncing up from the moving water, cast wavery reflections on the enormous, creaking wooden structure all around us and made the seaweed seem to slither unnaturally.

"Casting rod. Lying up there, somebody left it. I dropped it when I tried to snag it. And the platform was already loose, part came down earlier. The rest of it just now."

He peered into the forest of dock pilings. "Damn. Nice rod, too. A little too nice, actually. . . . You hear something else?"

"N-no. But I really think that . . ."

He swung the rowboat around, powered the engine up a little, and aimed us—how he knew this, I have no idea—out from under the dock. "There." He pointed.

A shape in the water, like a small, shiny rock, moving fast. A splash and a riffle of waves on the surface; then it was gone.

"Harbor seal?" I asked. Wade was motoring after it.

He shook his head. "Nope. Diver. God *bless* it."

Which is Wade's way of uttering a profanity. He swung the boat back toward the boat basin, didn't say any more until the boat was tied and we were making our way up the floating finger pier. "Well, so much for that."

"I'm not sure I get it. What would a diver be doing . . . Oh."

He slung the float cushions along with the rest of his gear into the bed of his pickup. "I guess somebody else saw the tide was right, just the way we did. Decided to come and collect a few things he'd left lying around. A platform, maybe. Tear it off the dock. And maybe a nice casting rod."

He started the truck. "I'll tell you, Jacobia, this idea of yours sounded like moonbeams to me. I mean, that somebody hooked Raines, pulled him off that dock."

"You mean you brought me down here to show me it *couldn't* have happened that way?"

Indignation struck me. I was cold, wet, and embarrassed at how scared I'd been minutes earlier; you wouldn't think a little seaweed and pitch-darkness could be so unnerving. But it was.

"Yup," he said. "Hey, there's no sense chasing a notion that couldn't physically be done."

Well, he had a point. "But now," he went on, "I'm not sure."

"Couldn't we have just followed that diver?" Mapes, I now recalled, was an urchin diver in season, and I'd seen his diving equipment out at his place.

He shook his head. "Can't spot him, not in this fog. Especially in the dark. He could go anywhere, and if he spots us, he's just not going to surface. Now he's probably got that casting rod I dropped, too, and by tomorrow that plywood'll be floating halfway to Lubec. I gave it a smack, tried to grab it up, all I managed to do was knock it away, then the rod fell off. I'm sorry, Jacobia."

He pulled into my driveway, mad at himself.

"Don't be," I said. "We're no worse off than we were, and at least now we know that what I suspected really could've happened. In fact, I think that now we can be pretty sure it did. Because there wouldn't have been a diver at all unless somebody wanted to get that stuff out of there. Would there?"

"Huh. I guess not. So now you can tell Bob Arnold that—"

"That we saw a harbor seal," I finished firmly. It

didn't have to be Mapes in the water. With the amount of diving gear on our little island in Maine, you could equip the Navy SEALs.

"Let's just keep this all to ourselves awhile, shall we? Because maybe the diver doesn't know we saw him. And anything we know that someone else doesn't could be in our favor."

Wade eyed me wryly. "If I'd known you were so devious, I'd have been afraid to get involved with you."

"Too late." I slid nearer to him. "It was awfully nice of you, going down there with me."

"Yeah? How nice?" he asked mock-innocently.

Suddenly I wasn't so sure at all about getting married. It would be a shame, I thought, to cast a pall of official sanction on our illicitness.

But I didn't get to go any further with the thought, or for that matter with anything else, because just then Jill Frey's car pulled into the driveway at an angle that put us out of her line of sight, so she didn't notice us. And in the truck's rearview mirror I could see that she and Sam had beaten us to it in the romance department. Two seconds after she turned the engine off, they looked like a couple of starfish that had gotten tangled in each other's arms. Or legs.

Or whatever. "Dammit. Now we've either got to get out and catch them necking or sit and pretend we're not here."

"No, we don't." Cheerfully, Wade leaned on the horn.

The doors on Jill's car popped open as if those two starfish had exploded inside there, and Sam and Jill hopped out looking startled.

Well, Sam looked startled, anyway. Jill looked furious. She slammed back into the car and roared out in reverse without another look at him.

"Jill," Sam called helplessly after her, but nothing doing. Wade got out and strode toward him, hands spread apologetically.

"Oh, man, I am so sorry," he said. "There was a spider on the dashboard, it was scaring your mother, and I gave a big swat at it and . . . man. Really, I am very sorry."

I got out, too, amazed at what I was hearing. To get Wade to lie, you practically have to torture him with electric wires.

"Hey, that's okay," Sam said, not very much to my surprise. It was what you would say if you were trying to be nice about it. And Sam was a nice guy, most of the time.

But then I got a look at his face, and what I saw there really did surprise me. Because it was. Okay with him, I mean.

Sam looked flustered: his hair messed and his lips puffy, as if he'd been kissing someone for a long, long time. But now that his surprise had evaporated, mostly he looked as if he'd just had a very narrow escape.

And . . . he looked relieved about it.

Wade and Sam went to bed while I took Monday outside, then sat alone in the darkened kitchen as she padded upstairs. Fog crept just outside the tall, bare windows, seeming to touch the old glass panes with insubstantial fingers.

It should have made me nervous, I guess, but it didn't. Not anymore; the feeling in the house was peaceful, as if it were getting what it had wanted for so long and didn't have to agitate for whatever it was any longer.

Or maybe it had only been my imagination all the while: the sense, so strong it was nearly a physical sensation, that someone or something in the house wanted—needed—something very badly. But now . . . nothing.

Later, upstairs with Wade in the dark: "Wade. Do you . . . do you believe in ghosts?"

A silence. He knew why I was asking. But he will do this: leave me alone to sort a thing out or get over it, not pestering me about it. It was why he wasn't mentioning the getting-married idea, either; not pushing it.

"Well. I'll tell you a story." He settled his arm around me, leaned his head down against my own. "After the old man got laid off from the paper mill and he'd started drinking heavy, Mom made him move out into the shed."

At the foot of the bed, Monday sighed and settled herself contentedly. "And some nights, if he didn't come home at all, I'd go out there, sleep in his bed."

I said nothing.

"So this one night I'm out there and I hear him come in. He didn't know I was there and I was scared I might give him a heart attack, startling him in the dark. But for once, I knew just what to say to him."

At night, in the dark, the house seems to breathe in and out very slowly, as if animated by the myriad lives that have been lived in it, all the sleeping and waking. "What did you say?"

"I said, 'Dad. It's me. Don't be afraid.' "

"And he said? Was he drunk?"

Another silence. Then:

"I don't think so. And he said, 'I love you, Junior.' Nobody ever called me that, see. Even he didn't, unless he really wanted me to listen up. I still don't know why I didn't get up, give him his bed. But somehow I figured he didn't want it, so I didn't. I just went back to sleep."

"That's nice." I wondered what the point of this was.

"Next morning, there was a cop car outside our house."

Oh.

"Dad," Wade said, "had been killed the night before. Beat up out in front of that bar in Derry."

A longer silence.

"Course, I guess I could have dreamed the whole thing, and him dying just that night could've been a co-incidence. It's not like I've got proof of anything."

Right. Me neither.

"So you ask me if I believe in ghosts, and I don't know what to say," Wade went on quietly.

He will do this, too: tell you a story suddenly, like a boy shyly offering you some small found treasure, a robin's egg or a bit of beach glass, after a long time during which you had begun thinking he might never tell you anything more of himself at all.

"I guess sometimes we make too much of old stories," Wade finished. "Or of feelings. But sometimes . . ."

His shoulders moved in the dark.

Yeah. Sometimes we don't.

Much later, in the small hours of the morning, I heard rain begin gurgling in the gutters, muttering in the downspouts. From the window I saw it slanting thickly through the cones of yellow light under the streetlamps, the pale spray gleaming.

I decided to pay a visit to Lillian Frey.

She lived on an old apple farm on the mainland, over-looking Clamshell Cove. The place had been a haven for swarms of young, mostly well-educated but disaffected back-to-the-land enthusiasts of the 1970s, when kids with physics degrees and fancy Manhattan upbringings decided to grow vegetables, haul water, and keep pigs on places that even native Mainers had abandoned as too stony and harsh to provide decent livings.

Some of those kids were so determined to give their wealthy parents the middle finger, they actually succeeded in becoming real farmers. But Lillian hadn't been one of them. She'd bought the place from a communal religious group that abandoned it to move to Belgium to await the millennium, and at just about the moment when the apocalypse disappointed them by not arriving, Lillian had been razing the old farmhouse which by then had nearly crumbled to sawdust.

In its place, she had built a trilevel cedar structure with windows and decks overlooking the water, planter tubs full of evergreens on the railings, perennial beds all around it. As Bob Arnold said, it looked more like California than Maine.

The rain, so promising the night before, had ended quickly and the fields around the house looked as dry and flammable as ever. A small sign said simply, FREY VIOLINS.

As I climbed the cedar stairs to the entrance level, I heard a band saw whining. Another sign by the door told me to RING BELL so I did, and the saw's whine cut off a moment later.

"Hi." Lillian was wearing jeans, a purple, paint-stained T-shirt, and canvas sneakers. Her blond hair was tied with a scrunchy, a few wisps escaping down over her face. Viewed close up, the long scar on the side of her cheek made me wince inwardly.

But not, I hoped, visibly. "I guess you must've come about Jill," she said before I could explain the real reason for my visit. I'd made a few stops in town before coming out here, and Teddy Armstrong down at La Sardina had confirmed what he'd told Bob: that Jonathan Raines had been in the place just before he went off the dock.

And as if Bob's comments hadn't been impetus enough for me, Teddy had also said—in answer to my direct question, or he'd never have mentioned it—that Lillian had been in there, too.

"I want to apologize for whatever behavior she's been up to," Lillian said as she led me into the bright, spare kitchen. It was furnished with the bare minimum of appliances, no clutter on the granite-topped counters, no dishes in the brushed-aluminum sink. A wall of windows looked out onto a field of gnarled apple trees and from there to a vast expanse of blue water.

Lillian put a blue-glazed teakettle on the gas stove and lit a match. A Siamese cat stalked in, stared imperiously at me for an instant, and stalked out again. Lillian's hand trembled the faintest bit, lighting the gas burner.

"I'm sure if I were Sam's mother I wouldn't appreciate Jill's ways," she went on. "I don't appreciate them myself. But she's angry. I just won a custody battle with her father, much against her wishes. I'm hoping she's going to settle down."

Her voice was taut; despite her effort at hospitality, I sensed the strain she was under. It couldn't be easy, having a daughter who fought with you right in the middle of the street with everyone watching. The scene of a few mornings earlier when Jill had confronted her at the crafts fair—with, to make things worse, a photographer around, for heaven's sake—was still fresh in my mind, as I was sure it was in Lillian's.

Also, there was a pile of what looked like bills in the cubby of a desk by the window, and it struck me that keeping this place running probably piled up a sizable nut each month. I wondered how she managed.

Meanwhile, though, I thought I'd better hear the rest of what she had to say. You never knew; Jill might end up being—perish the thought—my daughter-in-law.

"Custody battle," I repeated, puzzled. "Isn't Jill a little old for that?"

Lillian eyed me knowingly. "She's sixteen. She just thinks she's ten years older. And smarter than everyone else, of course. Thinks she knows it all."

She'd had me fooled, all right. In fact, I was stunned. "So she doesn't want to be here?"

Lillian shook her head. "To put it mildly."

Close up, she was even more fit and tanned than she looked from a distance, with cheekbones that were to die for. Even with the deep scar running angrily from the end of her eyebrow to her jawline, you could see how Jill got the good looks she traded so shamelessly on.

The scar itself, though was deep and seriously disfiguring. Once you got talking to her, you kind of forgot about it.

But if I'd been her, I'd have been shy of having my picture taken, too. She put mugs on the table and filled a teapot from the kettle. The spicy fragrance of Constant Comment tea floated into the air.

"She was living in Boston with her dad, not going to school. Not doing anything but hanging out. That's his lifestyle, you see."

She pronounced the word with an ironic twist. The tea was strong and delicious. "You didn't approve," I said. "That's why the custody fight."

It hadn't even occurred to me until now that Jill was young enough to be fought over that way. Her self-possessed manner was indeed that of a twenty-year-old, going on forty-something. "Even so," I went on, "she's got a car. Why doesn't she just leave?"

Lillian sighed. "Jill's dad is a loser." She glanced up at me. "And not just because he's my ex. I was nuts about him, and I would have stayed that way. But it's hard to stay romantic about a guy who keeps going back to jail for the same dumb stunts over and over. Fraud, mostly. Arts-type fraud. And theft."

She got up. "He's completely irresponsible and unpredictable and she can't stay with him if he won't have her. Which," she added, "he won't, now that he knows what it's like. It cramps his style. He never really wanted custody, just a fight with me. And Jill has no money, no other friends to go to."

"So she's stuck."

Lillian nodded tiredly. "She stayed with my brother for a while, but that didn't work out, either."

I felt again that she was putting up a good front, but the circles under her eyes, her stiff posture, and the harsh control in her voice all said she was a woman on the ragged edge.

She rubbed her neck, trying to get the tension out of it, then rallied with an effort. "Want to see my workshop? I've got some wood cooking up there, I want to check on it."

What I wanted was to go, quickly; despite the sweet scent of the tea, the air here was thick with anxiety and anger. But I wasn't finished with her.

"Sure." Carrying my mug, I followed her out a sliding door onto the deck, where the breeze whipped my hair wildly, then up a flight of open stairs to another doorway.

"Wow," I said when I got inside. The studio was a single open room, high-ceilinged and, like the rest of the place, almost fully walled with triple-glazed, enormous windows. It was like being in a fire tower, high above the treetops and the cove.

But in this tower, every bit of space was cunningly designed for a woodworker who despised clutter. There was a drill press, a planer, the band saw I'd heard running, and the nail gun I'd seen her using on Water Street at the crafts fair.

"Lots of tools." There was a device for heating, softening, and bending sheets of wood into shape for the violins' sides, molds and templates for the tops and sound holes. Racks of chisels, awls, knives, and wood shavers, plus dozens of other tools whose names and uses I had no idea of, were neatly arranged.

What there wasn't was any mess whatsoever. Sawdust had been swept into a single pile so tiny and neat, you got the feeling it didn't dare go anywhere. And I noticed no computers or other automated stuff; nothing to draw or cut shapes out of the wood except knives and pencils. Everything here was done the old way, by hand and by heart.

Lillian peered into a saucepan steaming on a small hot plate. In it were several thin sticks. "I'm boiling them so I can shape them," she explained. "But they're not done yet."

"Look," I said, refreshed by the sense of tradition up here, and by the change in atmosphere, "I didn't come to talk about Jill. I'm not crazy about her and Sam's relationship, but . . ."

Now that I knew how young she really was, the idea of her victimizing my baby . . . Well. The whole thing didn't seem so one-sided anymore.

Lillian looked curiously at me. "Really? I thought you'd come out here to demand I put my daughter in leg irons. Sam's always seemed so . . . I don't know. Just so clean-cut."

"Lillian, he's a big boy now." *And he's his father's son*, I added silently. Which could turn out to be as troublesome as Jill being her father's daughter. But that wasn't Lillian's problem.

Meanwhile, once I'd gotten used to the fresh smell of raw wood, I smelled something else: gun oil. It was so incongruous in these surroundings, I thought at first I was mistaken.

But nothing else smells quite like it, sweet and clean and a little oily. Then I spotted the familiar orange-and-red-striped box: Winchester.

It was tucked on a high shelf, above the chisels and router blades. I was so surprised, I reached up and grasped the rolled rag lying next to the box and brought it down before I realized how rude I was being.

When I turned, Lillian was watching me bemusedly. "Go ahead," she said with a wry smile.

"Sorry." I unwrapped the rag. "I just . . . it wasn't what I was expecting to find here, that's all."

The object in the rag wasn't what I was expecting, either. But I'd been around Wade and his antique gun catalogs enough to recognize the thing: a 1905 Colt .45 automatic with blued steel and a checkered walnut grip, in what looked like mint condition.

"It came with some other stuff from an estate sale," she said. "Go ahead, check it out."

Well, you can't live in a house with a gun professional and not learn a few things, including gun safety. Releasing the empty magazine, I removed it and pointed the muzzle safely, then pulled the slide back to check: no cartridge in the chamber. Markings stamped into the side of the slide read: *Automatic Colt/Calibre 45 rimless smokeless.*

Meaning the ammunition in the Winchester box. I released the slide again, let the hammer down slowly, and snapped the magazine back into the weapon. "Jesus, Lillian, this thing's a cannon."

And not locked up, either, I noticed.

She shrugged. "If I'd gone to buy one on purpose I'd have got something smaller, I suppose. But it's not that bad to fire."

Yeah, if you were used to getting kicked by a mule. I guessed the ear-protection headpiece on a hook by the band saw was used for more than woodworking. I wrapped the weapon again, put it back up on the shelf. Like so much else I'd been running into in the past few days, it was none of my business.

"Jill doesn't know it's here," Lillian added, reading my thoughts.

In my experience, kids know everything. For one thing, they start out so helpless, they pretty much have to be supernaturally perceptive about what their parents are up to, just to feel like they can survive.

Or Sam had been that way, anyway. "If you say so," I told Lillian. "You ever want a lockbox for it, Wade will sell you one at cost."

Hell, he'd give her one if she asked, and so would I. But she didn't. There was the tiniest awkward moment as she sensed my unease. I was thinking about the other thing that could make a fellow fall off the end of a dock: a gunshot wound.

But someone would have heard it. A sound from downstairs made Lillian flinch, but it was only a cat, its cross-eyed face appearing a moment later at the top of the stairway.

"Christ," Lillian said, letting a breath out. "I'm so wired up, I jump at shadows. I still keep expecting he's going to show up and grab her, maybe clobber me to get at her. Jill's dad, I mean."

Jumping at shadows is not a trait I like seeing in a person who has a weapon. But I said nothing.

She gazed out the big window. "Or maybe he would smack me around a little just because he feels like it. To show me who's boss, you know? It wouldn't," she added, "be the first time."

She put her hand to her face. "He gave me this. Box-cutter. He was drunk." A bitter laugh; I thought she was going to say more. But then she straightened abruptly.

"Let's get out of the poor-little-me groove," she pronounced as if instructing herself, and from her wry look

I could see she was not only talented; she was tough and smart, too. Maybe she was on the ragged edge right this minute, but the decision to survive was one she made every day.

Thinking this, I told Lillian about the violin I believed Raines had been looking for, and that I wondered if he'd mentioned anything about it in La Sardina.

I didn't tell her I thought he'd been murdered, or about the blind set up underneath the dock. Or about the diver Wade and I had spotted in the water, an omission I was glad of, later.

Also, I didn't tell her that I was concerned about her, or that I understood how difficult Jill was and sympathized. I had my plate full already, I thought, so I didn't ask her if she needed anything, or wanted to come by for coffee some afternoon when she was in town.

All omissions about which, later, I wasn't so glad. But as I say, that was later.

"Yes, I was at the bar, and I saw him," she agreed, meaning Raines. "But he didn't say anything about any musical instrument that I heard. Hecky Wilmot had him backed into a corner, cross-examining him about something. I wasn't really listening."

She began pressing the softened wood pieces onto a molding base, securing them to the curved shape by wrapping them with thick twine. "And as for some hidden violin, all I've got to say is, good luck."

She finished what she was doing, turned. "Look around you. I didn't put those triple glazings in for the fun of it, you know. They're all necessary, and so's the insulation you don't see, and the humidity control."

On closer inspection, I did see: three hygrometers spaced at intervals throughout the big room. Baseboard hot-water heat that must have cost a mint to put in.

Humidifiers, and a wall panel of dials and switches to control it all.

But it was still pretty low-tech as such things went. No computer-aided-design gadgetry or automated cutting jigs to make things come out exactly the same every single time. There was a handwritten checklist by the switch panel; the humidifiers were the kind you can buy at Wadsworth's Hardware. Like me, she was no devotee of twenty-first-century electronic stuff.

While I was wondering again how she'd paid for what she did have, I got the point. "It wouldn't survive. A fine old wooden instrument. . . ."

Lillian shook her head emphatically. Behind her in a corner were stacked thin sheets of wood on spacers, thicker lengths for, I supposed, violin necks.

"You could wrap it and seal it, but with so many temperature changes . . . And they didn't have the technology then to really pack things right. It could dry out and split, or get wet and rot. And the finer the instrument, the less has to happen before the tone is ruined. Because it's not just the glue joints, it's . . ." She waved a lean, muscular hand, trying to explain. "It's in the molecules of the wood and a million tiny decisions that the instrument builder made, the thing that makes the sound so . . ."

That was what Raines had been saying. "Anyway," she finished, "that's one reason I don't hold with high-tech ways of doing things, when I can help it. For me, they're a waste of time and money, mostly, and besides, they just don't interest me."

"So the bottom line is, if you're looking for an old violin, you might find something but it might not be the instrument that was hidden two hundred years ago."

She nodded. "Almost guaranteed not to be. Miracles

happen, I guess." But she didn't sound as if she expected one in this case.

Downstairs, I took a last look around Lillian Frey's nearly surgically clean household. The windows all shone as if they had been polished that morning, and the floors gleamed. Combined with the orderliness of her work area, it gave me an insight, one that caused me in spite of myself to sympathize with Jill.

Lillian, perhaps on account of the craziness of life with Jill's father—and partly because of the picky, detail-oriented care required to build musical instruments the old-fashioned way—was a control freak. That was another reason she didn't give over any instrument-building tasks, even the repetitive ones, to computers; she wanted to keep that control for herself.

She confirmed my opinion by rinsing the mugs and teaspoons and drying them—no dishwasher, either, I noticed—then putting them carefully away before walking me to the door.

And then I saw something else, on a hook behind the door so I couldn't have seen it on my way in: a small leather handbag. It was the one Charmian had been carrying when she first walked in my own back door. Lillian saw me spotting it.

"Oh, good," she said, "you can take it back to town. Do you mind? I called this morning to let her know it's here, but there was no answer."

After I'd gone out, probably. "Or I can give it to Charmian when I see her," Lillian said. "Whichever."

"I don't mind taking it if you'll tell me how it got here. I didn't know that you and Charmian were acquainted."

She met my gaze levelly. "We weren't until the other day. I was working at the crafts fair the morning after she arrived in town and she walked up to my booth. We got talking, and yesterday I brought her back here for tea. Was that not all right?"

She moved toward the door; I followed. "Perfectly all right. She's my guest, not my ward. Did she ask you any questions about Raines? Whether you'd met him, anything of that nature?"

"Oh, yes." Lillian smiled easily at this. "She was quite the little detective. Told me about his 'quest,' her uncle, how sure she is that Raines was murdered, and how she intends to find who killed him—*and* locate the instrument he was supposedly after."

We were outside now. "And you said?"

She spread her hands. "What could I say? I told her I was sorry to hear of her loss, wished her luck, and warned her."

My ears pricked up. "Warned her? About what?"

Or *who*. But Lillian only looked impatient. "The same as I've warned you—that no violin, priceless or otherwise, sitting all unprotected through nearly two hundred Maine winters, is going to be worth much. *If* it's there to find at all."

"Oh." That made sense. "You said you'd be seeing her again, though?"

I'd overstayed my welcome. But it seemed that I was just striking pay dirt, so I lingered rudely.

"I'm meeting her for coffee in town tomorrow. She asked me, and she seems like a nice person, and I accepted. Okay?"

At which it struck me what an awful busybody I must seem to her. "Of course it's okay, Lillian. I'm sorry to be so—"

"That's all right," she said, taking a step away from me like a hostess signaling firmly that the party is over. "Thanks for taking the bag back to her." She turned to go in.

"One last thing," I said. "Is Wilbur really your brother?"

It still hardly seemed possible. His chaos was the polar opposite of her cleanliness and order. But the face she made as she turned back said it was true.

"Oh, Wilbur," she sighed, half laughing.

But half something else; relief, as if she'd thought I was about to ask some other question.

"He's my cross to bear," she said resignedly. "When I moved up here from Boston, he just kind of tagged along, and . . . Is he in some kind of trouble again?"

"No." If I hung around in her driveway much longer I would have to pitch a tent. But she kept dropping bits of information; deliberately or otherwise, I didn't know.

"I'd just heard that he was your brother and didn't know if I should believe it," I said. "You know how the stories get going, and pretty soon the whole town thinks you're related to the Pope or something."

Under the deck, a familiar object caught my eye: a diving regulator, and behind it a drysuit.

Something funny about it. "Jill's diving gear?" I asked with a wave at it.

Lillian's face closed. "No," she said shortly, "it's mine. I've been diving for years, Jill only took it up recently. I'm surprised she cares about it, seeing as it's something I enjoy."

She regained her friendly expression with difficulty. "But maybe it's Sam's good influence. Let me know, please, if she's causing you any real problems?"

Right, I thought, if they run off and get married, you'll be the first to hear. Thinking this, I took my leave at last, not letting my glance stray again to the diving gear under the deck in case she was watching from inside, noting my interest.

But driving away, I thought hard about it. There were plenty of divers in Eastport, so there were also plenty of drysuits; in the cold bay, it was impossible to dive without one. Still, I'd now run into three of the specialized garments, not even counting Sam's and Maggie Altvater's, in three days:

One under Lillian Frey's deck.

One out at Wilbur Mapes's place, behind his trailer.

And one on the diver Wade and I had seen in the water under the dock.

On my way home I stopped at the IGA, and I was in the cereal aisle trying to decide between oatmeal and granola when the most astonishing thing happened:

"You were right," said Victor, coming up behind me.

"Really?" Victor was about as likely to begin dictating his medical notes in pig Latin as he was to pronounce that particular phrase to me. "About what?"

"That girl," he said severely. "Jill Frey. She's pretty, of course. But I don't like her."

Which was the second astonishing thing. To get Victor to dislike a pretty girl, ordinarily you would have to do something really drastic, like maybe weld her knees together.

"She stole my watch."

"What?" I turned from contemplating the boxes of cereal.

"We were on the boat," he said. "There was a lot of spray. I took it off and put it in the aft storage cubby. When we got in and the kids"—Sam and Jill, he meant—"had gone ashore, I remembered and went back for it. And it was gone."

"You're sure?" I asked Victor. "And have you mentioned this to Sam?" I began unloading my cart at the register.

"I'm sure. And yes, I've spoken to him. And he's made as hell about it—at me," Victor replied.

"I'll admit she's charming," he went on. "I can see

why Sam's taken with her." He drew himself up into the noble posture he always assumed when he was about to make a pronouncement. "But you know, Jacobia, even charming people can be villains."

Sometimes I wonder what Victor sees when he looks in the mirror. "I'll try to remember that," I said, and he eyed me to see if I was being sarcastic.

"Hmph," he said, as we left the store and started walking to my car. "You should take this seriously, Jacobia. I mean, Sam's involved with some little sneak thief, here."

"Oh, I do. Really, I do," I assured him.

I'd told Victor I thought Jill might be a problem, and he'd paid about as much attention as he always did, promising to talk with Sam and then doing nothing about it. But now something had happened to *Victor*.

So *now* it was important. Starting the car and beginning to back slowly away from him, I noted that nowadays it took hardly any willpower at all to keep from flooring it and running right over him.

At the same time I couldn't help wondering why he'd made a point of the incident to me, seeing as it confirmed something I'd said; ordinarily, Victor's tendency is the opposite.

Something funny going on there, I mused. But I didn't think much more about it than that, because for one thing something funny going on where Victor's concerned is pretty much standard operating procedure.

And for another, on the way home from Clamshell Cove I'd had what I thought was a brilliant idea. So after I put the groceries away I sat down in the telephone alcove and called another one of those old friends of mine in New York: an authority.

Not a mob authority, like Jemmy Wechsler. And not

a federal authority, like that trio of cousins Jonathan Raines hadn't really been related to at all.

A higher authority.

"Yes," he said, when I told him what I wanted to know and when I wanted to know it.

"No," he said, when I asked if he expected to have trouble finding out.

"Yes," he said, when I promised to call back the next day to get his answer.

Then I grabbed the invisible-ink manuscript we'd found in the wall, filched a roll of quarters I'd been saving for the day when the washing machine finally beat itself to death, and went out intent on getting to the bottom of at least one mystery once and for all.

Uh-huh.

7 The next morning Ellie and I went to pick blueberries behind Hillside Cemetery. There the granite that forms our island pushes up through thin topsoil matted with lichens, their tiny blooms dark orange against the pale grey of the foliage and the blackish emerging rock.

"You gave her the handbag?" Ellie asked, meaning Charmian's.

The blueberry shrub grows thickly nearby, its leaves a dark, glossy green; the berries are the size of pencil erasers but with a shockingly intense flavor.

"Uh-huh. I have no idea what to make of the friendship. Hers and Lillian's, I mean. If it is one."

Ellie got plastic pails and her sun hat from the car, while I sprayed my shoes, pants cuffs, and shirtsleeves with mosquito repellent. "Maybe nothing," she said, not sounding convinced.

I put shots of bug dope into my socks. People didn't come here to pick berries much, not from any superstition about the cemetery but because of the biting red ants that surrounded the bushes and just about everything else on the island—like armed guards. I must have had half a dozen of the little sprayers scattered around my house.

"Where's Charmian now?" Ellie asked, combing her fingers through the blueberry foliage and coming up with a handful.

"Still at the library. Volunteering, she says, to keep busy while she's in town. She *says* she's really given up on trying to snoop into the circumstances of Jonathan's death, after her scare out at Mapes's place. But I'm not sure I believe her."

The library was full of old manuscripts—not just Hayes material but a variety of stuff from the 1800s, some very valuable and some not—which Charmian had offered to help sort.

"She says she's only staying to wait for Raines's body to be recovered. But I think all hope of that is probably long gone—Wade says the way the currents are running, the guy who went off the cliffs at North End probably isn't going to turn up, either—and I think *she* knows it, too."

I ate a few blueberries. "At least, Bob Arnold's told her so a million times. I think she's got some other reason for sticking around."

"To finish the job Jonathan started," Ellie said, dropping another handful into the pail.

Monday snuffled nearby, plunging her nose into the shrub and snurfing up berries like a piglet rooting for truffles. "To find what he was looking for," Ellie finished.

"Right," I said. "Maybe with her supposedly evil old uncle's help. He, by the way, is still around Eastport, too. Staying like a bad cold, Charmian says. And turning into the town celebrity."

"So I've heard." More berries went into the pail. "Hecky's nose is out of joint, George says, because Winston Cartwright is a better storyteller than Hecky, and he doesn't get mad when you contradict him like Hecky does. *And* people haven't already heard Cartwright's stories forty times, the way they have Hecky's."

She ate a berry. "But Hecky's book is coming out any minute, so he'll be the nine days' wonder again soon enough."

Cartwright had made a bed-and-breakfast on Washington Street his home base. Days he spent moseying around town; evenings he sat in La Sardina, at the bar with the other regulars. And like the public library, the bar at La Sardina was full of interesting information; Teddy didn't talk, but everyone else in there did. You just had to keep your mouth shut and your ears open at the right times.

Which, it turned out, Winston Cartwright was also good at. "What are they up to?" I groused. "Charmian and Winston, whether separately *or* together?" But of course I got no answer.

"Any more luck with the invisible ink book?" Ellie asked.

"Nope. I copied the whole thing on the copy machine over at town hall—with Charmian at the library, I didn't want to do it in there—and sent it to a friend of mine at St. Patrick's."

The cathedral, I meant, in New York. Priests may still take vows of poverty, but the organization they work for most certainly does not, as I had learned back in my old money-management days. And the priest I'd dealt with back then had been a dab hand at reading Latin manuscripts.

Also, he was fast. "He called me back this morning."

Ellie looked up. "How? You can't mail overnight from here," she objected.

"I know. I put it on Tim Prouty's fish truck."

Laden with ocean delicacies, the truck made three round trips a week between here and some of the finest restaurants in Manhattan; I'd added the rest of those chocolate-cherry cupcakes for Tim, plus a thermos of coffee and a couple of live lobsters for my buddy over at St. Patrick's. The quarters were for tolls.

"So why didn't you tell me about this before? And what does it say?" Ellie wanted to know.

I hadn't told her because the result was so discouraging. I brushed an ant off my shoe.

"Not much. Or anyway, not much to help us. It's a record of Hayes's commercial dealings in the pirate loot he was selling for Josephus Whitelaw, as it turns out. So much for silver tankards, so much for Spanish gold."

Down the hill from us, a few people moved among the granite headstones: tidying up the plots, placing flowers, or making small repairs to the graves and accessories: flags, Masonic insignia, war memorial markers. Every so often one of them stopped to slap madly at a sleeve or pants leg: those ants.

"The accounts pretty much substantiate the story Winston Cartwright told," I went on. "That Hayes was crooked. And man, was he ever salting it away, all in gold. I mean a fortune. Guess that's why he was so secretive about it, with the Latin *and* the invisible ink."

Ellie looked glum. "But why would he hide his own account book in the wall?"

"Beats me." We resumed combing the bushes, but I soon thought Monday had eaten enough blueberries, snorting and snuffling along like a canine vacuum cleaner; if I didn't stop her, she would go on until she fell over in a bloated heap.

"C'mere, you," I told her, and spread a beach towel for her to lie down on in the grassy shade. Snarfing up a final mouthful of berries, she obeyed reluctantly.

"Was that *all* the book said?" Ellie asked. Her berry pail was half full.

"No." I dropped another handful into mine. "It was pretty sad, actually. When he wasn't keeping his accounts in the book, he wrote about Jane Whitelaw. How much he loved her and how she wouldn't marry him. He thought getting rich would help persuade her, just the way Cartwright said."

"What about the map?" Ellie said hopefully.

"No luck there, either. For that, we would need to make the visible out of the invisible, and my friend at St. Patrick's only reads Latin. He doesn't do magic tricks. There just wasn't enough he said, for him to decipher anything useful from it."

"Oh." Ellie fell disappointedly silent, thinking this over. Monday dozed, waking only to snap at a honeybee buzzing too near her nose. Out on the water, a little red and black boat puttered up the bay toward New Brunswick.

We picked steadily for another half hour; they were big berry pails, and we wanted enough fruit for making jelly and for the freezer. Then:

"Something's not right about all of this," Ellie said. "If Mapes was working with Raines—or if someone else was—it would be to that person's benefit to have Raines alive to help in looking for the violin. Unless . . ."

Right. "Unless Raines had already found it, or was about to. Then Raines's partner might want to get rid of Raines and keep the thing for himself."

"Scamper off to Boston or New York and sell it. But *then* Charmian and Winston arrived, so he's got to wait until the uproar dies down?"

"Assuming," I said, "it's a he, and that he's got the violin at all. But if it's Mapes we're talking about, then he hasn't got it yet, or I doubt he'd still be around."

"So maybe Raines knew, but he didn't *know* that he knew."

I stood up, feeling my knees creak. The mosquito repellent was wearing off; a couple of scout ants were clambering up the cuffs of my pants. I brushed them away as Monday got to her feet and yawned. Our buckets were full to the brim.

"Okay, so *what* could Raines know? He didn't see what's in the invisible-ink book, the words *or* what might be a map if the lines were all there. Because the words *weren't* there, and lines of the map still *aren't* there, so . . ."

We looked at each other. "Or did he?" Ellie said. "Did he see something *we* haven't seen?"

I let out a big breath. "What if there was something else in it that he took with him? Something he *could* read? And then, in a hurry but hoping to hide the book again, he dropped it back into the wall. In his hurry, he also dropped that fiber-optic-looking instrument he—"

"He wouldn't be careless with that," Ellie objected. "He didn't need it anymore, that's all, so he left it. He knew what he needed to know. And maybe—Jake, could he have made a phone call?"

I opened the car trunk and set the buckets inside, let the dog into the backseat. "I don't know that he *didn't* call someone, and it *would* make sense. 'Wilbur, I found something. Meet me,' he might've said."

"On the dock, and Wilbur did. Put Raines off an hour to give himself time, maybe?"

"He'd have had to," I agreed. "It's a five-minute

walk from my house to the dock, but Mapes would have needed longer than that to get ready."

I turned to Ellie as we got into the car. "What gave him the idea to do it at all, do you suppose? Mapes doesn't strike me as a quick thinker."

She frowned. "Maybe because that other fellow went off the cliffs at North End that same morning?"

"Right. It would not only give Mapes the idea, it would make it seem like the kind of accident that could happen."

I started the car. "So he put Raines off with some excuse, drove to town, took a rowboat, slammed that platform up there, tied up under the dock, climbed up, waited for Raines to arrive. Because he understood something from what Raines told him. And *he* wanted to be the one to benefit from it. Him alone."

I'd already told her about my watery expedition with Wade. "And he had the dive gear, for urchin diving. It could have been him last night, back to retrieve the evidence of what happened."

She sighed. "But even that's no help, because the evidence *is* gone now. So not a bit of this can we prove," she finished. "It's all speculation."

Drat, why did she have to be so right all the time?

"So what do we do?" I asked as we passed the high school and the remnants of Fort Sullivan, where seventy American soldiers first got a look at the British ships, their guns bristling, as they hove into the bay one ghastly morning in 1816.

Being outnumbered a hundred to one and also no fools, they lay down their arms. The British took Eastport without a shot and held it until the end of the war, which end was itself delayed by the occupation. That gave Andrew Jackson time to win at the Battle of New Orleans, made him a national hero, and eventually made him president.

Funny how one thing leads to another, and how you can't tell that it will. Jackson was probably mighty unhappy when he heard about those Eastport soldiers putting down their weapons. Later, of course, he felt differently about it.

"We look at the manuscript again," Ellie said. "And keep talking to people."

"Why? People, I mean. If we think that whatever Raines knew, he found it out from the manuscript . . ."

I pulled the car into my driveway. Monday dashed for the porch, where a pile of diving gear lay outside the door. *Gone to Boston. Maybe your friend can use this stuff,* the note pinned to the door read.

It was from Maggie Altvater. "Oh, damn. That son of mine's got his brains in his . . . I *told* Victor he should talk to Sam, but you know Victor."

Inside, we washed and froze some berries quickly, put some more into containers for Ellie to take home and make jam, and ate the rest on ice cream; unlike the watery blue objects you can buy in the grocery store, wild blueberries have to be used quickly or they will turn into blue goo.

"You know, though," Ellie said thoughtfully, "*if* it was Wilbur Mapes that Raines was teamed up with . . . Well. Then even if Wilbur didn't want to share the violin's proceeds with Raines, he still could not have gotten rid of it all by himself."

"Huh. That's true. Wilbur's claim to fame is getting hold of stuff around here, not selling it in New York."

"So Wilbur might try to team up with some *other* partner, one who would take less of a commission."

I ate some ice cream. "True again. So keeping in mind that Wilbur's been in trouble, before . . ."

"With Hecky Wilmot," Ellie agreed. "But he's probably still too riled up to talk to us."

"Right. So who else's cage could we rattle in case something useful falls out?"

But she was already nodding. "That's easy. Howard Washburn," she said.

Howard Washburn's barn full of auction items stood on a side road, west off Route 1, up in the hilly land where the comforts of town quickly began seeming like a distant memory. Small wooden signs by the roadside, each a mile from the last, directed us to the AUCTION SUNDAY!

I peered at yet another of the signs; unfortunately, they gave no clue as to how many more of them we had to read and pass before arriving at Washburn's place.

"Howard buys from everyone," Ellie said from the passenger seat. "Stores stuff up, then in summer all the tourists go out to his auctions. But the rest of the time . . ."

"A nine-month break in his business activity?" I negotiated a tricky S-turn. When these roads were built, fifty miles an hour was regarded as suicidal; that they had pavement on them at all was the height of modern convenience.

"Yep." Ellie gazed out the car window. "Look, an eagle's nest."

I glanced at the mass of sticks at the top of a wooden power pole, branches as big around as a man's forearm poking out every which way. It looked more like a beaver dam than a bird's nest and imagining the size of the eggs made you believe the theory that our feathered friends had descended from dinosaurs.

"So he's got some other way to make money." In the backseat Monday rode happily, tongue lolling, delighted to be in the car. "Moving illegal items, maybe? I thought Bob Arnold put a stop to that."

Ellie nodded. "He did. It's gambling now."

I shot her a look of surprise. Around here the football pool at the convenience store was big-time: maybe a hundred bucks.

"Howard has lots of friends," Ellie explained, "from when he worked at the Portsmouth shipyard. And when he was in prison."

Bigger surprise. Jail's one thing, prison another. "For what?" Thick forest fell away suddenly on both sides of the road and was replaced by spreading marshland, cattails massing thick at the edges of the blue, pearlescent pools.

"Something to do with some men getting together to hire a hit man," Ellie replied.

Coming out of Ellie's mouth, the phrase *hit man* sounded ridiculous. But her tone remained serious, and the authorities must have thought it was, too, if Washburn had gone away for it.

I glanced at her again, shocked. "So he was a bad guy, for what, conspiracy to commit murder? And now he's become a bookie, with the kind of old pals who could get bad things done here, too. Why didn't you tell me this before?"

She looked at me. "Jacobia, it was a long time ago. And lots of people have been in one kind of trouble or another. You can't assume anything from it."

True; George Valentine himself had had his little run-ins with the law in his younger days. "And the gambling can't be much because if local guys were losing much, we'd have heard of it."

"Good point. But you can't blame me for getting my hopes up, can you?"

"No. But just keep an open mind, that's all. I don't

think Howard's going to be quite the kind of major crime figure you're expecting."

Another sign advised AUCTION AHEAD! How far ahead, was my big question. We were high on a hill with what looked like all of Maine spread below us: the mill at Woodland puffing white smoke, a lake's irregular borders cut into the solid evergreen of a pine forest. Patches of pasture lay like quilt squares spread out on the hillsides.

Suddenly the biggest sign of all was upon us: YOU'RE HERE! A crushed stone drive cut through brushy undergrowth, bordered by a rail fence upon which bittersweet climbed with riotous vigor. At the top was a parking lot the size of a football field.

Well, half a football field, but it was big, and so was the barn: gambrel-roofed, four stories high, bright yellow. A big bay door stood open at the near end, the shadowy interior pitch-black by contrast with the brilliant day. Shafts of sunlight slanted down from hayloft windows onto a plank floor.

A beater of an old Ford Escort was pulled up alongside a shed. Other Fords, each one missing some vital component of its equipment—one had wheels but no tires, another four bald tires piled on its hood but no wheels—lined up by the Escort.

A man in a blue coverall slid from beneath the vehicle at our approach, a wrench in his greasy hand. Hopping up, he grinned eagerly, showing a set of false teeth that didn't fit and making me wonder uneasily where they had come from originally.

"Howard Washburn, good t'see ya, how ya doin'? Wonderful day, ain't it? How can I help you two young ladies? Got some fine bargains out there in the barn, new stuff every day."

The teeth clicked loudly with every syllable. "Got a new washing machine, poor lady died before she could use it." The knuckles on his right hand were bleeding through a coat of black grease.

"Mr. Washburn, we're not here to buy anything."

The teeth snapped shut. Sharp suspicion replaced the bright, false welcome in his eyes. "You cops?"

"No." I looked around curiously: no house. But a teardrop trailer was parked at the end of the row of Fords, a card table and two lawn chairs set up just outside it.

"Mr. Washburn, we need to ask you about Jonathan Raines."

I saw him jump before he could hide it. Prison, I suppose, can do that to a fellow. So he knew the name.

"Say, I know you," he said cheerfully to Ellie. "You're the one who came out here to . . . Oh. Now I remember." His eyes, brightening at the sight of her, narrowed with sudden caution again.

"Right," Ellie said gently to him. "I came out here one time to tell you that so-called colonial furniture you were selling still had the Sears tags on it."

She turned to me, her expression indulgent. "Howard found a way to distress furniture so it would look antique. But he kind of forgot about the undersides, didn't you, Howard? If you want to fake stuff, you've got to do the whole thing, take it apart to get at all of it. Howard just did the tops."

Clearly Howard wasn't the sharpest knife in the drawer. But he was a good sport about it. He grinned embarrassedly, looking down at his grease-stained hands. "I don't do none o' that stuff no more, anyway. All on the up-and-up now."

"Right, Howard," Ellie said. "Sure you are. Now, my friend here wants to know how you've heard of Jonathan Raines."

Howard Washburn made a show of trying to remember. "Wilbur Mapes said this Raines fella was from away and o' course I didn't like that, right off the bat."

He peered at me through the automobile grease that smeared his face. "They come here, think the home folks is idiots. Try to buy the fambly treasures for peanuts and a song."

And if anyone was going to do that, it should be Howard, he clearly felt. "Ain't right," he pronounced stoutly. "Ain't fair."

"Uh-huh. Did Wilbur mention an old violin?"

Washburn's look turned sly. "Might have. Might not. I wasn't payin' a whole lot of attention, tell you the truth."

There was a concept: Howard Washburn telling the truth. I'd already decided he couldn't have found it with both hands and a road map. I lowered the boom.

"Or maybe Wilbur had been in touch with you earlier about it? That Raines, I mean, was looking for one?"

Washburn looked from one to the other of us, cottoning on to what we knew already.

"Why," he wanted to know, "am I talking to you? Is there some benefit to me standing here shootin' the breeze?"

"Maybe it's because I've still got one of those 'colonial' tables you sold to the lady from Connecticut," Ellie said mildly.

"Now, you can't prove I had anything to do with—"

"I don't have to prove it, Howard," she told him sweetly. "I just have to talk a lot, especially to the people who run all the hotels and bed-and-breakfasts, where the summer tourists stay."

He took her point. Maybe there were some legitimate finds in that old barn of his, but no tourist would ever make the trip to see them if word of those Sears tags started spreading around.

"And then there's your other business," she went on. "Games of chance? Things no one wants to follow up on. Unless I persuade them."

Bob Arnold wasn't going to rattle Howard's chains about any minor-league gambling. He had enough to do chasing criminals whose victims hadn't gotten their own selves into trouble.

Not unless someone complained. Ellie smiled sweetly again.

"Mapes was out here, coupla weeks ago," Howard admitted grudgingly. "Said he had a sucker from Boston lookin' for an old Stradivarius."

"Go on."

"Mapes'd sold the sucker a buncha stuff out of an old trunk. Music books, sheet music as was handwritten, old ink pens, kind that're made out of a quill, you know? And a lot of other papers, old diaries and such. And a violin."

My heart thumped suddenly. "Not the one the sucker said he was lookin' for," Howard went on. "But I guess it encouraged him, the sucker, I mean. Stuff belonged to the right old guy, one as was supposed to have had the really valuable fiddle."

Jared Hayes. "Once he'd vanished, his house would've been emptied, eventually," Ellie said. "And at that point the story about the Stradivarius hadn't really heated up yet. An old trunk full of things could've gotten anywhere."

"Ayuh," said Washburn. "Up in an attic, Mapes said, house he cleared out for some people a long time ago, they'd had a chimbly fire."

Chimney, he meant. My house: the fire that hadn't burned it to the ground, by some miracle. And if some of Hayes's things had still been in it when the fire happened . . .

"Smoked up all their stuff, they just wanted to get rid of it all."

From the corner of my eye I spotted Monday, sniffing around the corner of the old barn. "Okay for the dog to run?" I asked.

"Oh, ayuh. Way out here, no cars. I don't put out no rat bait or no traps or nothin'. 'Cept in trappin' season, then I put out a coupla lines. Got me some nice fox furs."

He eyed me hopefully. I used to think foxes were smart, beautiful, and romantic animals, on account of the way they were portrayed in nature programs on television. Then I moved to Eastport, where they make their dens in the backyards of old, unoccupied houses and lope through the night like feral ghosts, emitting when confronted a cry like a cross between a rusty door hinge and person in the act of having his throat slit.

"No, thanks, Howard," I said politely. I don't care for foxes, but I am even less fond of the obscenity known as the leg-hold trap. Talk about a crime that actually does have an innocent victim: if you're going to kill something, put a bullet in its head and be done with it, is my attitude.

"Jonathan Raines," I reminded Howard. I got the sense that sticking to the subject was not his forte.

This probably accounted for him being the one who got sent to prison in the hit-man affair, since after ten minutes in his presence I had come around to Ellie's point of view. In fact, I was already certain that (a) he wasn't the hit man himself, and (b) he could not possibly have been ringleader of a plot to kill somebody.

Or any kind of a major player in any plot. What Howard was perfect for, in fact, was (c) the role of the fall guy.

"Yeah, him," Howard said. "I didn't know him. Knew the old man, though," he added. "Mapes mentioned him, my ears pricked up right quick."

"Winston Cartwright?" Here was a wrinkle I hadn't expected. "How do you know him?"

Howard spread his hands expansively. "Hell, he's legend. You deal in antiques, books, maps, anything old-like, you don't even need to know about him." Wondering at the idea, he shook his head slowly. "Even a little guy, likes o' me, bank on it. He'll know and get hold o' you."

Fascinating, and very likely true; the notion of Cartwright as a spider at the center of a web struck me once more.

But so did what Howard said. "Maps? What made you think of maps?"

He flinched guiltily; damn, there he'd gone again, saying more than he'd meant to. But once he'd done it, he stepped up to the result manfully and talked some *more,* yet another mark of the born blame-magnet. I began feeling sorry for Howard.

"Mapes said if the violin everybody says is so valuable was hid, stood to reason whoever'd hid it would've made a map to it," he said. " 'Cause everybody in town knows the old story about the violin, hid in that big old house in town. But it ain't there, 'cause that old house has been gone through. Gone through good. So if there is one, it's somewhere else." He said it with certainty.

"How do you know?" I gave him the stare I used to use on clients who were tax cheats, who wanted me to sign off on returns so fictional, they should have had literary agents instead of money managers.

"Well," Howard stalled, digging a hole in the dirt with the toe of his boot. "I know 'cause I knew a guy who did it. Had a gadget, it could see shapes right through the walls. Did it with sound waves, he could tell what was inside there."

Like a carpenter's stud-finder, I guessed. It senses

density so you can locate the solid structure behind the plaster.

Howard looked strangely at me, having figured out something. "Say, that ain't your house we're talkin' about, is it? I heard a lady from away bought it. That you? 'Cause if it is," he went on, "I bet you've seen some funny things."

"What're you talking about?" Meanwhile, I was still thinking about the search his friend had made. The book inside the dining room wall should have shown up if he'd looked with a device like Howard was describing. So why hadn't it?

Howard shivered expressively. "My buddy said that place gave 'im the creeps. And he wasn't the type to get spooked. He came out o' there, wouldn't turn the lights out for three nights."

Great, just what I needed. "And *if* he'd found it," I steered the conversation around again, "this buddy who I'm sure you were the one who told him to look there in the first place. Somebody from Portsmouth?"

Howard frowned. "No. Afterwards." Prison buddy, he meant.

"*He'd* have handed the violin over to whoever owned the house then, right? Because naturally the owners knew your buddy was doing this. He'd gotten permission."

"Well, not exactly," Howard admitted. "This guy, he was not exactly a big hander-over of stuff."

An unpleasant memory fled across Howard's face and was gone. "But it never mattered anyway. He didn't find nothing."

"But if it existed, and it's not in the house . . ."

He nodded vigorously. "Right. Then Mapes's idea made sense, see? Map to it, X marks the spot. Never found no map neither, though," he added mournfully.

Monday came back from wherever she had wandered off to. She always knows somehow when it is time to get back in the car and is so optimistic that she regards the end of one outing as merely a punctuation mark, signaling the delightful start of another.

My silence wasn't meant to be accusatory, but it must have made Howard nervous again. "Okay, you want to know about Raines, I'll tell you what he talked about," Howard said.

His own attention span had obviously been exceeded, and he'd talked more than he'd meant to about things he didn't understand, and it all made him uncomfortable. Very uncomfortable.

"You *met* him? Jonathan Raines?"

"Yeah. In La Sardina."

Oh, damn and blast the bartender's legendary code of ethics; maybe it was good business, but it was getting to be a pain in my tail. No one had asked Teddy Armstrong about Howard Washburn, so Teddy hadn't mentioned him.

"But all he talked about was a girl, about how she was so gorgeous"—*gore-juss*—"and smart. But she'd busted up with him. Busted his heart. Oh, but he was sweet on her. The old man broke 'em up, he said; that's how the old man's name came up. He was going to get her back, Raines was, if it was the last thing he ever did."

He folded his arms, glaring at Ellie and me. Apparently, telling the truth about anything went against his principles, but he had done it, by God, he had done it, and were we satisfied?

"Thank you, Howard," I said quietly, wanting to weep. Partly for Howard; you could see how he had wound up behind those prison bars. And he wasn't a bad guy, really, just terminally inept.

But also for Jonathan Raines. *The last thing he ever did*.

"You've been very helpful," I said.

Not really; coming out here, I'd had some idea he might be a part of some grand, nefarious scheme. Fat chance. But I found myself wanting to say something nice to him, the poor schmuck.

Howard brightened. "Well, then. Glad to do that for you two nice ladies. Now, how about a fine deal on a brand-new . . ." —the false teeth clicked like a pair of castanets—"well, *nearly* new," he amended hopefully, "Ford Escort?"

Driving back, I told Ellie about Victor's wristwatch, and she was all for finding Jill Frey and shaking her until her teeth rattled harder than Howard Washburn's.

"No," I said as we rounded the curve into town. "It will only make Sam want to defend her even more than he already does."

In the IGA parking lot a two-and-a-half-ton truck was unloading flats of annual garden flowers, the black-top a riot of geraniums and petunias, zinnias and marigolds. Next came a row of antique white clapboard houses snugged up to the sidewalk on Washington Street. In the eighteenth century, property taxes were based on the size of the front yard, so thrifty Mainers had promptly eliminated them.

"Well, then I guess we stiffen our spines and talk to Hecky Wilmot, if we can find him," Ellie said.

Hecky being the last of the varied group that had been in La Sardina with Raines before Raines took his unscheduled dive off the pier, and the third man in Mapes's old marijuana-smuggling operation.

"I guess," I said disconsolately. The thing was, in Eastport you could look for nefarious schemes, but what you found instead were flower sales, craft shows, and a freighter coming in, getting tied up at the town dock. That and fellows like Howard Washburn, who might look bad on paper but in reality were just guys trying to make a living.

"Ordinarily all you'd have to do is walk down the street," Ellie went on. "But I heard from Truman Daly that Hecky's book's due out today, so Hecky's routine has probably been disrupted."

"Criminy, that's right. Today's the day." With everything else going on, Hecky's big moment had slipped my mind. But bound copies of his memoir of Eastport were due to arrive at Bay Books any minute so he could sign them for people. "He must be . . ."

Thrilled, I'd been about to say. But:

"What's going on?"

Just ahead, at the foot of the hill leading down to Water Street, a group was forming. I saw several members of the Ladies' Reading Circle, men from the Elks Lodge, and more whose specific affiliation I couldn't identify, only that they were all angry.

"Traitor!" somebody shouted.

"Turncoat!" yelled somebody else.

"Goodness," said Ellie. At the head of the crowd, glancing over his shoulder as he hurried along, was an elderly-looking man with dyed black hair; sharp, suspicious little eyes that spied everything; and a look of terror on his age-mottled face.

"I don't think we'll have to go looking for Hecky," I said, slowing the car almost to a stop.

On the sidewalk, stroking his long, white beard, Truman Daly looked on in consternation and amusement. As a rule, Truman did not enjoy witnessing other people's troubles, but it was hard not to relish the sight of Hecky getting his comeuppance, for once.

The crowd wouldn't let me pass. "Hit the horn," Ellie said quietly.

"Huh?" Unless you counted Wade leaning over to honk it at Sam and Jill, I hadn't heard the horn on this car since I'd moved here; in Eastport, you couldn't very well blast today at someone you'd be sitting next to at the church supper tomorrow night.

Ellie reached out and leaned on it. The crowd jumped and scattered away like startled deer, with Hecky running ahead of them. I caught up to Hecky, who had a book in one hand, his hat in the other, and an egg splattered across the back of his plaid flannel shirt.

"Get in," Ellie told him, and he followed this advice without hesitation.

"Key-riminy." Hurtling into the backseat, he slammed the car door and we sped away. Monday began licking the raw egg from his shirt, which under the circumstances I thought was probably the best way to dispose of it. "Those people have gone nuts!"

"What seems to be the problem, Hecky?" Ellie inquired.

"Problem?" he sputtered. "Those folks just can't take a dose of old-fashioned home truth, is the problem. What'd they expect, a lot of dishwater-dull foolishness?"

"Oh," I said, suddenly enlightened. "The book."

"Damn right," Hecky said stoutly.

I glanced in the rearview mirror. Perspiration had dissolved the dye in Hecky's hairline and was running in inky rivulets to form black ruts in the wrinkles of his forehead.

"Cut a little close to the bone, did it?" Far behind us, the thwarted literary critics had stopped chasing us and were forming into angry little groups on the sidewalk in front of Wadsworth's Hardware.

Debating, probably, the merits of running Hecky out of town on a rail versus the equally attractive advantages of hanging him in effigy. Meanwhile, Ellie had taken the book from him and was paging curiously through it.

" '. . . fourteen illegitimate children, seven of whom had coffee cups with their names on them in the town jail, then located down in the ground-floor rooms of the bank building . . .' "

She looked up at him in alarm. "Hecky Wilmot, are you out of your tiny mind?" She flipped more pages.

" '. . . drove getaway car for the notorious Hoover boys . . . fan-dancer at a saloon in Nevada . . .' " She snapped the volume shut. "Is it all like this?"

"Every bit," Hecky agreed proudly. "Course"—he frowned—"I figured there might be some upset about it." But this idea seemed to bring on a flock of others he didn't find comfortable.

"You can let me off here," he said. He lived in a tumbledown Victorian mansion that had belonged to his great-grandfather, the Honorable Hector B. Wilmot: either the finest attorney the state had ever produced or a lowdown dirty rotten scoundrel, depending on whose version you accepted. I wondered which one Hecky had put in his memoir.

"No, Hecky," Ellie said firmly. "You're coming with us."

He looked mutinous. "Now, don't you try telling me—"

"Or we'll take you back downtown and let your fans tell you what a great author you are," she added, at which he fell silent and allowed himself to be driven to my house and hustled inside.

"You must have known something like this would happen," Ellie scolded the old man exasperatedly. "People around here don't take kindly to having their laundry publicly aired. Now the whole world's going to know Philomena Parr was a fan-dancer in a saloon out there in the gold rush in Nevada before she got so respectable here."

Philomena's headstone in Hillside Cemetery was so ancient and moss-ravaged, you could barely see the fan engraved into it—until now, I'd thought it was a religious symbol of some sort—and the gold rush had happened a hundred and forty years ago. But this, by Eastport reckoning, was only the blink of a gnat's eye; you didn't go casting aspersions on the acorns folks' family trees had sprung from in Eastport. You just didn't.

"There's plenty of people with stories about you they could be telling," Ellie went on sternly. "Certain dealings in certain substances. Growth and transport."

Hecky shifted uncomfortably under my gaze. "That's all past history. I don't have aught to do with any of that anymore."

"Hmph. But after the hoo-hah there was about it, and how you were so upset about the way people talked about you, I don't see how you missed realizing the way they would feel when you wrote about them. What's the title of this thing, anyway?"

She snatched up the book again. It was soft-cover, nicely produced, with a picture of a square-rigger plowing bravely up Passamaquoddy Bay. The artist had done a particularly good job on the Jolly Roger, a skull-and-crossbones insignia clearly visible from where it flew on the mizzenmast.

"*Rum-Runners and Downeast Scoundrels . . .* but that's not the title you told everybody it would be. Oh, Hecky," Ellie sighed, mortified. "How could you *do* this?"

"Well, I didn't want to publicize the real title in advance of it. I had a sneaking notion some people wouldn't care for it much." Under the kitchen light his black hair shone dully like a fresh lump of charcoal, and his wrinkles all sagged downward morosely.

"S'posed to be in Florida by now, tell the truth," he added. "But money for the ticket and moving tab didn't come through."

The penny dropped. He'd thought he could be a famous author *and* escape the town's wrath. Hecky Wilmot, grand old storyteller of Eastport, had meant to hightail it out of here ahead of the lynching party and relocate to warmer climes.

Eye for the main chance and the hell with all the rest, Bob Arnold had said about Hecky, and I guessed it was true. And for that, Hecky would have needed money. . . .

Just then Sam came in, glanced darkly into the kitchen, and thumped upstairs, not speaking. Ellie was still staring at Hecky.

"Florida?" She breathed it in disbelief, as if he'd confided that come the winter holidays, he was planning on having a roast leg of Rudolf for Christmas dinner.

"Time to make a change. Variety is important, you know," he said stubbornly. "Anyway, guess that ain't worked out. Mebbe I'll visit m' sister, down to Portland."

I thought if Hecky intended to escape to Portland, he ought to make it Portland, Oregon. The phone lines to Hecky's sister were humming right now, I had no doubt.

"What you got me over here for, anyway?" he demanded to know. "Now I got to find a way home, they're out there waitin' with the knives all sharpened up, a-ready to scalp me."

"Ellie will give you a ride home in my car," I said. "On the way, she's got a couple of questions to ask you.

About," I emphasized severely, "Jonathan Raines. And Hecky, I want you to tell her the truth, no nonsense and no embroidery."

If he'd been a rooster, his comb would have bristled up in reflexive anger. "Young whippersnapper, comin' in here where he had no business—"

"Yes, well, you *did* have business here, and you've mucked it up pretty well yourself, haven't you?"

He slumped, understanding: Hecky would have to go some ways to clean up the mess he'd managed to make in his own nest.

"All right," he allowed reluctantly, getting up. "Ask away. I guess it cain't do no harm now, can it? Me and my big mouth." He was beginning to accept the enormity of what he had done and the impossibility of taking it back.

"Well, Hecky, at least from the size of that crowd down in front of Bay Books, you have a best-seller on your hands."

He looked hollow-eyed at me. Ah, the perils of first-time authorship. For Hecky, I had a strong feeling it was probably the last time, too. "Ayuh," he agreed shakily, but turned at the door in a last burst of unfocused antagonism.

"You got it all wrong, you know, you and that know-it-all fella with the cane. Winston Cartwright," he sneered, giving the words a sour, frightened twist. "Him and his stories. He got the whole thing twisted up backwards."

"Really? In what way?"

Hecky gave a disparaging snort. "Jane Whitelaw. *He* says she fell off o' them cliffs the day *b'fore* Jared Hayes disappeared. But that ain't so. My fambly was livin' in Eastport already, even then, an' they carried the story down as it happened, not the way that blowhard got it from some old book."

"So how *did* it happen?" Micah Whitelaw could've gotten that detail wrong, I supposed. Still, what difference could it make?

" 'Twas the day *after*," Hecky asserted. "And it weren't any accident she died of, my fambly folks say. Story is, *she* wrote it all down b'fore *she* died, what her troubles was, in a diary. She was an eddicated girl, read books. Likely that was her trouble," he added with a dark look at me.

He had, in addition to his many other charming qualities, a suspicion of any female whose activities ranged beyond home and hearth.

"They say it's where the boy, Micah Whitelaw, got his diary-keeping habit," Hecky went on. "Nobody ever found what *she* wrote, that Whitelaw woman. One thing's f'sure, though." He aimed a gnarled finger at me. "Jane Whitelaw didn't die accidental. Nossir. My take on it, she was *kilt*!"

With that, Hecky stumped out, and I heard him muttering all the way down the back porch and out to the car. In the silence he left behind I watched the sugar bowl on the kitchen table move a quiet, deliberate six inches to the left and back again.

Whereupon I abandoned the kitchen and went upstairs to have a heart-to-heart talk with my son, and found him in his room with a gleaming object in his hands.

Victor's wristwatch.

"Mom, it was a joke," he insisted. "She was going to give it back. When I told her how upset he was, she was horrified."

"I see." I sat on the bed beside him.

Over the years, Sam's bedroom-decoration theme has gone from gangsta rap (hideous), through model shipbuilding (delightful), into a brief, intense infatuation with very old cars (messy), and finally to a crisp, shipshape arrangement of desk and bookcases, indicating his final decision to return to school in the fall.

"Jill's mom told me she's been having a bad time," I said. "Maybe she just wanted to get a little attention, huh?"

He nodded eagerly. "Right. Play a joke, everybody laughs. If they do," he finished, his face falling. "But instead, everyone's decided she's some kind of *criminal*."

"You know, Sam, when fall comes you're going to be involved with a lot of new things. Classes, meeting new people. . . ."

Other girls, I was thinking hopefully. But he was way ahead of me, shaking his head. "Jill's the one. I'm going to marry her. Mom, I've just never met anyone like her before."

Military school, I thought wildly; or a tough-love camp. But Sam was too old for those. In fact, he was old enough to do just about anything he wished.

Including ruin his life. "She's smart, she's funny, she's really brave," he went on.

She's blond, beautiful, built like a fashion model. She's got all the moral sense of a piranha. Perfect marriage material.

For another piranha. "She is a very attractive young woman," I allowed.

"Oh, yeah," Sam said impatiently, "humor me. You think I'm going to get over her. But I'm not," he insisted. "I'm just not."

I got off the bed. Gone were the days when I could smooth his hair and administer a baby aspirin. "Sam . . ." I hesitated at the door. "About the watch."

"Yeah?" He glanced cautiously at me.

"When you went to see her, how did you put it to her? I mean, did you bring it up first? Or did she?"

His face snapped shut as he took my point: would Jill have mentioned it if he hadn't? If Victor hadn't accused her? Or would she have kept the watch in that event, said nothing about it?

"What kind of a question is that?" Sam demanded. "Oh, man. Just leave it, Mom, okay? Leave it, I'll take care of it."

He turned his face to the wall, shutting me out.

"I'm sorry, Sam, I shouldn't have asked," I said, feeling the answer like a clump of cold seaweed gathering in my heart.

By the time Ellie returned and we'd gone out together, I'd thought it over.

"Sam's got to deal with it himself," I said as we passed the old redbrick library building.

Inside, Charmian was cataloging the historical collection. Inviting her to lunch would have been a hospitable action. But I wasn't feeling hospitable.

"Ever since we came here, Sam has been the absolute model of a good son. Funny, pleasant to be around. But now—"

"Separation," Ellie said succinctly. Out on the bay, the children's sailing class was having a practice regatta, a dozen small craft skittering across the waves like so many waterbugs.

"He's going away in the fall," Ellie explained to my look of surprise. "Living in the dorm in Machias during the week, away from here. Away," she finished, "from you."

"He'll be home weekends," I protested.

"And feeling of two minds about it, is my guess," she went on, ignoring me. "Because he likes you, you know. He does. And he likes it here. But he's got to go. So he's . . . at war with himself, sort of."

Of course she was right. It fit his behavior perfectly. Now that she'd said it, I wondered only why I hadn't seen it before.

"So you think he's fastened on to this unsuitable girl just as a way to . . . cut the umbilical cord in advance? So when the real separation comes he'll have already . . ."

"Dealt with it," she agreed flatly. "And more importantly to him, he will have made you deal with it, too; in some ways he's just trying to get a rise out of you, I think. Although of course he doesn't realize it."

"Maybe that's why he looks relieved to get away from her one minute"—the look on his face the night before rose up before me—"and in the next insists he's going to marry her? Because it's all about independence? Breaking the bonds with me?"

She nodded. "Sure. After all, he's only eighteen. It's natural for him to swing back and forth like a loose sail. And he's probably got a lot of . . . issues." She pronounced the jargonish word reluctantly, but it was right for the stuff she meant.

"And you're right: attacking her will make things worse. You know how gallant he can be."

"Yes," I said, thinking of the old days when Sam would run psychological interference between me and his father. It hadn't been good for him. But at the time I took any defense I could get.

We reached the stairs leading up past the shoe repair shop to the Starlite Café, above the antique stores looking out over the boat basin to the islands beyond. From the café floated the good smells of the Starlite's idea of lunch: homemade vegetable soup, toasted onion bagels, fresh chocolate brownies, and fresh-ground, brewed-a-heartbeat-ago Blue Mountain coffee.

My step quickened. At the top of the stairs was a barnlike room furnished with shabby-chic antiques, ferns on wire stands, and tables equipped with backgammon boards. The front was a wall of windows whose dazzling light mellowed as it poured in.

"Anyway, Hecky says the same as everyone else," Ellie said when she had ordered her usual: an avocado and Swiss sandwich with tomato and mustard sprouts on seven-grain bread. I had the soup and half a bagel, and not much later, our lunches arrived.

"Raines didn't say anything except about Charmian and how he meant to win her back, in La Sardina. But Hecky says Raines *did* look like he'd just swallowed the canary, and sounded very sure of himself, which of course just drove Hecky half nuts."

Hecky liked people to sound *un*sure, because it made him feel *more* sure. She bit into her sandwich.

"My thought is," she said when she had negotiated all the grains, greens, and other chewy stuff she was eating, "we need to, um, amalgamate. Or something."

She waved the sandwich; looking at all the things that were in it, I got her drift. "You put the different ingredients together and you get . . ."

All the bits of information we'd been gathering; no one of them was helpful on its own. But . . .

She nodded energetically. "Right. Something entirely new."

So, think: an old violin but not a precious one, along with an old book that Raines bought from Mapes. Add Washburn's habit of distressing new furniture to look like valuable antique stuff. Then there was Mapes's own cluttered dwelling: some treasures, but a lot of junk, too. And Hecky Wilmot and his book troubles; his big Florida hopes and his lack of money to realize them.

All mixed up with Charmian's odd talents, and Winston Cartwright's story about Jared Hayes's love for Jane Whitelaw. Hayes's plan to win her heart by getting fabulously wealthy.

Finally, there was Eastport itself: full of guys who might seem to be one thing—ex-cons, or junk collectors, or retired fellows puttering quietly in their gardens raising dahlias—but who were really another.

"We think of Hayes," I said slowly, "as this dignified man. A musician and composer, we think of a sort of high-flown, high-minded person. Someone who could write in Latin, for instance. The pirate association, his high style of living, his fencing of stolen goods—all this time later it just adds a note of glamour in our minds, doesn't it?"

Ellie nodded, understanding. "But what if he wasn't?"

"Precisely. Years later, we've turned him into a bigger-than-life figure. But what if he was more like the guys we've been talking to, Hecky and Mapes and Howard Washburn? Just . . . guys. The kind who, some of them, get bright ideas and pull a few schemes?"

As I spoke, Harriet put a CD into the player: Vivaldi's *The Four Seasons*. Spring trilled out of the speakers.

"What," I went on, "if Hayes really did get a Stradivarius? Say, in some pirate loot or something." There'd been no record of such a purchase in his account books. "And his first plan was to sell it, make money. But then, because at heart he was really just an ordinary guy like Mapes or Howard Washburn, Hayes got a bright idea."

"A scheme. Like Howard's 'distressed' Sears furniture: fake one, and sell *that*." Ellie's eyes shone.

"Uh-huh. He's got a model in the real one. So he buys, or has built, an inferior, cheaper instrument and alters it so that it looks like the real thing. If he can sell them both, he'll make twice as much. Only . . ."

"Not right away. It wouldn't be credible for him to have two of them, would it? So . . ."

"He hides the real one, meaning to sell it later, or even to keep it. But before he can do anything, even sell the fake . . ."

There'd been no record of any violin sale in the invisible-ink book, either.

"He vanishes," Ellie finished calmly. "Ends up in Pirate's Cove. And the fake article could be the violin Raines found. He would know how to tell a fake from the real thing, though, so he wouldn't be fooled by Hayes's counterfeiting attempt."

I spooned up the last of my soup, decided to indulge in a brownie for dessert, and accepted a refill on my coffee.

"Okay, so what does that mean? For all we know, he did sell a Strad, for instance, and never wrote anything down about it. We can only go so far on theory."

But Ellie shook her head. "No. If such a violin existed now, that had been sold from here back then, people *would* know about it. Cartwright would know, and Raines would've; the experts would be aware of such a thing, its history. Wouldn't they? Raines said individual instruments are so famous, they have their own names."

"Good point." I thought some more. "And Lillian Frey says if it is still here, it's probably sawdust by now."

"So it could've rotted away in a hiding place somewhere. But wouldn't Raines have thought of that, too?"

In other words, why would he be so hot to find a handful of wormy firewood? "Well, maybe he was hoping against hope. Or . . ."

Something else. But I couldn't quite latch on to the third possibility. It had to do somehow with Hayes's money and account books, and it hovered infuriatingly at the edge of my mind like something glimpsed unreliably from the corner of my eye.

Drat. "Anyway," I said, finishing up my coffee, "if Raines was on to something, it's almost surely something he learned either from that book in my wall—though I still don't see how—*or* from the diaries he bought from Wilbur, in the trunk of old stuff."

Ellie's brow furrowed as a new thought struck her. "Jacobia. Howard did mention old diaries in that trunk. But Winston Cartwright said *he* had all of Micah Whitelaw's diaries. And as far as we know, all Hayes's are accounted for, too. We've seen them. So *what* diaries do you suppose Raines bought from Wilbur?"

I stared at her. "Ellie. You're a genius. What if one of them was Jane's? Jane Whitelaw's?"

I got up and paid the check, followed Ellie down the stairs to the street. We walked in silence until we got to my house.

"The thing is, Hayes wanted Jane," Ellie said. "He meant to win her with money. So wouldn't he tell her what he intended to do? Confide his plan, sort of dazzle her in advance?"

"Never mind what *he* wanted," I said, letting us in the kitchen door. "What I want to know is, where are they now? Jane's diary," I mean, "if that's what it was, and the old violin Raines found, too. But I'd rather have the book."

Just then Sam came downstairs, looking slicked-up and ready for action. I didn't ask him who he was going out to meet, and he didn't offer to tell. But he overheard

Ellie's last comments, and in an effort to be congenial offered a smiling remark, along with a look at me that I interpreted to mean, *Truce?*

I nodded, just as he dropped his innocent bombshell.

"Always," he intoned, "hide where there are a lot of the same kind of things."

8 "No wonder she's been working in the library," Ellie said as we hurried back to it. "*She* knew Raines, knew how he thought. He might even have pulled the same trick in the past, and she knew about it."

"And he *said* he'd been to the library, that night at the dinner table. I should have thought of it myself."

We rushed up the steps. "He probably tucked it in with the other old books. It would look as if it's always been there."

"And for some reason he *wanted* it discovered. Otherwise he wouldn't have made a point of mentioning the library to you." But here she stopped. "Only, *why*? He couldn't have known someone was going to take him out of the picture."

"Maybe we'll figure that out when we find it. If we do."

Inside, we looked left and right: to the fiction collection jamming the shelves on one side, the reading room full of white light from the tall arched windows. No Charmian anywhere.

"Darn, don't tell me now *she's* disappeared," Ellie whispered, and a lady who was reading an old copy of Harriet Beecher Stowe's *Uncle Tom's Cabin* looked up admonishingly.

We moved toward the checkout desk, past the little

alcove that is the children's part of the library: small chairs and low painted shelves stuffed with brightly covered volumes. It wasn't quite time for story hour, yet; the area was empty.

Empty, that is, except for a decidedly non juvenile-looking book on one of the child-sized tables, lying there open as if it had been left only for a moment, its reader intending to return.

It was bound in old green leather, its pages brittle and foxed. "Ellie!" I whispered. The frontispiece, in spidery black ink, read: *Jane Whitelaw, this is her book*.

We took the book to the back of the fiction stacks and sat to scan it. The writing was faded, the spelling idiosyncratic, as was usual even for educated people then. But within moments Jane Whitelaw's personality came through as if she were sitting there with us. Not a pleasant personality; as we turned them, a whiff of brimstone practically rose up off the antique pages.

Sly and greedy, shallow and promiscuous. Self-dramatizing, too: "I want to live as the great ladies do, and I shall, if I have to kill them all to achieve it," Jane wrote on one occasion.

On a later date: "These simpletons do not amuse me, and Hayes is the worst of all, the silly little mincing braggart with his muddy boots and inky fingers, playing his love songs."

Ellie took the book from me. "'I bid him goodnight, let him think I go to my maiden's bed alone,'" she read aloud. "'But later I slipped away to the real men, as Hayes scratched out his farm-boy ideas of music. The fool could never imagine my plan or guard against it! Or my father, either.'"

The rest was the same: envy, greed. It struck me that Jane must have been a great beauty, to hide the venom that ran in her veins in place of blood.

" 'Hayes has returned. I've told him he will be hanged

unless he talks, and he believes,' " I read. "Ellie, I think this means *she* talked Hayes into betraying Josephus."

Ellie nodded. "But why would she do that?"

"Here," I said, putting my finger to a yellowed page. " 'The silly minstrel'—that must have meant Hayes— 'has stolen all he can. The golden goose has laid its final egg and now off with its head.' "

"Hayes's head? Or her father's?"

"Both, apparently," I said grimly. "One hanged as a pirate and the other . . ."

"Murdered by Jane," Ellie whispered. "He served his purpose. So she killed him?"

"Or had him killed. By one of the 'real men' she hung around with, probably."

Willful and wanton, selfish and self-obsessed: " 'I shall have my own way in all things or repair to my grave,' " Ellie read aloud from the final page, then looked up.

"This is so disappointing."

I felt the same way. "I'd been imagining her as more . . . noble. Or something. Romantic. Larger than life. Like Hayes."

"Finding out she was pregnant must have put a real hitch in her plans," Ellie commented. "There doesn't seem to be anything here about it, though."

"Maybe it didn't," I said, getting up to peer out toward the atrium. But Charmian had not returned. "Put a hitch in her plans, I mean. Jane doesn't sound like a woman who would let a child get in her way. Even her own child."

"And that's why she took the baby with her when she went to the cliff," Ellie agreed sadly. "Because all she thought about was herself."

It was the part I disliked most. I couldn't imagine that any sane woman—and Jane, however nasty, sounded in full possession of her faculties—would deliberately endanger her own child, no matter how urgent the errand.

"Hey," Ellie said softly. She'd come to the very back of the book, where the linen thread that fastened in the pages still gleamed faintly in the glow of the hanging light bulb between the stacks where we sat. "Look at this."

I peered over her shoulder. "It's torn?" I put out a finger to touch the break in the green leather binding, where the inside of the back cover met the final page.

"No," Ellie said, "it's . . ." She poked a finger into the open place. "The binding's slit, and recently. See? It's unfrayed."

A sudden memory of Charmian's fancy penknife came to me, in the handbag that I'd returned to her. "Raines got old books from Mapes. Mapes had read them, of course, but didn't examine them well enough. I think this might be one of them, and something was in the binding of this one."

"Another map, maybe?"

"It would've been the perfect spot for one. And what *else* would have sent Charmian off in such a hurry, she didn't even put the diary away again?"

Ellie nodded energetically. "And if Hayes *did* tell Jane about his plan, that he hid something valuable . . ."

"Wanting her to love him," I said slowly. "Bragging, maybe, about how much money he was going to make by his scheme: selling a fake Stradivarius *and* a real one. But not knowing . . ."

"How really, truly *bad* she was," Ellie finished. "He told her where he hid it. Maybe she even made him tell her where. And he *gave her a map*. A copy of his own, which is probably the other one, the one we can't read. Do you think?"

She jumped up. "If he did, maybe that's what Jane

was doing out at North End at the cliffs that night: trying to follow it. And speaking of sneaky women,
what'll you bet that Charmian's already hooked back
up with her supposedly evil uncle, whom she supposedly despises so much—"

"But she only despises him for our benefit?"

"Exactly. So she rushed out of here, and the two of
them are on their way to find Hayes's real Stradivarius
this minute?"

"Wait a sec." I followed Ellie from between the tall
stacks to the checkout desk. "I thought we decided it's
rotted away by now. The violin, I mean. And they must
know that. Or ought to. So why would Charmian and
Winston . . ."

"It depends on what the map said," Ellie replied.
"Maybe it says the violin's somewhere the weather
couldn't get at it, Jacobia. And it really *has* been here in
Eastport all these years."

If he'd wrapped it up properly, made it safe against
the elements . . . Something still bothered me about all
of this, but we didn't have time to worry about it. At
our question, Mina Sirois turned harriedly from guiding
the children in for their story session.

"She made a phone call," Mina confirmed, and then:
"Kids, let's sit quietly, please!" she appealed. At this a
crowd of youngsters charged into the reading room, to
the despair of the lady trying to read Harriet Beecher
Stowe.

But one of the older youngsters had escaped Mina's
expert supervision and was now busily copying his face
on the copying machine, on a low table by the front
desk. Grimacing, he closed his eyes and pressed the
copy button, having pushed aside the thin yellow volume still splayed open on the machine's glass.

It was a phone book from the collection behind the
desk: our local phone book, open to the pages of M's.

M for Mapes; I called the numbers. He answered on the fourth ring.

"Wilbur, if she's out there with you, I think you'd better tell me so right this minute, or the next call I make will be to Bob Arnold."

"Huh? Dunno what you're talkin' about. Who's out here?" But he sounded nervous.

"Wilbur, I mean it, you—"

He hung up. So I did call Bob, but the town dispatcher said there'd been a development in the arson case, and Bob was busy arresting a firebug—her tone implying there would be a parade later to celebrate the occasion—and did I want to leave a message or call back?

"What?" Ellie wanted to know, seeing my face.

"They got the firebug. Anonymous tip," I whispered. To the dispatcher: "Tell him I'm on my way to Wilbur Mapes's place and I need him to meet me," I said. "As soon as he can."

But when I'd broken the connection, I had second thoughts. "I couldn't tell if she's really out at Mapes's place or not," I said. "We'd better check around here before we go hightailing it out there, or we might miss her."

Which turned out to be a good idea, just not quite the way I expected. Charmian wasn't anywhere in town, but down at the breakwater we spotted Winston Cartwright, having a hot dog outside the small red snack stand called Rosie's, by the Quonset warehouses.

"Have you seen Charmian?" I confronted the big man.

Sharp eyes peered from under the disreputable slouch hat. At my words he tossed the hot dog into the trash abruptly, his jowly face creasing with concern. "No. What's happened?"

"I'll get the car," Ellie said.

"She found a map, we think, in Jane Whitelaw's old diary." I tried to summarize for him as quickly as possible. "Raines got it from Mapes, hid it in the library. Charmian found it there."

"And you think she might be trying to follow it."

"Yes. A map Hayes gave to Jane Whitelaw because he wanted Jane to love him. So he trusted her with it."

I took a deep breath. "It *might* be a copy of another map, an unreadable one. It could be, Jane's copy survived but the original didn't."

Saying this, I realized what was bothering me: if Raines knew the map was there—and why else hide the book?—why hadn't he simply taken it and used it himself?

"Anyway, we think she might be in trouble," I finished.

It was as slippery and treacherous a progression of thought as Eliza crossing the ice floes in Harriet Beecher Stowe's old story, but Cartwright followed it without any difficulty and looked horrified.

"She doesn't have a car," I added. "She called Mapes. Then someone, maybe Mapes, must've come and picked her up."

"Oh, dear God. Charmian, if anything happens to her . . ."

He seized my shoulder with his large, surprisingly strong right hand. "What are we waiting for? We've got to find her."

My thought exactly, but as Ellie pulled up and we piled into the car, I had an instant to wonder: just what was behind Winston Cartwright's sudden anxiety? Concern for his niece, or . . .

He caught my unspoken drift. "You're still wondering about my motives," he said heavily from the back seat as Ellie sped out Route 190. "The evil old uncle from the city, here to thwart his young relative's plans."

He didn't sound evil now. The contrary, in fact. "Why don't you tell me about it?" I said. "Maybe if I heard your side of the story . . ."

"I've tried my best," he said, as if trying to reassure himself more than persuade me. "Two lively little girls dropped on my doorstep. I was," he pleaded, "a scholarly, solitary man immersed in books and antiquities."

Right. And in twisting the collective earlobe of the art world's criminal scene to get at its secrets. But that all seemed far away now.

He sighed. "There were toys, tiny items of clothing, a trail of crayons and dolls all through my bachelor rooms. Dolls that *squawked*," he recalled.

I remembered it well, from Sam. But I wasn't interested in a tale of Cartwright's old domestic travails. It was current events I wanted some accurate reporting on, and fast.

"Winston, are you and Charmian in on some plot to find a long-lost Stradivarius and steal it away from here? Either with Jonathan Raines or in competition with him? Is that why Charmian's painted you as such an ogre, just as a smoke screen? But now maybe she's turned the tables on you?"

It could account for his shock at discovering she'd gone off without him. But when I turned to face him, the worry and grief in his eyes remained real.

And the regret. "No," he said gently. "Charmian hates me and it's all my fault. I wanted to save her from that foolish young adventurer Jonathan Raines. Like me, in my youth, always haring off after a new treasure. When my real treasure was right there at home."

I must have looked mystified. Meanwhile, Ellie drove as fast as she dared, slowing only for the speed trap at Pleasant Point.

"My wife," he explained. "She was ill—I didn't realize how ill. At the time, I'd located an ancient manuscript in Rome. It doesn't matter what," he added. "It wasn't worth the trip. She'd begged me not to go, but I told her I'd be back soon. It's what I always said when I left her. Only this time . . ."

His voice threatened to break. "She died. I broke my wife's heart, and she died before I could come back and make amends."

We crossed Route 1 and jogged onto the narrow two-lane that wound between widely spaced farmhouses, trees, and fields.

"What about the bet? Charmian says you were holding her to some silly wager, making her work for you instead of going off on her own with Raines. Holding her sister hostage."

He shook his head impatiently. "Charmian took it seriously. It was she who was holding herself to the wager, not me. A sense of honor I foolishly inculcated in her . . . but I'd have never held her to it myself."

He took a sorrowful breath and continued. "I didn't want what happened to my wife to happen to Charmian. So I opposed her romance with Raines. He'd do the same as I had, I knew. He's got the bug, it's in his blood, I saw it as I'd seen it in myself."

We passed the rusting railroad trestle, the salt marshes, and the grange hall, its white paint peeling gently in the sun. "And once a man's infected with the desire to find old things . . ."

Cartwright sighed miserably again. "Oh, I'm a fool."

"We'll find her, Winston," Ellie said quietly. She gunned the car onto the dirt part of the road, the car jouncing on the washboard surface littered with stones.

A partridge poked its head from the underbrush, cocked its beady eye. Overhead, a brown hawk circled serenely, riding the thermals rising from the warm, dry land. "We'll find her before anything bad can happen to her."

But the truth was, none of us was certain of that outcome.

Not at all. "So you wouldn't have destroyed a Strad if you found one, to save what remains of a professional reputation that is, according to Charmian, already badly fading?" I asked.

At this, his laugh was genuine. "Oh, my. That's what she's told you? No wonder she thinks I killed Raines. Encouraged that poor young vegetable-eater off the end of a dock to save people's good *opinion* of me? Oh, heavens."

Our eyes met, and in that moment I genuinely liked Winston Cartwright. He was a large, wheezy, gouty, opinionated old man, but with a steely will and a lot of good, old-fashioned spinal cord, not to mention the kind of wiliness it took to beat the professional art-world tricksters at their own game.

He had what George Valentine would have called gumption. But I couldn't help realizing, too, that I had no proof of the story he was telling. And he *had* tricked plenty of art-world criminals, to get their loot.

Which meant he could still be tricking me.

"My reputation," he said dryly, "is rather more secure than my dear Charmian understands. Not all one's exploits receive the sort of publicity that most academics secretly crave, you see. My days of *wanting* any reputation are rather ancient history."

Of course; getting your face all over the magazines, or even your name in professional journals read by others in the trade, could get in the way of achieving similar success in the future, in the kidding-the-kidders department. But I wasn't ready to let our large friend off the hook quite yet.

"How much farther?" he asked anxiously as we rounded a curve.

I fastened on the remark. "You ought to know. You must have been there." At which he looked taken aback.

"Charmian was quite certain he'd had dealings with you," I persisted.

"Indeed. By mail and phone. There was never any need to meet him personally." Understanding dawned on his face. "But you still think . . ."

I'd had enough. "Look, there's a very valuable object around here somewhere—or everybody seems to think there is, anyway—and you're a prime candidate for wanting to find it. Give me one reason why you're not as much a suspect as anyone else."

"Because it's not. Here, I mean. A Stradivarius violin—I'd wish it as much as anyone, but . . ." He made an impatient sound. "Can't you people get it through your heads? The odds against it are fantastic. Even if it once was here, time takes *everything*, my friends. Especially things made of organic materials like wood and glue. And," he finished resignedly, "us, sooner or later."

It was just what Lillian had said, and it still made sense, so I didn't bother arguing with him. We rode on in silence until we reached Mapes's trailer. Getting out, Cartwright gazed around in the unusual stillness: no dog barking, no angry thumping footsteps on the trailer porch. Nothing but sky and the wind moving distantly in the lines of trees at the far end of the clearing.

No Charmian. And no other car but ours, pulled up alongside Mapes's old pickup truck. I put my hand on the hood; it was cold.

"Look at this," Ellie said. "Looks like Wilbur was getting ready to head for the hills for a while."

Two big cardboard boxes of groceries sat in the truck bed: canned soups, packets of noodles, sacks of trail mix. Cooking implements, too, and jugs of water and a box of kitchen matches. Something pinged my memory as I surveyed the collection, but then Cartwright was shouting.

"Here, over here! Good heavens . . . where's Charmian? Tell me, man, what have you done with her?"

The dog crept from under the pickup truck, the fight gone out of him as he blinked nervously at me, then slunk forward as if to shove his big head under my hand.

"Okay, boy." He wasn't hurt, but something had scared him very badly. He padded alongside me, tail tucked, ready to bolt.

By the trailer full of Wilbur's hunting trophies and antique furniture, we found the reason why: Wilbur himself, bleeding onto a pile of cardboard.

"Someone shot me," he muttered, his eyes focusing on us with an effort.

"Who shot you?" Winston Cartwright demanded, but Mapes wasn't listening. Ellie ran for the trailer to call help.

"Damned fiddle," Mapes whispered, wincing in pain. The shot had gone through his shoulder, and he was losing a lot of blood.

"They're coming," Ellie called as she came back out of the trailer. "The ambulance is on its way."

"Don't talk now, young fellow. Save your energy," Cartwright said.

But Mapes shook his head. "Gotta keep myself awake. Couldn't find it until that Raines guy came around, talkin' about a lady who went over the bluffs. Long time ago."

Jane Whitelaw. The dog pushed forward and shoved his muzzle under Wilbur Mapes's hand and whimpered.

"Killer," Mapes said, smiling weakly. "Hey, boy."

The dog wriggled happily. "You mean you couldn't find the map? Did *Raines* mention a map to you?" I asked.

"Ayuh. Got it from me, trunk of stuff I sent him. Only he didn't *understand*. . . ."

A spasm of pain made his face twist. "And he wouldn't *show* me. Said I'd only get m'self in trouble with it. So I've been lookin' some underwater. . . ."

"What, boy? What've you been looking for?" Cartwright asked urgently.

"*Caves,*" Mapes breathed harshly. "Below the bluffs. From the story Raines told, I think the lady must've went in a . . ."

"When Wilbur here was young and foolish he used to ship marijuana from Eastport," I said. "But he'd have needed a place to store his shipments by the water where no one would notice."

Ellie looked enlightened. "In a cave, below the bluffs at North End. If he timed the tide right, they'd stay dry until . . ."

"Yep. Get 'em before the tide came in. The rest of the time the cave would be underwater."

"Is he trying to say he thinks the violin you've all been fixated on is in a *cave*?" Cartwright looked horrified at the idea. "Well, then, of course it couldn't have . . ."

Survived, he was about to say, but he didn't have to. He bent to Mapes again. "But Charmian, where is Charmian?"

Mapes shook his head painfully. In the distance, the howl of an ambulance siren was getting louder.

"Wilbur, have you told anyone else?" I asked. He was fading. "About the map, or the searching you've been doing on your own?"

Hecky Wilmot, for instance, with his eye for the main chance and his desperate need for money, so he could get out of Eastport before he became persona non grata on account of his new book. Or Howard Washburn, with his prison buddies and his habit of saying the wrong things to the wrong people.

Or all three of them together, like some ramshackle version of the Three Musketeers, although when I pictured them what came to mind was more like Curly, Moe, and Larry.

I wanted to know how the hell Mapes had gotten hold of the Wellington boots, too, and where they were now. But Mapes didn't look as if he were in any shape to be playing twenty questions.

And it was a cinch he hadn't shot himself. For one thing, no weapon was anywhere in evidence.

"Mapes! Dammit, man," Cartwright said, but Mapes had passed out. The ambulance pulled up the drive, causing the hairs on the dog's neck to bristle aggressively.

I shook Wilbur hard. "But Charmian called you. What did she want?"

He was nearly out cold. "Phone number," he whispered.

"Wilbur, *whose* number?"

But then he was gone completely, his breath coming in rough hitching motions that I didn't like the looks of. A scary growl came from the dog beside me as the EMTs approached.

"Killer," I said quietly, and the animal relaxed; the key, apparently, was knowing his name. "Come on, Killer, let's go inside and have a biscuit."

His ears perked and he followed me up the steps amiably, to the obvious relief of the ambulance guys, as Ellie began telling them what little we knew about Wilbur's injury. From inside I watched them load Mapes onto a gurney; they had an IV started and an oxygen mask clapped to his face as they slid him into the rear of their vehicle and backed out fast.

And then he was gone, leaving us all with a question: whose phone number? I tried thinking fast, which was, as usual, a nearly impossible stretch for me, but this time I managed it.

"Someone must've picked her up in town the way we first thought. That car she rented is still over at Havelock's garage waiting for a part. And we don't know Wilbur's the *only* one she called. Probably she's with whoever she called *after* she talked to Wilbur."

But that was as far as I got. It was Ellie who came up with the rest. "Lillian," she said flatly. "Wilbur's sister."

Lillian Frey was smart, feisty; a winner, I thought, despite her current difficulties with Jill and her ex-husband. I liked her and I thought she already had enough trouble.

I didn't want her to be involved in this. "She knows about violins," Ellie pressed. "Charmian's been seeing her."

And she kept a gun; something I hadn't mentioned to Ellie. But now Wilbur had a gunshot wound, didn't he? He hadn't had the chance to get to one of his own weapons, apparently.

Meanwhile, Lillian also had a good reason for an unlisted phone number: her ex-husband.

So Charmian might've needed to call Wilbur to get it.

"Okay," I gave in, "we'd better find Lillian."

Hurriedly, I put some food down for the dog from a sack Wilbur kept under the sink, and fresh water. The eyes of Wilbur's hunting trophies seemed to follow me as I moved.

"We're going to have to come out here, you know, and walk this animal twice a . . . Hey, where's he going?"

The dog had inhaled the food in a gulp and whirled, bolting for the door and dashing away down the grassy path leading from the back of the clearing, in its haste nearly bowling Cartwright over from behind. He'd been stomping around the clearing peering keenly at everything, but now he, too, was headed down the path that went into the pasture and brush land out back.

"Mr. Cartwright! Winston!" His only reply was an impatient wave of the carved walking stick.

"We can't wait for him," Ellie said. "I don't think Charmian knows what she's gotten herself into. Somebody's not kidding, and whoever it is hasn't got the nice manners she grew up with. Or at least," she added frowningly, "whoever shot Wilbur hasn't."

So we piled back into the car; we'd have to return anyway to care for the animal, and we could pick Cartwright up then. From the supplies in Mapes's truck, it was clear that at least the old man wouldn't starve, assuming he liked saltines and mushroom soup.

"We need to go to your house," Ellie said as we approached Route 1.

"Why? Lillian's house is—"

She shook her head emphatically. "We still don't know for sure it was Lillian. And if it was, we don't know they went to Lillian's house. In fact, that's the last place they'd be if Lillian's up to something. Also, there's something else going on, because why would she shoot Wilbur? He's her brother, for Pete's sake."

I'd heard of people who would kill their own relatives for money, or for things that were worth money. In fact, back in the city I'd worked for quite a few of them.

But I still couldn't believe that Lillian was one of them. I nodded, driving and listening.

"And Mapes said Raines already had Jane's diary with the map in it, before he ever opened up your wall. And *that* means . . ."

Right, it had bothered me when he said it. Why did

he tear down all that plaster if he already had what he wanted?

Ellie spread her hands in a this-is-simple gesture. "Raines didn't find that invisible-ink book in your dining room wall. He put it there himself."

The simple obviousness of this hit me like a hammer smashing through old plaster.

"Oh, my God. He put it there for us to find, didn't he? The same way he hid the other one in the library. Because he'd heard we were a couple of snoopy types. Thought we would have success where he couldn't, so . . ."

Clues, he'd left us clues. "But Ellie, we can't read that one, and he'd have known it. We've already tried."

There was something else we were missing, too, something important, but I just couldn't put my finger on it.

Ellie nodded firmly. "Right. But maybe we *can*. I've been thinking about that, because of the Fourth of July quilt."

Any minute now, I was just going to lose my mind completely. "Ellie, what's a quilt got to do with "

She talked over me. "Remember how I said the quilting is in two colors, the stitching, I mean, and you can't see the pattern until both colors of it are done?"

I nearly stalled the engine. "Ellie, that's it." We rushed back to town, slowing only at Pleasant Point, and pulled into my driveway, then ran for the house.

"Because it just makes sense," Ellie said as we laid the map out on the kitchen table: the invisible ink map from the book we found in the wall. "Doesn't it? That a man who writes in Latin *and* further disguises his writing by other means, like invisible ink, might have a few *more* tricks up his sleeve, too."

From the refrigerator she pulled the remains of the cabbage water Raines had stored there after making his cabbage rolls. A few minutes later we had our answer: a pattern. But just as in Ellie's quilt, you had to have all of it to see what it was.

"Two," Ellie said, "*different* invisible inks."

With heat *and* chemicals, the whole thing had come clear. But it still wasn't an easy read. "It's a map, all right. But I don't see—"

Just then Wade came in, his work satchel over his shoulder and his face full of the cheerful know ledge that he had the rest of the day off. "What's up?"

I explained the situation. "We can't just start looking in caves randomly," I said. "There are too many of them."

As I finished, Sam slammed in, too, his face like seven days of rain. "She stood me up. I waited *hours* for her."

"Jill?" But of course it was Jill. "Sam, I'm really sorry."

The words *I told you so* wanted to come out of my mouth. I clamped my teeth down on them.

"Something very important must have come up," I said instead. "I'm sure she'll have an explanation."

He studied the floor. "I guess so."

"Oh," Wade said as he turned the map sideways. "I see. The brown lines are north-south. The purplish lines"—they were the ones we'd revealed by spraying the map with cabbage water—"are east-west. Which makes this . . . Okay, I get it now. The shoreline from the ferry landing out to Dog Island."

Ellie and I looked at each other. Dog Island was the northeasterly dot of land just off North End. "Where the caves are."

"Yeah," Wade said, unsurprised. "Although they're probably some different now. A hundred and fifty years," he explained, "of wind and tides working on that cliff. You've got to figure you're going to get some erosion."

Then he frowned. "But I don't see any specific place marked. Anyway, you're not going to try going *in* those caves, are you? Because it's almost high tide. You want to wait till the tide's ebbing, then maybe—"

"We can't wait," I said, hearing my own words as if from a far distance. Because suddenly it was all coming together for me like the pieces of Ellie's quilt: different shapes and colors.

But just one pattern. "They're down there. Charmian and Lillian . . ." I grabbed up the map, now so murderously legible, newly deciphered but telling the same old deadly story: love and money. "We're just going to have to try to find them without this."

"I know those places," Sam said, already gathering his diving gear. "They'll both drown."

"Sam." Wade was hauling rope and the first-aid kit down from the hall shelf. "You told me you weren't cave diving."

Sam met my gaze. "Yeah. I did. But I've been out there. Jill wanted to go. I'm sorry, Mom."

"We'll talk it over later," I said, and he went out, lugging his equipment.

"Come on." Wade touched my shoulder, the map in his hand. "Ellie, call George and let him know where we're going, okay? And then catch up with us."

She turned to the phone. I followed Wade to his truck, where Sam was waiting.

"Jared Hayes told Jane Whitelaw that he'd hidden a treasure on the island. And he gave her a map to it, too, hanging on to the invisible-ink copy for himself."

On Water Street we made our way past the storefronts, among strolling groups of tourists, past the fish pier and the Quonset warehouses of the freight dock. Wade aimed the truck toward North End; I glimpsed the yellow buoys of the sailboat race course bobbing on the bay. Finally we reached a stand of white birches marking the beginnings of the wide, grassy bluffs.

"*Why* did Hayes give Jane Whitelaw a map?" Wade wanted to know, pulling the truck to the side of the road. Over the water, drifts of seagulls circled. Waves boomed distantly, a constant bass note that seemed to come from everywhere.

"Because she wanted it and he loved her, I suppose. But that was his mistake. She double-crossed him. And I think I understand what must have happened next."

We got out. There was no sign of anyone on the bluffs, but something glittered in the sand by the pavement.

"Charmian's ring." The blue stone shimmered at me, its milky iridescence cold and somehow malevolent, like a dead eye. I imagined her dropping it, hoping someone might find it.

Holding it, I squinted around. "Where's Lillian's car? They had to've come in one. Pulled back into the birch stand, maybe?"

But the tide was running fast, the turbulence of the massive whirlpools far out in the channel testifying to its power. And chances were good that wherever Lillian's car was hidden, they weren't sitting in it having a pleasant chat.

We could find it later. A path led to the cliffs, through weeds and tall grass. "*What* must have happened?" Wade prompted me as we sprinted along it.

"The old stories are wrong. Hayes didn't die the day after Jane. He died the day before, the way Hecky Wilmot says. She was a pirate's child, remember. With pirate instincts."

We peered over the cliffs. Most of the edge was precipitous, yet studded with trees growing precariously from the soil formed by the crumbling shale. Here the drop was straight down to where the water moved massively far below.

"This is where that other fellow went off," Wade said, his tone grim, and the strangeness of that event struck me again, too. It was an odd place to try scrambling down for a snapshot, if that was what he'd been doing. But we had no time to ponder it.

"Over here." Through the trees that clung to the cliffside I could see a steep, slanting sort of trail. The stones and twigs on it were freshly disturbed.

"Jane killed Hayes, or had him killed, *because* he'd given her the map. So she didn't need him anymore."

"And because he'd betrayed her father, the pirate Josephus?" Wade reached a hand up, steadied me as I made my way down.

"No. They did that together. She planned it all, Wade. She meant to be the last one standing, and have the money Hayes stole for herself. After she'd got rid of Hayes, though . . . *Oof*."

I grabbed a protruding tree root, caught my breath as loose shale slid out from under my shoe.

"After that," I went on when I'd reached the bottom, "she had Hayes's body dumped at Pirate's Cove, where Josephus's ship had been burned to the waterline by the townspeople after he was hanged. It's how the skull ended up there."

A wave crashed onto the wet rocks protruding from the water, boomed in an explosion of spray, and fell back for another onslaught.

"Probably," I finished, "it was a kind of joke to her. The pirate wanna-be buried with a pirate ship. God, how she must have despised him with his fake respectability, his pretensions to education. Everything she didn't have and wanted so badly."

"What about his head?" Wade swung down expertly. "You think Jane's boyfriends actually cut it off?"

Here at the foot of the cliffs with the water pounding, the waves hurtling in, and the gulls crying, the world of streets and houses seemed like a distant country. "The ocean did that. Two hundred years and a lot of water . . . the rest of the bones probably just washed out to sea."

I gazed around at the wild landscape. "But the skull rolled into a backwater, got covered up with peat and silt, and it just stayed there."

No other human beings were in sight. The footing down here at the water's edge was treacherous, slippery rocks shifting as we tried stepping on them. We covered as much of the narrowing shoreline as we could, but it was useless. There were dozens of openings, no way to tell which ones led to caves or had anyone inside.

Wade shouted inaudibly, his voice swallowed by the pounding of the rising tide, then shook his head and pointed up. It wasn't as difficult climbing back up the cliffs as it had been trying not to tumble going down, but the earth and rocks were unbelievably treacherous. I slid a few times and once nearly lost it entirely in a clatter of stones, before finding an outcropping I could put my whole weight on.

Finally, I hauled myself up to seize Wade's reaching hand, as he looked out toward the swirling blue channel and the islands beyond. He pulled the invisible-ink map out, scowled at it again as I peered at it with him.

"Look, it shows these cliffs," I said. "And there's the rocks we were just standing on. The entrances to some of the caves. But . . ." A stiff breeze off the water made the old paper flutter and threaten to tear; I steadied it. "But if it's a map *to* something, where's . . ."

"I still don't see anything specific. No X to mark the spot. Or if there is one, we're just not recognizing it.

Hayes could read it because he already knew what it indicated, and as far as he knew, he was the only one who
would ever need to follow it," Wade theorized.

So we were stonewalled. Meanwhile, Sam had been
pulling on his drysuit, checking his tanks and regulators. But there was nowhere for him to dive. The idea of
checking every possible cave remained ridiculous, as he
had already concluded.

"If they're in there, they're trapped," he said. "Tide's
so high, it's filling the entrances to the caves. Even if
there are pockets of air inside, they won't last. Hear it?"

I hadn't. But now I realized: the booming sound of
the waves was coming not only from the foot of the
cliffs, but from the earth beneath my feet, the water
hammering inside the rock that was the foundation for
this whole end of the island. Filling the caves, making a
drum of the earth itself as it pounded with the force of
billions of gallons of icy water.

The sound of an engine made me look up.

Ellie arriving, I thought.

But it wasn't.

Instead, it was the important thing that we'd been
missing.

It was Jonathan Raines, highballing toward
us in Mapes's old pickup truck, with Winston
Cartwright riding a massive shotgun and
Ellie clinging in the truck bed, her red hair
flying.

The truck skidded to a halt and Raines jumped out. I
didn't know whether to kiss him or kick him.

Kick him, I decided. "You faked it," I said. "You faked

your own murder and left us this mess to try to sort out. You lying, sneaking, dirty rotten little son of a—"

"Right. I apologize." He gazed around urgently. "But I'll do my penance later, if you don't mind. Where are they?"

Ellie leapt from the truck bed. "Bob Arnold's gone out to Lillian's place, see if he can find out anything there," she said as Cartwright lumbered down from the passenger seat.

The old man leaned hard on the carved cane, anxiety etched on his face. "Winston, what the hell is going on?" I demanded.

He waved at Raines. "He intended for Charmian to have a change of heart at the news of his death," Cartwright said. "*And* to spur you two to further detective efforts. Mapes was hiding him, in hopes of learning more about that blasted map. But—"

"I think Charmian and Lillian Frey are down there. No sign of them now, though," I told him. "I don't know what more to do or where to look. And the caves . . ."

His sharp eyes took in the situation. "The tide," he uttered gravely. "Oh, dear God in heaven."

But Raines didn't pause for praying any more than he had for penance. Instead, he pulled a much-folded sheet of paper from his pants pocket.

"Sam," he said crisply, "look at this. Do you think you can find this opening?" He pointed at a spot on the paper.

"Where did you get . . ." I began, then stopped as it hit me. He'd made his *own* copy of the map he'd found in Jane's diary, of course. The one that had been so legible, it had sent Charmian out to try following it at once.

"Wait a minute," I started again. "Sam's not going to . . ."

Sam just looked at me, and all at once I noticed how tall he was: as tall as Wade. Bigger through the shoulders, actually. And while I wasn't looking, something had happened to his face.

That jutting jawline, the shadow along it because he hadn't shaved. And the eyes, so calm and confident. Much more than mine had been when at that same age I had married his father.

"Oh," I said, and the hint of a smile creased the corner of Sam's mouth; he bent back to the paper Raines was showing him.

"Right here," he said seriously. "Yeah, I can do it."

I turned to Cartwright. "But how did you know? That Raines was alive, I mean."

He snorted disparagingly. "Mapes is a hunter. Guns, antlers, trophies. But the box of food and supplies in his truck consisted entirely of vegetables."

Cartwright's voice was a low rumble as he watched Raines and Sam. "Thus I concluded the supplies were not meant for Mapes."

"You remembered Raines is vegetarian," I said. "Brilliant."

He shook his head sadly, removed the disreputable slouch hat to gaze at it before resettling it. "Not quite brilliant enough, apparently."

He caught his breath as Sam disappeared over the edge of the bluffs. Wade went down behind him, carrying the coil of line that Sam would use in case it was murky or he lost his bearings. The very idea made me want to hunker down on the grass and cover my eyes.

"I still don't understand why Lillian Frey thinks she'll find the Strad down there." I waved at the water. "She's the one who first told me it couldn't survive the elements, and surely Hayes would've realized that, too. I mean, I'd say a flooded cave is a pretty harsh—"

But here I stopped, as my tactless musing brought a look of anguish to the old man's face. After that, we waited for twenty long minutes until Sam reappeared over the edge of the bluffs. Even from this distance I could tell his search hadn't been successful. The target cave, the one marked on Raines's copy of the map, was empty.

"I went all the way back," he said as we gathered around him. "Nothing. But you know, once you get in there it's not what the map shows."

He peered again at Raines's tracing of the sheet from Jane Whitelaw's diary. "See, you start here, but when you get here . . ."

His finger moved along a line Raines had marked. Watching, Winston Cartwright paled. Then he understood, too.

"Idiot!" he bellowed, clapping a massive hand to his forehead. "Oh, I am a foolish old— Give me that."

He lumbered hastily to Raines and Sam, snatched the copy of the map from Sam's hand, scowled blackly at it. "Oh, of course, any *infant* could surely predict that . . ."

"What?" Raines demanded, as Cartwright took the map Wade had been carrying and held the two maps up side by side: the invisible-ink map from my dining room wall, and the tracing Raines had made of Jane Whitelaw's map, the one from her diary.

And finally, finally, I understood what must have happened: two books. Two maps. One for Hayes, one for Jane.

Different maps. "Compare," he demanded. "Here, and here. You see?" He looked triumphantly at us. "The maps don't match. Hayes gave Jane Whitelaw a map, all right. But it was a fake."

"Of course," Ellie breathed. "He didn't trust her."

"He wanted to appease her, and he loved her. So . . ." I tried picturing it: the beautiful woman he adored, his growing sense of something amiss, perhaps. He just didn't know how amiss.

"Oh, Lord." Cartwright's voice was despairing as he examined the map we now believed to be the true one: the one Hayes kept for himself. "Haven't any of you any classical learning at *all*?"

We shook our heads. "Greek to me," Sam said as a joke, but shut up as Cartwright glowered at him.

"What does this word say?" he demanded, shoving the frayed sheet of old paper under my nose.

"It's Latin," I said. "It says '*ex*,' which I think means out. But we don't want to get out of somewhere, we want to get . . . Oh."

"Oh," Ellie echoed comprehendingly. "Ex. And not as in FedEx, either, but as in . . ."

I clapped a hand to my head. "Ex marks the spot. Do you mean to tell me that on top of everything else, this annoying little jerk had to be a bilingual joker on his own damned *treasure map*? Oh, that's just . . ."

I stopped. They were staring at me, Cartwright in despair.

"If I'm not mistaken," he said heavily, waving at the water, "the spot this map marks is now entirely submerged."

Sam's shoulders slumped. "Yeah. I'm afraid so. When I was down there I saw the opening. Saw it from above, I mean, it's way below the surface now, this entrance."

He put a hand on the old man's massive shoulder. "I couldn't have gotten in even if I'd known it was the right one. I'm sorry, Professor. But this cave here . . . Well. It's been flooded for quite a while, now. Without air tanks, they couldn't . . ."

Cartwright looked up. His face was desolate. "Thank you, my boy. Thank you for trying to save my niece. You've been so kind."

He turned away, and we watched him walk slowly back to the pickup truck, leaning on the walking stick. When he got there, he looked at the vehicle as if he couldn't remember what it was for.

So there we were, helpless and miserable. It was over for Charmian and Lillian Frey. And there wasn't a damned thing any of us could do about it.

"That lying bastard," Ellie said vehemently, and I knew who she meant: Hayes.

"He was a fake, and a thief, and a liar. He betrayed the man who helped him. I don't care if Josephus *was* a pirate, he was a friend to Hayes. And I hope he's rotting in—"

"Look!" Sam shouted, pointing.

A hand flopped up over the edge of the cliff, scrabbled for purchase in the crumbly soil, slipped, finally found its hold. As we stared, a black-clad arm followed, then a face. Blond hair stuck in sodden wisps from a closely fitting drysuit helmet.

"Jill!" Sam ran a few steps and stopped, just as a car sped down the road at us and swung over.

Lillian Frey jumped out, her face distraught. In her own car and driving alone. Which meant that the car we were going to find backed up into that birch stand belonged to . . .

"Have you seen Jill?" Lillian demanded worriedly.

"Over there," I said.

"Thank God," Lillian said, "I've been frantic. People downtown are saying something happened to Wilbur, and . . ."

Then she caught my tone, as Jill climbed over the cliff edge and got to her feet, tugging off her headgear before she saw us all standing there.

I showed Lillian the opal. "Charmian's ring," I said.

And now here was Jill. "She's done something, hasn't she?" Lillian said.

"Yes," I said. "Yes, I'm afraid she has."

Jill decided how to play it. "Oh," she cried, "someone help! I saw Charmian fall, she's down there, somebody's got to—"

None of us moved. Jill came toward us, her face a mask of urgency. As she walked I could see her eyes flicking from one to another of us, deciding which one to manipulate.

Finally she decided. "Sam, come on, you have to—"

"Sam doesn't have to do anything, Jill," I said.

She stopped, a glimmer of uncertainty in her eyes. Then her chin jutted, her shoulders straightened, and she stalked past me; she was going to try to bull it through.

"You don't know anything," she snapped. "Sam—"

"Where is she, Jill?" Sam asked quietly.

"I *told* you, she—"

"Yeah, she fell." His tone was icy. "So instead of calling the cops or getting an ambulance, you went home and got dive gear and came out here, all on your own."

Jill stared at Sam, her face like that of an animal caught in a trap.

"I think you brought her here," Sam said.

"I didn't!" She clenched her fists as Lillian put a hand out to her. "Get away from me!"

"You know what I think? I think Charmian called your mother to tell her about her find. The original map, she thought, and it was readable!" I said. "But you answered, and she was so excited, she told you instead. That's what I think happened."

No reply from Jill.

"You've been planning something all along, haven't

you?" I went on. "Hanging around with Sam, pumping him for information. A pretty girl, and smart. You probably knew Raines was coming and why long before he even got here, from when you were staying with your uncle Wilbur. You know where Wilbur was searching, too."

She smirked at what she thought at first was a compliment, scowled resentfully as I went on.

"Too bad you take after your father, instead," I said. "Who thinks life is about expensive toys, and the money to buy them."

Something sparked in her eyes at the mention of her father, a look of sharp caution. But I didn't care about that now.

"I'll bet we find out that your mother's gun is the one that shot Wilbur, won't we?"

New knowledge creased Sam's face. "So that was why. A girl like you, wanting to hang out with me . . ."

"Oh, shut up!" she spat at him, then whirled on me. "If my moron uncle Wilbur would've just . . . None of this is my fault. I just wanted to move back with my dad," Jill insisted.

"And bring him something when you went?" I suggested.

"Yes," she hissed. "Something to make us *rich*. I *want* it. Or do you think I should stay here in this hick town, marry someone like your son? So sweet," she added venomously. "And *dumb*?"

Sam flinched once, but that was all. For an instant I wished she'd known him a few years ago: angry and strung out, crippled with dyslexia but not knowing what was wrong, hooked on anything he could get his hands on, and so afraid. Afraid that he was stupid.

Maybe she'd have liked him then, I thought, wanting to slap her. But I didn't need to. Sam had gotten over lots worse things than Jill, mostly without my help. Now he turned away, walking back toward the car where Cartwright leaned against the bumper.

The rest of us followed, leaving Jill. By now she'd begun stripping off the drysuit; Lillian got a blanket from the trunk of her car and brought it to the girl, saying nothing. Without many clothes, Jill looked more her age: young. Very young.

And scared; with the blanket around her she peered up and down the little road for some way of escaping us. But there was none. She walked as far as the pavement, picking her way in bare feet, before Wade seized her arm.

"Let *go* of me, you—" She tried to jerk away, at which Wade grasped her other arm and turned her to face him. He outweighed her by a hundred pounds, but that wasn't what stopped her.

It was the look on his face. I'd never seen it before, and you wouldn't want it aimed at you. Wade went along so peacefully most of the time, you could forget that such a look might be in there.

But of course it was; the look of a boy whose father has been beaten to death outside a bar. Anger and grief, the wanting to hurt someone, wanting to be able to undo some terrible thing that has happened and not being able to: all the fight went out of Jill at the mere sight of it. She sat down hard on the side of the road and began crying.

Wade called police dispatch on his car phone and asked them to send the ambulance; by now, it would have finished delivering Mapes to the hospital. After that he called Bob Arnold, who was returning from the mainland, filled him in, and got him to send a tow truck to take Jill's car.

And that, we all thought, was all we could do.

Until Jonathan Raines spoke: "Sam. Give me your dive gear."

"Oh, hey, you can't— Listen, it's way dangerous. You don't even know how to—"

"Sam." In that moment the shark's tooth Raines wore at his throat looked suddenly appropriate. Remembering the snapshot of him at the edge of that cliff, I knew any fears I might have had about his inexperience were groundless.

He checked the tanks and regulators while Sam watched, but didn't pull them on; the cliff was too steep for their weight.

"Lower these down for me, will you?" he said to Sam. "I'll put 'em on down there." Then Sam had another bright idea, one I thought was even worse than Raines's brainstorm.

"Your tanks down there?" he asked Jill, and she shrugged in sulky assent, not looking up at him.

The gun, probably, too, that Lillian had thought Jill didn't know about, and that I thought Jill had used to menace Charmian into doing as she was ordered: it hadn't been in Jill's hands as she came up over the cliff. By now it had likely been swept out in the torrent of tide and currents.

"Sam, don't you think you should wait for—"

"Hey, Mom, I'll be fine." He grinned briefly at me, but I could see the smile was only for show.

The set of his jaw and the toss of his head as he bent to gather the rest of Jill's gear—were all business.

Ellie saw it, too. "He looks like Victor," she said.

"Yeah. Doesn't he, though?"

"Except for the eyes. The eyes are all you." She meant well, but it wasn't true.

Like the rest of him, Sam's eyes were a mixture of traits I would never be able to sort out. Nor could I stop trying.

But I could stop taking it out on him. As he went over the cliff edge I gave him a small salute, two fingers touched to my eyebrow: *Good luck*. But I wasn't sure he saw it.

"What are the chances?" Winston Cartwright asked Wade. His voice craved reassurance, though he must have known it wasn't possible to give any honestly. "Of being alive in . . ." He angled his massive head slowly at the churning water. "In that," he finished brokenly.

Wade didn't lie to him. "I wish I could say something more optimistic to you, sir. But . . ."

Cartwright nodded. "But the tide is high, and the water is cold, and the current is swift and vicious. Jonathan's bravery is admirable. I only hope his life, and that of the boy, aren't put at risk, too."

"They are, sir." Wade shot a swift glance at me. "But Sam's a good diver, and I gather Raines has some experience?"

Cartwright laughed harshly. "More than you would believe. He is, despite his scholarly appearance, a very physical young man."

Time passed with excruciating slowness until Sam's head popped up over the side of the cliff. It was all I could do not to run over to him and fling my arms around him, gear and all. Instead I waited.

"No go. Currents are murder," Sam said when he got to us. "Raines went ahead. I tried to wave him back, but he wasn't having it, he went in a cave."

He coughed, and I realized it was worse in the water than he was letting on. "He's trying to save her," Sam finished.

Jill, silent and resentful over no longer being the focus of everyone's attention, looked up and laughed bitterly.

"Grow up. He's not saving anybody. He's finding the gold."

Cartwright's head turned slowly, and his stare made Wade's earlier look resemble a loving glance. "What do you mean?"

She tossed her blond hair carelessly, recovered a bit now, and pleased to have information that someone wanted. And a way to feel she was both superior and interesting to us again.

"That's what's down there," she replied scornfully, as if this must be obvious to all but the fools we were. "Not some old crummy violin. Mom *told* you it couldn't be. I knew it, too."

Right. Everyone knew it. And yet . . . "What's there, Jill?"

She smirked at me. "Gold. And another way out. A tunnel."

Those account books, I realized; the hidden one, especially, where Hayes had written the truth about his illicit income. And then I wondered all at once: so *much* gold. Where *had* it all gone?

"How do you know?" Cartwright's big fist tightened on the head of his walking stick; Jill caught the movement and flinched away from what it implied.

"Well," she quavered, then regained her confidence, secure in her belief that we wouldn't let an old man beat her to death, although in this by now she was only barely correct.

"I found a piece of it. A big gold coin, when I was diving here with Sam. But of course I didn't show *him*," she added with a scathing twist.

Sam's face remained impassive. "And just now?" I prodded. "More when you were down there with Charmian? Or is this all just another lie, something to keep us fascinated?" I turned away.

"No!" As I'd expected, she reacted swiftly to the

threat of being ignored again. "I could prove it, I'd show it to you, but I gave it . . ."

And there it was, the lie within the lie. Her mouth snapped shut as she realized what she'd nearly said. More tiny pieces of the puzzle fell into place for me, like the glass bits at the end of a kaleidoscope.

"A friend," she finished weakly.

"No," I said. "Not to a friend. You haven't any of those."

Mapes would live, unless I missed my guess; there'd been a lot of blood, but the ambulance fellows hadn't looked desperate. They'd known what to do, and Victor had assembled a crack team of trauma experts at his medical facility.

So Jill wouldn't be guilty of murder in the shooting attack on her uncle Wilbur, assuming it could even be proved without a gun.

The ambulance still wasn't here, or Bob Arnold, either. I wished they would come. I wanted to be away, back in my own house with its familiar haunts.

"Anyway, he can't save the girl *and* grab the gold, can he?" Jill's tone was smug now.

Raines, she meant. "And that tunnel goes a long way," she went on, "probably all the way to the other side of the island."

She shuddered. "When you get way in there, it goes uphill, and then it's all red ants and spiders, crawly roots hanging down. Ugh."

Wade nodded minutely. It was what he'd been telling me about the caves earlier: that they were supposed to go, some of them, for miles. Although until now, no one had believed it, because no one had been foolish enough to try following them wherever they led. Or to where they ended in a flood of icy water, down there in the dark.

Cartwright's face darkened further. "That young

blackguard," he began. But just then Bob Arnold screamed up in the squad car and skidded to a halt in the sand by the side of the road.

We told him what had happened. "His air's run out by now," Sam added glumly, meaning Raines.

The ambulance pulled to a halt behind Bob's car and the fellows got out of it, looking around for someone to rescue but not finding anyone. Bob waved at them to wait.

"Let's just have a look-see," he said in the patient tones that meant he was on the very edge of losing his temper, which if he did we were all going to be very, *very* sorry, indeed. He went to the edge, and we followed him.

But there was nothing at the foot of the cliffs but water and rocks, their bare top surfaces sloshed over with foam. We all looked hard, too, praying to see something: an arm, a face, some hint that someone might be recovered out of this disaster.

There wasn't any. "Better get the Coast Guard out, tell 'em we're looking for bodies again," Bob Arnold said reluctantly. "Divers need to check inside the caves again, too, far as they can go, see if there are any remains caught up in the entries."

Wade headed back toward his truck. I took a deep, sorrowful breath, looking out over the water on a bright summer day with the seagulls circling and the white clouds floating carelessly.

Jill hunkered on the pavement, her lips a tight, thin line of sullen resentment. "I don't see why you think all this is *my* fault," she said injuredly to no one in particular.

"Okey-dokey," Bob sighed, and trudged on over to collect his prisoner as the rest of us made our way to our own vehicles.

At the car, Winston Cartwright gazed sadly at

Charmian's opal ring. "If I'd let her marry him, she'd be alive now," he said.

Lillian came over, too, looking beaten. "Jacobia, I just want to say I don't hold any ill feeling on account of—"

Jill turned as Bob Arnold was putting her in the squad car. "Say so long to your dad for me, Sam," she called. "Tell him I'll miss him." Her eyes glittered with this last malicious thrust.

Damn you, I thought, knowing suddenly what she meant. What she must mean, because in spite of it all she was a pretty girl. And a pretty girl is like a melody, I thought with bleak sorrow.

A melody to the same old song. I didn't look at Sam.

"Get in," Bob Arnold told Jill, holding the squad door open. "Watch your head." Through the cage that divided the car front from rear, I could see her face: even more frightened now. Beginning to wonder if she would get out of this at all.

Then they were gone. Wade and I looked at each other across the pickup hood. The whole thing just felt so unbelievably not possible, everything gone so hideously wrong, so fast. Not until we'd actually gotten into the truck and were preparing to drive away did one of the ambulance guys come over and peer in at us.

"Folks?" he said in tones of puzzlement. "You sure we're all done here? Because . . ." He waved toward the cliff edge.

"Yeah," I began dully. "We're done." And then I saw a figure staggering toward us across the bluffs. It was Jonathan Raines. And with him was . . .

A great bellow of joy erupted from Winston Cartwright.

"Charmian!" He stumped as fast as he could across

the bluffland, practically pole-vaulting with the walking
stick over scrub brush and stones.

"Well, I'll be damned," Wade said.

"I guess there was a kind of treasure out there after
all," I said, gazing through the pickup's windshield.

Out on the bluffs, the three adventurers laughed and
hugged one another, Charmian drenched and tottery
but apparently none the worse for wear, and Raines—

Raines allowed Cartwright to seize him in a bear hug
and clap him on the shoulder, but his attention was
only for Charmian.

Slowly, he reached out and took the opal ring the aging man still clutched and put it back onto Charmian's
finger. She smiled up at him with a look suggesting that
he could save her out of a drowned cave any old time he
wanted. Then she kissed him.

It was a long, lingering kiss, framed by the bright
water. "I think Jonathan has recovered the only treasure
he really cares about," I said, and Wade nodded, drawing me toward him.

"You know," he allowed, laying his cheek which was
prickly with stubble against my hair, "you might be right."

10 "If she'd let me carry her," Raines groused
affectionately, "it would have been a whole
lot faster."

"In your dreams," Charmian retorted,
mussing his hair. "The day I need rescuing like some
helpless damsel in a fairy tale, do me a favor and just
leave me in the water, all right?"

"In the future," Winston Cartwright advised Raines

severely, "please just make up the quarrel in person instead of faking your death. I'm an old man, I can't take much more of this."

Because that, of course, was what Raines had done: jumped off the dock with the fishhook already stuck into his jacket, wearing neither it nor the boots we'd seen out at Wilbur Mapes's. He'd put the platform there earlier and left a fishing rod on it, too, all to further the notion that he'd drowned, not accidentally, to spur Ellie and me to further investigation.

Then he'd made his way out to Mapes's trailer and waited. It was Raines, too, that Wade and I had seen under the dock, taking advantage of the tide just as we had.

"It was the fishing rod, wasn't it?" I said. "That you had to get back before we found it."

He nodded wryly. "Right. I got to Mapes's place, looked at the stuff he's got, and realized nobody from around here goes fishing with an Orvis graphite. Borrowed Mapes's dive gear, then I saw the rod and platform go into the water and thought you'd taken care of it all for me," he added to Wade. "One minute you'd nearly caught me, and the next I thought my troubles were over."

"You wish," Charmian said. "From now on, to prevent these little errors, I insist on being a part of all your plans."

I doubted she'd get much argument over that.

"Did you really crawl to the other side of the island?" Maggie Altvater wanted to know.

She, it turned out, had not gone to Boston at all. Instead she'd gone to Bangor, done some shopping, had her hair cut, eaten three different varieties of ethnic food—Chinese, Mexican, and rathskeller-style German—and seen three first-run movies one after another. And when Sam asked her if she'd been lonely doing all that by herself, she said cheerfully that no, she'd been too busy.

Returning, she'd taken over my house with calm efficiency, having walked Monday, bought groceries, and put a fire in the outdoor grill, covering the big old wooden picnic table with the summer tablecloth: red and white with a pattern of sailboats.

Now she regarded Charmian Cartwright in much the same way as, I imagine, little children regard their favorite action heroes. "But you went in. Spiders," she went on, "and red ants, and all?"

"Red ants and all," Charmian confirmed. "Fortunately, I had a sprayer of mosquito repellent in my pocket. I assumed," she added to me, "that's why there's one of them in the bathroom, one in the kitchen, and another in the back hall—that people use them. And when I noticed the number of red ants on the island, I made the connection. The spray works," she added with satisfaction.

We sat on lawn chairs, sipping the beverages that Maggie had provided: iced tea with mint leaves from the garden for Ellie, me, and Sam, beers for George and Wade, wine spritzers for Jonathan and Charmian, who were toasting their engagement. In the largest chair sat Winston Cartwright, nipping at his flask of cordial.

"That's why it took me so long to find her," Jonathan said. "She was so far into the cave."

In the fire foil-wrapped potatoes baked, while on the picnic table similarly wrapped ears of corn waited. Beside them stood a platter with a whole fresh salmon on it: stuffed with onions and shellfish, garlic and lemon slices, and other delicious items; Maggie had marinated and baked it and would finish it atop the grill.

"How'd you know to do all this?" Sam asked as she tossed the salad, and she looked wise.

"You know I've got a scanner in my car, Sam," she replied patiently. "It was pretty obvious what must be going on, and there were already plenty of EMTs on the job, so they didn't need me for that. But I knew everyone would need to eat when it was over. People were going to be hungry, whichever way it went."

She set napkins out. "And," she added, a somber note coming into her voice, "if it turned out badly, people weren't going to feel like shopping or cooking. But they would still need fuel."

"Oh," he said, a new kind of assessment in his eyes as he watched her work. "Say, that's a nice outfit you're wearing."

It was, too: green canvas camp shorts, a short-sleeved white shirt, and a silver-buckled belt. On her feet were a pair of top-stitched leather tie shoes, with white rolled-down hiking socks. Altogether she looked neat and complete, her glossy honey-colored hair tied back with a green ribbon.

"Thank you," she said mildly, and brushed past him to reach the barbecue tongs. He looked a little shell-shocked, but that could have been on account of the events of the day; naturally, I didn't mention it to him.

And then, just when I thought things had finally settled down and we could eat our dinner in peace, Victor drove by in his little sports car and noticed us all out in the backyard, and included himself.

"Got something for you, Dad," Sam said, and handed over the wristwatch.

Victor glanced at me, and I'm not certain, but it might have been my clear, unspoken promise to whack him upside the head with an entire cooked salmon that zipped his lip for him.

"Well," he said. "Glad it turned up. Your . . . friend found it for me, I gather?" He put it on.

"Yeah," Sam said. "She found it."

A beat. Then: "Thanks for straightening that out for me," Victor said, and turned to accept a glass of white wine from Maggie as if nothing had happened.

It had, though, because Victor hadn't left that watch in the aft cubby of his boat. And Sam knew it, although Victor didn't seem to understand this yet.

"How's Wilbur?" I asked as Victor plopped onto the last lawn chair, leaving me standing.

But I didn't care; when he was sitting down with a drink, at least he was firmly in one place and could be better controlled.

"Not too bad, considering." Sipping his wine, he looked happily over the proceedings as if he had arranged them himself.

"Lost blood. His sister went over and donated, though, so that's all right." His face clouded. "But about the girl thing . . ."

I waited, wondering what he could possibly say, because sleeping around was one thing, but doing it with your own son's girlfriend was something else again.

Way something else. And that wristwatch of Victor's went two places: onto Victor's wrist or into the drawer of his bedside table. Nowhere else, as I knew very well and so did Sam, once Jill's parting shot—*say so long to your dad*—had made him think of it.

He frowned seriously. "I think you should pay more attention to Sam's companions. I know he's nearly grown up now, but in many ways he's an impressionable boy, and it seems to me that you could take more care over who he sees. I want you to do that."

Whereupon, of course, I did not wrap him up in aluminum foil, tuck him neatly in among the red-hot barbecue coals, and fasten down the lid of the cooker.

Instead I took a long, calming swallow from my own glass. "You're absolutely right," I said. "I am going to pay more attention, from now on, to the habits of Sam's companions."

Hearing my tone, Victor glanced alertly at me; he was, as we both understood, also one of Sam's companions.

"And when I disapprove of those habits I am going to say so. To him. Loudly and clearly, and in a great deal of very accurate, well-researched historical detail."

It may have been the threat in my voice that made Victor choke, spluttering white wine. "Now, Jacobia, I don't mean—"

I lowered my voice, kept an amiable expression on my face, and went on. "You son of a bitch. I don't care what you mean. You don't change, do you? You'll never change. You're the problem."

I aimed a finger at him. "Because where women are concerned, you're a low-life, sludge-dwelling, slime-sucking little predator, and now you've gone too far."

He opened his mouth to object, then thought better of it and writhed guiltily as I continued. "Do you know they've got a scorecard for you behind the counter down at Leighton's Variety Store, right beside the one for the Boston Red Sox?"

He looked aghast, and I finally felt I might be getting somewhere. Around here an individual's personal and professional reputation were the same, and if only to hang on to his job, he wouldn't want people thinking he was daydreaming of young ladies' anatomies while delving into patients' brains. Also, he'd lived in Eastport long enough to know that the scorecard idea was not only possible, it was likely.

"Listen, Jacobia, I didn't sleep with that girl."

"Yeah, right. Where've I heard that one before?"

"I mean it. I didn't."

Something in his voice made me look at him. "Why not?"

He slumped in the chair. "She looked old. She *acted* old. But when I got a good look at her . . ."

Unclothed, et cetera. I turned away in disgust.

". . . I knew," he finished miserably. "I'm a doctor, for God's sake. I can tell. Not her date of birth precisely, but . . ."

I understood; I'd seen her, too, out on the bluffs. And with no clothes on, she was just a skinny—scrawny, even—kid. "So," he said, "I sent her home."

I had an instant of mean glee as I imagined the moment when it dawned on him. Just the memory was shriveling him now to a cinder of shamed misery.

"She must have been furious," I said. "That's probably why she took the watch."

He shot his cuff reflexively to glance at it. "Uh-huh. She didn't think I'd tell anyone, I guess, on account of the circumstances."

But Victor loved that watch. He didn't love much, but when he did, he found a way. "Anyhow, I wanted you to know," he said.

Poor Victor. The only time he seemed really real to me anymore was when I pitied him. It's part of my karma, I guess, that I have to learn over and over again: wishing won't make it so. If I want something a certain way, I have to make it that way.

Victor, in the long run, had turned out to be a good lesson in that regard. Maybe it's why I bought an old house, too: to get another one. And maybe it's why once I knew—or thought I did—what had really happened out at North End, I couldn't let that go, either.

He got up. "Tell Sam I'll see him later." The little sports car pulled out and roared away as the aroma of grilled salmon began wafting deliciously from the fire.

And then we all had dinner. Bob Arnold and his wife Clarissa showed up; Maggie had invited them, also based on information gleaned from her scanner. With them was their year-old baby, the devastatingly handsome Thomas, googling and smiling in the way I remembered so well; why, *why* can't they stay that way?

"Can't hang around long," Clarissa said, pouring herself a glass of lemonade. "I promised that I'd help Hecky Wilmot arrange a book-signing party for tomorrow."

"Really? I thought it was going to be a lynching party."

She laughed. "It was, until the *Times* review came out. They called it a work of naive genius, said he was the Grandma Moses of historical narrative, and that Eastport was a 'gem of unspoiled Americana' that Hecky had polished."

"Yeah," George put in. "And this afternoon I had a look at the book, and you know, it's pretty darned good. Folks around town are starting to think so, too, now they've got their breath back. Got over the shock of seein' all their skeletons marched out of the closet."

Which solved all Hecky's trouble; between George Valentine's recommendation and that of the *New York Times,* I guessed his book was going to do very well, indeed, and that the Florida literary lights would have to shine on without him a while longer.

"Course, he'll complain that all the autograph-signin' is makin' his arm hurt," Bob Arnold said wisely, and we all laughed, imagining Hecky finding the dark side of a lot of royalty checks.

A short while later, while we were still eating, one of the fellows from town stopped to drop by the Johnson trolling motor I'd bought for George, and as I'd expected, George turned all pink and allowed that it would be just the ticket, up at the lake next time he wanted to drown some night crawlers.

"Thank you, Miz Tiptree," he said. No matter how I tried, I never could get him to call me Jacobia. "It's a wicked nice one."

Wicked nice; it was George's highest compliment. At which it was my turn to go all pink, and the party went on happily, except that the little motor reminded me of the day I bought it down at the Quoddy Marine Store.

And after that I remembered once more the other thing that happened that same day:

The guy who'd gone off the cliffs. As Sam had predicted, his body never had been recovered. And except for the moment when I'd seen where he went down, we'd all kind of forgotten about him.

But now I realized: we shouldn't have.

"The tunnel had a cave-in," Charmian was saying matter-of-factly, as if she were discussing a minor delay on the causeway to the island. "While I was in it, actually. Sand and centipedes, a few other critters."

I, by that point, would have been hysterical. "So I had to stop," she finished.

"Let me get this straight." Bob Arnold had Thomas seated on his lap and was feeding him bits of salmon with his fingers while Clarissa looked on dotingly.

"You got down there when the girl forced you. Why didn't you come up the same way, over the cliffs where you went down?" Bob wanted to know.

Charmian shrugged, swallowed some corn, which was fresh, hot, and dripping with butter. "The whole edge of it is sliding. But of course you all knew that. I'm surprised Jill got back up it, herself, and after she'd kicked all the rocks and whatnot loose, we certainly weren't going to try it."

She glanced happily at Jonathan. "We like our cliff edges a little more solid, don't we, dear?" she asked.

"So *that's* what happened." Ellie speared herself a baked potato, peeled back the foil. "Jane Whitelaw knew where the gold was, or thought she did, killed Hayes, then headed out there to collect it."

"But in her haste," Winston Cartwright intoned, "Jane missed her footing and the soil crumbled away beneath her just as it nearly did beneath Jill Frey today. A sad end."

Clarissa took little Thomas from Bob, wiped his lips with a corner of her napkin, and cuddled him tenderly. "And wasn't it said that she had a baby with her?" She pressed Thomas's forehead to her cheek and made motherly noises at him. "And that it was saved?"

But Raines shook his head. "That must have been just part of the legend," he said definitely. "I can tell you for sure no baby would ever survive what I saw down there today."

He smiled at Thomas, reached out to dandle the child's tiny finger, then looked indulgently over at Charmian, who blushed.

"It was," George Valentine said, "all a mish-mash, some true and some not, like any old story as gets started around here. If any baby survived it's 'cause she left it home."

He said it the Maine way: *stahted*. "Rescued babies and old violins and witch's curses . . . and if the lady screamed, this Jane Whitelaw lady, likely she was a-screamin' at her own bad luck."

Sam applied himself to his potatoes and salmon, his

misery over Jill's betrayal assuaged somewhat by food and friends. From across the table, Maggie watched him eat with a look of pride in the fine meal she had accomplished and, I thought, the tiniest bit of feminine calculation, too.

Sam brightened further when Maggie brought out the chocolate cake. "I didn't know you could do this," he said wonderingly as she set a slice in front of him. On the table now were a pitcher of milk and a pot of hot, fresh coffee; somehow she'd managed to whisk away the main course as unnoticeably as a magician.

"You," she said with a twinkly smile she aimed straight at him, "don't know a lot of things."

Sam blinked, as with a glance around the table she made sure all was well; satisfied, she sat down to enjoy her own cake.

Me, too, and as I did so the lingering sense of something unresolved nearly faded from my mind, pushed out by the pleasure of chocolate butter-cream frosting. But not completely.

"So Jared Hayes marked an especially unstable area of those cliffs on his map?" Cartwright's tone was contemplative, his old eyes sharpened by the possible implications of this.

"Seems so," George agreed, forking up cake. Which was when it hit me, but Winston Cartwright had begun speaking again.

"Hayes," he said having come to a conclusion, "marked the bad part of the cliffs on purpose, on the map he gave Jane. She knew they were all unstable, of course; everyone did. But he realized that if she betrayed him, her greed would probably drive her to try it, anyway. So he got the last laugh in the end. Got it," he finished rumblingly, "from the grave."

A little chill went over me. It was getting on for

evening, the shadows lengthening over the green grass, and the breeze off the water had grown damp and tangy with the smell of sea salt.

"So there was never any violin," Wade said. "And no gold in the cave, either?"

He turned to Jonathan. "Jill Frey told us you'd probably got it and vamoosed with it. But—"

"Oh, yes." Jonathan dug in his pocket. "There was gold."

Whereupon he produced the largest gold coin I had ever seen: as big around as a cookie cutter, flatter than a modern coin, and irregular at the edges, stamped with a sun pattern and engraved with some kind of legend in what appeared to be French.

"It's just," Raines finished in tones of faint sadness, "not there anymore."

He tossed the coin onto the table. "Jill told the truth on that. Until she got there, there was a great deal of old Hayes treasure in that cave, hidden under those bluffs. "This coin," he added, "belongs to Wilbur. I think he's earned it."

George gazed fondly at the outboard motor. "Kinda makes me glad I went in and fixed that plaster for you, Miz Tiptree. In the dining room. I hung Elvis back up, though," he added seriously. "I wasn't sure but maybe you might want to keep 'im."

I looked at Ellie, and she looked at me. "The plaster," we breathed together, and hurried into the house. I got the hammer, and she got the crowbar, and together we demolished George's new repair job in no time flat, while he watched astonishedly.

"Jared Hayes cut a hole in this wall," I said.

"And he cut it," Ellie said, "for a *reason*."

"Below the floor level," I said, shining a flashlight down there. "That's why Howard Washburn's friend didn't find anything. He wouldn't have been able to sense anything with a stud-finder through the baseboards and flooring."

Excitedly they all crowded around behind me, waiting for me to find . . .

Nothing. "You'd think he could at least have dropped one little bag of gold down there," I complained.

"Oh," Charmian said disappointedly. "All he hid there was the book, after all. Oh, Jonathan, I'm so sorry."

But Jonathan's face was shining.

"Never mind," he said quietly. "That's not the treasure I was really looking for, was it?"

He put his arm around her, drew her near, and spoke to us all. "I've found the only treasure I need, and from now on I'll never forget it. Thank you, Charmian, for coming to find me. Please don't let me get lost, ever again."

She looked up sweetly at him, and with a tart little edge in her voice that I thought boded well for both of them, replied:

"You needn't worry. You're going to marry me without delay, and afterwards I'm not going to let you out of my sight."

She turned to her uncle. "This means I won't be working for you anymore, you know. I'm welshing on that damned bet we made."

Jonathan squeezed her shoulders as Winston replied with a harrumph. "I told you I never meant to hold you to that wager."

She stepped forward and kissed him soundly. "Then you'll give me away at the wedding?"

Whereupon he blushed, and harrumphed some more, and tapped on the old floor with his ornately carved cane, finally allowing that if pressed he would do so.

"With great," he averred, nipping from his flask of cordial, "pleasure."

"So," George said slowly, eyeing the destruction Ellie and I had wrought. "Guess that new plaster never needed to come down, then. I expect somebody had better get busy."

Which was when I realized that what we had, yet again, was a hole in the wall, and I doubted that George would fix it for me a second time; the goodness of his heart is plentiful but it is not inexhaustible.

Bucket, I thought; *trowel, drop cloths, plaster mix.* But somehow the list, and the thought of using all the items on it, didn't lower my spirits. The opposite, actually.

"Oh, Jacobia," Charmian said, "we can fix the wall for you. Can't we, Jonathan?" she added with a bright glance at him.

To his credit, Jonathan didn't agree immediately. The hole was rather large, and he eyed it with all the respect it was due.

"Never mind," I said, thinking about the old days when the house was built: when ships filled the harbor, Lewis and Clark's great adventure remained vivid in living memory, and a person who could put up a plaster wall, erect a brick chimney, or glaze in a window was a valued craftsperson.

Now, the house depended on me. Maybe I could even find some horsehair to put into that plaster. "Somehow I think that this is a repair I want to make myself," I said.

"Good thing I hung onto that Elvis painting," George commented. But he was smiling when he said it.

Later, as the streetlights came on and the last birds of the evening began calling from yard to yard, Sam and Maggie started clearing the picnic table while I found Bob Arnold.

Because, although Jonathan Raines had lost one

treasure and recovered another, there was still a final bit of the tangled skein left to unravel. "Bob," I said quietly, "where's Jill Frey, now?"

Behind him, Clarissa jounced baby Thomas gently on her hip. Sam reached out a tentative hand and the baby grabbed it, crowing with infant delight.

Bob shrugged. "Mapes wouldn't press charges, and Cnarmian, either. No weapon found. So I had to release her."

". . . in leather bags," Jonathan Raines was saying as the rest came out to help Sam and Maggie. They were all talking about the treasure, again; the *other* treasure.

The gold. "Inside an old wooden chest," Jonathan went on. "For a while it was probably safe, but the tide's come up farther over time as the land erodes away."

He shook his head. "Bags and chest both been getting doused twice a day, every time the tide comes in, over a hundred years."

"She opened the chest," George Valentine said, stacking the plates. "Jill Frey. She couldn't resist."

Raines nodded. "And that was it. Next wave hit, that's all she wrote. I got one look at what was left, grabbed this . . ."

He waved at the glittering gold object still lying on the table. Wilbur wasn't ever going to be short of money again; he could fix up his old trailer.

If he wanted to. "But by now those coins are all over the bottom of the bay," Raines said, "some halfway to Nova Scotia, the rest on their way to Lubec. They'll be getting found one at a time for a thousand years."

"To her mother?" I asked Bob. "Jill's back at her house?"

"Uh-huh." He paused on the porch, glancing at Clarissa and the baby framed against the gathering darkness, as Ellie came up behind us carrying the salad bowl.

"I still don't understand how Charmian and Jill got into the right cave, the one with the gold in it, when they had the wrong map. I mean, how did they know?" Ellie asked.

Raines followed her, the charcoal bag in his hand. "Hayes annotated his maps, as you figured out, in Latin. And Charmian is," he pronounced proudly, "a cool customer in tricky situations."

"Because," Charmian added, appearing out of the gloom with the cake plate, "I didn't *know* it was the wrong map, you see."

She stepped up beside Jonathan. "And I certainly wasn't about to lead Jill to where that map said the entrance was."

"So?" I held the door open for them.

"So I marked it myself with an X," Charmian replied simply. "With my handy-dandy little jacknife pen when she wasn't looking. Jill ignored the Latin she couldn't read, followed the X-mark."

She set the cake plate on the sink. "I'd already decided if she asked, I'd say the *ex* on the map must stand for *exit*."

All this while being menaced by the gun Jill held; Charmian had confirmed this detail, as well.

"Remarkable," I said dryly, beginning to fill the sink. "So you just happened to pick the right cave." I squirted dish soap into the steaming basin. "By luck?"

"Um, not exactly. That wasn't all of it." Charmian examined the opal ring on her hand. "You see, by then I was thinking about how I would get out alive."

"And about time, too, I'd say," Jonathan said sternly, but he couldn't sustain it; you could see he thought she was the best idea since the invention of sliced bread.

"Anyway," Charmian continued, "by then I didn't care about finding anything. I just looked at the map we *did* have, picked the cave that looked to be the highest above sea level, that's all. So I'd have a long time before it flooded. Time to escape."

"Which," Jonathan concluded, "made it also the one Hayes had picked to hide his treasure. It was highest above sea level back then, too, and that made it the most accessible to him without the special equipment we've got nowadays. So it worked out."

"Jonathan," I said, "there's one thing I still don't quite see. What happened to the old violin you bought from Mapes? It's not by any chance—"

"A Stradivarius, too?" He laughed comfortably. "Oh, would it were so. But no, I'm sorry to report I only took the violin to get the trunk Mapes had described on the phone to me, of moldy sheet music that stank of a house fire . . ."

The things Howard Washburn had mentioned.

". . . and old books," Raines finished.

Which accounted for the whiff of smoke I'd smelled back in the library; not brimstone at all. Just the smell of my poor old house's chimneys, and the fire one of them had started long ago.

"I'm afraid I fooled Wilbur a little on that one," Raines said. "I didn't want him to know what I thought he really had, so I let him think I wanted the violin. It's a perfectly playable instrument, though," he added, "now it's cleaned up. I gave it to Maggie."

He and Charmian joined hands; clearly these two were going to make a formidable team, a fact Winston Cartwright seemed to realize with considerable pride as he gazed at them.

"I had meant to return at once to Boston," Cartwright said when some of the others had repaired to the parlor and Clarissa had taken the baby upstairs. "However, I have been inveigled."

From the parlor came the sound of Maggie's new fiddle tuning up; we were to have, I gathered, a musical evening.

Or some of us were. Bob Arnold sat patiently at the kitchen table, waiting.

Soon, I telegraphed to him, and he nodded, not happily.

"Inveigled?" I wiped my hands on the dish towel.

"Indeed." Cartwright had put on the disreputable slouch hat and draped the vast folds of the huge trench coat around himself. Now he gripped his walking stick firmly in preparation for an evening stroll.

Exercise, I thought; regular meals, congenial company: the town was good for him.

"The ladies of the Eastport Reading Circle have asked me to speak at their annual summer picnic," he announced.

"How delightful. And have you accepted?"

"I have," he intoned gravely. "However, to do them justice I must move considerable of my research materials. Therefore I have engaged lodgings in town."

So he was staying. It happens; some urban person who thinks life begins and ends on the island of Manhattan or in Cambridge comes to our little island and is captured, and decides to stay. It had happened to me.

"Jonathan," I said, finding him a little while later in the butler's pantry; he was putting away unused paper plates. "Tell me the truth. I know you called, but *did* I really invite you?"

He shook his head ruefully. "No. I knew of your sleuthing reputation from the cousins. Yours and Ellie's reputations, that is. But I couldn't risk actually trying to wangle an invitation. You might refuse, or talk to the cousins before I got here."

"Whereupon your scheme to actually stay here in the house so you could put the book in it, thus getting Ellie and me curious and involved, might fall apart."

He nodded. "Exactly. When I showed up, I needed you to have spoken to me before, so I'd be at least a little familiar, *and* I needed a connection you'd trust as a reference. But not one you'd actually go to the trouble of checking with care."

He looked a little shamefaced. "And," he admitted, "I made sure I came when the cousins were tied up in projects that meant you wouldn't be able to reach them, anyway. I didn't expect you to check me out any further than that."

"Meanwhile, you didn't tell me the truth about yourself and what you wanted in the *first* place because . . ."

He nodded again; that much was obvious. Of course I would've said no. And he'd known that, too, not just suspected it, because . . .

"That Australian guy," I said. "Who called before you did. I told *him* no, although he was very persuasive, so you knew . . ."

"Roight," Jonathan replied, sounding for all the world as if he'd been throwing shrimps on the barbie all of his life. "Also, it was a last-minute check to make sure you'd be here, yourself."

Oh, boy. "Jonathan, with the kind of nerve you've got, it's a good thing you *didn't* have evil intentions."

A shadow touched his face; the notion, apparently, was not a new one to him. "Yes," he said quietly, pressing his fingertips together. "I suppose it is."

Then in the parlor fiddling began, along with a sound that meant George Valentine had found my old banjo and was remembering how to play it. Jonathan went to join them.

"Five minutes," I said to Bob Arnold. Nodding, he went to drive Clarissa and Thomas home before coming back for me, and I walked through the dining room to the front parlor, expecting to find a happy throng, Sam included.

Instead I found Sam sitting alone at the dining room table with Jared Hayes's skull in front of him, staring disconsolately at it. "He died for love, didn't he?" Sam said.

By *he,* Sam meant Hayes. "Because he loved a woman."

"Because he loved the wrong woman," I said. "Wrong for him."

He sighed hugely. It wasn't just Jill. For the first time in his life, Sam had come up against the sad fact that wishing won't make it so. "People don't change much, do they?"

I hadn't said anything to him about Victor and Jill. But it was there between us, like the skull on the table, and I thought that was what he meant.

"I guess Jane Whitelaw didn't go around pretending she was some kind of a Girl Scout, either," he said.

"Oh," I said, understanding my mistake. "You mean people changing over time. From one era to another."

"Uh-huh. Poor old Jared, he was crazy in love with Jane, and never mind he must've known she was bad news. You idiot," he told the brown-stained relic on the table.

A few teeth were missing, the arrow-point in it jutted up roughly, and the hole in the cranium was jagged-edged, beginning to crumble. Altogether, it looked as if it ought to have a black candle burning inside it.

"No," I agreed finally. "Neither one of them, Jared

Hayes nor Jane Whitelaw, was much different from any of us, at heart."

Love and money, pride and ambition. And lust. The same old song. In the parlor Maggie's fiddle danced with brisk confidence into "Pirate's Revenge."

And nailed it, negotiating the weird intervals, syncopated rhythms, and sad, minor-key melody flawlessly.

"How *did* I know that tune?" I heard Jonathan say. "As far as I can see, it's the only mystery left to be solved."

But it wasn't; not quite. Bob Arnold returned. "You're sure about this, are you?"

"Yes." Suddenly I didn't want to go where we were going; not at all. But there was no help for it: murder had been done. And—

—so I thought in my innocence at the time—

—murder must out.

11 It was nearly eight-thirty and the last deep pink shreds of the dying evening lay on the western horizon, the smell of low tide floating in from the calm flats as we went over the causeway to Lillian Frey's place on the mainland.

A few cars still lingered in the parking lot at the New Friendly Restaurant on Route 1, but the Farmer's Exchange Market was closed and shuttered for the night; behind them, cattails bristled against the dark gleam of the tide marshes.

At the turnoff, an eighteen-wheeler roared by in a sudden boom of sound and headlights, its turbulence buffeting our car briefly. Then it was only a set of cherry-red taillights in the rearview, and we were alone.

"Nice kid," Bob Arnold said from the passenger seat. The road here was narrow and curving, fields and scrub trees drawing right up to the edge of the pavement.

We had thought it would seem less threatening if we arrived in my car. And this wasn't an official visit.

Yet. "Raines," he added. "A little crazy, but okay."

"Uh-huh." I took the left fork onto the Shore Road, past the little white church with the scattering of graves in a fenced plot behind it.

"He caused us a lot of trouble," I said. "I can't say I'm entirely pleased about all of it."

"But all's well that ends well?"

"Maybe." I wished I shared his confidence. The road led through a stand of pine, past a rail-fenced corral, a dozen white-faced cattle standing at the far corner of it, waiting to be let into the gambrel-roofed barn.

"Right here's where the old school burned," Bob said, his head angling toward the roadside. A whiff of charcoal smell came on the damp night air, through the open car window.

"It was Raines," Bob said, "that called in the anonymous tip."

On the arsonist, he meant. "You're kidding. How d'you know?"

Bob shrugged. "Thought I recognized the voice, meeting him on the cliffs. Asked him about it, he just looked clever. Said he thought anonymous tips ought to stay that way, wouldn't say more. Did a lot of walking, saw things, out to Mapes's place, I guess."

Walking down those country roads. "I guess."

"He saw a guy toss a match. Took down the plate number."

There was, we both knew, a reward. But if Raines accepted it, considering the way firebugs tended to hold grudges, my house might be the next target for the arsonist's friends.

And Raines had understood this.

Bob sighed; we were approaching Lillian's long, down-sloping driveway. No streetlights here; I squinted so as not to miss the entrance to it.

"Tell me again what I'm going to find?" Bob said.

A thump of misery struck me. Now that we were arriving, it all seemed more real. I hoped I was wrong.

"Wallet. Identification, probably. And car keys. They were not in the vehicle when it was towed, were they?"

The stolen one, that the guy had been driving who went off the bluffs. Bob shook his head as we pulled up to the house.

"No. And if you can't ID a fellow, it's hard to figure out who might've offed him. If someone did."

With all its lights on, blazing in the darkness against the water, the house resembled some ghostly ship asail on an ocean of midnight, the false blue dawn of moonrise brightening behind it.

I shut off the ignition. Part of me wanted to just let it all go by. But if I did, sooner or later someone else would get in the way, present an obstacle or trigger a murderous rage.

And then that someone would die; maybe someone like Sam.

Or even like Victor. "She didn't push him," I said.

Meaning Jill's father. Because when you came right down to it, who else would it have been? "He knew her, he wouldn't have let her get close enough, right there by the edge of the bluffs."

Because she was her father's daughter: he would know.

"And she didn't shoot him; Lillian's gun was here when I came out here. And it hadn't been fired recently."

You could smell it, if it had, and all I'd smelled was gun oil. I doubted Jill was clear-headed or knowledge-able enough to clean the weapon, to kill the burnt-powder reek.

As we approached the house, a shape moved in one of the big windows; they knew we were here.

"So?" Bob asked.

"Nail gun," I said. "If you find him, he'll have a nail in him. Probably it killed him, but it didn't need to. Just . . ."

"Send him over the edge. Lillian Frey's ex-husband. Jill's dad."

"Right." I got out of the car. My old mobbed-up friend, Jemmy Wechsler, had a cell phone, and I was among the half-dozen people in the world with the number. And Jemmy knew everyone—that is, if they were crooked enough. "Jill's dad was a bad guy. Habitual wife-beater, stalker. Big criminal record in Massachusetts, too; fraud, theft. You know the type."

I looked up at the house. "But then he made one big mistake, this tough guy. This guy no one ever dared to say no to."

We started up the steps. "Which was?" Bob Arnold asked.

I knocked on the door. No answer. Knocked again.

"He said no," I replied to Bob Arnold, knocking harder, "to his teenage daughter."

The door opened. Lillian Frey stood in the entryway.

"Thank God you've come," she said.

She took us into the big room overlooking the water. The moon had risen, sending a wash of silvery glitter onto the dark waves. Behind, the lights of the villages on Campobello sparkled. At such a distance, everything always looks so peaceful. A fire burned in the woodstove, though the night was too warm for one.

"Jill's locked herself upstairs in her room and won't come out," Lillian said. "I don't know what to do. She's so upset, I'm afraid she might . . ."

Around the room an eclectic collection of small objects stood on display: a metronome and a music stand in one corner, in the other a lectern with an antique dictionary open on it.

"The gun you showed me?" I asked. "Jill hasn't . . ."

She hadn't used it the first time, on her dad; the second time, though, to threaten Charmian, she must have. And even though I didn't *think* Jill could have salvaged it—she'd had no place to hide it, coming back up the cliffs—I wanted to be sure before Bob or I went upstairs to talk to the girl.

And to my relief, Lillian shook her head no.

But what she said next confused me completely. "I just went to my studio and checked. It's still there."

Curveball; so what *had* Jill used? To cover my confusion I turned from Lillian and examined the room. On a table were ranged small procelain items: a pair of red Chinese fighting dogs, a bowl marked with the insignia of the City of New York, showing the opening of the Brooklyn Bridge.

"Mrs. Frey, have you had any contact with your ex-husband in the past ten days or so?" Bob Arnold asked.

She looked startled. "No. Why?"

"We think Jill might have met with him. Here, I mean, not in Boston. We think he might have come here."

She nodded slowly. "It would make sense. He's always saying he'll do something. Follow me, the way he has before."

"I don't think that's why he came," I told her. "Jill

wanted more than anything to go back to Boston; if she called him, told him there was something valuable to find here, he might come and take her back with him, she'd have thought."

Lillian said nothing. "I wonder, has Jill's attitude toward him changed?" I asked. "In the past few days? Because they might have quarreled. Over whether she could go back with him, maybe."

When he rejected this idea—rejected her, even after she'd told him a potentially valuable secret—she'd have been angry.

Very angry. But Lillian only shook her head ruefully again. "He always manages to convince her I'm the villain," she said. "I doubt he was here, though. His business"—she gave the word a bitterly ironic twist—"keeps him occupied in Massachusetts."

Silence from upstairs. If Jill was having a tantrum, she was keeping it pretty quiet.

"What business would that be?" Bob Arnold asked.

I browsed on: books on a shelf behind the table. A stack of sheet music for violin. A fancy tool catalog. Books about wood, and instrument construction. Lots of antique knickknacks.

"Electronics," Lillian replied a bit impatiently. "At the moment. He says he's a dealer. The truth is, he fences things after other people steal them: computers, cell phones, all that kind of thing."

She got up. "Look, I don't see why you want to know anything about him. I hoped you could talk to Jill. Straighten her out and make her see reason."

"What was it you wanted us to say?" I turned from a group of crystal paperweights on a shelf, like a collection of glass eyes. And something behind them, something that was not an antique.

Lillian waved a hand. She seemed particularly to

want to engage my attention. "Well. That she's got to behave. That she's lucky no one's pressed charges. That from now on—"

A bang from a room above. Bob turned and headed for the open stairway. "What's that?" he demanded as he went, and after a moment of hesitation Lillian ran toward the sound, too.

But I already knew what it was: a nail gun firing, loud and concussive. I'd seen it in Lillian's hands that day at the craft fair, when Jill and Lillian had been arguing.

The sound wouldn't carry far, but inside the house it was like the *crack!* of a pistol being fired. Again. And again.

Bob pounded. "Jill! Hear me now, girl, I want you to open this door!" He rattled the knob, gave the door a solid kick, and another. "Jill!"

No answer, and he was too late anyway. I cursed myself for trying to be tactful, trying to save Lillian's feelings instead of just laying it on her: that her daughter was a killer.

Jill had gotten about six shots off from the nail gun. The door was effectively barricaded now, until someone went after it with a crowbar. I pushed the glass paperweights aside, grabbed the thing I'd seen tucked behind the old books: a camera.

And not some cheap, quick-print item, either: this was the camera Sam and Maggie had been yearning for, that put the visual images onto a disk to be loaded into a computer. It was a digital camera like the one Winston Cartwright had explained to me.

Then I had it: *electronics*. And remembered again the rest of what the unidentified man had been carrying with him as he walked out onto the bluffs. Camera equipment.

At the same time I heard the creak of another door upstairs. And knew what it meant.

Another time, another set of circumstances: no moon, maybe, or the scent of wood smoke not floating quite so poignantly in the air, though the evening was warm. The tide was coming in; below the big windows, foam showed like lacy trimmings around the slick black rocks.

Any other time I might not have understood. But now as I ran out into the darkness, searching for the outside stairway to the second-floor balcony with its awe-inspiring view of the drop over the cliffs, the truth flashed over me, the one fact that no one else understood about the pirate girl Jane Whitelaw:

That when she went over the cliffs to perish in the ice-cold waters, she did it in the dark. It was why they saw her torch as she ran; why men built bonfires on rafts they towed behind their boats, to light their way when they went searching for her.

And the dark of night was a very strange time to search for a hidden treasure, carrying an unfamiliar map.

Jane hadn't fallen accidentally from that cliff, as we'd surmised from the dangerousness of the crumbling edge. And she hadn't been *kilt,* as Hecky Wilmot and — Winston Cartwright believed.

And it hadn't been the first time she'd gone there, I was willing to bet. She'd been there before, searching, figured out that Hayes had given her a fake map, and understood: without him, she would never find the treasure she lusted furiously for.

But she'd already killed him, hadn't she? She was a girl with an eye for the main chance, and now it was gone because she had destroyed it herself. So Jane Whitelaw had jumped.

From grief, or guilt, or fury that her scheme hadn't worked? To that question I would probably never have a certain answer, but as I found the outside stairs and began scrambling up, I knew Jill was about to do it again.

"Stay where you are." Her voice quavered at me from above.

I stopped, trying to catch my breath. Inside, Bob still tried to break the door down, slamming himself against it.

"Hey." I managed a weak laugh. "Guess he's not going to get very far, is he?"

No answer. My eyes began adjusting; when they did, I wished they hadn't. She was perched on the railing, looking out into a yawning space of nothing. I forced myself to keep my eyes on her.

"Jill? Listen, I know it must seem—"

"No, you don't. You don't know how it seems at all." Her voice was oddly patient, as if I were the child. The nail gun lay on the deck by her feet.

"Anyway, I know you hate me. Because you think I'm not good enough for Sam. And now you've got another reason."

"Jill, I don't—"

"That I killed my own father."

And there it was, as pretty a confession as I'd ever heard. I sat on the steps with the camera in my lap. She hadn't seen it; I hadn't brought it out here for any particular reason. I'd had it in my hands and never thought to put it down, that was all.

"I don't hate you," I said. She made a skeptical face.

Truth time: "Or not the way you mean, anyway. But there's something I don't understand. Your mother still has her gun, she says. So . . ."

The gun business just didn't compute. "So what did you use to get Charmian down those cliffs and into the cave?"

I gestured toward her feet. "Not the nail gun. You didn't bring anything back up the cliffs with you, but here it is."

She looked at me, her surprise genuine. "Mom has a gun? Oh, that's funny. That's a real scream. I never even knew it. So I never needed . . . but Uncle Wilbur has lots of guns," she explained. "And ammunition. Everything I needed."

She stayed with my brother awhile, Lillian had remarked.

"I never meant to hurt him. I just went out there to get one of the guns, to use to make Charmian show me where the gold was on the map she found. I wouldn't have hurt her with it, either," she added earnestly. "I tried to get her to go back *out* of the cave when the water was rising. But she wouldn't."

"I see." Charmian hadn't agreed with Jill's assessment of her own harmlessness, apparently. Nor did I. But I was beginning to feel differently about this girl, nevertheless.

"Uncle Wilbur came around the corner of the trailer and surprised me, that's all. The gun went off, I thought I'd killed him. Then I got scared."

"So you ran." Instead of calling help for him; Charmian had been right. Jill wasn't harmless.

Still, as I sat there I got less of the sense of the malignant criminal I'd thought Jill must be, and more the impression of a sad, screwed-up sixteen-year-old mess.

"I don't know what's wrong with me," Jill said from the high railing, her tone conversational. "All my life I was more like my dad, that's all. Bad, like he was. Wanting it all. Not like Mom, I mean. She's got a lot on the ball, actually."

I looked down at the camera in my lap. Anything I said could be the wrong thing. "But you were in the middle. Between them."

She glanced gratefully at me. "Right. When he hit her, when she screamed at him for it. When he cut her, that time. Gave her that scar. I had to pull them apart, call the cops."

Suddenly I felt like the world's biggest jerk, because all at once I realized that I'd had it all wrong. "So is that why you wanted to go back to Boston? To keep him from coming up here?"

She nodded minutely. "It was the only thing that ever worked to keep him away from her; me being there. Even if he didn't want me there, it kept him focused on something but her."

"But . . . why didn't you just say so?"

"To who?" she demanded, suddenly angry. "I tried to tell it all at the custody hearing. But nobody ever listens to me."

And it wouldn't have gone over well, anyway: *Judge, I've got to live with my repeat-offender father, so that he won't slice my mom up with a box-cutter again.*

Oh, sure. "So you went out to North End that morning. Your mother followed, I saw her go. And . . ."

And what? It was the next part I couldn't quite picture. Had Lillian's ex attacked her, and Jill intervened?

I didn't have to ask why Jill had made a point of telling Lillian where she was going, whom she would meet. I already knew that now; it was because Lillian's reaction was so important to Jill. The way mine was to Sam.

The pounding on the door stopped.

"Tell him if he comes out here, I'll jump right away," Jill said.

I shouted to Bob. Lillian's face showed in the darkness behind him, at the foot of the outside stairway.

"Jill," she said pleadingly, "I—"

"Say one more word and I'm going right this minute," Jill threatened, her voice wavering near tears suddenly. "I mean it, Mom. There's nothing you can do. Because I'm up here, I'm calling the shots, so you just keep your mouth shut."

About what? Because sure, she was a real mess, and considering what she'd been through in her sixteen years, I had to admit I didn't think a lot of it was her fault.

But there was more in her voice now than the guilt-ridden, hysterical bossiness of a seriously distraught kid. Something . . . as if they both, Jill and Lillian, knew something I didn't.

"Jill," I said, "Sam's going to feel very bad about this. He really cared a lot about you, you know. There must be at least something good about you, for him to feel like that. Some part of you that deserves another chance."

But this was the wrong tactic, too. "Yeah, his good opinion of me just lights up my life," she sneered.

In the moonlight, her swaying body cast a thin shadow on the cedar decking. "You listen to me. You know what I'm like? I'm like a picture somebody's drawing, they wreck it, and they should tear it up and start over. If Sam liked me, he's stupider than I thought, got it?"

A little flicker of intuition seized me; I glanced down at Lillian. *Swinging like a loose sail*, Ellie had said of Sam, and Jill was nearly the same age as he was. "Unlike your mother, who is worth saving? Don't you want to be around to help?"

No answer. I looked at the camera. Why had Jill put it in the bookcase, I wondered, instead of taking it up-stairs with her? It was, I thought, a sort of keepsake to her: something that had belonged to her father. But why hide it?

"Jill, why are you telling me all this? If there's nothing I can do, I mean. If you're going to just end it?"

"I wanted someone to know, that's all." Her tone remained stubborn; hanging on to the little, proud part of herself that she had left. "I just wanted someone to know."

"Yeah." I could understand that. Sitting there trying to come up with something to say in reply, I pressed a button on the camera in my lap. Not for a reason; just fiddling with the thing.

A two-inch video display lit up on the back of the device.

And suddenly everything was different yet again. "Jill?"

"What?" Distantly, as if for all but the very most practical purposes—pulse, a blood pressure—she was already gone.

I stared at the picture on the display, not believing it: a small, extremely sharp color photograph. A dateline in the corner of the screen told me when it had been taken: date and time.

Then Jill saw it. "No!" she shrieked, lost her balance for an instant, and swayed. "Give me that! Give it to me, you—"

It was a picture of Lillian. Rapidly, I clicked through all the images on the disk: her face, getting closer and closer. The scar all down one side of her face, ruddy with emotion, and the pictures one after another, like a mean joke.

He must have known she hated it and you could practically hear the guy laughing as he took the shots, firing it at her as if it were a weapon.

But she had the last laugh because in the final picture, the nail gun was in her hand. You couldn't see his face, but you could imagine the look on it as he realized what she could do.

And then she'd done it. She must have grabbed the camera as he staggered, in case it should be found with his body, tell the truth of how he'd died.

And at whose hand. "Jill, I see that you mean to sacrifice yourself. You feel like you've done so many bad things. So why not confess to this one, too, and then die—so your mom can have a life, right? Presto, everything taken care of."

But I still couldn't figure out why Lillian kept the camera and the disk with the damning photographs on it.

Until I remembered: Lillian was like me. Low-tech, out of the stream of electronic progress. The two of us were a couple of stones on the banks of the river of progress as it went rushing by. Which meant:

She didn't know how the camera worked any more than I had, and what she'd needed was to be *sure* those images were absolutely unrecoverable. And maybe—just maybe—she had wanted to gloat over them, too.

But finally she'd come to the only truly reliable solution: she'd started the woodstove though the night was warm, and gotten it blazing.

All the high-tech in the world wouldn't survive the inside of that woodstove. Then Bob and I had arrived, whereupon she hadn't had much time to hide the camera, so she'd simply shoved it behind the old books and put her game face on:

Thank God you've come. We would give Jill a talking-to, she must have thought, and then she could finish what she'd started.

But Jill didn't know Lillian had the camera at all.

And with our arrival she had come to a decision of her own.

"I thought it went over with him," she said, staring at the camera. "But everything happened so fast, and I was crying, and I didn't see it. I kept thinking that his body would wash up and then they would find the pictures. I was so scared. But she had it all along, didn't she?"

"Yes. And eventually you decided she was safe, didn't you? Until we drove up here tonight. You thought we were after her."

She nodded. Suddenly I wanted to put this whole evening on rewind and start over, but of course I couldn't do that, either.

"What I've got here is proof of who really killed him, Jill. And you know it. Your mother was going to burn the camera, but we showed up, so she didn't get the chance. Still . . ."

Under the circumstances I thought this could still turn out all right, I was about to say. A history of abuse, violence, and criminality: I felt sure a good lawyer could help Lillian Frey out of the trouble she was in.

But Jill didn't give me a chance to say any of that. "Give it to me," she wheedled. Her voice turned threatening. "Or I'll tell you something you'll really wish you didn't know."

"Wow, Jill. Way to win me over."

You had to hand it to the kid: even teetering on the edge of a railing, pitiful and wretched as she was, she could still make you want to give her a push.

But I hadn't spent all those years of my life dealing with another monster of emotional arm-twisting for nothing. "You're going to tell me that you slept with Sam's father. You're going to say that was how you really got his wristwatch. Right?"

Rage twisted her face. And pain; humiliation. Seeing it made me stop, put the film on rewind at last.

Made me say the one thing I should have said to her in the first place: "Ever since Sam met you, Jill, I've treated you like a thing, like an obstacle in my way, nothing more. I never really saw you as a person at all. And I'm sorry. So very sorry."

Because she was a twisted little brat, all right, but she was also a scared kid; even Victor's stolen wristwatch was only a bid for attention, a plea for help.

As I spoke she looked straight at me, and I'd like to think it made a difference, what I'd said. I like to think she already had let go of the railing with her other hand.

It would be nice, thinking that.

Wicked nice. But wishing won't make it so.

She let go with her other hand. I rushed at her, screaming something, I don't even know what—

—as Bob Arnold hurled himself at her from behind, from the darkness at the other end of the deck.

"No," she sobbed, heartbroken as he hauled her back up. "You should've let me go, you don't *under-stand* . . .

But I did. Bob Arnold, too,

And so did Lillian. When we got Jill to the ground, Lillian was standing there, looking as if all the blood had been let out of her and replaced with embalming fluid.

Her scar was dead white in the moonlight, like a lightning bolt down the side of her face. In her hand were a man's wallet and some car keys. Stolen with the car, I supposed.

"Here," she said, dropping them.

"Lillian," I said. "It's going to be . . ."

Okay. Yeah, sure it was. She wasn't listening, anyway.

She looked at Jill with . . . what? Regret? Apology? I couldn't tell. "I'm so tired," she whispered.

Then I saw what was in her other hand, close by her side.

Too late. "I'm sorry," she told Jill.

And then, before we could do anything to stop her, she shot herself with that old Colt pistol she kept.

That cannon, I'd called it.

She was dead by the time we got to her.

12

It was midnight, but the lights were still on in the kitchen and parlors when I pulled into the driveway. Wade came out to the yard to meet me, and threw an arm around my shoulders.

"Hey," he said.

"Hey." I'd called him from the hospital, told him the nuts and bolts of what had gone on.

Basically, Bob Arnold had signed a petition for Jill Frey's involuntary temporary commitment, and a judge had gotten out of bed to grant it. But after the ninety-six hours specified in it were up, I had no idea what would happen to her.

Even if no charges were brought, I doubted Wilbur Mapes would be judged a fit guardian when she was released, and I felt like somebody who'd just dropped an unwanted dog off at the pound.

"Wade, I couldn't just bring her home."

"No. Don't beat yourself up. Some jobs need professionals."

Still, I couldn't get her face out of my head: through the window of the van that had come to take her. She'd put her fist to the glass as if to pound on it, then let it fall. I couldn't hear her, but her lips were moving: *Tell Sam I'm sorry*.

We went up the porch steps. "Bob went through

Lillian's desk while we waited for the ambulance," I said. "It was all going to crash down on her: her ex had gotten the custody order appealed."

He didn't want Jill and probably couldn't get her, but he wasn't going to let Lillian have her without a big fight, either. "And she had money troubles, more than we knew. It costs way more than she was making to live the way she lived."

Then she'd killed someone, and while Bob and I were trying to save Jill, Lillian had realized that I had the camera. "Love and money and the end of her rope," I said. "Like Jane Whitelaw."

Same old song. And much as I knew it was probably not a good idea, I knew, too, that whenever Jill got out of that clinic, I was going to be there. Counseling, therapy: possibly something could still save her, and I was going to try to find it. I was going to make Victor help, too, whether he liked it or not.

Because maybe it was the same old song, but somebody's got to write a new verse, now and then.

Somebody's just got to.

"You know, I keep thinking," Wade said slowly, "about all those years ago. When Jared Hayes was alive and none of us had even been born yet. Then it was his turn to live. And now . . ."

Now it was ours. "Let's do it, Jacobia. Let's just go ahead and get married. As soon as we can." He opened the door.

"All right," I said calmly, amazed that in the end it was as easy as that. We went into the house together.

In the phone alcove, the little red light on the answering machine was blinking. I pressed the button and it was the cousins from New York, the federal fellows, wanting to know if they could visit again this summer: two weeks in August.

From the phone I could see into the dining room where a lamp burned, illuminating the Elvis painting. In it he was still young and handsome, a touch of pale blue putting a glint in his hair and his grin rakish. Painted on velvet, frozen forever in Day-Glo acrylics, he was not yet the sad, sick old man his life had made of him at the end.

Spread out on the table like jewels at his feet lay Ellie's finished quilt, all bright geometry and careful handiwork in red and marine blue. I thought a minute and then I erased the message on the answering machine: sorry, guys. Maybe next year.

In the kitchen, Sam looked up. Wade had filled him in on the evening's events. Now Wade went upstairs to his workshop.

I sat in silence as Sam put the kettle on and made cups of tea. Finally: "If I hadn't gone out there tonight . . ." I began.

"If I'd never gotten involved with Jill . . ."

"If I hadn't been so stubborn, so worried you were turning out like your father . . ."

"If only I'd listened." Monday padded in, settled in her dog bed.

"You planning to say anything more to him?" I asked.

To Victor, I meant, about Jill Frey. Sam understood.

"Nah." He shook his head. "Besides, he already knows I know. He didn't mention it to me, but you know Dad. What he's got of a conscience is written all over his face."

I thought about leaving Victor there, wriggling on the hook. It would've been poetic justice. But in the end I couldn't. There was enough grief and guilt in Eastport tonight.

Enough to go around. Besides, something about the decision I'd just come to with Wade made hitting out at Victor pointless.

Even more so, I mean, than before. "Sam. Things didn't get as far as Jill wanted you to think. Between her and your father."

He glanced at me, unable to keep the relief out of his face. "Yeah, huh? You know that?"

"Yeah. I know that."

He considered. "It's complicated, isn't it?"

The house felt . . . empty. It was gone, that *occupied* feeling as if any moment the doors would bang open and the windows slam up and down. Whatever had wafted in and out of the old rooms—

I just wanted someone to know. The sense of many lives lived within the old walls still remained. But that unhappy *particular* presence, wanting and waiting . . .

Gone. "Sam, your father is a very complicated and screwed-up guy," I began. "But . . ."

"Yeah," Sam said. "But that's my dad, huh?"

He was silent a moment. Then: "Hcck. Maybe Maggie and I will go over to his place tomorrow, help him move some of those books of his out to the clinic. Probably he could use a hand with some of the heavy lifting."

Couldn't we all. And some of us were lucky enough to get it, weren't we? Some of us, like me.

"This other thing, though . . ." Sam said, meaning the trouble between his father and himself, and in his voice I could hear him letting go of it.

Just letting go. A breeze drifted in, smelling of the sea at night: cold salt water and the place, invisible from shore, where the sky begins.

You can't see it until you get there.

ABOUT THE AUTHOR

SARAH GRAVES lives with her husband in Eastport, Maine, where her mystery novels featuring Jacobia Tiptree are set.

If you enjoyed Sarah Graves'
REPAIR TO HER GRAVE, you won't
want to miss any of the exciting books
in her *Home Repair Is Homicide*
mystery series. Look for
THE DEAD CAT BOUNCE,
TRIPLE WITCH, WICKED FIX,
and WRECK THE HALLS
at your favorite bookseller's.

And turn the page for a tantalizing
preview of the *Home Repair Is
Homicide* mystery, UNHINGED,
available from Bantam Books.

UNIIINGED

A *Home Repair Is Homicide* mystery by
SARAH GRAVES

H arriet Hollingsworth was the kind of person who called 911 the minute she spotted a teenager ambling down the street, since as she said there was no sense waiting for them to get up to their nasty tricks. Each week Harriet wrote to the *Quoddy Tides,* Eastport's local newspaper, a list of the sordid misdeeds she suspected all the rest of us of committing, and when she wasn't doing that she was at her window with binoculars, spying out more.

Snoopy, spiteful, and a suspected poisoner of neighborhood cats, Harriet was confidently believed by her neighbors to be too mean to die, until the morning one of them spotted her boot buckle glinting up out of his compost heap like the wink of an evil eye.

The boot had a sock in it but the sock had no foot in it and despite a diligent search (one wag remarking that if Harriet was buried somewhere, the grass over her grave would die in the shape of a witch on a broomstick) she remained missing.

"Isn't that just like Harriet?" my friend Ellie White demanded about three weeks later, squinting up into the spring sunshine.

We were outside my house in Eastport, on Moose Island, in downeast Maine. "Stir up as much fuss and bother as she could," Ellie went on, "but not give an ounce of satisfaction in the end."

Thinking at the time that it *was* the end, of course. We both did.

At the time. My house is a white clapboard 1823 Federal with three full floors plus an attic, forty-eight big old double-hung windows with forest-green wooden shutters, three chimneys (one for each pair of fireplaces), and a two-story ell.

From my perch on a ladder propped against the porch roof I looked down at Ellie, who wore a purple tank top like a vest over a yellow turtleneck with red frogs embroidered on it. Blue jeans faded to the color of cornflowers and rubber beach shoes trimmed with rubber daisies completed her outfit.

"Running out on her bills, not a word to anyone," she added darkly.

In Maine, stiffing creditors is not only bad form. It's also a shortsighted way of trying to escape your money troubles, since anywhere you go in the whole state you are bound to run into your creditors' cousins, hot to collect and burning to make an example out of you. That was why Ellie thought Harriet must've scarpered to Vermont or New Hampshire, leaving the boot as misdirection and her own old house already in foreclosure.

From my ladder-perch I glimpsed it peeking forlornly through the maples, two streets away: a huge Victorian shambles shedding chunks of rotted trim and peeled-off paint curls onto an unkempt lawn. Just the sight of its advancing decrepitude gave me a pang. I'd started the morning optimistically, but fixing a few gutters was shaping up to be more difficult than I'd expected.

"Harriet," Ellie declared, "was never the sharpest tool in the toolbox, and this stunt of hers just proves it."

"Mmm," I said distractedly. "I wish this ladder was taller."

Shakily I tried steadying myself, straining to reach a

metal strap securing a gutter downspout. Over the winter the downspouts had blown loose so their upper ends aimed gaily off in nonwater-collecting directions. But the straps were still firmly fastened to the house with big aluminum roofing nails.

I couldn't fix the gutters without taking the straps off, and I couldn't get the straps off. They were out of my reach even when, balancing precariously on tiptoe, I swatted at them with the claw hammer. Meanwhile down off the coast of the Carolinas a storm sat spinning over warmer water, sucking up energy.

"Ellie, run in and get me the crowbar, will you, please?"

Days from now, maybe a week, the storm would make its way here, sneakily gathering steam. When it arrived it would hit hard.

Ellie let go of the ladder's legs and went into the house. This I thought indicated a truly touching degree of confidence in me, because I am the kind of person who can trip while walking on a linoleum floor. I sometimes think it would simplify life if I got up every morning, climbed a ladder, and fell off, just to get it over with.

And sure enough, right on schedule as the screen door swung shut, the ladder's feet began slipping on the spring-green grass. I should mention it was also *wet* grass, since in Maine we really only have three seasons: mud time, Fourth of July, and pretty good snowmobiling.

"Ow," I said a moment later when I'd landed hard and managed to spit out a mouthful of grass and the mud. Then I just lay there while my nervous system rebooted and ran damage checks. Arms and legs movable: okay. Not much blood: likewise reassuring. I could remember all the curse words I knew and proved it by reciting them aloud.

A robin cocked his bright eye suspiciously at me, apparently thinking I'd tried muscling in on his worm-harvesting operation. I probed between my molars with my tongue, hoping the robin was incorrect, and he was, and the molars were all there, too.

So I felt better, sort of. Then Ellie came back out with the crowbar and saw me on the ground.

"Jake, are you all right?"

"Fabulous." The downspout lay beside me. Apparently I'd flailed at it with the hammer as I was falling and hooked it on my way down.

Ellie's expression changed from alarm to the beginnings of relief. I do so enjoy having a friend who doesn't panic when the going gets bumpy. Although I suspected there was liniment in my future, and definitely aspirin.

"Oof," I said, getting up. My knees were skinned, and so were my elbows. My face had the numb feeling that means it will hurt later, and there was a funny little click in my shoulder that I'd never heard before. But across the street two dapper old gentlemen on a stroll had paused to observe me avidly, and I feel that pride goeth before *and* after the fall, like parentheses.

"Hi," I called, waving the hammer in weak parody of having descended so fast on purpose. The sounds emanating from my body reminded me of a band consisting of a washtub bass, soup spoons, and a kazoo.

Some were the popping noises of tendons snapping back into their proper positions. But others—the loudest, weirdest ones—were from inside my ears.

The men moved on, no doubt muttering about the fool woman who didn't know enough to stay down off a ladder. That was how I felt about her, too, at the moment: ouch.

In the kitchen, Ellie applied first aid consisting of soapy washcloths, clean dry towels, and twenty-year-old Scotch. A couple of Band-Aids completed the repair job, which only made me look a little like Frankenstein's monster.

"Yeeks. All I need now is a pair of steel bolts screwed into my skull." The split in my lip was particularly decorative and there was a purplish bruise coming up on my cheekbone.

"Yes," Ellie said crisply, putting the first-aid things back into the kitchen drawer. "And you're lucky you *don't* need bolts."

Responding to her tone my black Labrador retriever, Monday, hurried in from the parlor, ears pricked and brown eyes alert for any unhappiness she might abolish with swipes of her wet tongue.

"You could have killed yourself falling off that ladder, you know," Ellie admonished me. "I *wish* you'd let me—"

Wriggling anxiously, Monday threw a body-block against my hip, which wasn't quite broken. Monday believes you can heal almost anything by applying a dog to it, and—mostly—I think so, too.

But next came Cat Dancing, a big apple-headed Siamese with crossed eyes and a satanic expression. "Ellie, I'm fine," I said, trying to sound believable. "I don't need a doctor."

Except maybe a witch doctor if Cat Dancing kept staring at me that way. She was named by my son Sam for reasons I can't fathom, as the only dance that feline ever does will be on my grave. She wouldn't care if I died on the spot as long as my body didn't block the cabinet where we keep cat food. We'd gotten her from my ex-husband Victor, who lives down the street and is also reliable in the driving-me-crazy department.

"Right," Ellie agreed. "Why, you're just a picture of health." *Pick-tcha*: the downeast Maine pronunciation.

When Ellie's Maine twang gets emphatic it's a bad time for me to try persuading her of anything. Fortunately, just then her favorite living creature in the world padded into my kitchen.

"Prill!" Ellie's expression instantly softened as she bent to embrace the newcomer.

A ferocious-looking Doberman pinscher, Prill sported a set of choppers that would have felt right at home in the jawbone of a great white shark. But the snarl on her kisser was really only a sweet, goofy grin. Prill was an earnest if bumbling guardian of balls, bones, dishrags, slippers, hairbrushes, and cats.

Especially cats. Squirming from Ellie's hug, Prill spied Cat Dancing and greeted the little sourpuss by closing her jaws very gently around Cat's head. Then she just stood there wagging her stubby tail while the hair on Cat's back stiffened in outrage and her crossed eyes bugged helplessly.

"Aw," I said. "Isn't that cute?"

Cat emitted a moan keenly calculated to warm the heart of a person who has just pushed the cat off the kitchen table for the millionth, billionth time, and that was about how many times I'd done just that Cat's first week here.

"Prill," Ellie said in gentle admonishment. Days earlier she and I had found the big dog alone and tagless on the town pier, gamely trying to steal a few mackerel heads from the seagulls. No owner had yet claimed her, and I doubted now if anyone would.

Cat's moan rose to an atonal yowl as Sam came in with his dive gear over his shoulder, wearing his new wristwatch which read out in military time. It was, my son had informed me happily, the way the Coast Guard did it. In love with all things watery, this summer he'd signed up for an advanced diving-operations seminar so risky sounding, I disliked thinking about it.

But if he was going to be in and on the water for a living, as seemed inevitable, I guessed as much supervised practice as possible was only prudent. Now he dropped his gear beside the buckets of polyurethane and tins of varnish remover I'd put out a few days earlier. Besides the gutters, I was also refinishing the hall floor that spring.

"Wow, where'd you get that big shiner?" Sam asked with the half-worried, half-admiring interest of a young man who thinks his mother might have been in a recent fistfight. At nineteen, he had his father's dark hair, hazel eyes, and the ravishing grin—also his dad's—of a born heartbreaker.

"Oh, no." I rushed back to the mirror, finding to my dismay that Sam's assessment was correct. An ominous red stain was circling my right eye; soon my face would be wearing two of my least favorite human skin colors: purple and green.

And *speaking* of green . . .

A bolt of fright struck me. "Ellie, come and hold my eyelid out, please, and look under it. I think when I landed I shoved a contact lens halfway into my brain."

One blue eye, one green; oh, blast and damnation. But just as I was really about to panic, Sam's girlfriend Maggie arrived with a tiny disk of green plastic poised on her index finger.

"Did you lose this?" Maggie was a big red-cheeked girl with clear olive skin, liquid brown eyes, and dark, wavy hair that she wore in a thick, glossy braid down her plaid-shirted back.

"I spotted it on the sidewalk," she added. It was Maggie who'd bought Sam the military wristwatch, shopping for it on-line via her computer.

Then she saw me. "Jacobia, what *happened*?"

Well, at least the lens wasn't halfway to my brain. "I was testing Newton's law. The demonstration got away from me." I popped the other lens out. Suddenly I was blue-eyed again. Both eyes. "I'm okay, though, thanks."

Actually parts of me were hurting quite intensely but if I said so, Ellie would insist on taking me to the clinic where Victor was on duty. And rather than submit to my ex-husband's critical speculations on how my injuries had happened, I'd have gone outside and fallen off that ladder all over again.

"I guess I can't be in your eye-color experiment, though," I said. Like Sam, in the fall Maggie would be a sophomore at the University of Maine. "I don't think I should put the lens back in right away," I explained.

The experiment, for a psychology-class project, was to see how long it takes a person to get used to a new eye color. If my own reaction was any indication, the answer was *never*. It was astonishing how jarring the past week had been, seeing a green-eyed alien with my face looking out of the mirror at me.

Disappointment flashed in Maggie's glance, at once replaced by concern. "Oh, I don't care about that silly experiment," she declared.

But she did. She had designed it, proposed it, and with some difficulty gotten it approved, to get credits while staying in Eastport—where Sam was, not coincidentally—for the whole summer. It wasn't easy getting people with normal sight to wear the lenses, either. I was among the six she'd persuaded, the minimum for the project. "It's you I'm worried about," she added.

The girl was going to make someone a wonderful daughter-in-law someday. But it wouldn't be me if Sam didn't hurry up and get his act together. Other mothers fret if their kids get romantically involved too fast, but my son's idea of a proper courtship verged on the glacial.

Luckily in addition to her other sterling qualities Maggie was patient. "You should put something on it," she said. "A cold cloth or some ice."

"That," Ellie interjected acidly, "would mean she'd have to sit still. And you're allergic to that, aren't you, dear?"

Dee-yah. Catching the renewed threat of a clinic visit, I sat down and accepted the ministrations she offered: aspirin, a cloth with cracked ice in it. If I didn't, she might hogtie me and *haul* me to Victor's clinic. She could do it, too; Ellie looks as delicate as a fairy-tale princess but her spine is of tempered steel.

Also, I'd begun noticing that something about Newton's law had hit me in a major way. Sunshine slanting through the tall bare windows of the big old barnlike kitchen wavered at me, and the maple wainscoting's orangey glow was shimmering weirdly.

"Oh," I heard myself say. "Psychedelic."

"Jake?" Ellie said in alarm, reaching for me.

Then I was on the floor, Prill's cold nose snuffling in my ear while Monday nudged my shoulder insistently. Faces peered: Sam, Maggie. And Ellie, her red hair a backlit halo, green eyes gazing frightenedly at me and even the freckles on her nose gone pale.

"Okay, now," I began firmly, but it came out a croak.

". . . call the hospital?" Sam asked urgently.

"Lift your feet up," Maggie advised.

So I did, and felt much better as blood rushed back downhill to my brain again. Newton's law apparently had advantages, although if my brain planned depending on gravity for all of its blood supply, I was still in serious trouble.

Which was how things stood when my husband, Wade Sorenson, walked in. Tall and square-jawed, built like a stevedore, with brush-cut blond hair and grey eyes, he surveyed the scene with an air of calm competence that I found hugely refreshing under the circumstances. And while Sam asked again if he should phone the hospital and Maggie insisted I put my feet up higher and Ellie was all for summoning an ambulance right that instant, Wade said:

"Hey. How're you doing?"

He doesn't freak out, he doesn't screw up; he's the only man in the world into whose arms I would trustingly fall backwards.

Or forwards, for that matter. Crouching, he assessed me, smelling as always of fresh cold air, lime shaving soap, and lanolin hand cream. He'd already noticed that I was breathing and had a blood pressure. The dogs backed off and sat.

"Your pupils are equal," he commented mildly. Meaning that I likely did not have the kind of brain damage that would kill me. Or not right now, anyway.

Victor would have scoffed at the notion of Wade assessing anything medically, but guys who work on boats learn how to eyeball injuries pretty accurately, reluctant to forfeit a day's pay for anything but the probably-fatal. And as Eastport's harbor pilot, guiding freighters safely through the watery maze of downeast Maine's many treacherous navigation hazards, Wade works on boats pretty much the way mountain goats work on mountains.

Eager to lose my invalid status, I sat up. Not a good move. "Hey, hey," Wade cautioned as the room whirled madly. "Take it slow."

"Okay," I said grudgingly. That Newton guy was beginning to be a real pain in my tailpipe. But I was *not* lying down again.

Ellie was just waiting to bushwhack me into the clinic, Sam resembled a six-year-old who wanted his mommy, and Maggie—

Well, Maggie looked solid and unruffled as usual, for which I was grateful since I had an idea I'd be needing her, later.

For one thing I'd planned a special dinner in honor of the tenant who'd moved into my guest room that morning, an aspiring music-video producer filming his first effort here in Eastport.

For another, somewhere between the ladder and the ground I'd had an important epiphany. Harriet Hollingsworth wasn't just missing.

She was dead. And she'd probably been murdered.

"She had no car, no money. No family as far as anyone knows. So how did Harriet drop off the earth without a trace?" I asked a little while later, sitting on the edge of the examining table at the Eastport Health Clinic.

The clinic windows looked out over a tulip bed whose frilly blooms swayed together in the breeze like dancers in a chorus line. Across the street, a row of white cottages sported postage-stamp lawns, picket fences, and American flags. Beyond gleamed Passamaquoddy Bay, blue and tranquil in the spring sunshine, the distant hills of New Brunswick mounding hazily on the horizon.

"Well?" I persisted as Victor shone a penlight into my eye. "Where'd Harriet go? And how?"

The clinic smelled reassuringly of rubbing alcohol and floor wax. But years of marriage to a medical professional had given me a horror of being at the business end of the medical profession. Ellie had brought me here while Wade finished the gutters, knowing that otherwise I'd go right back up the ladder again; if you let any element of old-house fix-up beat you for an instant, the house will get the upper hand in everything. And although I wasn't graceful or sure-footed I was stubborn; so far, this had been enough to keep my old home from collapsing around me.

Victor snapped the penlight off. He'd tested all the things he could think of that might show I was *non compos mentis,* which was what he thought anyway. When I came here from New York and bought the house he'd had a world-class hissy fit, saying that it showed my personality was dis-integrating and besides, if I moved so far from Manhattan, how would he see Sam?

I'd said that (a) at least I had a personality, (b) if mine was disintegrating it was under the hammer blows he had inflicted upon it while we were married, and (c) as it was, he hadn't seen Sam for over a year.

That shut him up for a while. But not much later he'd moved to Eastport, too, and established his medical clinic.

"Normal," he pronounced now, sounding disappointed.

"A person needs money to run," I reminded Ellie, "even when money trouble is why they are running in the first place."

"She scavenged, though," Ellie countered. "Cans, return-able bottles. Over time, Harriet could have gotten bus fare to Bangor from that."

"Then what?" I objected. "Start a new life? Harriet was barely managing to hang on to the old one. And what about all that blood at her house?"

"Nobody reliable ever saw any blood," Ellie retorted.

After her boot was found, a story went around that a lot of blood had been seen on the top step of Harriet's porch. By whom and when was a matter of wild speculation, and when I'd gone to see for myself it hadn't been there, so I'd discounted the rumor. But now . . .

"Ahem," Victor said pointedly. He had dark hair with a few threads of grey in it, hazel eyes, and a long jaw clenched in a grim expression. Partly this was his normal look while ferreting out illness and coming up with ways to knock its socks off.

Also, though, it meant I was not regarding him with sufficient awe. "Could you," he requested irritably, "pay just a little more attention to the situation at hand?"

Reluctantly I focused on him. This took some doing, a fact I'd failed to mention when asked about symptoms; blurry vision, I understood, could mean Something Bad. But I was determined not to become a patient if I could help it, and I *had* just taken out the contact lenses . . .

"You might have a mild concussion," he pronounced at last.

"That's all?" Ellie questioned. "She seems quite shaken up."

She was complicating my exit strategy: find the nearest door and scram through it, lickety-split. I rolled my eyes at her to get her to pipe down; the room lurched, spinning a quarter turn.

"The simplest possible explanation is usually correct," Victor intoned. " 'Shaken up,' is as good a description as any."

"So I can go?" I slid hastily off the examining table. If it meant getting out of here right now, I'd have hopped off a cliff.

Which, it turned out, was just exactly what getting off that table felt like. Somewhere were my shoes, making contact with the tiled floor. They seemed far away and not entirely reliable as if connected to my body by long, loose rubber bands.

Feets don't fail me now, I thought earnestly. If I had to, I would take floor-contact on faith.

The way, once upon a time, I'd taken Victor. "Someone would remember if Harriet took the bus," I told Ellie.

Victor frowned. He feels everyone should keep silent until he finishes giving *his* opinions. And as he will finish giving *his* opinions a day or so after his funeral, mostly I ignore him.

But now we were in the land of traumatic head injury, where Victor is king and all he surveys is his to command. He'd gotten reeducated for country doctoring, but back in the city Victor was the one you went to after all the other brain surgeons turned pale and began trembling at the very sight of you.

So this time I listened. "Twenty-four hours of bed rest," he decreed. "Watch for headache, disorientation, and grogginess."

Breathing the same air as Victor made me groggy. We'd had a peace treaty for a while, but now Sam was away at college most of the time and without him to run interference for us, Victor and I were about as compatible as flies and flyswatters. And guess what end of that charming analogy I tended to end up on.

"Great," I said glumly. It wasn't enough that I looked like I'd gone nine rounds with a prizefighter. My X rays were clear but my face was a disaster area, and the click in my shoulder had gone silent, probably on account of the swelling.

But I *couldn't* lie down. I had *things* to do: dinner guests.

And Harriet's murder. First, I had to convince Ellie that it had happened. I had a pretty clear idea of how to do that, too; Harriet hadn't owned much, but she had possessed *one* thing . . .

"Well, maybe not actual bed rest," Victor allowed. "But if you won't take it easy," he added sternly, "I'll admit you to the hospital for forty-eight hours of observation."

An odd look came into his eye, and I realized he could make good on this threat if he came up with dire enough reasons, Wade might believe Victor, if he sounded sincere; Ellie, too.

And Victor was good at sincere. "I will," I vowed, "take it easy. Um, and is it okay to put the contact lenses back in?"

Because if I could, Maggie's project might get saved. Victor looked put-upon.

"Oh, I suppose," he replied waspishly. "It looks bad but the orbital processes were spared, the swelling's minimal, not *in* the eye at all, and you have no signs of neurological dysfunction."

Never mind if your face looks like road kill; if you can follow his moving finger with your eyes and touch your nose with your own, you're good to go. "But why in heaven's name are you participating in amateur-hour science?" he wanted to know.

"Thank you, Victor," I cut him off. It's yet another of his talents, making me feel like a rebellious child.

Leaving Ellie to settle up at the business desk I made for the exit before he could decide to prescribe a clear liquid diet. Maybe I'd learn later that I'd knocked an essential screw loose and it needed replacing right away, before my brains fell out.

But I doubted it. And I doubted even more that the gleam in his eye had been benevolent, when he realized that if only for an instant there, he'd had me in his power.

Again.

So I was getting the hell out of Dodge.

My name is Jacobia Tiptree and once upon a time I was a hot-shot New York financial expert, a greenback-guru with offices so plush you could lose a small child in the depth of the broadloom on the floor of my consulting area. I was the one rich folks came to for help on the most (to them) important topics in the world:

(A) Getting wealthier, and

(B) Getting even wealthier than that.

Everything was about money. Fallen in love? Break out the prenuptial agreements. Somebody died? The family is frantic not with grief for the dearly departed but because the old skinflint stashed his loot in an unbreakable charitable remainder trust.

Loot being the operative term; most of my clients were so crooked their limousines should've flown the Jolly Roger. But I didn't care, mostly on account of having started out with no loot whatsoever, myself. Until I was a teenager my idea of the lush life was glass in the windows, shoes that fit, and not too much woodsmoke from the cracks in the stove chimney, so I could read.

At fifteen I ran from the relatives who were raising me, trusting in my wits and a benevolent universe to pave my path, which is why it was lucky I turned out to have a few wits about me. Getting through Penn Station I had the sense I'd have been safer in a war zone; men sidled up to me, crooking their fingers, weaving and crooning. In my pale shiny face and hick clothes, lugging a cheap suitcase and in possession of the enormous sum of twenty dollars, I must've looked just like all the other fresh young chickens, ready for plucking.

Fortunately, however, all my cousins had been boys. Something about me must have said I knew precisely where to aim my kneecap, and the nasty men skedaddled. Before I knew it (well, a couple of weeks after I hopped off the Greyhound, actually) I was living in a tenement near Times Square where I'd found the best job a girl from my background could imagine: waitress in a Greek diner.

My feet were swollen, my hair stank of fryer grease, and in the first couple of days I learned thirty new ways to buzz off a lurking creep-o. Meager wages and no tips; Ari's Dineraunt wasn't a tipping kind of place, except on the horses. But it was all-you-could-eat and most of the other girls didn't enjoy the food. Too foreign, they said, turning up their well-nourished noses.

Which left more for me. Short ribs and stuffed grape

leaves, moussaka and lamb stew; ordinarily the owner was tighter with a dime than a wino with a pint of Night Train, but for some reason Ari Kazantzakis thought it was funny to watch me shoving baklava into my mouth.

Maybe it was because he had enough family memories of real hunger to know it when he saw it. Ari had a photo of Ellis Island behind the counter, and one of the Statue of Liberty in his fake-wood-paneled office. The tenement where I lived was just like the one his parents had moved into when they got here. Or exactly the one.

Whatever. Anyway, one day Ari's accountant didn't show up and the next day they found him floating in the East River, full of bullet holes. Suddenly it wasn't all sweetmeats and balalaikas at the Dineraunt anymore. More like hand-wringing and sobbing violins until I said I was good at math and that when I wasn't slinging hash I was taking accounting courses. By then I'd gotten a high school equivalency and talked my way into night school.

I'd figured it was the only way I would ever get near real money, which was true but not in the way I'd expected. Two days later I was carrying a black bag, the one the accountant had been expected to pick up and deliver. That was how I got to know the men at the social club, several of whom later became my clients.

They thought it was hilarious, a skinny-legged girl with big eyes and a hillbilly accent running numbers money. But they didn't think it was so funny a few weeks later, when every other runner in the city got nabbed in an organized crime crackdown.

All but me. Like I said, I'd had boy cousins, and if there was anything I was good at besides math, it was evasive action. A few years later when I'd finished school, gotten married, begun solo money management, and had a baby, one of the guys from the social club came to my office.

He wore an Armani suit, a Bahamas tan, and Peruggi shoes. The diamond in his pinky ring was so big you could have used it to anchor a yacht. His expression was troubled;

they always were on people with money woes. And this guy's familiar hound-dog face was the saddest that I had ever encountered. But when he saw me behind my big oak desk, he started to laugh.

Me, too. All the way to the bank.

And there you have it: my own personal journey from rags to riches. Victor's another story, not such a pleasant one; first came the hideous coincidence of our having the same uncommon last name. At the time, I regarded this happenstance as serendipity. And I'll admit I was still full of bliss when our son Sam appeared. But soon enough began the late-night calls from lovelorn student nurses whom I informed, at first gently and later I suppose somewhat cruelly, that the object of their affections was married and had a child. And in the end I got fed up with the city, too.

I'd thrived in it but when Sam hit twelve it began devouring him: drugs. Bad companions. And our divorce half killed him. So I chucked it all and bought an old house that needed everything, on Moose Island seven miles off the coast of downeast Maine.

It's quiet: church socials and baked-bean suppers, concerts in the band shell on the library lawn when the weather is warm. There's the Fourth of July in summer, a Salmon Festival in fall, and high school basketball during the school year, of course.

But that's it. Not much happens in Eastport.

Unless you count the occasional mysterious bloody murder.